Two Weeks At Hotel Alyeska

TULSA

ISBN: 978-1-957262-24-6 (Hardcover)
    978-1-957262-18-5 (Paperback)

Two Weeks at Hotel Alyeska

Yorkshire Publishing
1425 E 41st Pl
Tulsa, OK 74105
www.YorkshirePublishing.com
918.394.2665

Published in the USA

Two Weeks At
At
Hotel
Alyeska

Ashlynn
Ford

DEDICATION

Those of you who have encouraged me toward this moment since the very beginning and have given me that extra push when I needed it.

I never thought I would make it here. Thank you.

And to those who look at their dreams believing that they are just too big to ever happen.

Let this be a physical reminder that it is all possible. Just dream, chase it hard, and be brave.

1

I'll take this red ribbon
Stitch my heart together
It will heal, given time
It beats a strange rhythm
But I'll go on living
When I don't get it right

In the famous words of a certain Anne Tyler; once upon a time, there was a woman who discovered she had turned into the wrong person.

"Quoting Anne Tyler?" The voice over her shoulder observed, "Ambitious."

"Thanks," Aspen Vilein-Astankova gave a wicked smirk, her eyes trained on the bright screen of her laptop, "I figure even though she is American, we have to give her some credit for knowing what she's talking about."

Collapsing across her friend's bed, Lena let her head hang over the edge, and she took in their dorm from her favorite angle, upside down.

"You think this is the one? Will you be the student to finally stun ol' prune face?"

"That's the plan," she murmured, "He certainly won't forget about me; I'm going to make sure of that."

"Of course, he won't," Gemma, the last of the trio, shut their door behind her with little grace, "Who are we talking about?"

"Professor Fernsby," Lena answered, lifting her head so her face could just barely be seen peeking over the bed.

Gemma, affectionately known as Gem by over half the university population, made a gagging sound and sat down with her friends. "Why in Lucifer's reach would you want him to remember you, Azzie? You could do so much better and younger. Have higher standards, babe."

"Not like that," Aspen chuckled.

"Oh good. You'd kill the man," Gem laughed, "I mean, he's basically knocking on the door anyway. If he tried to keep up with you, that would definitely do him in."

Lena hummed in agreement.

"He's going to remember my name when we get back from break, and this piece is going to seal the deal for me," Aspen stated, still typing, her focus only half on her friends at the moment.

"Yeah, let me see," Gem reached over and, grabbing the top of the laptop screen, she turned it to face her.

"I was working on that!" The aspiring journalist protested and threw her hands up, already knowing she was defeated.

"Mm, an American author," Gem quirked a brow as she met her friend's gaze over the screen. "Bold choice."

"He'll remember," she shrugged.

"Alright, you're the writer."

Shaking her head, Aspen allowed herself a few minutes to relax while her friends read over her piece. The corner of her lips lifted a little to reveal a small dimple that was almost identical to her mother's. Where would she be without these two?

The three of them were an odd little pack and always had been from their first moments sharing this dorm room two years ago.

Three girls, new to university life, thrown together by random chance, found themselves trying to make little places of their own in this room they would call home for the rest of their time at university.

* * * * * * * * * * * * *

"Who are they?" Lena inquired, watching as Aspen placed a family photo on her nightstand.

"That's my family," she answered fondly, "We were on vacation in Alaska. That's my Mum, my nuisance of a little brother, and that's my Dad," Looking back at her new roommate, Aspen flashed a bright smile, "What about you? Did you bring any pictures of your family?"

Lena cleared her throat and glanced down at her feet for a moment, "No. I—I don't have too much of a 'family.' I mean, I've got my Mum but. . . I never knew my father."

"And I wish I had never known mine," Gemma added from her side of the dorm, raising her tiny flask in the air. "I had the chance to kill him. I still wonder to this day if I made the right choice."

"Is that. . .?" Aspen glanced at the silver tin, suddenly a little nervous.

"Oh yes," Lena nodded, "She's troubled. I have no control over her."

"How do you know?" she continued to speak softly, "That she's troubled, I mean."

"She's my cousin."

Aspen's brows nearly met her hairline, but she wasn't given a chance to respond before Gemma finished her inspection of the room and turned her attention back to them.

"What about you, Blondie?"

"Wh—what about me?"

"How's your father?" She gestured toward the framed photo.

"Oh, I love my Dad," Aspen answered without hesitation.

"Right," Gemma drug out the word, as if already annoyed but trying not to show it, *"Oh well, we can work with that."*

* * * * * * * * * * * * *

"What are you smirking about?" Lena asked, looking up from her reading.

Aspen shook her head, "Nothing. Just thinking."

"Fine, don't tell us," Gem teased, "But I'll tell you this, if Fernsby forgets about this paper, it's because he's got dementia. This is excellent."

Aspen blushed and took her laptop back, closing it and putting it away for the day, "Thanks, girls. I really hope you're right."

"Have I ever been wrong?" Gem asked, but quickly added. "The question was rhetorical. Don't answer."

The moment passed with some stifled chuckles, and the three sat enjoying each other's company.

"So, dinner with the family today?" Lena broke the quiet, making a statement more than asking a question.

"Yeah, I'm meeting up with them down by the boat club, and I may show them around the underground bar. We'll see," Aspen shrugged, her eyes holding a far-off look.

Most kids identify the year they turned sixteen as the year they began preparing to get their driver's license, and the fear of forever being hulled around by their parents was beginning to fade. I identify that year of my life as the year my parents separated. I would have been fine with my parents having to drive me around for the rest of my life if it only meant they stayed together.

"What's the face?"

"I'm not making a face," the blonde replied, her brows knitting together momentarily as she shook her thoughts away.

"Oh yes, you are," Gem agreed, "You're making the sad thinking face."

Shaking her head with a half-hearted laugh, Aspen had to admit she was dumbfounded, "What are you two talking about?"

"It doesn't matter," Lena answered, "What's on your mind? Where are you at?"

"Nothing really. . . I'm just thinking. . . Another birthday spent with my parents who desperately miss each other but can't, or won't, give being together another chance."

The cousins nodded thoughtfully. They had been around Aspen's parents, and anyone could see that there were still feelings between them. But there was also an undeniable tension.

Little could be said to explain it, except that when two people genuinely love each other and can't make it work, that's real tragedy.

"I just. . . I have these vivid memories of them together. Over half of my life, they were one of the best couples, and then everything changed so quickly. Looking back on it, I realize that there had to be subtle shifts that I was missing there toward the end, but I was so caught up in high school and everything else that. . . somehow I missed my parents falling apart and drifting away from each other."

Lena rested a comforting hand on Aspen's knee and gave it a gentle squeeze. She hardly ever talked about her parents this way. The subject of her divorced parents was just another one of those things that Aspen tucked away for her alone to deal with.

"They were so happy, such a team, and then one day I woke up and there was this thick air between them, and the magic was gone. They were different. So severe and silent with each other. They didn't even hold hands anymore. Sometimes the softness would come through, but it would never stay long."

Gem, being secretly sensitive to matters concerning family these days, flicked an escaped tear away and wondered what that must have been like. Having a good family and then one day waking up to it all being ripped out from under you. Aspen had something to miss, while Gem never knew family before moving in with her cousin.

"For as long as I can remember, when Zayden and I would go off to study after dinner, we could hear them laughing in the kitchen or even just the murmured sounds of conversation between them while they talked about their work. And when it had been a hard day for either one of them, I would look out my window after going to bed, and I could see them standing out on the deck just holding each other. No talking, no attempts to fix whatever went wrong, just together in the quiet."

"And then one day, it was all just gone. No more laughter, no more quiet nights on the deck, just silence, and then it was all over. We weren't a family anymore. Dad moved to our little house in Hoylake and Mum stayed in the house at Liverpool. . . and Zayden and I were caught somewhere in between."

A few heavy moments passed with Aspen still lost in her thoughts before she quietly voiced the truth that had been following her around the last few days.

"I guess, no matter how old you get, you always want your parents together, you know. Anyway. . ."

Uncomfortable, but not at all unfamiliar with heavy life situations like this, Gemma was the first to break the silence.

"Well. That was a nice birthday conversation."

Lena laughed a little awkwardly, "Yeah, happy birthday, I guess."

"Thanks, girls. Really, I don't know what I'd do without you."

"Ah, you would be fine," Gemma waved her words away. "You would have a lot less fun without us, but you would be fine."

Don't beat myself up about the
things that didn't work out

Least I can say is that I tried

I'll take this red ribbon

Stitch my heart together, and I know I'll be fine

A bright smile breaking across her face, Aspen closed the remaining distance between her and the tall man approaching the riverside.

"Hi, Dad!" Throwing her arms around the man's neck, she felt the deep rumble of his laughter and squeezed a little tighter.

She could hear the smile in her father's voice, "Hello, sweetheart."

Releasing him from her iron embrace, Aspen smiled up at him and immediately fell into their teasing ways.

"Something really important must be going on to have you show up somewhere on time."

"Oh, you know, just celebrating my daughter's birthday," he shrugged playfully. "Can't be late for things like that." Cradling the back of her head like he had from the first moment Aspen was placed in his arms, Ian smiled softly at her before ruffling her hair just a little, "Happy birthday, baby girl."

"Thanks, Dad."

Wrapping her arms around her father's, Aspen lead them down the riverside to watch the rowing society practice for their final races coming up in a few weeks.

"Mum got held up at the station, by the way," she informed as they walked.

Chuckling softly, Ian couldn't help but ask, "What did your Mum do to get picked up?"

"Not the Nick, Dad," Aspen chortled in that funny way that always amused her parents, "She's at the train station. Which is good because I want to talk to you."

"Ooo, you sound just like her when you say that," Ian replied, his brows coming together briefly, knowing he was in for something by the tone of his daughter's voice.

"I don't think that's the best idea, sweetie," Ian shook his head. "Your Mum really won't like it."

"Dad, all I am saying is that this is going to be our last Christmas before I start traveling for internships, and Zayden starts spending his breaks with some girlfriend. You and Mum can get along for a couple of weeks."

"Yes, we can," he nodded thoughtfully, "When we are a few towns apart, sometimes cities apart, and have absolutely zero communication, we get along perfectly well."

"Dad."

"Penny, please don't press this. It is not going to happen, and I don't want you to get your hopes up. When Perri and I are in the same room—."

"Fireworks fly?" Aspen cut in, wiggling her brows at her father.

A quick burst of laughter was the prelude to his response, "More like live grenades are tossed."

"Can we at least talk about it more at dinner tonight?" she asked, cognac brown eyes twinkling with mischief.

When Ian hesitated, Aspen whipped out her most winning pout. Sad eyes and quivering bottom lip.

Ian looked away, and taking his daughter's hand in both of his, he squeezed gently. A few moments passed. Finally, he sighed and shook his head.

"You know that little pout of yours isn't going to work on me forever."

"Well, I'm twenty-two, and it hasn't failed me yet," Aspen smirked triumphantly, "So I'll take my chances for now, thank you."

Patting her hand before letting go, Ian smiled too, "Of course you will."

Planting a kiss on top of his daughter's head, he rested his chin there. Playfully tugging at the ends of Aspen's wavy hair, Ian couldn't stop the second sigh from escaping his lips.

My gorgeous girl.

She was the spitting image of his ex-wife, Perri. It was almost shocking when you saw them together, but for Ian, it both warmed and broke his heart to this day.

"Yes. Fine. But only because it is against the rules to deny the birthday girl anything she wants on her birthday."

"Yes!!" Aspen pumped her fist, not even trying to hide the extra skip in her next step.

Convinced that she at least had a shot at getting her request, Aspen allowed the comfortable silence to rest over them, knowing there was no need to harass her father on the matter anymore.

I just have to get Mum sold on the idea.

Father and daughter watched the slim boats slice through the water with unearthly grace and waited for the rest of their family group to arrive.

Aspen always missed quiet moments like these with her father. They brought a sense of tranquility with them, even if the world around them was going mad. Being next to her father and just sharing some stillness with him. The quiet made Aspen feel like everything was going to be alright in the end.

"How's your Mum been?"

If he had been talking to anyone else, Ian knew the soft hesitance in his voice would have never even been noticed. But, he could tell by the look in his daughter's quick eyes that she sensed it.

"Good, I think," Aspen nodded thoughtfully, looking back out at the rowers. Her brows drew together as she continued, "Busy. She's been keeping herself very busy."

Ian felt a painful twist deep in his chest. He hated the idea of his wife—ex-wife—being alone so much. She hated it, and for good reason.

Feeling a gaze on them, Ian looked around, and a unique warmth settled over him, swelling in his chest.

"Hey," he gently bumped Aspen with his hip, "Looks like they finally let your Mum out."

Snapping her head in the direction her Dad was looking; a wide smile broke out across Aspen's face at the sight of her mother coming toward them.

The woman lit up with a smile almost identical to Aspen's own, "There you are." Her voice was heard just over the sound of a passing boat.

Slipping out from under her father's arm, Aspen closed the remaining distance at jogging speed. Colliding with her mother, who couldn't help but laugh a little with excitement at seeing her daughter, the girl locked her arms around the woman.

"Hi, Mum!"

"Happy birthday, my love," Perri squeezed the girl tight for a long minute.

Aspen hummed softly and took a deep breath of the woman's perfume. A smell that the girl always associated with comfort and safety.

That was something that, even after her parents separated, Aspen knew to be true without question. If anything ever happened and she needed them, all she would ever have to do was run to them, and she knew deep within her that those two would band together and protect her against the world. Those arms would keep her safe at all costs, and she never worried it wasn't true.

Nuzzling just a little closer into her mother's hair, the girl sighed contentedly.

"I told Dad they kept you at the station," her mischievous smirk could be heard in her voice. American's had such strange meanings for words, but they came in handy every now and again. Mostly when teasing her mother about being carted away to prison because of her shirty ways.

"Oh, did you know," Perri chuckled, giving her girl a final squeeze before letting go.

Taking a short step back, her mother reached forward and caressed the shaved side of Aspen's blonde head.

"And I love this even more in person."

Reaching up to run her fingers through the long tresses left on the other side, Aspen smiled shyly, "Thanks, Mum."

Looking over her daughter's shoulder at Ian, who had remained a quiet presence in the background, Perri gave a tender, close-lipped smile.

"Ian," she greeted, her voice carrying on the London breeze.

Looking into someone else's eyes is a form of nakedness all on its own. Far more vulnerable than any sort of physical bareness.

"Hello, Perri," he returned the smile and approached the two, his hands tucked deep into his jacket pockets like the day they first met.

Mm, that leather jacket. Perri both hated and loved it. It just wasn't fair how he still had such an effect on her after all these years.

Quickly shaking away the thought, Perri turned back to their daughter. "Does anyone know where your brother is?"

Aspen shook her head, amused, "Mum, we all know that no one can ever really keep up with where Zayden is these days."

"Well, in case he has beaten us there," Ian reached out to place his hand on Aspen's back, "let's get to the restaurant before he causes trouble."

"Or runs up a massive bill," the girl added, wrapping her arm around her mothers as the trio turned to walk back up the riverside.

Ian opened the door to the restaurant, and Perri's eyes were instinctively drawn to his hand. Catching sight of her mother so quickly falling into the old habit of checking for new wounds, Aspen tried not to smile as she ducked inside.

Ian's hands and arms were littered with scars of varying shapes and sizes, all of them from pets of wide variety as well. Aspen knew that no matter how much time had passed, her mother could still tell you what had happened when it came to the scars that looked deep and angry despite being healed. Especially the scar on his face. She would catch her mother staring at it with a far-off look every now and again. That was one injury her father received that Aspen was glad she wasn't old enough to remember.

Although she did recall the day that Ian came home with a black eye and swollen nose. Aspen chuckled to herself as they made their way to the table.

* * * * * * * * * * * * *

Ian shut the front door behind him and listened for sounds of his family. Hearing muffled conversation coming from the kitchen, he went in to say hello.

"Hello, everyone," he greeted cheerfully.

Perri turned from shooing the dogs away from the stove, and her typical 'how was your day' was replaced with a much more urgent question.

"What happened?!"

Ian gave a tired chuckle, "It's been a long day."

"Well—yes, I can see that, but what—"

Looking up from their homework spread near and far on the kitchen island, Aspen and Zayden's mouths fell open.

"Dad! What happened to your face?" Zayden seemed more excited than concerned.

Smiling in a lopsided way that looked honestly painful, Ian leaned against the bar allowing his children a closer look at his black and purple skin and the blood from his nose that now stained his shirt.

"I had this horse of a dog who didn't like his nails getting trimmed. He decided the best course of action would be to headbutt me in the eye," he explained, shrugging casually, "I guess it got him what he wanted."

"Did you do anything for that at work?" His wife questioned from somewhere close behind.

Ian could see her hands on her hips and the stern expression on her face without even turning around. Flashing a nervous expression to the children, he ran his hands through his hair.

"Afraid not."

The only reply was the sound of their freezer opening and closing, then Perri's bare feet softly slapping against the tile floor as she came to a stop beside her husband.

"Ice that."

She held out one of the soft icepacks she kept ready in for such times.

Dutifully taking the pack from her, Ian gingerly placed it against his face.

"Oh yes, madam."

"Please," Perri added, "Thank you."

* * * * * * * * * * * * *

Just flashes in time. Flashes that made Aspen both smile and want to cry. They had all been so happy.

Where had it all gone wrong?

But before she had too long to ponder the question, they arrived at their table.

"At least he's not here making trouble," she remarked.

Perri shook her head in exhausted affection, "Which means he's just out there—"

"Making trouble," Ian finished.

Remember all of the pain; was it all too much?

Remember falling apart every time we touched

Remember going insane, but I'll never give up

A heart that's been broken is a
heart that's been loved

Ian pulled out a chair for Aspen and kissed the top of her head as she took a seat.

"Thanks, Dad."

"It is your birthday after all," he replied.

Turning, Ian's hand brushed Perri's as she passed him. She couldn't help but jump, eyes a fraction wider, as she immediately withdrew her hand back to the safety of her side. She could still feel the hum under her skin where their hands met, and her heart had yet to slow back down. Then she made the mistake of looking up into those sea-green eyes and seeing the flash of hurt that passed through them. If only he knew that her reaction wasn't because she didn't want him touching her. It was because she just ached for him to hold her close. Casual touches, even if they were accidental, made it so much worse, no matter how much time had passed. Because now, not only would she have to sit across from him all through dinner, but she would also have to try and make herself forget how soothingly warm his skin had been seconds ago. Then when she couldn't make that happen, she would have to just try and smother the longing she had to get up from her seat and close the distance between them. Even if it was to do no more than hold his hand, she doubted that if she ever allowed herself that she would not stop there.

Perri mentally shook herself. That was enough of that. If she thought too much more about it, she would end up falling down that rabbit hole and never pulling herself out. Perhaps she brought most of that feeling on to herself, but she couldn't deny how those last several months had weighed her down.

Perri Vilein-Astankova had left her husband.

It wasn't something she liked to talk about. She was never proud of it. If she told the truth, she was actually a little ashamed and defiantly still heartsore about it. She loved Ian. Always would. She was sure of it. But the biggest problem she faced in their marriage was that for the last part of it, she always felt like the only adult.

To be frank, Ian had somehow become the cool parent, and Perri was always the disciplinarian. She made the hard decisions, ones that usually left her standing outside of slammed doors or on the dead-end of abruptly ended phone calls. And it had seemed to Perri that Ian was more than happy to keep on going as if nothing were wrong. *"They'll get over it"* had been his favorite phrase, followed by a kiss to Perri's forehead, until one day, the stress pushed Perri to snap.

Ian's concern, verging on problem, with Perri was that she had forgotten how to just enjoy life and have some fun every now and then. That wasn't the woman he married. Perri had become all seriousness and solemn, always straight to business and getting things done. Which was probably why she had gotten divorce papers filed so quickly. And it was exactly why Ian had 'accidentally' misplaced them. . . *twice.*

So, here they were, six years after their divorce was finalized, sitting across from each other at dinner to celebrate their daughter's twenty-second birthday.

Staring.

Well, Perri was casually glaring.

And Ian. . . He had this strange smirk on his ruggedly charming face, and he held Perri's gaze with those quick eyes of his.

Stupid perfect eyes, Perri thought before she could stop herself.

"Why don't you have a drink, Perri?" Ian suggested, sliding his Bellini across the table. "You look like you could use it."

Ian wasn't going to lie; he was fishing for a reaction, of course. There was no denying that Perri looked amazing, except for the irritated expression on her face now. But with those waves of honey gold that drove Ian wild, she was in killer shape, and the flawless skin, well, he could easily overlook the wrinkle-inducing scowl.

"Not quite strong enough," she retorted, sending it back in his direction.

"Sorry, I'm late!"

Aspen gave a sigh of relief and allowed her eyes to fall shut for just a moment. It wasn't often she was this grateful for her brother's late arrivals, but this was perfect timing.

"Hello, Mum," he leaned down and kissed his mother's cheek.

Reaching up, Perri cupped his cheek briefly, "Where have you been?"

"Around," he shot her an impish smile that they all knew he learned from his mother.

Straightening, he went over and hugged his father in more of a choke-hold manner than an embrace.

"How are you, mate," Ian smiled, affection evident in his eyes.

Zayden Vilein-Astankova chuckled when his father's arm came up around the back of his neck, "I'm good."

Turning, he held out a large shopping bag, "Happy birthday, big sis. You are *officially* ancient."

"Respect your elders then, fetus," Aspen playfully pushed him away after snatching the bag from his grasp.

"Rude, Penny," Zayden replied, "Mum would be ashamed."

Sticking out her tongue, Aspen tried not to smile. Bringing her bag into her lap, she went to excitedly rip into the tissue paper.

"I'm opening this now."

"At least wait until after dessert," Perri interjected.

"Live a little, Perri," Ian countered, laughing at his daughter's childish excitement.

Aspen and Zayden gave each other a look. Instead of opening the gift, Aspen sat it on the empty chair beside her.

There was a long moment of awkward silence in which Ian looked across the table at his ex-wife.

"Forgive me for trying to teach my children something called etiquette, Ian," Perri replied to his expression.

"Etiquette is nothing but fancy rules for fancy people. And rules are made to be broken, or at least that's what a wise young woman once told me," he stared pointedly at the blonde woman glaring at him, "Especially the fancy rules, I believe she said."

Perri scoffed, "You *would* remember that."

Aspen half-expected, half-hoped that Perri would stick out her tongue at Ian and for Ian to reach across and tweak her hair. The couple's playground antics had been a constant theme in their household. Before the divorce, of course.

But now, where playfulness used to be, comedic relief was required to handle the situations.

"I will turn this car around this instant, and no one will get dessert if you two don't stop this right now," Zayden cut in.

The table fell quiet again, but Aspen was the first to break it with a snort of barely concealed laughter. Her small family followed suit, laughing at Zayden's well-timed interruption. And when their parents were distracted by the arrival of the appetizers, Aspen mouthed a quick thank you to her brother, who threw her a wink of acknowledgement.

"So, how was the last building job, Mum?" Zayden inquired, reaching across the table for one of the extra plates.

"Ehm," Perri made the thoughtful sound that her children also picked up, but they refused to believe that anyone but their mother made that sound, "It was exhaustin'."

Aspen's brows drew together, a concerned expression in her dark eyes.

"Mum, don't wear yourself out alright."

Perri waved her words away casually, promising that she was fine and had actually recovered quite well from her traveling in the few days she had been home.

But her family knew her a little better than she sometimes liked to believe. They all knew that Perri's once very heavy Scouse accent usually only came out when she was exceptionally tired.

Aspen watched her mother silently as she took a sip of her drink in hopes of taking everyone away from the subject at hand. And Aspen's mind was once again drawn to a memory she had tried to forget. Not that she was traumatized in any way, it just made her so sad. She hated thinking about it.

But isn't it odd how the memory works? The things you can't remember, even though you wish you had a shred of something to look back on, and then the things you will never forget despite how much you want to.

* * * * * * * * * * * * * *

Sixteen-year-old Aspen walked on cats' paws down the stairs to the kitchen. She didn't sleep a whole lot recently. Not with everything that had happened and all the changes. Her mind hardly ever stopped working long enough for her body to drag her into sleep. So it was better to have a full stomach and a full mind at this point than a full mind and an empty stomach.

Padding around the banister, she passed the living room that was lit by the soft blue light of the tv. Pausing in the doorway, Aspen wondered why it had been left running. Her mother would have gone to bed hours ago, and she always turned everything off and checked all the locks before going to her room for the night.

She probably just forgot. Aspen crossed the room and went to switch off the quietly murmuring late-night comedy show. Bending down to click the button at the base of the screen, she jumped when she heard a rustling behind her. Quickly turning, she was shocked to find her mother sleeping, rather restlessly on the sofa. One arm thrown wildly above her head and hanging over the edge of the arm, and the rest of her limbs tucked close around her. Her breathing was gentle and rhythmic, though her forehead was creased even in sleep.

Closing the distance between them, Aspen knelt down and gazed at her mother with confused and worried eyes.

"Mum," she whispered, and the woman stirred, slowly opening her eyes.

"What is it? What's wrong?" Perri asked, not fully conscious yet.

"Mum, are you aright? What are you doin'?"

Glancing around for a moment, recognition flashed across Perri's face, and she sat up a little.

"I'm sorry, love, I guess I just got so tired."

They held gazes for a moment too long, and they both knew that the other understood exactly what had happened.

Perri had not wanted to go up to bed at all and had instead decided to sleep on the couch in hopes that her children would not find her there.

A sad, half-hearted smile rested on her closed lips as she swung her feet onto the floor.

"Let's go up to bed, yeah?"

"Yeah, let's go to bed," Aspen replied, standing and walking beside her mother all the way up to her room. Sliding her eyes over to watch her mother as they went along.

"I'm a'righ', love," Perri remarked, feeling her daughter's gaze.

The girl quickly looked away, "Yeah, I know."

"There's nothin' to worry about," the woman finished, staring down the hall with an unreadable expression, and Aspen knew she was talking mostly to herself.

Never in her life had she seen her mother like this. Her mother had always been so strong, a little on the hotheaded side, but she always seemed to have everything under control. She seemed almost at a loss.

Reaching over, the girl brushed her hand down her mother's arm and gave her a soft smile as they stopped in front of Perri's bedroom.

Returning the smile, her mother leaned down a fraction and planted a kiss against her forehead.

"Thanks for wakin' me," she squeezed her shoulder tenderly, "Love you."

"Love you," Aspen replied and watched the woman walk silently into her room and close the door, leaving only a small sliver open for the lamp light to pour through into the hallway.

Aspen stood outside for a minute or two, knowing her mother would not be sleeping in the room that now seemed all too empty.

* * * * * * * * * * * * *

"Penny."

"Hm?" Aspen looked up, her mind breaking free of her thoughts, "Sorry, what?"

"I asked where we were going tonight," Zayden repeated.

"Oh, yeah!" Her heavy thoughts passed, Aspen smiled excitedly, "Z-man, you and I are going to go pub crawling."

"Oh dear Lord," Aspen heard their mother murmur in the background, and the girl smiled, imagining Perri shaking her head and trying not to smirk.

"But before you get too excited, you're with me tonight. Which means you're not allowed to pick up any girls."

"Really, Penny," Zayden almost whined.

"Really," she answered decidedly, "Suck it up."

Just before dessert, Aspen decided it was as good a time as any to throw out her idea of a holiday in Alaska. One like when she and Zayden were kids, and they were all happy for a change.

"I don't know, Penny," Perri shook her head before turning to thank the waiter as he placed her dessert on the table.

"Look," Aspen told the table, watching their expressions with dread in her heart, "I'm not pressuring anyone into it. I just think it will be good for all of us to be someplace where we all have fond memories."

Before anyone could answer, a lovely trio of three waiters with surprisingly beautiful voices arrived at their table to serenade Aspen with a rendition of 'Happy Birthday.' They finished off their song and placed a masterpiece of a French pastry in front of her, the flame from a single candle still dancing along to the fading song.

Aspen stopped believing in magic as a teen, but as an adult, she would reconsider her position on its existence. As it stood, she sent her birthday wish curling into the heavens along with the smoke from her birthday candle.

I wish my parents remembered why they fell in love. Or, at the very least, didn't hate being around each other.

Zayden claimed he was happy and didn't mind their being separated, but Aspen knew better. During the 'secret party' for Zayden's sixteenth birthday, the one where Aspen had bought some cheap red wine, he had gotten incredibly sloshed and confessed that he missed the days when their parents were together.

As soon as the dessert was gone, Zayden was up and harassing Aspen to go. She kept waving him away, still hoping for an answer from their parents, but neither of them brought it up. After her fifth attempt at hinting for an answer, Perri started shooing them on their way.

"I want you two back in the safety of one of one of your homes before midnight," she insisted.

"But, Mum—"

"No 'buts,' young man."

"Fine," Zayden sighed and then smirked at her, "Good night, Mum."

"Good night, trouble," she replied and wrapped him up in a tight hug.

Flashing that winning smile, Zayden then turned to hug Ian, trading parents with his sister. Leaving Perri at the mercies of Aspen's pleading eyes that were so much like her own.

"Please, *please* think about it, Mum," the girl begged.

Reaching out, Perri pulled their daughter into her arms and held tight.

"Oh baby girl. . ." she sighed heavily before leaning away and pushing a lock of hair behind Aspen's ear, "I promise I'll think on it, yeah. Until then, have fun celebrating with your brother."

Trying not to be too disappointed, Aspen attempted a smile but could only bring the corner of her lips to lift a fraction.

"Thanks for dinner, Mum."

"Happy birthday, my love."

"Come on, Penny, let's go already!" Zayden threw his arm around her shoulders and turned them toward the door.

"Be careful, you two," Ian called after them.

The siblings didn't even respond. They just continued on their way out the door, leaving their parents to watch them go.

"Do you think. . ." Perri's voice broke the silence between the once happy couple, "Do you think we did this to them?"

"I don't understand the question," Ian looked down at her, his brows coming together, creating a familiar crease between them.

"I mean, with Penny becoming a journalist, always out to discover and write the truth and nothing less. And then Zayden in Peace and Conflict Studies. I just. . . I feel like we did this to them."

"You say that like it's a bad thing," Ian replied, "I think we've done a pretty good job with them both."

"I just can't help but sometimes wonder if," Perri paused, "If things had been different, would they be doing something else? Would they be different?" *If I hadn't done what I did, would we all be different?*

"I guess that's just one of those things we'll never know," he replied gently, "But I still think we've done a great job with them, even if they were maybe meant to do something else. They're amazing."

Perri nodded, "That's something we will always agree on. They are amazing."

"Are you ready for the bill?" their waiter inquired, ripping the couple from their thoughts.

"Sorry," Perri flashed a smile, "Yes, we're ready."

Walking out into the cool London night, Perri wrapped her long coat a little tighter around her body and Ian tucked his hand back in his pockets.

"My car is just around the corner," Perri gestured to their left.

"Wonderful!" Ian's face brightened, "So is mine. I'll walk you to yours, if I may. That way we can discuss. . .?"

He allowed his words to drift off into the night, hoping Perri understood what he was referencing.

Looking up at him, Perri tried not to let herself hesitate too long, "Sure."

Rounding the corner, they passed a young couple nestled close together even as they walked, using the slight chill as a reason to be pressed as near as possible to one another.

"If our young selves could see us now, do you think they'd believe it?" Ian inquired thoughtfully.

For a moment, he wondered if she had even heard him, then finally,

"I don't know if I'd want young Perri to know me."

"Well, I for one, think she would like you."

Perri gave a small, closed-lipped smile, something that Ian sadly noticed had replaced her once vibrant grin, and hummed softly in response.

"You're definitely everything young Ian wanted to be," she offered, "He'd be proud."

"I suppose," Ian gave a single shoulder shrug, "I'm only lacking one thing that he loved."

Perri's head snapped in his direction to meet his gaze, knowing exactly what that 'one thing' was.

They couldn't look at each other long before she panicked and quickly looked away again, her heart speeding up.

Feeling the knife in his chest twist just a little more, Ian turned his attention back to their walk, scanning for Perri's car.

"Sooo," he drug out the single word like a question, "What do you think? Our daughter makes an excellent case for herself. Who knows where she'll be at Christmas time next year and what she'll be doing. Same with Zayden. He could be completely out of the country by then."

Ian glanced back at Perri, who nodded silently, wearing that same expression she always did when really weighing a decision.

At least she actually has to think about it. Ian remarked to himself. *I'm glad the time spent having to be around me isn't that repulsive.*

Giving her a moment more to think on it, Ian continued almost cautiously, afraid his voice might make her decide against the trip immediately.

"Do you think we could put aside this reality for. . . a fortnight," he suggested the time frame on a whim. Two weeks in Alaska with Perri and their children would be a dream. And since Aspen didn't suggest a length of time, he would, "Just go back to a place where we were always happy, and none of this had ever happened. Can we pretend to get along for that little amount of time for the sake of our kids?"

Perri remained quiet for several long moments, making Ian want to fidget.

"Yes."

He looked up from his shoes, shocked at what he had just heard. "Yes?"

His ex-wife turned her attention to him and, stopping, gave a single nod, "Yes."

"Thank you, Perri," Ian's smile spread across his lips in the most wonderful way and traveled all the way up to his eyes. Taking her hand in both of his, he pressed a gentle kiss to the back of it.

Gazing at Ian as he performed the achingly familiar gesture, Perri longed to tell him that she didn't really hate him at all. She never had.

And her chest ached with a tightness like she was being squeezed by an iron fist. *He was so surprised that I agreed. If only I could be kinder without showing how much I still care. If I could tell him how sorry I was without giving him hope. . .*

"Aspen knew I was all in for the idea," Ian straightened, still smiling but promptly releasing her hand, "so I think she would love to hear from you that we're spending Christmas in Alaska."

Turning on her heels, Perri began closing the remaining distance between herself and her car, "I'll call her on my way home."

Ian, jogging a few paces to catch up with her, fell in step beside her once more, "Are you driving home tonight?"

Never turning her eyes from her car that sat waiting a few parking spaces away, Perri replied simply, "I am."

"Perri. . ." Ian's voice took on a concerned tone.

Oh no please, please don't do this to me. Perri's expression remained neutral, but her stomach knotted in anxiety. *I don't deserve how kind you are.*

"I can tell you're exhausted. I can see it in your eyes," he said, laying a hand on her shoulder. "Should you really drive home this late? It's quite a drive for this hour."

Feeling the warmth of his hand burn through the shoulder of her coat, Perri slowed to a stop beside her car.

"I'm sure I can manage."

Silence reigned between them once again, and Ian decided to try something else. Leaning against Perri's car, he smirked a fraction, hoping his nervousness didn't shine through instead.

"Come back to mine instead."

Again, his ex-wife's eyes snapped up to his.

"What?" she questioned as if she thought she had misheard him.

"Come to mine," he repeated, leaning down a little closer, "We can order Chinese takeaway, and you can make fun of me for still not knowing how to use chopsticks. Then you can soak in the bath and munch on fortune cookies. Let yourself recover from a long job well done."

Still staring up at him in disbelief, Perri tried to appear unaffected by his suggestion.

"We just ate, Ian."

His smirk grew a little, and suddenly the closeness had all of Perri's senses in overdrive.

"I'm sure we can find a way to work up an appetite." Ian's voice was low, more of a rumble from his chest than anything else, "Don't you think."

Perri clenched her jaw to keep her mouth from falling open and slowly narrowed her eyes, hating how she had to tilt her head back ever so slightly to look him in the eye.

"Who are you, and what have you done with my ex-husband."

"My game has improved over the years, Perri," came his simple answer, "Are you impressed?"

Keeping her eyes quizzical, she retorted, "Oh yes. I can imagine every other woman you've enhanced it on before now was very impressed. Shame they didn't know you had no game not so long ago. But I'm sure it does wonderful things when you're on the pull."

Finally looking away, Perri unlocked her car and moved away from Ian, taking a deep breath and trying to clear her head.

His newfound bravado fell away to reveal the same tender, quiet man she knew and loved. Straightening, Ian gave her a soft, less smug smile, "Actually, I've been practicing in the mirror hoping to get your attention and win you back."

Perri was getting tired of his words making her physically pause. But here she was again, halted in place, staring at him over her car. One look at his face, and she could tell he wasn't lying. Eighteen years of marriage to a person gives you that kind of insight.

Her mouth opened and closed a couple of times before Ian's smile gained a little confidence.

"It's okay, Per," he finished, "At least I left you speechless. Whether that means my game has improved or not, I don't really know, but a man can try. You sure you won't let me at least drive you home? I won't try anything."

A few seconds ticked by before Perri shook herself enough to answer, "No, no, I've got it."

"Alright," Ian lifted his hand in a motionless wave, "I'll see you in Alaska then."

"Yeah. . . See you."

Getting in her car, Perri watched Ian walk away, back up the street and around the corner to wherever his car was actually parked.

He was going to be the death of her.

"Alaska was such a bad idea," she stated into the emptiness. As much as Ian's acquired boldness was delightful and gave her the feeling of electricity crackling through her veins, Perri knew it would lead to no good the longer they were forced to be around each other.

Perri tossed her briefcase onto the armchair and went to find her little family.

"Darlings, I'm back," she called, going further into the house. "Sorry I'm late. Traffic was mad as a bag of ferrets."

Following the sounds of voices, she finally found them all in their favorite place to gather, the kitchen.

Peeking in, she smiled softly. Their children, who in Perri's mind's eye had so suddenly grown up, were seated at the kitchen island, watching their father stirring some kind of batter.

Those arms, *Perri mused for a moment,* And those shoulders. Mm, what a man.

Entering the room, she tossed a wink to Aspen and Zayden and moved up behind her husband.

"Can I help?" she offered, resting her chin on his shoulder to sneak a look into the mixing bowl.

"No, thank you, love."

"Oh, okay," Perri took a step back and placed a kiss in the valley of his upper back. Feeling his spine shiver beneath her lips, she smirked, pleased with herself. "I won't refuse the opportunity to just watch."

Looking over his shoulder when he heard Perri's retreating footfalls, Ian smiled, "You know I hate to tell you no and ask you to leave. But I just love the chance to watch you walk away."

"Ugh, Dad!" Aspen gagged, chuckling a little, "You have absolutely no game!"

"Yeah, that was pretty awful," Zayden agreed, still wincing.

"Hey!" Ian pointed a batter dripping spoon in their direction, "I try, okay."

Perri came to stand between the two teens, planting a kiss on each of their heads. "You have to forgive him, my loves," she dropped her voice a fraction but still spoke loud enough for Ian to hear and smirked the whole time, "He's never had any game. I find it very sweet."

Ian met her sidelong gaze and laughed good-naturedly, "See, your Mum has game enough for us both, thank God. Otherwise, I don't know how we ever would have ended up together."

"I'm sure we could have figured it out," Perri replied, "But my flirting definitely saved us time. We may not even be married yet if it hadn't been for that."

"I was trying to be a gentleman!"

"You were scared of me."

"You do tend to make me nervous, Per."

"In the best way," She shot him an exaggerated smile, all teeth and mirth in her eyes.

"How do you know?" he questioned, to which Perri promptly stuck out her tongue, scrunching up her nose, and turned her attention to their children.

* * * * * * * * * * * * *

Aspen's memory was interrupted by her phone vibrating in her pocket. Pulling it out to reveal the screen, she was greeted by a text from Ian.

Please tell me when your Mum makes it home.

Looking up briefly to make sure Zayden was still with her and had not run off to the nearing pub, she typed out a reply.

Will do. Thanks for tonight, Dad.

She watched the three dots appear and do their dance in the bottom corner of her screen.

It was my joy, sweetheart. Love you.

Love you too.

For a moment, she thought about asking if their mother had agreed to family vacation but decided she'd rather enjoy the rest of her evening with her brother.

"Hey," Zayden's voice broke through the quiet between them, "You're giving your phone the scary face. What's going on?"

"I just really wanted us to go on vacation together," she answered, releasing a heavy sigh. She had known since she had the idea that it would probably never happen, but she had went for it anyway and possibly just hurt herself more. But she couldn't help it, both of their parents were that way, and she just happened to inherit the innate ability to cause herself pain when trying to mend things around her.

Wrapping his arm around her shoulders, Zayden pulled her close to his side, and Aspen tucked herself up under her not-so-little brother's arm.

"Listen, it's going to be alright," his finally deepened voice rumbled against her ear where it rested on his shoulder, "You may not have gotten them together this year, but you sure as hell tried, and I love you for it. You're both braver and stronger than me for trying."

"That's not true," Aspen mumbled, forcing back the tears that stung her eyes.

"You are, though," Zayden insisted, squeezing her arm gently. "We both want them to be with each other, but you are the only one willing and ready to try whatever it takes to make that happen. Whereas I've just resigned myself to it and try not to hope that one day things will be like they were."

They continued down the sidewalk toward the bright lights of the pub.

Not knowing how else to respond, Aspen reached up to lay her hand over his, "I love you, you big wanker."

"I know," Zayden smirked with that playful twinkle in his pale eyes.

Rolling her eyes, Aspen smiled. Of course, she knew her brother loved her, he adored her even, but he hardly ever said so.

Before she had time to sass back, a group of several sloshed young men came stumbling out of the pub. It appeared that they were attempting to swagger but were definitely too drunk to do so. Elbowing Zayden, Aspen only had a moment to open her mouth to remark before the wolf whistles and catcalling began. Immediately, her brother's face lost all twinkle of amusement and took on a dark expression Aspen rarely saw.

"Zayden, just leave it," she whispered, not wanting to ruin their evening because a pack of boys didn't know how to respect a woman.

"If you're not going to take care of it," he growled, "I will."

"Zayden—"

"Oi! Listen here, you tossers, this is my date," Zayden had drawn back his shoulders, making himself appear taller and broader than Aspen was used to, "And I know a handful of sergeants who wouldn't take too kindly to you harassing this lovely lady."

The group fell quiet, and they passed by with most of their eyes on the ground, all except one. He flashed a cocky smile and shot Aspen a wink.

"If you change your mind and want to hit the pub two blocks over with me, I'll wait around."

"Shove off, you chav," Aspen snapped.

With a shrug of indifference, he followed after the rest of his group.

Taking Zayden's arm, Aspen pulled them in the opposite direction and up the stairs to the small shack-like pub.

"What a slag," she stated, opening the door, "He was very fit, though."

Zayden stopped in his tracks, "Are you serious, Penny?! He just treated you like that, and you still think he was worth looking at."

"When you're fit, you're fit," she shrugged, "I can't help that he was easy on the eyes. Now, come on, it's my round."

Shaking his head, Zayden finally moved from where he had cemented his feet and reached around his sister to open the door. As she passed through the door, he ran his fingers over the small braid laid tight against her scalp that divided the shaved portion of her head from the rest of the thick waves of blonde hair.

"So I guess this punk rocker look is really doing it for you, huh."

Laughing, Aspen brushed his hand away, "Shut up, fetus."

I've got stitches and scars
I've got yards of yarn
Got miles of string running under my skin
I've got so much to give so I'll give it
Again and again and again.

— "Red Ribbon" by Madliyn

As fate would have it, Aspen and Zayden were still together late into the night. They had walked to his loft apartment, where Aspen had left her car before beginning their pub crawl and were settling in for the night.

"This is awful close to River Irwell," she said, making herself comfortable on his couch. "I still don't think you make this much money."

"You're going to have to face it one day, sis," Zayden shrugged, straightening from digging in the refrigerator with bottles of water in hand, "Your little brother has made it big."

"Zay, your phone's ringing." Aspen yelled from the living room and peeked at the lit-up screen, "It's Mum!"

Hearing his sister practically throw herself over the back of the couch onto his catch-all table where his phone was vibrating, Zayden chuckled.

"Hey, Mum!" she greeted loudly without meaning to.

Zayden shook his head and murmured, "Sure, go ahead and answer it then." But he couldn't help the smile that lifted the corner of his lips at the sound of his sister trying not to sound too enthusiastic and failing so miserably.

"Hello, love," Perri smiled at her daughter's poorly concealed excitement. It never failed to brighten her world. "What are you two up to? Since I assume you're both still alive, and you're not the only one left."

"We're just faffing around at his loft," Aspen replied, settling back down on the couch, "Is everything okay? Are you home yet?"

"Everything is fine, but no, I'm not home yet."

"It's late, please be careful, Mum."

"I'm fine, sweetheart," Perri chuckled, "Now, is your brother around since I called his phone."

"He's here," Aspen swiveled around and, reaching out toward her brother, snapped her fingers to get his attention. "I'll put you on speaker."

"I spoke with your Dad about your idea of going to Alaska for Christmas."

"Yeah?" Aspen could feel the hope bubbling up inside her, despite how hard she tried to push it down.

"I hate to admit when he's right, but he is. We should enjoy our last Christmas together before you two are off to do your own things."

"Soooo," she drew out the word like a question, "Hotel Alyeska?"

"I did want it to be a bit of a surprise, hence why I called Zayden, but since you picked up. . ." Perri trailed off teasingly.

"Yes?" Aspen bounced in her seat as Zayden sat down beside her.

"We're going to Hotel Alyeska for Christmas," their mother confirmed.

Letting out a shriek that was part triumph, the rest pure joy, Aspen latched onto her brother's shoulder and shook him almost violently, and he laughed.

"Family spa days! Seven Glacier restaurant for dinner! Hot tubs! Nature trails! And skiing!" Aspen's pitch hit a new level with each memory she recalled.

"Yes," Perri chuckled, her own giddiness blooming in her chest. She would do anything in the world to see her children smile, and if this was what Aspen wanted, well then, a family vacation was what she would surely have.

"So, I suppose it is safe to assume that you guys are in?" she inquired, mostly teasing.

"We are *so* in!" the two yelled into the phone.

"I'll make the reservations as soon as I get home."

"Okay!" Aspen exclaimed, "Let us know when you get there."

"I will," their mother replied, "I love you both."

"Love you too," they answered, and the line went dead.

"Must be that candle magic, huh," Zayden shot her a wink.

"Holy crap," Aspen's mouth fell open in complete shock, "Do you know what this means?"

"Yeah," he chuckled, "Instead of Mum and Dad fighting in the UK, they're going to fight in the US?"

"I don't think that even their bickering could ruin this moment for me right now." Aspen admitted as she fell back into the couch,

"They got along well enough to discuss the idea of a family trip. That's promising."

"Maybe."

"That's progress. They normally use us as messengers."

"That is very true," Zayden nodded, holding out a bottle of water, "Here, drink this."

"Mark my words, Zay," Aspen giddily twisted open the bottle, "I've got a good feeling about this."

2

And I remembered everything
And every windowpane
Every word came back to me
The way it used to be
Then I saw your face across the street
And my heart was home again

— "My Heart Was Home Again"

Nestled close against the breathtaking Chugach Mountains, Hotel Alyeska offers year-round adventure, but it's always a little special around Christmas time. In December of 1998, Alyeska broke its previous record of the most snowfall within a month when 283 inches fell, covering the whole resort in almost 24 feet of snow. During Christmas week alone, Alyeska received 100 inches of snow in a seven-day period.

To the west and north of the resort, the mountains of the Chugach State Park provide a spectacular backdrop over Alyeska. At 495,000 acres, Alyeska Resort is the third largest state park in the US. In 1954, eleven of Girdwood's residents passed a tattered hat and raised enough money to purchase what became the land base for the major ski area. Through much perseverance and initiative, they developed a small ski area that held much promise. Coming upon a French Baron who shared their dream, Francois De Gunzburg installed a Poma chairlift, built ski trails, and a day lodge. Then he ordered Chair 1, a 5,700-foot double chairlift that rose 2,000 vertical feet into the air.

Today Alyeska Resort is an established ski destination known around the world for its steep terrain and deep snowpack. With expansive mountains and ocean inlet views at your very fingertips, Alyeska boasts an average of 650 inches of annual snowfall at the summit.

And at the base of it all stands the 300-room Hotel Alyeska.

"Penny," Zayden's voice made Aspen look up from her laptop, where she was rapidly typing to try and soothe her anxiety.

"Are they here?!"

Laying one of his surprisingly large hands on her shoulder, Zayden held her gaze with his own pale blue one.

"Take a breath. They're going to be here. They promised, and they won't break a promise to us."

Nodding and inhaling deeply, Aspen released it slowly, "You're right. It's going to be fine. They wouldn't stand us up without an explanation."

"That's right," he agreed in a calming tone, "So there's no need for you to worry so much. Calm down, look around, get some inspiration from the airport atmosphere, and write about something. *For fun.* Not like you have been hired to write the resort's next brochure."

Turning her dark eyes back to the open document with its blinking cursor, Aspen tried to slow her racing heart and not panic that their parents had changed their minds and decided they couldn't—or wouldn't—cohabitate the same resort for just two weeks.

"Now, I need to go see a man about a dog," Zayden stated, standing up from his seat, "Will you be okay out here and not have some psycho anxiety attack while I'm gone?"

Giving his hip a shove, Aspen shooed him away and told him he had better be careful calling her psycho.

"Don't leave without me, yeah," Zayden chuckled over his shoulder as he walked off.

"No promises, fetus."

Lifting her gaze from the screen, Aspen looked around for a moment, hoping to find their parents somewhere in the crowd.

Instead, her eyes caught on a small girl running a few steps ahead of a watchful-eyed man, straight into the waiting arms of a woman who had knelt down at the sight of her approach.

"There's my favorite girl!" the woman squeezed her tight and stood up, holding the girl close.

Beside the woman whose arms were now full of what appeared to be a small seven-year-old was another kind-faced brunette who was trying her best to look offended.

With a tap to the little girl's shoulder, "Excuse me. Where's my kiss? I mean, I know you haven't seen Auntie in a long time, but I still exist too."

The small brunette head untucked itself from her aunt's shoulder, and the woman was greeted with a bright but tired smile.

"Hi, Mum."

Reaching out to caress her daughter's hair, the woman paused as her eyes locked in on a scuff mark on the pale cheek before her.

"What happened, baby?"

Slipping up behind her, the man placed his hand on her shoulder before leaning close, "There was a little mishap at school today."

Deep green eyes filled with tears as the little girl looked up at her mother, "They were saying mean things. I just wanted them to stop."

"It's alright, baby," the woman assured, laying a tender hand on her back, "We'll talk about it when we get home, yeah?"

She nodded against her aunt's shoulder, and the woman instinctively tightened her embrace. As the family passed by Aspen to exit the airport, she overheard the aunt lean down and ask softly, "Do you want Auntie to go talk to their Mummies and get them in trouble?"

Being a woman to get lost in her own head much of the time, Aspen's mind drifted back to her own primary school days and an experience similar to the one she had just watched unfold.

* * * * * * * * * * * * *

Perri's car practically flew into her daughter's primary school parking, throwing loose pebbles as she whipped to a stop.

Catching sight of seven-year-old Aspen seated on the large steps outside, Perri was out of the car in a flash and racing up to her daughter's slump-shouldered formed.

"Love, wha' are you doin' outside?"

Finally looking up from her scuffed shoes, Aspen met her mother's eyes with a red-rimmed gaze of her own.

"I didn't want to sit inside any more."

Knelling down and pushing a lock of hair behind her ear, Perri cupped Aspen's face in her free hand. Looking past her daughter, she met the teacher's gaze and nodded. Understanding the que, the young woman returned the gesture and slipped silently back inside.

"Are you ready to go home?"

The blonde head nodded, and Aspen whipped her eyes with her sleeve.

It was then that Perri caught sight of her daughter's knuckles. Feeling her chest tighten with deep, burning anger, Perri took as deep a breath as she could manage. Scooping up her daughter, Perri cradled the back of her head tenderly and turned to take her to the car so that she could get them home as quickly as possible.

"What happened, Penny girl?" Perri swallowed down the churning apprehension she could feel crawling through her stomach.

"They were saying mean things. I couldn't get them to stop, and I got mad," the girl explained, her chin quivering. "And when I went to hit them, they moved out of the way, and I hit the wall instead."

Depositing her daughter in the backseat, Perri sighed and hung her head for a moment.

"Baby, you know we can't make things better with fighting."

Aspen nodded, and a tear escaped from her eye to make a tiny path down her cheek. Planting a kiss on top of her head, Perri went to open the boot and take out a mini first aid kit she kept neatly tucked in the back. Between her husband and her children, she needed more than one if she were honest.

"Hold still, love," she said, and taking Aspen's small hand in hers, she wiped at her bloody knuckles with an antiseptic wipe.

"Why did they not clean this up for you?" Perri tried not to let her anger boil over.

"I didn't want them to. I wanted you to do it."

Wrapping some gauze lightly around her hand and taping the wrap in place, Perri pressed a kiss to the back of her hand and reached around to buckle Aspen in.

"Let's get you home. We'll talk about it all later, okay."

Later that evening. . .

Coming into Perri's drawing-room, Ian peeked inside to find his wife hard at work in front of her drafting table with one arm securely around a sleeping Aspen's back. Their daughter's head lay contentedly against Perri's freckled shoulder.

"How are my girls?" he asked softly.

Perri lifted her eyes from the building plans and gave him a close-lipped smile, "Tired. Both of them."

Coming up to stand beside her chair, Ian leaned down to kiss the corner of Perri's lips.

"I can see that," he remarked, taking in his wife's lead smudged hands and the plans on the table, "It's looking great, darling. When do you show them what you've made?"

"A couple of weeks," she answered, "I'm not satisfied yet."

"Of course, you aren't."

His low chuckle rumbled near Perri's ear, and she tried not to smile but cut her eyes at him instead.

Kneeling down, he brushed a finger over the thick bandages on their daughter's hand.

"What happened?"

"We talked about it," Perri leaned back in her chair and stared up at the ceiling, "Apparently, some of her classmates were saying that Zayden is not her real brother. So after they wouldn't stop, she took matters into her own hands. . . Or fist, in this case, I suppose."

Lulling her head to the side, Perri met Ian's gaze, "They moved, and she ended up punching the wall instead. Unfortunately."

"Perri," Ian chided laughingly.

"What?" she insisted, "I know their mother's. They sit in local coffee shops and talk shite about people all day. I swear it's what they do for a living."

Ian was silent for a long moment and stared at Aspen's sleeping face.

"Is Zay still with Mum?"

"Yes, they're out taking care of the horses, and then she's bringing him home."

"Maybe we should talk some things over with Penny."

"I agree. Then we go to the school tomorrow and have a nice little discussion with those mothers at drop-off."

Bedtime. . .

Carrying Aspen across the hall to her room after reading stories in their bed, Ian held the freshly wrapped hand tenderly in his and felt an ache in his chest. Laying Aspen down in her bed, he tucked her in and kissed her forehead.

"One more story?" Aspen pleaded.

"Not tonight, sweetheart," he replied, "Two stories tomorrow, how about that."

Aspen's mouth opened wide in a big yawn, "Okay."

"You were very brave today, but we don't want you to use violence to express what you're feeling. You might get seriously hurt," Pushing the blonde bangs from his daughter's face, Ian continued, "And then who would I have tickle fights with? Your Mum can't handle too much tickling. She would scream and scare all the neighbors."

Aspen giggled, her eyes scanning the glow-in-the-dark stars on the ceiling before landing back on Ian's face.

Coming in from putting an already sleeping Zayden in his bed, Perri joined her husband in Aspen's room.

"Good night, love," she bent down to kiss her cheek, "Fais de beaux rêves."

Aspen mumbled a garbled version of the French phrase in return, and her dark eyes drifted closed.

Leaning back against Ian, Perri sighed and allowed her own eyes to close.

"It's going to be alright, isn't it," she asked more than stated, "Someday, they'll understand, and we won't have to worry so much."

Wrapping his arms around her middle, Ian rested his chin on her shoulder, "Exactly. Until then, it will be alright, and after that, it will still be alright."

Somewhere outside the London Airport. . .

The mist fell thick onto her windshield as she pulled to a stop behind the line of cars looking for places to park. Glancing over to the passenger seat, she quirked a brow at Perri, who sat anxiously rubbing the soft skin of the scar that divided her eyebrow into uneven halves.

"Per."

The blonde gave a quiet hum in response, her dark eyes locked on the line of people making their way into the airport.

"Calm down. Ya actin' like it's ya first date or somethin'."

Head snapping to glare at her best friend, Perri's hand dropped, "I am not. In case you don't recall, our children will be there too, not just Ian and me."

Aliyah laughed, "I think you're the one who needs to remember."

"Shove off," Perri mumbled.

"Whatever ya say, princess," Aliyah shrugged as she set the car into crawling motion. "Ya can just get out 'ere then and run all those bags inside through this dreary weather."

"I'm sorry," she sighed, letting her head fall back against the headrest. "I didn't mean it."

"Ya only sayin' that because you want me help."

Lulling her head to the side, a wicked smirk grew across Perri's face, "Maybe."

Shaking her head, a blinding smile lit up Aliyah's features, "Hag."

As they snaked through the rows of parking in comfortable silence, Perri glanced over at the woman across from her.

"Thank you for doing this, babe."

Reaching over, Aliyah squeezed Perri's arm, "Any time, chick."

Perri smiled softly and remembered a time back in primary school all those years ago when she and Aliyah had first met. The two had always been just as opposite as yin and yang, only compact versions compared to now. When the two first met, things were so much different it was almost hard to believe how different they were.

Perri was small, a darkness resting under her young but tired eyes, and strikingly blonde. Primary school Perri was not bold or confident just yet, given time, she grew into both, but having just lost her mother, she was timid and trying to sort out what life had become for her.

Aliyah, on the other hand, was tall for her age and strong; her dark hair bounced in delightful corkscrew curls every which way, her bronze skin dotted with soft freckles across her cheekbones and nose. It was her kind, black eyes that first caught quiet Perri's attention and then her unbridled ways that drew her young classmate in. Not to mention the heavy Cockney accent that fascinated the little blonde as soon as she heard it. The accent had lessened as Aliyah grew up and traveled more, but the basic sound still lingered and would really come out on occasion, mostly when she got upset or was in what she called "safe" company.

As the song goes, ebony and ivory live together in perfect harmony. It had been that way since the beginning. And as time went on, the pair found themselves picking up mannerisms from one another. It was inevitable, their parents noted, with how the two were attached at the hip they were bound to act like blood sisters. As the years went by, Perri knew that even if she were offered as many blood sisters as she ever wanted, she would never trade Aliyah. It was just that simple.

Looking over at Aliyah, Perri watched her determined expression for a long moment. Determination just seemed to be her friend's resting face. Aliyah smooth skin was still sprinkled in freckles that she made no efforts to hide, her dark eyes gleamed golden in the sunlight and were accented by smile lines at the corners, and her thick chestnut hair was beginning to gray in a single strip sprouting up from the center of her forehead.

"You're really going to make me go in by myself?"

Aliyah glanced over at her passenger, her brows knit together in confusion. "You're actin like I'm sendin' ya in to take down a whole secret agency. Per, you are goin' in to get on a plane with ya family. And being that I have seen my niece and nephew very recently, I will not come in and take up time. You're all scotch mist about nothin', chick."

Coming to a stop behind yet another motionless car, dark eyes turned to meet Perri's gaze.

"You are goin' to be fine. You're doin' this for your kids, remember, so be kind and try to enjoy yaself."

Huffing out a sigh, Perri fell back against her seat, "I will. I'm looking forward to it, I really am. I'm just. . . anxious."

"I know, I can feel that," Aliyah laughed, "But I'm serious, there's nothin' for you to worry about. Unless you are worried about not bein' able to hide your feelin's for Ian for two whole weeks. Then that's a legitimate concern."

"Shut up!" Perri gently shoved her and looked out the window, trying to hide the blush creeping up her neck.

"Oh, remind me to never tease you again," Aliyah replied in mock fear, "I may end up seriously injured. Maybe even down below with the brown bread if I'm not careful."

"You are driving, I can't risk any more than a good shove. Just wait until you don't suspect me anymore and then we'll see who's laughing," Perri shot her a wicked smile.

"Sure, babe," came the laughing response, and the car turned into a parking spot finally close to the entrance of the airport, "A'ight, woman get out of me car."

"Rude," Perri grabbed her purse and went to open the door, "But fine."

Stepping out into the chilled London air, she popped the collar of her coat and leaned down to smile in at Aliyah.

"Thanks again for the ride and all that *wonderful* moral support."

"Ya welcome," Aliyah shot her the tooth-rotting grin. "I'll talk to you la'er on, okay."

Perri nodded and straightened to her full height, "Open your boot, I've got to get my things."

"There you go, chick."

She couldn't help it. Aspen continued to scan the constantly moving crowd and then glance down at her watch to check the time. Their flight would be boarding soon, and there was still no sign of their parents.

"You ever feel like an owl, sis?"

Zayden's voice startled her a bit, and she turned to quirk an eyebrow at him in question.

"Your head is always swiveling, and it makes you look a lot like a tiny, angry owl."

"Shut up, fetus," Aspen tried not to laugh, shoving his shoulder.

Zayden shrugged, smirking a little, "I was just wondering if you felt like you were ever an owl in your past life."

He always knew how to make her laugh and take her thoughts away from whatever was wearing her down. But Zayden was also not someone to deflect for too long. He was the one to ease the moment, bring about some relaxation, and then approach the subject. By "approach," he typically charged the subject at high speeds.

Laying his hand on Aspen's shoulder, he squeezed gently.

"Like I said, Penny, they'll be here."

Aspen turned to look out the massive window wall instead of focusing her eyes on the ever-changing mass of people and hummed softly in response.

"They wouldn't let us down like that. Not without good reason."

"What if they both came up with good reasons?" she asked so softly Zayden almost missed it over the collective buzz of airport chaos.

"It's a real pea-souper out there today."

The siblings nearly leaped out of their seats at the sound of their father's voice. But instead of tackling him out of pure excitement, much like when they were children, they settled for jumping up and taking turns hugging the broad-shouldered man instead.

"Well, I didn't expect you two to be this happy to see me," he laughed as he planted a kiss atop Aspen's blonde head.

Throwing a wink Zayden's way, Aspen replied, "I *really* didn't want to spend two weeks alone in Alaska with my brother."

"Very funny. You're not always my cup of tea either," Zayden shot her a wicked smirk, "You're something more akin to. . . a bucket of bog water."

Aspen's brows nearly touched her hairline, and she stared at him, momentarily shocked, "Bog water? Really?"

"And to think I get to experience two full weeks of your bickering," Ian smiled at his children and looped his arms around their shoulders, "Where's your Mum?"

"Not sure," Zayden leaned forward to meet Aspen's eyes, "Do you want to go call her, Penny?"

"Sure, I'll be right back."

Stepping away to stand by the window wall, Aspen pulled out her phone and dialed her mother. She started counting the number of rings.

One.

Two.

Three.

Four.

Aspen could feel this invisible fist squeezing around her chest, crushing her lungs. Her heart was next.

Five rings.

She really wasn't going to pick up. Aspen took a deep breath and hung up just as the sixth ring began, her eyes stinging with the tears that threatened to escape without her consent.

Tucking her cell back in her pocket, she went to rejoin the father-son pair who were laughing about some story Zayden had just told in his very animated way.

It just wasn't like their mother not to answer at all. Even when she was busy, she would at least pick up and say she would call right back when she could.

But it also wasn't like her to just not show without an explanation. Deep down, Aspen knew that, but it didn't take away the panic that this time just might be different.

Putting on a smile, Aspen tried not to let her overthinking mind choke her.

Looking up, Ian smiled brightly at her, "Did you get an answer, sweetheart?"

Returning the smile, she hoped it reached her eyes but when she opened her mouth to reply her phone began to ring instead. Quickly reaching into her pocket, her eyes snapped to the screen, which was now illuminated by a picture she had taken with Perri a few weeks ago while walking around the university campus with her.

"Wait! This is her!"

Bringing the phone to her ear, she tried not to sound too frantic. "Hey, Mum!"

"Love, I'm sorry I missed your call."

The relief washed over Aspen like a tsunami wave at the sound of her mother's voice. Now, for the moment of truth. And just like that, her heart rate was back up all over again.

"It's—it's okay," she replied, "Um, so are you still coming or. . .?"

"Yes, baby, of course," Perri replied, *"I'm actually heading your way right now. You're near our gate, yes?"*

Aspen squealed into the phone and heard her mother laugh. "I'm so excited! Yes, yes, we're waiting near our gate! I'll see you in a few!"

"Actually, I think I see you now."

Her eyes searched the crowd for her mother's face and, finally, she spotted her. Ending their call, she closed the distance between them as fast as she could while trying to go against the flow of airport traffic.

Perri came to a stop. Immediately putting down her carry-on bag and setting her roll-away up next to her just as Aspen collided with her and latched on tightly.

"Hi!" Perri greeted, a little surprised by the enthusiasm but readily returning her daughter's embrace, cupping the back of her head. "I'm sorry it took me so long. They were taking their time at security."

Aspen snuggled closer, her response muffled by her mother's coat, "S'okay. You're here, that's all I wanted."

Aspen could smell the crisp London air still clinging to Perri's coat and mixing with the familiar scent of her green apple shampoo. She couldn't recall feeling such a soothing warmth blossom in her chest in a long while.

"Darling, you act like I wasn't just at your dorm," the woman chuckled but dared not let go of her daughter.

That was one of the things Aspen loved so much about her mother. Perri was never the first to let go in a hug. She would hold you as long as you stood there and wanted to be held. And after a certain length of time, if you were still holding on, she would wrap you tighter, not by much, just enough for you to notice. And she always, without fail, would cradle the back of your head in the most caring way. That was something Perri didn't even realize she did until Zayden pointed it out years ago. Aspen remembered the way their mother seemed to think on it for a moment, then she shrugged and smiled, *"I had never even noticed."*

Not wanting to be utterly selfish, Aspen let go and moved to her mother's side, picking up the carry-on bag so that she could stay tucked under Perri's arm.

When they finally made it to where Zayden and Ian still stood waiting, Perri planted a kiss on the side of Aspen's head before letting go to hug her son.

Bending down just a little, Zayden eagerly enfolded his mother, and his chest rumbled in a chuckle as she had to reach up to hold the back of his head.

"My boy," she greeted, squeezing him tightly. Well, as best she could anyway.

"Hi, Mum."

Taking a step back after a few more long seconds, Zayden smiled down at the woman. Feeling himself relax at last and allowing himself a little glimmer of hope that maybe, just maybe, his sister's scheme would work out after all.

"You must be as tall as your father now," Perri marveled, looking over her son's shoulder at Ian, who stood smiling not too far away.

Turning to look at his father, Zayden beamed with pride, and Ian decided it was time he joined the little group instead of just watching from a distance.

"Hello, Perri," he greeted, and Perri returned his smile softly.

For a moment, she didn't know what to do. Shaking his hand was much too formal, but hugging him was so *so* dangerous. She could already feel the familiar ache in her chest just at the closeness of him. If she hugged him she knew the turmoil that would break loose inside her. And she knew she would not want to let go.

Ian, though he seemed to be having the same internal struggle, somehow reasoned that a hug would be fine. Stepping forward, he wrapped his arms around his ex-wife and pulled her close against his chest. The familiarity of his embrace was enough to almost bring tears to Perri's eyes as she slid her arms around him in return, her chest tight and eyes stinging.

Her senses were overwhelmed by all things Ian. His arms, his hands against the small of her back and holding on to her shoulder, and the way she would have to lift her chin to rest it on his shoulder. The way he rested his jaw gently against the side of her head and his cologne. Ian still smelt of the same cologne that haunted Perri's memories. She tried not to breathe so deeply that he noticed, but it had been so long since Ian had held her this close. She wanted to breathe in what it smelt like. Try, in the smallest way, to bottle up how it felt so she could hold on to it long after these two weeks were over.

Just as quickly as it happened, the embrace was over. A handful of seconds passed, both like a flash of light and yet seemed to go on for more than forever. As if time itself had stopped, but it still wasn't long enough.

For a fraction of a moment more, Ian's hand remained on Perri's arm, and she relished the soft, warm pressure of it, despite the barrier of extra layers between their skin. He allowed his hand to drop back to his side, and Perri did her best to ignore her heart clenching in her chest.

"Uh. . . Do you need help getting anything from your boot?" Ian offered, not really knowing what else to say but feeling like he had to say something.

Perri smiled a little, "No, thank you. I got it all through the first time."

"Right," he rubbed the back of his neck and chuckled a little awkwardly, "Of course."

Perri watched with a wicked smirk growing across her lips as her ex-husband's eyes drifted from her face, slowly slowly all the way down and then back up. Of course, she knew that Ian was attracted to her still, even after all these years, but it was always a boost in confidence every time he so blatantly stared at her with slowly roaming eyes.

Yep, still got it.

But she wasn't doing much better herself if she was honest.

The balancing act between not being allowed to love each other anymore and still deeply loving one another was beginning to become too much for them to keep up. These days they could feel the hum of electric attraction between them. At just the right moment, the sickeningly polite voice of a woman announcing that their flight was ready to board cut through the air.

Once the voice went away, Ian smiled at their children and picked up his bags.

"Well, time to go!"

"Yes," Perri quickly agreed, "Everyone have their tickets?"

While tickets were being retrieved from pockets and everyone was distracted, Perri pulled out her phone and sent a quick text.

He's wearing that bloody sweater.

"Mum, come on," Zayden called, pausing as they began to walk toward their gate.

Perri looked up and smiled, "Coming, love."

As they approached the gate, she felt her phone vibrate in her pocket. Bringing it out to glance at the screen, she found a reply from Aliyah.

Oh, the grey sweater ;)

Shaking her head but unable to not smile a bit, Perri's thumbs tapped across the screen.

Don't text and drive, stupid.

Not even a minute later, the response came back.

Well, don't text me important stuff while I'm driving :p

"Madame?"

The voice startled her, and Perri swiftly put her phone away and greeted the man with her bright, business smile.

"My apologies," she passed him her ticket and followed her family.

Aspen and Zayden walked close together, talking softly as they took casual glances back at their parents.

"Gosh, I hope this doesn't turn into a dog's dinner," Zayden leaned closer to murmur in his sister's ear.

"*You* hope it doesn't turn into a dog's dinner? I've dedicated weeks of planning to this. I may throw myself into the ocean if this turns into a fiasco."

"Well, if you do that, at least I'll get the window seat."

"Quit your whinging," Aspen shooed his words away with a wave of her hand with mannerisms much like their mother. "I called bagsy on the window seat long before you did."

Searching the aisle for their places, the two quickly slid into one pair of seats, leaving their parents with only one option; to sit beside each other the whole ten-hour flight. Settling in like two mischievous and excited children, the siblings smiled at their parents as they came into view. The realization of their current situation only made Ian and Perri pause for a moment before continuing their approach, just a little more hesitant now.

Could they handle ten hours in such agonizingly close proximity to each other without one of them combusting for one reason or another?

Seems there was only one way to find out.

Stepping aside, Ian allowed Perri to take the window seat where she had always been the least unperturbed. Planes, despite her constant travel on them, had never been something Perri enjoyed. Did she endure it? Yes. Did she like doing so? Definitely not.

Putting their carry-ons into the overhead, Ian sat down and prepared for takeoff. Cutting his downcast eyes briefly in Perri's direction, he took note of the slight tremor of her hands but decided it was best not to say a word.

Instead, once she was belted in and as ready as she was going to be, Ian leaned slowly into her space, giving her time to back away if it made her too uncomfortable. When she didn't move away from him but instead glanced up at him with a curious expression, Ian smiled a little and whispered to her.

"I didn't want to get the kids all excited, but I wanted you to know," he paused a moment, and Perri's heart raced with both anticipation and dread, "You look beautiful, by the way."

His eyes drifted over to meet her gaze for a handful of seconds before turning his attention to the flight attendant that had just appeared to give the safety demonstration.

Perri's eyes fell on the black screen on the headrest in front of her and remained unmoving for the longest time. She could faintly hear the voice prattling on about oxygen masks and seatbelts, but she knew the whole speech by heart anyway. Her thoughts were elsewhere and better occupied.

That was something she loved about Ian. When he said things like that, he expected nothing in return, unlike most men. It still did funny things to her chest, and try as she might, Perri still couldn't shake it.

The feeling of the plane beginning to roll forward brought Perri from her thoughts and back to the semi-frightening present as she latched onto the armrest between her and her ex-husband.

"They did say there may be a little extra turbulence due to the weather. Nothing bad, just a little more noticeable than usual," Ian reported, knowing Perri hadn't heard a word of what was said and would have to struggle to mask her panic when the flight wasn't as smooth as most.

Perri nodded and murmured her thanks, attempting to nestle herself back into her seat and maybe relax.

She did this alone all the time. This time would be better, even if there was some added turbulence. Because this time she had her family with her. Her people. It would be okay; she wasn't alone.

These eyes cry every night for you
These arms long to hold you again

— "These Eyes" by Lisa Lambe

Once in the air, Perri found her body uncoiling from its previously taut position and her lungs were able to fill themselves without her anxiety getting in the way. She knew that no one in the line of sight had noticed, she had tamed her nerves about planes enough to see to that, but she also knew that Ian had been silently taking in the whole thing. He still knew her too well to not pick up on her behavior, and she could see it in the long side glances that studied her.

She noticed something else as well.

"Are you going to sleep?"

Surprised by the sound of her voice, Ian turned and shot her an inquisitive look.

"No, I don't think so," Perri tried not to seem relieved at his reply, "Why?"

She paused for a moment, trying to find words to express what she saw in his face.

"Your eyes look tired. That's all."

"Yeah," Ian sighed and leaned his head back against the seat. "It was a rough day yesterday."

Perri knew what that meant, and her chest clenched painfully. She hated that her body still responded in empathy to the man she had left so many years ago. It wasn't supposed to be like this.

"I'm sorry. Do you. . . want to talk about it? I have plenty of time, and they tell me I'm a good listener." She tried shooting him an encouraging smile.

Turning his attention back to her, Ian smiled a fraction, "No, no, I'm okay. I'm officially on vacation with my family for the next two weeks. I'm okay."

Perri nodded, smiling sadly but with a softness in her eyes that she didn't quite realize still resided there when she looked at her ex-husband. She understood.

But she couldn't stop the twist of jealousy deep in her chest. Who did Ian talk to about his hard days now? And why was she suddenly upset that it wasn't her?

Ian laid his head back again and gazed up at the pristine white ceilings of the plane, trying desperately not to go down the rabbit hole of memories that Perri had just accidentally drug up.

He couldn't help but wonder if, just maybe, she was thinking about it too. But that was one thing about Perri. You would never know for certain what exactly she was thinking about unless she told you. It was part of her mystique, and despite being occasionally inconvenient, Ian had loved that about her. Still did.

* * * * * * * * * * * * *

Ian entered the house as silently as possible, hoping their dogs wouldn't make too much racket at his arrival just in case Perri was asleep. He hoped she hadn't waited up for him this whole time. It was incredibly late, and he knew it. He felt terrible about having missed dinner, again, after promising he would be home.

That will be the last time I do something stupid like that. *He thought as he eased inside.*

All was quiet. A lamp was left on in the living room, and so was the hall light. Following the path of light she had left for him, Ian looked into their bedroom and found his wife in a deep sleep atop the blankets of their bed. Her foot was resting on their Anatolian Shepherd's broad chest as if she had been rubbing it before they all fell asleep. And one of her arms was looped around their King Charles Spaniel, who slept contentedly tucked as close to her as possible. Perri's free arm was left resting akimbo, her fingers laying against her forehead, almost as if she had been thinking as she fell asleep.

Ian approached the bed softly, both dogs opening their eyes to thump their tails gently in greeting. Too exhausted to change, he laid down gently next to his wife and rested his head against her chest. The top of his head tenderly lying against her clavicle, where his cheek could just barely feel the beating of her heart beneath her ribs. Within minutes of laying down, he was lulled to sleep by the rhythmic rise and fall of Perri's chest.

Perri awoke almost an hour later, her fingers buried in the thick hair at the back of Ian's head, which was tucked up under her chin. Filling her lungs, she moved her head to look down at his sleeping face and smiled softly. She was glad he finally got to come home. Lifting her hand from his head, she draped her arm over his side and laid her hand on his hip. Discovering her other arm to be Spaniel free now, she reached up to lay her hand over his that had found a resting place on her stomach.

Humming quietly in content, Perri went to close her eyes again but was stopped by the rumble of Ian's voice, gravelly with sleep.

"I'm so sorry I missed dinner."

Tightening her hold on him as best she could, Perri planted a kiss on his hairline, "That's all right. This is much better anyway."

Rolling onto his stomach, Ian raised himself up to gaze into his wife's face.

"How did I manage to make you love me like you do?"

Perri shrugged, "Just luck, I guess." Reaching up to cradle his face in her hand, she studied him in the dim light that was pouring through the window. "Your eyes look tired."

"Rough day, that's all," he replied, smiling with a hint of sorrow peeking through.

A sadness came to rest in Perri's dark eyes, and her brows knit together, "I'm so sorry."

"It'll be alright," he answered simply, but she noticed the sigh that followed, whether he meant for her to or not.

Feeling helpless against the things Ian had to see and do, Perri turned to something that always soothed her when she was upset. Consistent strokes of some design, gentle against the skin to distract from madness in the mind. So Perri brushed her thumb back and forth across his cheek, then trailed her fingertips down his jaw to his chin before sweeping up again with the back of her fingers. Slow, calming motions in hopes of easing him somehow. Finally, she tunneled her fingers into his hair and just held his still tired gaze.

Ian was still so focused on the tender caressing pattern she had started that he almost missed her question of whether he wanted to talk about it or just leave it alone for tonight.

Pausing a moment, he gazed down at his wife and debated, could he stay awake to talk right now, or did he just want to go back to sleep.

Sleep won out.

"I think I really just want to get in some more comfortable clothes and go back to sleep."

Chuckling, Perri brushed her thumb across his cheek a few more times, and Ian could see the outline of her smile. "Okay. Make tracks then because I'm chilled and would like my personal heater back."

"Of course, that's the only reason why you're not wanting me to talk about my feelings," Ian lowered himself to kiss a now laughing Perri's cheek before rolling off the bed to change.

* * * * * * * * * * * * * * *

Ian's chest both warmed and ached at the memory, and having Perri so close just made it even more painful. But at the same time, there was no way he was leaving this spot so near to the woman who still held his affections after all this time. He hadn't had a reason to be this close to her for this long in years, and he wasn't about to give it up.

Glancing over at his ex-wife just to look at her for a moment, Ian noticed Perri's tension and instead turned to watch her. He said nothing, looking back to the tiny TV in front of him even while his attention remained on the woman beside him.

A few seconds later, Perri was briefly startled when she felt the tentative pressure of Ian's pinky finger on the back of her hand. Her gaze snapped down to where her hand lay on the armrest, and her eyes followed the pattern her ex-husband was making with his finger against her skin. Perri hadn't even realized that she was clenching her fist. Slowly relaxing her white-knuckled grip, Perri flipped her hand over and allowed Ian's fingers to trace a gentle path along the creases of her palm.

He gives me shivers even today. It's not fair.

Lifting her gaze Perri watched as Ian's soft stare flicked down from her eyes to her lips and then back up guiltily. He didn't miss the raise of Perri's eyebrows, followed by the slight curve to her mouth that shot a spark of warmth through him.

Maybe, just maybe, there would be a chance for them again one day. A man had to have some reason to hope, didn't he?

3

And still
The world stood still
I couldn't move
And all I could feel
Was this aching in my heart
Saying I loved him still

— "And Still" by Reba McEntire

"How's it goin', chick? Did ya make it?"

"We landed, and we're getting ready to head to the hotel," Perri confirmed as she grabbed her roll-away bag and popped the handle into place.

"All of you? Ya mean to tell me that ya didn't murder Ian or make him jump out of the plane in self-preservation from all your passive aggressiveness?"

"Yes, Ali, *all* of us," Perri rolled her eyes, "And I'm not passive-aggressive."

"Sure ya not. Anyway, I'm proud of ya, sweet thing."

Sighing, Perri wished she could tell her best friend how hard the flight had been and at the same time how wonderful. But that was definitely not a conversation to have with everyone else listening, mainly her children. "Thank you."

"Text me when ya get se'led, okay."

"I will," Perri promised and smiled as Aspen and Zayden yelled out jumbled greetings to the woman on the other end of the line. "Did you get any of that?"

Aliyah's laugh met her ear, and Perri couldn't help but chuckle along.

"I have a good idea what it was supposed to be." Finally came the response, *"Tell them I said 'ello and that I love them too."*

"Aunt Ali says hello, and she loves you," Perri relayed the message and then directed her attention back to the call, "Talk soon, yeah?"

"Sure thing, chick."

The two never said goodbye. Not when leaving each other's homes, parting ways from meeting up somewhere, or even hanging up a phone call. Neither of them liked saying good-bye, so they simply made the unspoken decision that they would not.

Sliding her phone back into her coat pocket, Perri turned her attention to finding the ride she had scheduled to take them to the hotel. After making this trip annually for years, she still would never chance either her or Ian trying to drive through this frozen world.

Meeting the eyes of a man wearing a thick coat and a bright green scarf, he called out, "Hotel Alyeska?"

Smiling in acknowledgment, Perri gave a wave, "That's us."

Aspen and Zayden sprinted over and began putting their things in the back of the vehicle, leaving Perri and Ian to just smile and shake their heads, following behind. Putting their own bags in with the rest, Perri had a lapse in judgement, but realized it all too late. Feeling his presence beside her, Perri's memories decided to flash with the image of the bright Alaskan sun and how it had always made Ian's dark hair shine a little like gold. Looking up only to sneak a glance at her ex-husband, just to see if all things really do change, she instead met his eyes, and she found that she couldn't read the expression in them. It terrified her. Quickly turning her attention back to her bags, Perri got everything settled and went to climb into the cab.

Ian wasn't far behind and reflexively placed his hand on Perri's back as she went to step up into the vehicle. He was like a moth to a flame; he couldn't resist her. Something in him just would never allow him to turn his attention elsewhere. Then again, it was something he never tried too hard to fight either.

Perri paused for a fraction of a second. His hand was warm against the small of her back, and she battled momentarily with stepping away from the touch entirely or reaching back to keep it there. She somehow decided on neither. All she knew was that his hand on her back was something she had missed more than she was truly willing to admit.

But she couldn't think about that now. They had a bit of a drive still to the hotel, and she was tired. She just didn't have the energy to think about it at the moment.

That's what she told herself anyway. That's what she told herself every time.

So Perri did what she normally did, turned her attention to their children, and acted as if nothing had happened to invoke any thought at all.

The door of her room clicked shut behind the bellhop, and Perri allowed herself a moment to relax.

Some days just last too bloody long.

Letting her head fall back, she closed her eyes and breathed deeply.

Hearing a muffled *thump!* on the wall that separated her room from the adjoining one, her thoughts were back on the one thing she was trying to forget. Ian would be spending the next two weeks sleeping in the room right next to hers. Their children had simply repeated their actions from the plane and quickly claimed the adjoined rooms a few floors up, leaving Ian and Perri with neighboring rooms. Of course, what did she expect? Aspen and Zayden were a hard pair to separate once you got them together, and the fact that their parents were separated but still drawn to each other like magnets didn't change that.

You are a grown woman, Perri! Just don't think about it.

Looking down at her bags, Perri decided she would just unpack them tomorrow. The change not only of time, but *days*, was hard to adjust to, and she would like to get used to it as quickly as possible. Which meant to bed with the sun and up with her tomorrow. Or, at least up around the same time as her.

Placing her suitcases on the floor against the wall, Perri popped one open to find something to wear to bed. Rifling through it all, she caught a quick glimpse of a shirt she had packed without really even thinking about it. Of course, she had discovered what she had done when checking her bags to ensure she had everything, but Perri, being Perri, had simply turned a blind eye and just let it be. There was no harm in just tucking it at the bottom of the case. It was there, and if she remembered, she could return it to him. Simple as that.

Oh yes, return it to him still smelling like his cologne. Then he'll just know you've been knowingly keeping it all this time <u>and</u> making sure it continued to smell like him. That's a great idea! Completely crush the *idea that it got lost during his move and just prove that you're still as hung up on him as you were the day you ended it.*

Perri couldn't fight with that sarcastic voice. Believe it or not, it was right more often than not. Maybe it was best she kept it tucked in her suitcase.

Then again, it was chilly here, and she would be much more comfortable if she wore something a little warmer to bed.

Just one more night won't hurt. Maybe some of the cologne will wear off.

Bringing the flannel out of the corner of her suitcase, Perri held the shirt in both hands for a long moment, fighting the urge to breathe in the smell of it. Then grabbing a pair of shorts, she went to change and lay down.

Surrounded by the warmth and the smell that her brain still connected with comfort, her mind subconsciously turned to Ian, and she wondered what he was doing in the next room.

Thoughts from the day came pouring in, as they typically did when Perri was trying to sleep. Her plane anxiety had not gone unnoticed by her ex-husband, and his work scared hand had still reached out to hold hers, even after all the pain she had caused over the years. Tears stung the back of her eyes at the memory of it. He had always been too kind to her for his own good. She had felt that way when they started out. It had faded with the years as she became less insecure and had come back full force the moment she decided to leave him. But if she was going to get any sleep, she definitely couldn't think about that now. Perri quickly rolled over to try and force herself to fall asleep.

The funny thing about a dream is that everything makes perfect sense when you're in it. You could wake up with a tail or find yourself with hooves instead of hands, and you would still just shrug it off with a "right then" and go on.

So when Ian felt the familiar tickle of hair against his collarbone and warm weight tucked into the crook of his arm, he didn't panic or even think twice.

Instead, he could simply feel one thing; Home.

"Per?"

He received a barely-there hum of acknowledgement and felt Perri's breath puff against his skin.

"What's the time?"

He felt her shuffle nearer, tucking her head a little closer under his chin.

"Shhh," she whispered back, "Go back to sleep."

"But what time is it," he asked again.

Silence prevailed, and Ian grumbled to himself before shifting around to see the clock. He opened his eyes.

Ian was alone.

The hair tickling his collar had been the tassels of the throw pillows they had on the bed that he had failed to put away before falling asleep. Gripping the corner, he threw the pillow across the room and fell back against the others with a huff. A part of him always missed Perri, but this, this was so much worse than normal. He blamed it on being in such close proximity to her for so many hours. That had to be why the memories seemed to be flooding back so strong in his tired state.

But just because the memories made him sad and still wonder what he could have done differently to make it where this was never their reality, Ian didn't stop his mind from carrying him back to a time when he and Perri were much younger and slightly different people.

* * * * * * * * * * * * *

"What are you doing?" Ian chuckled as Perri turned to snuggle deeper into his chest.

After a few moments of soft cuddles and quiet sighs, she rested her chin on Ian's shoulder.

"I don't know," Perri paused in thought. "But I don't think I hate it."

Ian held his girlfriend a little tighter, and a smile grew across his lips, "I don't either."

Even though sitting up on the couch wasn't the most comfortable position, he could feel the sleepiness envelop him, and Perri's finger's scratching gently through the hair at the base of his skull was not helping him fight off his drowsiness.

"One thing, though," Ian said after several moments of contented quiet, his words coming a little slower than normal. Perri leaned back just enough to press their foreheads together, her chest warming at the sleepiness in his tone. She found him adorable.

"Anything," she breathed, "Anything you want."

"You've always got to keep your nails this length because otherwise, the scratching won't feel as good," he replied, the corner of his lips barely lifting.

Bolting upright, Perri attempted to shove Ian away, but he was already laid back against the couch and so the action only made him laugh.

"I thought you were going to say something meaningful!"

"That was meaningful!" Ian's face was still lit up with an amused smile, "It would really mean a lot to me if you kept your nails this way."

"Blimey, Ian, I'm so glad you're easy to please," she retorted, *"Tosser."*

* * * * * * * * * * * * * *

Ian finally faded back into sleep and was dreaming more peacefully now of years passed, little knowing that just next door, Perri was doing just the same.

"Mum?" Aspen peeked into her mother's room, sliding the key card out of the slot and entering quietly.

There lay her mother, still sound asleep beneath a small mountain of blankets and surrounded by maybe a dozen pillows.

"Mum, time to get up."

She approached the bed and opened the curtains that had been keeping out the sun, "You'll never get used to the time change at this rate."

Perri groaned and threw her arm over her eyes.

"Leave my curtains and sleep schedule be, you li'le ankle-biter. I don't want that manky sunlight all in here." Her voice, though typically raspy to a degree, was always more gravely and rough when first used in the morning, and her children still found it amusing how mean she could sound but had never been.

Taking a seat on the edge of the bed, Aspen pulled back the blankets a bit, "Sorry, Mum, but I'm not afraid of you, and I'm doing this for your own good."

Jerking the blankets all the way off, Perri glowered up at her daughter, who simply smiled.

"Good mornin!"

"Mm-hm." Was the only reply the young woman received, and she couldn't help but chuckle. Until she stopped short as her brain made a connection that she needed confirmed.

"Mum? Isn't that Dad's old shirt?"

Even though Perri was not moving around all that much yet, Aspen could sense the pause in her movements. Much like a teenager being caught slipping in past curfew.

Finally, Perri's face appeared over the blankets, and she seemed to be studying the sleeve of the shirt she was wearing. "You know what, I think it is actually."

Aspen tried not to look too smug about her suspicions being confirmed, so she merely hummed in reply and tried to act as if she didn't find it interesting enough to give much thought on. When in all reality, she couldn't wait for there to be a moment her mother wouldn't notice her texting Zayden to fill him in. Maybe she would put a call into their Aunt Aliyah too. Just for information gathering purposes.

Left alone to her own devices while her children went out to see what kind of mischief they could get into before noon, Perri laid in bed and hoped that Aspen had not realized the slight panic she went into when her choice of sleepwear was noticed. She hadn't planned on being caught wearing Ian's shirt, especially not on the first day of their vacation. In fact, she had had every intention of tucking the shirt back in her suitcase and everyone staying blissfully unaware for the entirety of the trip. But, of course, she hadn't planned on a morning wake-up visit from her daughter either.

Pushing herself up to lean back against the headboard, Perri subconsciously grabbed the collar of the flannel and brought it up to her nose, breathing in deep.

After their divorce, there were many things that Perri was able to let go of. She had helped him pack his things and had sifted through all of her drawers and her closet for him since his clothes had migrated into hers over the years. But when she came across the slate blue flannel with its red and white lines and its hints of green, she found she couldn't part with it. The material was strong but soft with age and somehow still brought back all the feelings from the first time she saw it. It was as if it had some spell woven into the material that almost made Perri believe in magic. There were very few objects that could take back time for Perri like that old flannel. And she thought, maybe, that's why she had never let it leave her like she should have years ago when she and Ian began living separate lives.

If this shirt could talk, o, the stories it could tell. It carried a simpler but much finer tale of love than any Shakespeare could have ever written. Something that gave no unattainable expectation of love or false hope for "the moment" where you "just know." Instead, it gave an unassuming narrative of what it means to truly love another human being. A love the inches into existence in the most unexpected people and times and how those that find themselves caught up in this astonishing state have accepted the work of loving the other person and knowing that, even if they lose them in the end, it would have been worth it.

It all began on a sunny day in Liverpool. . .

* * * * * * * * * * * * * *

Home on break before starting the final year of her postgraduate degree in architecture, Perri was enjoying the peace that comes from returning home to find everything just as she had left it. All the people she had known most of her life, all doing the same things and content as ever with the beautiful normalcy of their everyday lives. It was something reassuring to think about when she was away in big cities that hummed with constant change. The knowledge that back home in her little part of Liverpool, everything remained the same. Everyone knew everybody else, and life seemed simpler. And as wonderful as that was for everyone who decided to stay and build a life there, Perri just knew that, as much as she loved it, if she didn't have her pursuit of a career getting her out, she would certainly lose her mind with the monotony of it all.

But her mother was here, and time seemed to stop and take a breath here in this small corner of the world. Which was always a welcomed change from the hecticness of the world she regularly occupied. A Scouser through and through, Perri Vilein was usually always ready to slide back into the quiet life that awaited her at her childhood home. So, to say that she was glad for some weeks back home was an understatement.

Waving to an "old family friend" that Perri couldn't really recall how they came to know each other in the first place, she turned her attention to the shop on the corner that always seemed to have a flow of people coming in and out. And of all the people she expected to come out of said door, he was not one of them. Which means she definitely wasn't prepared for the small jump of excitement she felt in her chest at the sight of him.

Ian Astankova.

They had met months prior and had kept in touch. The two of them met up every now and again when their university schedules had allowed it. He was easy to talk to, relaxing to be around, and so much fun to make blush with her brashness. Despite being fond of flirting and exceptionally good at it, Perri was never one to chase after a man. She was determined to never appear so needy but having settled into the gentle pace of break, she found herself really wanting to chase this one. Knowing *he lived less than a thirty-minute drive from Liverpool made it all the harder. But something in Perri was fighting for her to hold out and see if perhaps he would try to find her first. Was her stubbornness in this area a good thing? Probably not, but she couldn't help if she unintentionally played hard to get.*

Rolling her eyes at what she was about to do, Perri quickly closed the distance between her and a still unsuspecting Ian. Reaching out to touch his shoulder, she couldn't stop the megawatt smile that he was met with when he turned to look at her.

"Ian!" she greeted, more excitedly than she planned, "Fancy finding you here."

There was a strange glint of nervousness behind his eyes, and Perri didn't quite know what to make of it. That charming, shy hesitance of his had seemed to fade away a little once they were able to steal some time together after their first encounter and this new anxiety in Ian's expression unsettled Perri a bit. Had he never intended on making good of their agreement to reach out and spend some real time together over break?

Then, to Perri's shock and excitement murdering dismay, the potential reason for Ian's uneasiness came out the door.

"Sorry, Ian, I got distracted by the—" The woman stopped mid-sentence when she noticed Perri's presence and smiled brightly, "Who is this?"

She was lovely, with a kind face and ready smile. And that voice all women seem to carry around inside their heads began whispering in Perri's ear.

Ian opened his mouth to introduce her, but Perri quickly cut in with a sharp, on the verge of chilling smile.

"Just a friend."

"Perri—"

Turning to meet Ian's gaze, she once again stopped him before he could finish.

"It was so good to see you."

And with that, she walked away.

Perri made sure her walk carried a noticeable level of confidence, and she fought the hot, stinging tears behind her eyes when she heard Ian call her name. Hoping he knew better than to follow after her right now. Or ever again, for that matter.

Weeks of radio silence followed, despite Ian's attempts to make contact and explain what Perri had thought she saw.

Ian's elbow dug into his thigh as he held the crown of his head in his hand. He couldn't shake the feeling that even if he did get Perri to answer his calls, she would never believe him.

All he could think about was the flash of emotion he caught a glimpse of as Perri turned to walk away. He had almost gone after her but recalled a conversation they had shared a few weeks prior, and he decided it would be best if he didn't. But he couldn't help calling out to her in hopes that maybe she would turn around and let him explain. He hadn't known her long, but he knew better.

"She wasn't just a friend, huh," Stephanie from the Veterinary Department winced knowingly, "And she also didn't know that I'm part of the teaching staff at the university."

"No," Was Ian's single reply.

Needless to say, the meeting ended quickly thereafter, and that was when his sixteen-day pursuit for contact began. It was futile, but he wasn't giving up. It wasn't every day you met a woman like Perri Vilein, and for the first time, he wasn't about to let this woman slip through his grasp.

He looked down at the phone in his hand and debated on calling again. Upon looking at the clock ticking the seconds away, Ian decided it was best not to try again. It was late, and he knew either Perri was in bed or spending time with her mother that she probably wouldn't want interrupted.

"Not that she's going to answer anyway," he murmured.

His thumb hovered over the Call button for a long moment, but ultimately, he placed the phone on the table and fell back against the couch with a growl of dismay and dug the heels of his hands into his eyes.

Ian was unsure how much time had passed, but the shrill ringing of his phone ripped through the quiet of the dark living room. Bolting upright, he fumbled with it until he finally got a good look at the bright screen and fell completely motionless.

He would know that number anywhere. He had dialed it so many times by now there was no way he would ever forget it.

The seventh ring finally got his attention, and Ian snapped out of whatever daze he had gotten trapped in. Quickly accepting the call, he was almost breathless when he answered,

"Hello."

"Look, I know I've been ignoring you," her voice was so wonderful to hear, "But I didn't know who else to call."

Pulling up to the address she gave him, Ian paused momentarily to try and take it all in as fast as his mind would allow. Telling himself he would absorb it all later, Ian jumped out of his car and went to the front door which was opened before he even had the chance to knock.

"Thank you so much for coming," Perri greeted, "I really wasn't sure if you would."

"Of course. Where is she?"

"Out back in the stables. I'll take you."

The barn door was ajar, and warm light spilled out into the dark as the two raced to it.

"She's been struggling for a little while now, but she's only been in labor since this afternoon," Perri informed as they slowed their pace.

Throwing the door open, a woman whose features resembled Perri's own stood from her spot kneeling in the hay.

"Oh, thank God," came the only welcome, "I didn't know if he would come after what you've been doing."

"Not now, Mum," Perri growled.

But the interaction went unnoticed by Ian, as he was already taking in the mare's distressed condition.

"Thank you so much for coming. Our regular vet is away, and Perri said you were the best."

"Ian; my Mum, Laurel," Perri quickly went about introductions, "Mum; Ian. And this is Nyx."

The mare's velvety, black coat was glistening with sweat, and her brown eyes pleaded for help. Ian was immediately on the barn floor, stroking her tenderly and speaking to her in calm tones. After a few moments, he turned his attention to the women behind him, "I'm going to need some things if I'm going to help her."

"Yes, of course," Laurel nodded, "Anything you need, if we've got it, you can use it."

Quickly firing off a list of things, Laurel went to find what she could, and Perri came to kneel next to him with a determined expression.

"How can I help?"

Ian's chest did this strange warming thing that he couldn't define, and he fought the smile that tugged relentlessly at his lips. "I could really use some extra hands when we get started. I'm not sure exactly what I'll need until I know what we're dealing with, but I know I'll need some help."

"You've got it then," she replied.

"Before we get started, though, can I put this somewhere?" Ian shrugged the flannel off of his shoulders to reveal a gray shirt underneath that was wrinkled with obvious signs of being slept in, "I think we're going to be here a while, and it's not going to be easy."

"Sure, I'll take it and put it out of the way."

* * * * * * * * * * * * * *

That was the first time this flannel ended up in the hands of Perri, and she hadn't let it go since. There was a time when she might have blushed about how she had so willingly lied about keeping it, but that time was long passed.

Taking another deep breath in, Perri allowed her mind to wander back for just a little while longer.

* * * * * * * * * * * * * *

They passed through the house after leaving the barn from checking on Nyx and her foal.

"Both of them are doing very well. I can't wait to see how handsome he grows up to be."

"Thank you again for all your help with this," Perri said, "I know you really don't get anything out of it except for more work."

"I could always use the extra experience. And besides, I get to see you," Ian ventured, clearing his throat a little awkwardly, and Perri chuckled.

"Yes, I suppose that is convenient, isn't it. Sorry I couldn't find your shirt. Whenever it turns up, I'll get it back to you."

"Don't worry about it," Ian shot her a quick smile, "It's not like it was my most favorite shirt or anything."

After a whole night spent saving both Perri's mare and her colt, the two had found time to discuss their last interaction over breakfast that Laurel insisted on Ian staying for. Mostly embarrassed and slightly exhausted from avoiding him for so long, and now for no reason, Perri was glad to have the air cleared between them. With apologies on both sides for their own hand in the situation, things were finally on the mend.

Days passed and the contact between them started back again, slowly, but it was there. It seemed after the hiccup in their growing. . . something. . . the two were able to pick up mostly where they had left off. Both found themselves a little surprised that there was even a chance for anything to grow after both of them were certain that they would never speak again, although both thought so for different reasons.

They slowed to a stop near the front door, trying to put off his leaving for just a bit longer. Soon their hectic schedules at university would start again, and calm moments like this would cease to exist and be mere memories until they were able to return home again. No words were necessary. They just stood with each other, happy to be in the other's company after thinking it was something they would never share again.

It was Perri who moved first, disrupting the quiet between them. Ian turned to meet her upturned gaze as the blonde took a careful step closer. She carried herself like one approaching a skittish horse, especially since she knew she was about to push Ian a fraction more than he was used to. She silently prayed that her actions in the next few minutes didn't scare him away altogether.

With her hands folded calmly in front of her, by the time she halted her approach, there were barely a few inches of space left between them. Lifting her chin and tilting her head with a curious and hopeful smile pulling at her lips, Perri swayed into his space just a little more.

"You could stay the night, you know."

Struggling to not reach up and rub the back of his neck, Ian smiled awkwardly, "Your Mum would never approve."

Perri held his gaze for a moment, then broke into a full smile and chuckled, "You're right, she wouldn't like that very much. But you could stay a little while longer at least."

"I—I don't know if that's a good idea. . ."

Leaning further into his space, Perri reached up to slide her hands on to shoulders, keeping him from backing away but also still giving him the chance to leave if he really wanted to.

"Wait."

It was barely audible, but Ian was certain that he would be able to hear her voice anywhere, always, no matter how softly she spoke.

"Perri. . ."

"Don't," Cupping his jaw, she grazed her thumb across his lips, "It's okay. And before you ask me, yes, I'm sure. Just let me."

Ian made no move to protest or step away. Instead, his hand came up to cradle her elbow, causing a smile to break out across Perri's face.

Keeping one hand on his arm, Perri reveled in the warmth of his palm radiating through the material of her sweater. Still cradling his face in her hand, she took in his features with soft, though no less intense, eyes. She had never been this close before, and she was going to take advantage of it. Her observation allowed them both a chance to acclimate to the new and very close proximity they now found themselves in. But Ian, not used to being knowingly stared at in the way Perri was staring at him now, got a little uneasy after several seconds.

Still giving him time to back away if he wanted, Perri slowly, cautiously, closed the scant distance remaining between their lips and felt her body tremble in anticipation. Their lips met, and within moments, Perri's hand was at the back of Ian's neck, pulling him down and closer. His arms snaked around her, but gently, and his hands splayed out between her shoulder blades and against the small of her back.

Pulling away, blue eyes met brown and Perri gave a relieved laugh that came out barely more than a soft breath passed her lips. She rested her forehead against Ian's and nuzzled her nose against his, smiling contentedly for a few moments and sighing a sigh that seemed as if she had been holding her breath for years. And without any of the hesitation, she thought she would feel, Perri moved in to kiss him again.

A strange warmth exploded in her chest, and she felt that if she could kiss this man for the rest of her life, she would be just fine. But that cold sliver of—was it fear, or maybe doubt that this could last—snuck its way into that warmth. Maybe, if she just ignored it, it wouldn't last long. It would fade as she grew accustomed to being cared for. Right?

But I never told you
What I should have said
No, I never told you
I just held it in
And now I miss everything about you (still
you're gone)
I can't believe it, I still want you (And I'm lovin'
you, I never should have walked away)
After all the things we've been through (I know
it's never gonna come again)
I miss everything about you

— "I Never Told You" by Colbie Caillat

A knock on her door broke through the quietness of Perri's room as she stood beside her bed that evening, finally unpacking for their two-week stay.

"You can use your card key," she called, turning back to unpacking after glancing at the door. She fully expected one of her children to appear, searching for something they thought she might have with her. And it was very likely that she did have it.

"I can't," a surprisingly older masculine voice replied, "I don't have one."

Straightening to her full height, Perri stared at the polished door for a moment before regaining her senses and going over to let in her unexpected visitor.

"Hi," she greeted softly.

"Getting settled?" Ian inquired, pointing at her face, "You're making your unpacking face."

A familiar crease appeared between her eyebrows, and he had the urge to reach out and smooth it away with his thumb like he would have years before. But that was a different time.

"I don't have a—" Cutting herself short, Perri shook her head, "You know what, what do you want?"

"Easy killer," Ian lifted his hands in surrender. "I just heard that they are opening up the lobby tonight to a local band, and they are doing 'A Night in the 80's'. I wanted to invite you to go with me. Just for fun, of course. We could just enjoy the music together, and it would give us the wonderful opportunity to embarrass our children before they go off to their college dorms again where we no longer can."

He shot her a charming smile, that boyish twinkle that she loved so much appearing in his eyes, "What do you say?"

She knew she should say no—there was no question that she definitely should—but as usual, her mouth opened before her brain could communicate to it what to say.

"I suppose I'll come down for a while. I could use a break from unpacking anyway."

"I thought so," Ian smirked knowingly, "You know, with the face and all."

"I don't make a face!" Perri insisted, then sighed and turned back into her room. "Wait on me."

The door clicked shut, leaving Ian to stand in the stillness of the hallway, staring at the door in a sad sort of contentment.

"Always," he murmured and then chuckled softly to himself, knowing Perri would hate the "mushiness" of the statement.

Several minutes passed and Perri reemergesd to find Ian leaning back against the wall beside the door. She had dressed down but was still the most noticeable woman in the whole hotel. At least that was Ian's opinion. In a light royal blue turtleneck with sleeves that hung down to her mid-palm and black jeans tucked neatly into her boots, she still had the familiar air of confidence even in casual dress. But her softer side was able to show through just enough for those who knew it was there.

"Ah, the lady emerges at last," he smiled, "And stunning as ever."

"Oh please, you're being a suck-up," she rolled her eyes, "Where are our children?"

"Already down at the open bar, I'm sure."

"Blimey," she mumbled, "Come on, we had better get down there and embarrass them quick before they get too sloshed to care anymore."

Ian studied his ex-wife out of the corner of his eye as they followed the sound of some 80's funk song down to the lobby. She had taken on softer features in her middle age. The sharp angles of her face were less imposing than years earlier. Perhaps it was because he was no longer intimidated and had come to know the woman hidden underneath the edges. Or, at least, he thought he knew her.

"Mum! Dad!"

The sound of their children calling for them pulled their attention to a table tucked to the side. When they had arrived the day before, there had been large, leather chairs and potted ferns lining the massive lobby. All of it had been mysteriously removed and hidden away for the night. Leaving a few round tables with tall chairs along the outskirts of the room and a large open space in the center for couples brave enough to initiate dancing. Aspen and Zayden were waving them over, faces lit up with wide smiles. Without hesitation, Ian and Perri smiled brightly in return. After all, those young humans were the best things they had ever done with their lives.

An hour or so in and many 80's jams later, Aspen and Zayden couldn't stand sitting still anymore. So, instead of just going themselves, they drug their parents out on the make-shift dance floor. Playfully grabbing up his mother, Zayden swung her around, singing loudly to the chorus of the song, with Perri's laughter dancing its own way through the room.

"Oh! I wanna dance with somebody!" Zayden beamed at the woman and tried not to start laughing himself, "I wanna feel the *heat* with somebody! Yeah! I wanna dance with somebody!"

"With somebody who loves me!" Perri surprised him by singing along.

"Come on, Mum, try this!" Zayden encouraged excitedly and began to attempt to vocalize like Whitney Huston, only making his mother laugh even more.

And the woman could feel her heart get a little lighter.

A few more fun songs played through, and the family didn't leave the floor once. They had not been together like this, this care-free, in years, and it was something they had all decided to embrace.

"Okay, okay," Aspen laughed giddily, closing the distance between the four of them, "We're done. We're done."

She rested a hand on her brother's broad shoulder, leaning into him, and smiled brightly at their mother. "You and Dad do whatever. We need to sit down."

"We can come with you," Perri replied, gesturing back toward their table, knowing exactly what their children were up to.

"We're not as young as we once were," Ian agreed.

"Speak for yourself!" Perri interjected, mostly mock offended.

Aspen shrugged, "Besides if you do come sit down with us, we'll just harass you until you dance at least once."

Zayden nodded in agreement.

"How about one turn around the floor?" Ian asked softly, holding out his hand, giving his ex-wife ample opportunity to refuse.

"If they'll leave us alone, I suppose I can spare a few minutes." Perri tossed a wink at their children.

With a deep breath and a hope that this would be over quickly— but not too quickly—Perri took the offered hand and went out on the dance floor. The soft sound of a filler tune being played on the keyboard occupied the space between them while the band changed instruments for the next song.

Keeping hold of her hand, Ian turned and wrapped his arm lightly around her waist.

"Is this okay?"

Lifting her eyes from their feet, Perri laid her hand confidently on his shoulder, "Of course. Why wouldn't it be."

"Now time for a favorite from a late great."

The voice of the man on the keys made the couple start slightly and look toward the stage. Then the band began to play a familiar tune that hit them both like a bucket of ice water straight from the ocean that wasn't so far away. A song that had a whole new meaning for the two of them these days.

"It all came so easy
All the lovin' you gave me
The feeling we shared. . ."

Perri's dark eyes snapped up to meet Ian's for a moment, and the next few lines faded away into the sound of panicked blood rushing in her ears. But there was no way she was going to back down now. She had a good reason to let her husband—ex-husband—hold her for just four minutes, and she wasn't about to waste it. She could be waiting years for this to happen again.

Even though she knew all she ever had to do was ask. But that would just be unfair. She wasn't that selfish, or at least she liked to think she wasn't.

"We had a once in a lifetime
But I just couldn't see
Until' it was gone
A second once in a lifetime
May be too much to ask
But I swear from now on. . ."

Perri was going to die before this song was even through its first chorus, especially with the way Ian was looking at her so intensely. Seeing all the emotions swirling in his own expression, Perri knew she definitely wouldn't make it if she held his gaze. So, she looked down at her feet as if to make sure she wasn't going to trod on his toes, even though they both knew there was no chance of that ever happening.

"Now I'm seeing clearly
How I still need you near me
I still love you so
There's something between us
That won't ever leave us
There's no letting go. . ."

"Per?" His voice, soft and low, drew her eyes up a fraction to stare at him from beneath her lashes.

"What?" she murmured, "I know I didn't step on your feet."

"Are you okay?"

The gentle inquiry was all she needed to push her over a cliff she had been so close to tottering off of since the song started. Inhaling deeply, she cleared her throat and swallowed back her tears with the flash of a breathtaking smile.

"Don't worry about me," she replied and quickly tried to make a joke, "I'm more worried about you, old man. Do you need to sit down?"

"Perri. . ."

"We had a once in a lifetime

But I just didn't know it
'Til my life fell apart
A second once in a lifetime
Isn't too much to ask
'Cause I swear from the heart. . ."

She hated crying. Especially crying over this, which was something she brought on herself, in front of the man she wanted most.

But here she was.

A small sniffle that could barely be heard above the music escaped her, and she knew she was done for.

When his hand was suddenly empty, Ian just knew Perri was going to make a run for it. Back to her room, back to the hard and razor-sharp shell she had built herself, and he wouldn't see his Perri again the whole vacation.

But instead, both of Perri's arms were suddenly around his shoulders, and her fists were clenched tight into the softness of his shirt. Tucking her face safely into the curve of his neck, Perri tried to maintain what remained of her composure. Before he lost his chance, Ian wrapped her up in a warm embrace and held her close. He kept moving minutely to the music, knowing she wouldn't want a big scene to be made.

"If ever you're in my arms again
This time I'll love you much better
If ever you're in my arms again
This time I'll hold you forever
This time we'll never end. . ."

Feeling her tears drop onto his skin, Ian tried to ignore the aching tightness of his chest and the stinging behind his own eyes. Resting his cheek against her hair, he just held on and allowed himself to feel for a time.

"The best of romances
Deserve second chances

I'll get to you somehow
'Cause I promise now. . ."

"If ever you're in my arms again. . . This time I'll love you much better," he whispered the lyrics tenderly into her ear, recalling how she had once loved to hear him sing whenever she was upset. His voice was nothing special, but it was soothing to Perri even if he couldn't understand why. "If ever you're in my arms again. . . This time I'll hold you forever. . . This time we'll never end."

The band repeated that aching chorus a couple more times, and at last, the song was done. Perri knew she had to make a move to step out of Ian's arm; she just really did not want to. She told herself it was because he would see the tear clouding her vision still, but she knew the truth.

They both did.

She just never wanted to let go, and neither did he.

Back at the table, Aspen and Zayden sat watching with concern, and the knife in their hearts just twisted deeper.

"Maybe. . ." Aspen began, "Maybe we haven't done such a good thing after all."

Zayden sighed, "Yeah, maybe not this time."

Sometimes love is simply not enough. It was not enough for us.

Perri's words from years prior echoed in her head as she leaned back against the door of her hotel room.

She had not remained in Ian's arms for very long after the song had ended, just long enough to give herself time to muster up the courage to pull herself away. Whispering a quick good night without meeting Ian's concerned gaze, Perri went to kiss their children before going upstairs. She wanted so badly to run, to be in the safety of her room where she could mourn what she was missing so deeply. So Perri took the stairs as fast as she could without looking like she was trying to escape and hid behind the door of her room. This is where she would keep herself until well into the next morning.

Even as Perri leaned back against the door, Ian took the last flight of stairs two at a time, hoping to catch her before she had disappeared behind her door. Slowly approaching his ex-wife's room, Ian stood and stared, wondering if he should knock.

But for the third time in his life, Ian decided not to chase after Perri, no matter how much he wanted to.

Despite his decision not to follow her, Ian would always make the choice to be with her, even if she didn't want it. He hoped that someday she might. So, he went to his room and sat on the other side of the adjoining door.

As he listened to the silence, Ian's mind wandered back to their shared minutes downstairs, and his heart both ached and swelled with warmth. This was a terrible place to be, so pained by someone's presence but also too deeply in love to push it away.

He had fallen for her long ago, and it wasn't changing.

* * * * * * * * * * * * * *

"So, what did I interrupt when I showed up unannounced today?"
Ian asked.

"Nothing, really. I found this book in a box of my mother's things, and Mum found some of their favorite records, so I've just been reading and listening to some music. It's all been. . . so quiet these past few days."

Ian, who had taken a seat beside her on the bed, took the book tenderly from her hands and placed it on the other side of the bed. Perri shot him a curious look, and he got to his feet, shooting her that charming smile. Crossing the room to where the record player stood in the corner, he turned up the volume.

"I have a better way to spend some time."

"Oh yeah?" Perri asked, a smile growing across her lips, "What's that?"

"Dance with me."

"Ian. . . I'm not. . ."

He crossed his arms and gave a single-shoulder shrug, "A dancer? Blimey, love. Neither am I."

"What if we just—" Perri tried to barter with him, but Ian was having none of it.

Moving back to stand beside the bed, Ian took his girlfriend's hands in his and pulled her up. "Dance with me. Please?"

Perri rolled her eyes and allowed Ian to lead her closer to the record player. Sliding an arm around her waist, Ian pulled her close and let his hand settle on the small of her back. They started to move, and Perri felt a little awkward at first until Ian planted a kiss against her temple, and she settled into the soft movement as they swayed back and forth. It was comforting, being so close to Ian and moving to the gentle music.

"You're so beautiful," Ian whispered in her ear, and the feeling of warm breath and the conviction behind the words was almost over-whelming. Perri rested her head on Ian's shoulder and hid a shy smile.

"I've never done this before," she said, her voice uncharacteristically timid.

"You've never danced?" Ian asked with a laugh and slipped his hand up under the hem of Perri's shirt so that his palm pressed against her skin. "Now we both know that's not true."

Perri shook her head and took a deep breath, letting the scent of com-fort—of Ian—wash over her completely.

"Fallen for someone this way."

For a moment, the only sound that filled the room was the music, though Perri was sure that her heart was beating loudly enough in her chest for Ian to hear.

He may not have been able to hear her heart beating, but Ian could feel it. He could feel it beating as if it were his own, and in a way, it had become his own. Perri was his heart. Taking in a shaky breath, Ian hugged Perri closer to his body as they continued to sway along with the gentle notes that poured from the record player.

"I've never fallen for someone this way either," he answered.

Perri leaned back slightly to look into Ian's eyes. She was surprised to find them a little glossy, but she knew hers were too. A small smile lifted the corners of her lips, and she nuzzled her nose against his, kissing him sweetly.

Meanwhile, in a room a few floors up. . .

Aspen and Zayden sat on the bed in his room and huddled into the frame of Aspen's phone while they waited for their aunt to accept their Facetime call. Aspen was anxious to hear if the woman knew anything about their mother holding on to some of their father's things. Maybe this would distract them from the cloud that had hung around after watching their parents earlier.

"It's almost," Zayden looks at his watch, "Eleven o'clock here, which means it's almost eight in the morning back home. She's definitely awake. Do you think she's ignoring us?"

"She would never ignore us," Aspen replied without hesitation.

Finally, Aliyah answered the call, and the siblings smiled brightly, moving in close to one another again so they could both be seen by the woman on the other side.

"'ey, you lot!" Aliyah greeted excitedly, "'ow are my wee gremlins?"

"We're good!" Aspen answered happily as Zayden sat beside his sister and waved at their aunt.

"You look lovely today, Aunt Ali," he said.

"You li'le charmer," Aliyah shook her head with a knowing smirk, "Just like your Mum."

Zayden chuckled a bit, "Yeah. . . It may have gotten me in trouble a time or two recently."

"I can imagine it 'as," the woman on the screen laughed, "I know it did your mother too. *Don'* tell her I told ya that!" She pointed a threatening finger at them both before continuing, "But don' worry, it gets be'er. That same charm will probably help you find your one in the end." Then she shot him a wink and that encouraging smile.

Aunt Aliyah had always been good about saying just the right things, in just the right way. She gave solid, strong advice but without seeming like an overbearing adult who just thought they knew best, whether they actually did or not. She was a kind, listening ear that truly heard what you were saying, with the desire only to help you. Despite her sassy and occasionally abrasive behavior, Aliyah was someone people knew they could go to no matter the situation and she would always do what she could.

Aunt Aliyah had always been one of the most consistent aspects of Aspen and Zayden's life, especially during the divorce process. Don't misunderstand. Their parents made the transition as easy as possible for them, but there is nothing "easy" about your happy childhood being so violently interrupted with one home suddenly becoming two and your parents struggling to be in the same room anymore. Aliyah made sure the two had regular distractions and a safe place to talk about all the new and unsettling things taking place in their lives.

But their bond had been a powerful one long before then. It stretched back to before either of the siblings could really remember.

They both recalled evenings spent with Aunt Aliyah sitting on the floor with them, feet widespread, settling in for whatever movie her niece and nephew had picked to watch before bed. Of course, their parents were there, but Perri and Ian knew when Aliyah was around, well, they just weren't as much fun. So, they would sit on the couch and watch. Sometimes Perri would work on a sketch she had to have done soon, and sometimes Ian would study up on a specific case he was trying to manage at the clinic. But at least one night a week found them all together in one room. Just being close and relaxing together.

Aspen would always make herself comfortable between Aliyah's legs and lean contentedly back against the woman's chest. She would feel her eyes growing heavier and heavier, until the sensation of being scooped up and carried let her know that she must have nodded off *at least* twice.

Zayden, on the other hand, would come to stand behind their aunt and throw his little arms around her neck, resting forward into her back. His chin rested on top of Aliyah's shoulder, and the side of his head leaned contentedly against her cheek. Looking back on it, the siblings were surprised she didn't throw them off of her after a while. They all but wallowed the woman to death every time she walked through the door.

"Now, why are you two callin' me when you're supposed to be on vacation with your parents?"

Aspen gave a small smile, a little unsure of how to say what she called to ask.

They watched their aunt's face drop a fraction, "Oh Poppins, boy trouble? In Alaska? Already?"

Laughing, the girl shook her head, "No, Auntie! Well, at least not this time."

"Oh good," Aliyah looked visibly relieved.

"Actually, I need to ask you a question about Mum."

"A'ight, I suppose I can try and answer it."

Aspen thought about it a moment longer, then proceeded to blurt out the question with little to no grace.

"Did you know Mum kept and slept in one of our Dad's shirts?"

Aliyah seemed taken aback and a handful of seconds ticked by in silence.

"No, I 'ad no idea," she looked genuinely puzzled.

"Auntie Ali, you're basically Mum's walking diary," Aspen stated, almost rolling her eyes, "Surely you know something about it."

"I swear I don', Poppins." The woman held up her hands as if to prove she held no secrets. "I 'ad no idea she kept anythin' of his."

"Maybe you could. . ." the girl hesitated a moment and then shot a hopeful smile her aunt's way, "Find something out?"

The woman laughed, "And if I did wha' makes ya think I'd report back to you?"

"Because, Aunt Ali, you love getting into mischief as much as we do," Zayden replied knowingly.

A familiar smirk grew across the woman's freckle dusted face.

"You li'le devils," Aliyah shook her head, "A'ight, I'll see wha' I can drum up, yeah?"

The siblings replies of thanks mingled together, and the woman felt her chest warm. She loved these two more than words could say. And that was exactly why she was about to go dig herself into a mess with her best friend.

Aliyah's smile stayed bright for a long while after she hung up from her niece and nephew. Those two had been some of the best things to ever come into her life, aside from her best friend and, of course, her husband—can't forget about him. They had known her back before she was much of anything, and they still thought she had hung the moon, and she, for one, was still convinced those two troublemakers helped throw the stars into place.

Aliyah had been with Perri the day she went into labor and had been the first to even hold Aspen. That day was one that Aliyah would not soon forget, even after these twenty-two years.

* * * * * * * * * * * * *

Aliyah hadn't thought it was the best idea to begin with, but Perri had insisted.

"I'm turnin' into a daft cow, Ali," she had insisted early that morning while following her best friend around her house, "I'm so bored I could nod off just standin' around these days. Ian's been called into work so much these last few weeks I feel like I've barely seen him, and now that I've finished the plans for the new hospital in Manchester, I have nothin' to do."

Aliyah looked over her shoulder, "Ya could always read a book, Per."

"And fall asleep? No thanks."

"Babe, you're growin' a whole other human <u>inside</u> ya body, ya need to just enjoy relaxin' for a while," Holding up a hand to stop Perri's protest, she continued, "I know that's somethin' ya have never done before in your life, but just try it now. Ya may end up likin' it."

"Ali," Perri whined, just a little, and Aliyah could almost hear her foot stomping like a petulant child.

The woman laughed and shook her head, turning back to watering her plants, "I don't know what ya want me to do about it, princess."

Sliding up behind her to rest her chin on Aliyah's shoulder, Perri made sure she had her friend's attention again. "Take me to London," she smiled brightly.

And so, here they were, walking around some shops in the middle of London. It was a quieter day, by London standards, and that made shopping with a pregnant lady much easier. They had made it to the eleventh store after a solid two hours and Aliyah was about to suggest a break and some lunch when she looked to her right where Perri had been moments ago and found that she was no longer there.

Before she even had time to react,

"Uh, Ali," came Perri's shockingly wavering voice, "I don't feel. . ."

Whirling around, Aliyah closed the distance between them and held onto her best friend's shoulders, leaning down a bit to see into her face.

"Yeah? Wha' don' ya feel, chick? Oi! Per, speak!"

"I think my water just broke."

The statement was calm and made without Perri once looking up. So Aliyah followed her gaze and found Perri's jeans to be a shade darker along the inner seam of her legs.

"Blimey! Okay, okay," Aliyah looked around, trying so hard not to appear frantic, "To the 'ospital. To the 'ospital now!"

Aliyah swerved in and out of traffic, only breaking several traffic laws, in hopes of getting Perri to the hospital before she gave birth to her daughter in the front seat of a rapidly moving car.

"'ow could ya not tell ya were havin' contractions?!" Aliyah tried not to yell, but she just couldn't understand how someone missed that.

She looked over at her passenger, who was trying too hard not to appear scared as she anxiously rubbed the soft skin of the scar through her eyebrow. Her other hand was resting over her round belly all the while.

"I don't know, okay! I just thought it was some back pain and that I needed to walk it out!"

"Walk i' out?! Ya sure did walk i' out! Ya walked this baby righ' out of ya!"

"Will you please calm down!" Perri shouted, "I'm freakin' out as i' is! You can yell at me for this later once I'm not in labor anymore!"

Coming to a tire screaming stop at the entrance of the hospital, Aliyah jumped out of the car.

"Don'! Move," she demanded, "I'm comin' around to get ya out."

Perri rolled her eyes but didn't protest, and listened as her friend yelled for a wheelchair and some help.

Opening the passenger door, Aliyah helped Perri to her feet and glanced over the woman's shoulder at her seat. "I hope ya plan on paying for my seat to be shampooed."

Lifting her eyes back to Perri's, she smirked, both nervous and excited, "Come on, let's go meet my niece."

Squeezing Ali's hand, Perri clenched her teeth and screwed her eyes shut. A strangled cry managed to escape against her will, and Aliyah held her hand tighter in both of hers.

"Jus' breathe, chick," she said soothingly, "You're doing great."

"I want my Mum!" Perri insisted and tried to swallow back the tears, "Where is she?"

"I don' know, Per. She's comin' though, I do know that much." Aliyah snuck a look at Perri's monitors and brushed the hair back off her forehead, flashing her a smile.

"And where is Ian? It's his fault I'm here in the first place!" Another contraction made her body tense in pain. "I want to yell at him <u>so much</u>," Perri growled through clenched teeth.

"He's comin'. Ya can tell 'im all you want, but don' be too mean, yeah."

"I'll be as mean as I want!" Perri insisted, "He's not pushing a human out of his—"

Cut off by another contraction, Perri's eyes screwed shut, and she all but crushed Aliyah's hand in hers, "Ali, I can't handle much more of this!"

"I know, love, but you're doing so great," Aliyah did her best to soothe her through it.

"Madam," a nurse's voice interrupted, and Aliyah looked up. "There's a woman outside saying she's meant to be in here, that she was running behind, but we can't just let her—"

"I'll be right back, chick," Aliyah assured Perri, who nodded silently, her lips pressed tightly together.

"Move," she pushed past the nurse a little more aggressively than she intended, but she would apologize for it later. Racing out the delivery room doors, Aliyah looked frantically around for the woman she knew must be outside waiting.

"Auntie!" Aliyah sighed like a prayer and went over to assure the woman forward, "Thank God ya 'ere! Where 'ave ya been?!"

"I'm sorry, love, I got caught in traffic," she explained, crossing the room, "I wasn't expecting this."

"Me either," the concern she had tried so hard to keep hidden bubbled up momentarily in her eyes, "She's early."

"Everything will be alright, love. You'll see," Laurel reassured with a tender squeeze of her hand, "Let's get back to the girls, okay."

As soon as they entered the room, Perri's face crumpled like a worn-out piece of paper, and tears escaped out the corners of her eyes.

"Mum."

"Hey, baby," Laurel greeted softly, coming to stand beside the bed and gently cupping her daughter's face in her hand, "How's my girl?"

"This is terrible. Be glad you never did this," Perri's voice quivered as she held the woman's gaze.

"I'm so sorry, precious," Laurel swiped away the tears before taking Perri's hand and holding it against her chest as she leaned down to kiss her daughter's forehead. "Just a little longer now, and it will all be over, okay. And Ian's coming, he'll be right outside waiting to come in as soon as they'll let him."

Time passed in days, it seems, until suddenly it didn't anymore, and everything was moving at the speed of light. And as quickly as it had begun, it was over.

Ali watched the nurses as they cleaned and checked over the tiny human who was now crying in protest at the bright harshness of this new world she found herself in. Turning, one smiled and passed the small bundle to Aliyah, who cradled newborn Aspen in her arms.

"Oh shhhh, love," she spoke gently, "Ya safe 'ere."

The infant stretched her small body for the first time and quieted slowly, nestling into the warmth of the blankets.

"There now," Aliyah smiled down at her niece as she began to cross the room where the exhausted mother lay recovering, "'ello, Poppins. Oh, ya are goin' to be beautiful, my darlin'. Even if ya turn out to not look like ya, Mum, ya Dad isn't so bad either. So, either way, you'll be gorgeous.

More impor'an'ly than that, ya goin' to have an amazin' mind. Ya parents are geniuses."

Aliyah whisper-spoke the last sentence more to a tiredly smiling Perri as she looked up to meet her best friend's gaze.

"Time to meet Mum, li'le one."

Aliyah watched as the bond between mother and daughter began growing in their first moments of meeting after months of knowing each other more intimately than one else ever had or ever would. And she smiled softly.

Looking up, she met Laurel's eyes and gestured to the door, "I'm going to go get Ian."

Opening up the door, she stepped out into the hall and was immediately greeted by an anxious Ian.

"Ali? H—how are they?"

Smiling up at the man, she laid her hands on his shoulders, "Rest easy, Papa Bear. You have a lovely baby girl and a very tired mum waitin' in that room to see you."

"Now?" his smile could have put the sun to shame and the excitement in his eyes, well, let's just say not even most children have that much spark in their eyes come Christmas morning, "I can go in now?"

"Yes, yes," Aliyah began shooing him into the room, "Go!"

Years later, Aspen had grown into a small, seven-year-old version of her mother, and both she and Zayden had their aunt wrapped around their little fingers.

That is one of the reasons why Aliyah found herself taking care of the two of them when Perri and Ian both had to be out of town for the same stretch of days.

Having long since put the children to bed, Aliyah laid down on the couch and began clicking through channels as she willed herself to become tired. It wasn't going as quickly as she would like, but her eyelids were slowly getting heavy.

Moments before falling asleep, she was jerked awake by the sound of crying and the swift pattering of bare feet running down the hall. Leaping into action, Aliyah moved to meet the scared little one as fast as she could.

"Mummy!" Aspen sounded so afraid it broke the woman's heart. "Daddy!"

Turning on the nearby lamp, Aliyah knelt down, and the small blonde raced to close the remaining distance between herself and her aunt. The woman caught her niece up in her arms and held her tight, rubbing her back soothingly.

"Ya a'ight, Poppins. Ya a'ight," she spoke softly, "Come on, sit with me for a spell."

Scooping the girl up in her arms, Aliyah walked them back to the couch and settled them in nice and cozy under the blanket she had been trapped in moments before when trying to scamper out of the makeshift bed.

Aspen nestled close, and her tears slowly became sniffles. She focused intently on the softness of the sweater her aunt was wearing and how Aliyah's light bronze skin was always so warm and soft and smelt of eucalyptus and the sea.

"Ya safe, love," the woman reassured, "I'll let nothin' get to ya. Especially considerin' that ya Mum and Dad would 'ave me 'ead."

The little girl giggled just a little, and it warmed her aunt's heart. "There we are. Gettin' be'er?"

Aspen nodded against her chest, and Aliyah leaned back to relax.

"Good. Good. Now, wha' ya say we 'ave a sleepover right 'ere?"

"Sound's nice." Came a barely murmured reply.

"Good then," Aliyah swung her legs up onto the couch and laid back down once more with her niece clinging to her like a furless Koala bear.

Minutes passed, and once again, the sound of tiny footsteps met Aliyah's ear. Not frantic this time, they approach slowly and curiously. Then Zayden peeked around the corner into the living room lit by the soft light of the tv screen.

"Auntie Ali?" he asked and yawned, his eyes still dull with sleep, *"Is Penny otay?"*

"Sure she is," Aliyah assured and held out her free arm to him, *"Wan' to come 'ave a sleepover with us? Ya small enough, I think you'll fit just fine."*

Shuffling across the room, Zayden protested as he rubbed his eyes, *"I'm not small."*

"Oh of course not," the woman agreed, scooping him into her arm and lifting him up onto the couch to lay next to her, *"I must 'ave been mistaken. I do beg ya pardon, kind sir."*

Looping an arm over Aspen's back, Zayden laid his head on his aunt's shoulder and was back to sleep in moments. Aliyah, not always one to willingly give up sleep, would have gladly given up night after night of sleep if it meant getting cuddles from these two. She knew that the day would come when spontaneous living room sleepovers with auntie wouldn't be something her niece and nephew sought out, whether they needed the time or not. So she savored it and slept very little that night.

The teen years came, and with it, teenaged problems.

Letting herself into her second home, Aliyah was thinking she would be alone until Perri got off work. But instead, she was greeted by a surprisingly distressed-looking Aspen, who had obviously not been expecting anyone home just yet.

"Auntie Ali!" The girl did her best to compose herself.

"'ello, Poppins," Aliyah greeted, eyeing her and trying to figure out what was happening. "'avin' a rough go of it today?"

"No, no," Aspen waved her aunt's words away, which received a skeptical raise of an eyebrow in return. "I'm fine, really."

Just as Aliyah opened her mouth to reply, the phone lying on the counter rang loudly, startling Aspen and bringing that unsettled look back to life.

"Who's that then?"

Aspen's head snapped in her aunt's direction once more, and she smiled, "No one."

"It 'as to be someone, Poppins."

Lowering her head a fraction, Aspen started at the floor and Aliyah waited.

Leaning a hip against the counter, the woman watched her niece's face as she knew the girl was building up the courage to voice what was bothering her so deeply.

A story of a fellow classmate who had shown interest in dating her began to shed some light on the situation and Aspen's distress. Having agreed to spend some time with him, Aspen came to find he just wasn't all he had seemed and had told him that she simply didn't have the time to have a relationship at the moment. That answer had proven to not be enough, and he had made it a habit to call Aspen every day during the brief window of time that he knew she was at home alone waiting for her brother.

"Penny, I don' like that," Aliyah shook her head and tried to curb the strong emotions doing their best to blaze to life.

"*I've got it all under control, Auntie,*" *Aspen reassured,* "*Really, I promise I do.*"

The phone on the counter rang again and the girl fell silent.

Leaning close and speaking gently, Aliyah tilted her head to catch her niece's eye.

"*I can sort 'im out if ya need me to, Poppins.*"

"*I—I don't—*" *Aspen shook her head.* "*I can't—*"

She grabbed up the still ringing phone and held it out to her aunt.

Nodding once, Aliyah took the phone and quickly answered before she lost her chance.

"*Oi! I hear you're the ex-boyfriend. Wait, that's not even the case,*" *Aliyah's face dropped with annoyance, and it was evident in her tone,* "*Look. Let i' go, mate. It's over. And don' let me ever 'ear of ya so much as lookin' at my niece again or you'll find ya lack some thin's.*"

And with that, she hung up and handed the phone back to her niece.

After a moment or two of silence, Aliyah met Aspen's wide-eyed gaze.

"*Well,*" *the women smiled,* "*I hope that was him and not anyone else.*"

Giggling, Aspen's dark eyes danced, "*You're the best.*"

Shooting her a quick wink, Aliyah took a seat across the counter from her niece, "*You're not so bad yourself, love.*"

Perri came home a little while later to find her daughter sitting contently in her aunt's lap, her head resting on her shoulder and sleep having taken over.

Aliyah smiled and lifted a finger to her lips. "*She hasn't been asleep long, and I don't want to wake her.*"

"*What happened?*" *Perri tried to hide the concern in her eyes.*

"*Nothing Auntie Ali couldn't fix,*" *the woman assured,* "*I promise you it's all taken care of.*"

Shaking her head, Perri smiled and took a seat next to them, "I guess a girl just needs her aunt sometimes."

* * * * * * * * * * * * *

The door to their bedroom opened, and Liam appeared around it.

"Was that our niece and nephew on the phone, and you couldn't even keep them on long enough for me to say hello."

Laughing, Aliyah shook her head, as she met his gaze in the mirror, "You really are such a child, ya know that."

Coming over, Liam wrapped an arm around her waist and kissed her temple.

"You know you love me for it."

Rolling her eyes, Aliyah did her best not to satisfy him with a smile, but she could only hold back so long, "Idiot."

"I love you too."

Planting another quick kiss to her head, he let go and went to head back downstairs, "I have tea waiting when you're ready to come down."

She would never tire of this man.

A soft knock at the door brought Perri from her quiet gazing out the window-doors of the balcony, and with a jump in her chest she had not felt in several years, she knew. Or a secret part of her hoped, at least.

"I, uh, I still don't have a key," Ian called through the door. "Alright, if you let me in? Or is it better that I stay out here?"

Crossing the room, Perri opened the door, and Ian fell unexpectedly quiet. She watched as his bright eyes took her in, and she felt an unusual heat crawl up her neck and onto her face.

Ian had not seen Perri blush in such a long time, and it made his heart clench within his chest. He didn't understand how she could still make him feel this way, even with the way she made no pretenses of ever returning those feelings or even allowing them to come close to it.

But here she stood, in a deep blue, waffle knit thermal undershirt and thick flannel pajama pants with her hair tussled almost wildly by sleep, and she was as beautiful as always. As cliché as it may sound, it was true. Though he dare not voice it, knowing how much Perri would hate it, especially now.

"She's got quite the moxie, doesn't she, our daughter?"

Ian rubbed the back of his neck and chuckled quietly, "Yes, yes, she does. But. . . I think we both know where she gets it from, don't we."

"I don't know at all what you mean," Perri retorted, "She certainly didn't get it from me."

Ian smirked, "Ah, of course not."

The silence that settled between them held no discomfort, as was often expected between a couple that had separated on such terms as they did. It was easy and peaceful, despite the things said to one another in the heat of painful moments and the years spent knowing that, though neither of them was dead, it felt as if they only existed in each other's minds. But the quiet still had no need to be filled, so they stood in it and simply allowed it to be.

"If you could go back, still knowing everything you do now," Ian began, his voice low and heavy with all the emotion that last night had rekindled, "All the trouble we'd go through. . . How it would—how it would all end. . . Would you still marry me?"

Leave it to Ian to put words to the heaviness that did always seem to lurk.

Briefly glancing up at the ceiling, then turning earnest eyes back to her ex-husband, Perri knew exactly what she wanted to say.

"For the existence of those two alone, I'd marry you a thousand times over. But even if it weren't for them, all the good that came from us being 'us' would be enough to sell me on marrying you every time."

She paused, only for a moment, and held his gaze.

"We were happy, Ian."

"Yeah," he gave a mournful smile that almost reached his eyes, "Until we weren't."

Her eye flitted away from his, and she echoed the harsh truth that still pained her, "Until we weren't."

"Mum!" Zayden called as he, and Aspen came down the hall, "Dad! Come on! It's way passed time for us to be doing what we actually came here for."

And the moment was over. The truth laid bare and hearts aching anew, mother and father smiled at their children and moved on.

4

Unforgettable together, held the
whole world in our hands

Unexplainable, a love that only
we could understand, yeah

I know there's nothing I can do to change it

But is it something that can be negotiated?

My heart's already breaking,
baby, go on, twist the knife

— "Love You Goodbye" by One Direction

Ian had always had a strange fascination with Alaska. Laurel knew that and found it very amusing, so when he and Perri got married, she paid for their honeymoon and sent them straight to Alaska. That was their first time staying at Hotel Alyeska. And snuggled up in bed, trying to warm up after a day spent attempting to learn to ski, Ian had made the sales pitch that started their annual trips to Alyeska.

We should move to Alaska. You can design luxury cabins, ours first preferably, and I'll take care of the animals, and we could get this skiing thing down.

To which Perri declined and suggested annual visits instead.

With each trip, they promised to try something new, be it a new trail or something from the menu at Seven Glaciers, and eventually become brazen enough to try the double black diamond ski run. They did conquer that run eventually, but it wasn't fast enough for Perri, who tended to be the more impatient of the two. For years Ian's steady voice and affectionate hand on her shoulder had stopped her from leaping headfirst into a run she was far from ready to take on.

"Only a matter of time now, Per," Ian had always said, and that was enough for her to realize that he was right.

Time, Perri thought as she made her way downstairs to meet her family. *Do I even have much left?*

Smiling brightly at her children as they came into view, Perri briefly met Ian's gaze, and it was all coming back again and that heavy twinge of sadness with it.

It seemed so long ago that Ian and Perri had met in Hobbs on a spring day in London. Ian was trying to find a birthday present for his mother and found himself more confused now about what to get her than he was before he even entered the shop. Perri just happened to be in the same shop, trying on a red suit that had obviously been tailored specifically to fit her. One salesman and a seamstress were working on the finishing touches and Ian gawked at the gorgeous blonde through the trifold mirror. He had no intention of ever gaping, much less being caught, but Perri's eyes had flickered upward from watching the suit come together and caught his gaze in the reflection. And a wicked grin grew across her sharp features. Adjusting the lapels of the suit as the seamstress requested, Perri held Ian's gaze and threw him a wink.

Once Ian had gathered his jaw off of the floor and mopped up the drool, he had hurriedly decided on a handbag in his mother's favorite color and made his way quickly to the register. As he dug through his shockingly chaotic wallet, he could feel someone's presence come up beside him. The blonde from earlier had leaned casually against the checkout counter, an amused expression on her face.

"Can I—Can I help you with something?" Ian asked, finally locating the money he needed for his purchase.

"No," she drawled, her Scouse accent evident and beautiful in her raspy voice, "but I am about to help you."

Of course, she's beautiful and has an accent, Ian thought and found himself waiting, holding up the line, even though he wasn't exactly sure why.

"That handbag won't hold a thing. She'll never use it. Come with me."

And for whatever reason, Ian found himself following the blonde like a puppy being led by treats. About thirty minutes later, he and Perri walked out of the shop with her suit and a lovely but practical sweater for his mother.

"Um, thank you," Ian finally spoke as Perri passed through the door he was holding. "I never would have found this."

Looking over her shoulder at him, she smiled understandingly. "It can be a bit much in there sometimes, all the displays and sales-people. I don't go in there often, but my Mum was havin' this," she lifted the bag, "tailored for me and they have to see you to tailor somethin'."

This surprised Ian a bit, from the way Perri carried herself, he would have thought she was no stranger to luxury stores and tailored suits.

"I know my way around that sort of thin'," she continued, "But I also don't see myself enjoyin' it for the rest of my life. I'm more like my Mum, she likes livin' in the happy in-between."

"Well, you knowing your way around certainly helped me out today," Ian replied.

She hummed and shot him a smile, "Glad I could help."

Taking a pen out of her purse, Perri touched Ian's arm for him to stop, and he felt the strangest sensation that both warmed him and made his stomach do flips.

"Call me," she said as she began writing on the corner of his bag, "And tell me what she thinks, yeah?"

He nodded dumbly, and she just smiled.

Perri had always had that effect on him, and Ian didn't ever try to deny it. Ian also found that he was most adventurous with Perri. The blonde had pulled him out of his quiet shell, and two decades later, he was still grateful. But now, all that the two had were memories, spaces of time filled with images of their small family and their life together.

Time. If they had just had a little more time.

But those were thoughts for another place, for now, Ian was heading out to the slopes with his family just like years before. And while they were there, perhaps he could imagine that nothing had truly changed.

With the knock on her door, Perri resigned herself to the fact that any time she was wanted, it was going to be Ian who came to her door.

Having gone up to their rooms after skiing, the family made plans to change and then meet downstairs again for a late lunch. Perri, having taken up as much time as she could "changing," hoped she was calm enough to be around Ian for at least another hour or more.

He was still so attractive, and she was having a hard time ignoring it the more she was around him, especially after him holding her so close the night before.

No. Stop. That's enough. Perri told herself sternly. *You have to answer the door, and you know it's going to be him on the other side. So you have to pull it together.*

And she had been right. There stood Ian, leaning against the door frame, leisurely, arms and ankles crossed, patiently waiting for the door to be opened.

"I thought that might be you," Perri greeted.

Ian stood to his full height, and it still somehow surprised Perri when she had to look up at him. She didn't know why really, considering she had spent so many years married to the man, but after not standing remotely close to one another for so long, Perri supposed she did have some right to be shocked at just how tall he was up close.

He rested his forearm against the door jam and tilting his head, Ian's eyes drifted down, giving his ex-wife a once over. "Could you just sense it was me, or did my knock tip you off?"

"My eyes are up here," Perri replied and couldn't stop her own smirk from growing when she saw Ian's slipping into place.

His eyes moved up to hers, and he held the impish grin, "I know. You just look very lovely and I was appreciating the view."

Shoving past him so he wouldn't be able to see how his words affected her, Perri moved out into the hallway. "This just leaves less to the imagination than the snow pants and a ski jacket. There's nothing better about this sweater than the one I was wearing last night."

Perri paused in all her movements for a brief moment, her brain panicking at her own mention of the night before.

One second.

Then two.

Three.

And there was Ian at her side.

"Well, even if that is the case, I think you look lovely."

She murmured a soft thank you, and the pair continued down the hall toward the stairs.

* * * * * * * * * * * * *

Entering Seven Glaciers, Ian's hand came to rest so very lightly against the small of Perri's back as he pointed to a table near the back.

"We're over here."

Perri only nodded in reply, not really trusting her voice. She hated that he still had this power over her, but there was little she could do about it, and she had to come to terms with it eventually.

May as well start now.

"I swear, I saw *your* life flash before *my* eyes!" Aspen laughed, her hand on her brother's arm. "All I kept saying was 'don't die, don't die, don't die'."

"Yeah, and when I finally stood up, having to hold my broken arm to my chest, you *punched* me in it."

Aspen laughed all the harder, "It was a love tap! I was showing you that I was grateful you were still alive!"

"Oh, wow, thanks," Zayden rolled his eyes playfully, "Yeah, I really felt the love that day."

"What are you two carrying on about?" Perri asked, already finding herself smiling.

"We were trading stories on the most memorable things that have happened to us here. Mine was the time I accidentally hit Zayden's skis with my own pole, and he fell down the rest of the slope."

The younger of the two siblings looked thoughtful for a moment, "I have to say, I think that was the most memorable time for me too."

Aspen pretended to cough, "Bollocks!"

"What?" Zayden asked, turning his attention to his sister, "What's that supposed to mean?"

"I shouldn't say," she tried to backtrack, but it was too late, "Mum and Dad are here."

"Oh! Now you *have* to tell us," Ian laughed.

"Yes," Perri agreed, picking up her freshly filled wine glass and sitting back in her chair, "I am *all* ears."

"Wait!" Zayden reached out and hovered his hand over his sister's mouth, "Whisper it to me first."

Aspen looked at their parents and then raised her cloth napkin as a barrier and leaned over to whisper their secret to him.

"Oooooh," Zayden's face darkened a shade or two, "Whatever, I'm grown now."

"Well yeah, considering you were thirteen the last time we were even here!"

"Spill it," Perri cut in.

"Zayden had his first make-out session here."

"What?!" Perri turned to look at Ian, whose jaw was dropped in shock.

"With whom?"

"I think her name was Anna," he answered a little nervously.

"You think?!" Ian stage-whispered. "Son, have I taught you *nothing*? A real man always remembers a lady's name."

"Oh really?" Perri asked, leaning forward and resting her elbows on the table. "Like that time you remembered my name when we ran into each other unexpectedly in Liverpool?"

"I never forgot your name. You know that, Per."

"One of the things that I have lived to regret."

A heavy pause fell over the table for a long moment.

"You don't mean that."

Ian's voice had dropped an octave. If it were anyone else he were speaking to, they would have been a little intimidated, but Perri could never find it in her to actually be afraid of Ian. Instead, that drop in tone did the exact opposite, and the woman shifted uncomfortably in her seat. Looking at the offending glass of wine in her hand, she placed it back on the table and pushed it away from her. Things always seemed to get cloudy between them when alcohol was involved.

* * * * * * * * * * * * *

Seven years and some-odd months ago Perri sat on the couch, an arm wrapped around her knees and wine glass in hand. She was unsure of how long she had been sitting there in her own miserable thoughts, but it must have been long enough for her to begin to dissociate because she nearly jumped out of her skin when she heard someone knock on the front door.

She placed her glass on the coffee table and headed to the front door. Their children were with Aliyah, and her mother was out of town for a horse auction. There was no one else it should be, especially in a storm like this. But she opened the door anyway.

Ian stood on the porch, soaked from the pouring rain. Perri stared for a long moment, then quickly hid her real emotions behind an eye roll and moved to close the door. But his hand shot out and caught it.

"Come on, Per," his voice soft, and if she really thought about it, Perri thought she heard a hint of sadness in his tone, "Don't be that way."

Hesitating, Perri took a half step aside and allowed Ian to enter the home they had shared as husband and wife up until that very morning. Standing in the vestibule, Perri refused to let him in any further. She couldn't let him in that far, or she would never allow him to leave.

"What do you want, Ian?"

"To celebrate with you. It's our divorce, after all," Ian replied, only a hint of malice in his voice, and Perri acknowledged that she did deserve it.

"People don't celebrate divorces."

"Of course they do, Per. It's all the rage," he teased, and it was then that he really saw his now ex-wife's face. Red across her cheekbones, slightly puffy, watery eyes. Gently and non-accusatory, Ian told her, "You wanted this, Perri."

"I know I wanted this, but so did you."

A single stupid tear escaped from Perri's clutches as she took a step back, giving herself more space between them before she threw herself into her ex-husband and begged to be forgiven and for him to just come home. But she didn't beg. She would never.

"You know that's not true." Ian reached out and tenderly wiped the tear from Perri's cheek and then ran the back of his hand down it. "Come here."

And Perri allowed herself to be gathered up in a warm embrace, and she wanted to cry all the harder when she felt Ian kiss the top of her head. Then her temple. Then it was the bit of the tear trail left behind on her left cheekbone that he kissed away. Her right cheek, her nose. And with his lips so close to Perri's, breaths intermingling and hearts pounding, Ian stopped.

The pair that had woke up just this morning as husband and wife and were now nothing to each other but a past life made a choice. Still, in perfect unison with one another, they shifted and lips met in the same passionate dance as they had for years before. Ian cradled Perri's face in his hands, and she practically purred at the sensation of his hands on her.

Pulling away, Ian brushed his thumb across Perri's lips as she attempted to chase the kiss he had ended. Her eyes opened slowly, and she met his intense gaze.

"You want this?" he asked, his voice barely above a whisper.

"Yes."

"So do I."

Reaching up, Perri's hands cupped his neck and pulled him back in, crashing their lips together in a desperate kiss. She felt Ian's fingers tunnel into her hair, and she sighed into his lips, allowing his tongue to slip past. Hands moving from his neck, Perri's hands fisted into the back of his shirt and brought herself even closer as the kiss deepened.

There were too many layers between them, and Perri was getting impatient to have them out of the way. As if reading her thoughts, Ian slid his hands under her blouse, and he felt the muscles of her abdomen jump in surprise and anticipation. Pulling away for some much-needed air, Perri gasped at the feeling of his skin against hers. But she relaxed just as quickly back into Ian when he pressed his forehead to hers.

"We can stop," he offered so softly Perri almost missed what he said. But she had heard him and wasn't about to let him go that easily. She wanted him too much.

"Don't you dare," she murmured, tightening her hold on him and looking up into his suddenly dark eyes.

Ian's chuckle rumbled from deep in his chest, and Perri pressed a brief kiss to his lips.

"In fact," she purred, her lips a mere breath away from his, "We should probably get you out of these wet things."

Ian hummed in the back of his throat and kissed the soft skin, which divided her eyebrow into two parts, feeling the slightly raised scar against his lips. And Perri felt the fire that was already building inside her spread even further through her veins.

Tantalizingly slow, Perri moved her hands up his chest and over his broad shoulders, slowly pushing the age-softened leather jacket off him. It fell to the floor with a quiet rustling, and she allowed herself a mere moment in time to take it all in. Lifting her eyes back to his, Perri grazed her hands up and down his back and enjoyed the feel of his muscles rippling under her touch.

Closing the distance, Ian brushed his lips over hers, pressing a kiss to the corner of her mouth and trailing them along her jaw to the spot just behind her ear that made her crazy. Perri moaned softly and tilted her head to the side, giving Ian more access to place open-mouthed kisses on her sensitive skin.

She breathed his name and, gripping the thick hair at the base of his skull in desperate fingers, drew him closer somehow in an attempt to keep his lips working their magic over her skin. Breathing deeply, Ian tried to memorize the smell of her shampoo, mixed with the scent that was distinctly Perri, and the softness of her skin. With a quiet growl of his own, Ian scooped Perri up into his arms and continued his unbridled attentions to her now flushed skin.

Wrapping her legs around his waist, something in Perri's subconscious registered that she was being carried in the direction of their once shared bedroom. This version of herself could easily silence her more sensible self. Especially when Ian pressed her back against the wall just next to the door of their room, as if he simply couldn't wait anymore. With another purr of contentment, Perri smiled against his lips, "I've really missed. . . the way you. . . taste," she admitted between strategically placed kisses of her own. Ian heard the soft breaking of her voice and hesitated for the briefest moment, making his next kiss, placed in the slope between her collarbones, slow and tender. Closing her eyes, Perri's head fell back with a gentle thud against the wall and brought Ian's focus to one of the many features of his wife—ex-wife—that he loved to lavish attentions on.

Pressing in a little closer and keeping her in place with one arm, Ian lifted his hand from her back and glided his fingertips from under her chin down to her chest. His eyes trained on the subtle jumps of muscles and tightening of tendons that were left in the wake of his touch. Leaning forward, he laid a hot kiss over a specific freckle just to the left of Perri's throat that she had made reference to many years before about hating so much. He received a whimper in response, same as all the times before, and his knees felt a little weak at the sound.

Unable to stand it any longer, Ian stepped back from the wall, taking Perri with him and into their old bedroom. Back over to the bed they had shared for eighteen years and had signed papers just this afternoon to never do so again.

Yet here they were.

They both hit the bed with a soft hmph! And Ian continued what he had started just inside the front door of their home—Perri's home. Perri's fingers slipped under the hem of his black shirt and tugged lightly, but enough for Ian to know what she meant by it. Sitting them both up, he leaned away enough for her to remove the piece of clothing in one fluid motion, tossing it somewhere across the room to have to be found whenever this escapade was over. Laying her back down, he slowly and precisely began opening the buttons of her blouse, his gaze locked onto hers as his fingers brushed newly exposed skin with each freed button.

With golden hair splayed out on the pillow around her head and her dark eyes even darker than normal, Ian was as captivated as ever. Their breathing ragged but somehow still in unison, his hands inched passed her open blouse and wrapped around her waist.

"You are so beautiful, Perri," he whispered, "Do you have any idea what you still do to me."

Reaching up to interlock her fingers behind his neck, she pulled him in to where they shared the same air once more.

"Show me."

* * * * * * * * * * * * *

It happened only once more after that. It would have been their anniversary, their nineteen. But never again since. It ended up just being more painful than anything else.

Trying to hate someone you once shared your whole life with was harder than people made it out to be. Something that was made ten times harder by lapses in judgement when the attraction between them was just too strong. And especially when, deep down. . . they were still both so desperately in love with each other.

"No," Perri replied, her tone soft, "I don't mean it."

Ian looked almost shocked to hear Perri admit as much but couldn't seem to find his voice.

"So, are you two going to kiss or can we get back to your disgusting son?" Aspen asked, pulling their parents out of their moment.

"Penny!" Perri exclaimed

"Don't call your brother names," Ian said, stepping in to give Perri some time to recover, and Zayden smiled smugly at his sister.

"You'd be calling him gross too if you knew *where* he had his little snogging," Aspen said, munching on her pre-dinner salad.

"Penny!"

"Where?" Ian had to know if only to see Perri's reaction.

"Janitor's closet," Zayden confessed, his voice softer than normal.

"What?!" Both of his parents looked utterly horrified.

"Mate," Aspen laughed around a crouton, "you broke our parents."

Zayden chuckled and shook his head, "I hate you."

Oh, why you wearing that to walk out of my life?

Oh, even though it's over you should stay tonight

If tomorrow you won't be mine

Won't you give it to me one last time?

Oh, baby, let me love you goodbye

One more taste of your lips just to bring me back
To the places we've been and
the nights we've had

Because if this is it then at least
we could end it right

— "Love You Goodbye" by One Direction

Going their separate ways for the afternoon, Aspen and Zayden decided to find more trouble at the indoor pool, and their parents went to their rooms before all of them met back up for some night-time skiing in a few hours.

As they walked up the stairs to their adjoining rooms, Ian nudged Perri gently with his elbow and smiled down at her.

"I think we are doing pretty well. Giving the kids a nice vacation like old times. Getting along and all."

Perri nodded in agreement, "We're not doing so bad. For two slightly mature adults, I suppose."

"I've grown up a little since we were here last, Perri," Ian joked lightly, "You have to give me some credit."

Perri stopped and looked up at him quietly, her dark eyes intense with a hint of pain behind them.

"Don't. Don't do that."

Ian didn't know what to say in reply, so he simply held her gaze and tried to read what was going on inside her head. But time and distance had dulled his ability to read her that clearly, which made his heart clench in his chest.

"I'll see you in a few hours, yeah," Perri stated and turned on her heels, retreating to the safety of her room and once again leaving Ian to stand in the hall.

Perri sat on the other side of the desk, bouncing her leg anxiously as she waited for the silver-haired man to get the papers necessary for what she was about to do.

"Have you been married for over a year?" His deep, very professional voice startled her at first.

"Yes," she answered, surprised at how easily she was being rattled, "Yes, we've been married for eighteen years."

"Is your relationship permanently broken down?"

Like a knife twisting deep into her chest, Perri took a deep breath and replied with a simple, "Yes."

Perri heard the next couple of questions he asked, but only well enough to answer them, not enough to be able to tell anyone what they were.

"And the grounds for the divorce?"

"What?" Perri inquired, leaning a little closer to the desk.

With a soft sigh, the man repeated himself, "What grounds are you filing for the divorce?"

Chuckling nervously and shaking her head, Perri attempted a smile, "I'm sorry, I've, ehm, I've never done this before."

The man finally lifted his eyes from the papers before him and raised a brow at Perri, "I can see that. Do you need me to give you the list of facts?"

"Please," Perri answered softly and looked down at her hands.

"Desertion?"

A pause followed as he looked back up at Perri, who shook her head.

"Separated for two through five years?"

Again, a pause, to which she shook her head a second time.

"Unreasonable behavior?"

Perri paused, "Are there any other grounds?"

"Adultery, of course," the man answered, "But I assumed if that were the reason you would have said so by now."

"No, there has been no adultery." Her statement was matter-of-fact, and he nodded.

"What are your grounds then?"

Her chest felt as if it were being crushed in a metal vice. The grounds were none of these things. None of this was truly Ian's fault, not in the way they were going to make it seem. But there was no mending what had been broken, and Perri had to end this before they both ended up just hurting each other more.

With a deep breath and lifting her chin a fraction, "Unreasonable behavior."

"May I ask in which form?"

"You may not," Perri replied, "I don't know you, and the law need know nothing more than the facts."

With a nod and a slight raise of his brows at her boldness, the man-made some notes on his papers, "Very well."

The scratching of pen on paper was the only sound for a long moment.

"And have you made agreements about issues involving any children or properties?"

"He and I have not spoken of this," Perri admitted.

"Ah, I see," he scribbled some more, "You do understand you will have to speak about it sooner than later."

"I do."

After spending a little more time completing some basic information and paying the 550 pounds for the application process, Perri was sent on her way being curtly told she could return in a few days and finish everything.

* * * * * * * * * * * * *

"There they are," the man slid papers across the desk to Perri, who sat silently in her chair, "All finished. We will send them out this afternoon?"

"No!" Perri exclaimed, reaching out to grab the papers.

"But, you said you wanted—"

"I know what I said," she shut her eyes and sighed deeply, "But I can't do that to him. I will not have papers sent to him at his business. He—he carries enough as it is. I need to do this myself."

The man softened a bit toward her unexpectedly, seeing that Perri wasn't doing all of this out of selfishness and this woman was capable of some kindness in this situation.

"If you're certain."

She nodded decidedly, "I am."

"He will have eight days to respond. If he does not, we will have to re-issue the papers."

* * * * * * * * * * * * *

Sitting on the couch, Perri felt her stomach twisting in knots as she listened to the clock tick away the minutes as she waited for her husband to arrive home.

Everything was filed. There was no turning back now. And if this was going to happen, Perri was going to be the one to deliver it. She wasn't supposed to be. She had been instructed to ask a family member or a friend to hand Ian the papers. But what the law didn't know wouldn't hurt them. And she wasn't doing that to Ian.

The silence of the house was deafening and so the sound of Ian finally pulling into the driveway was both a welcomed and dreaded interruption. The sound of his footsteps on the porch and the knob turning sent a wave of nausea so strong that Perri feared she may chunder onto the papers before Ian even had a chance to see them.

And there he was. Standing in the doorway, looking as tired as he did most days, but always with a smile at the ready for his family.

"Hello, love," he greeted and took in her face, "You seem tired. How was your day?"

She paused a moment. *How was your day, Perri?* She questioned herself accusatorily. *You're about to get what you've been working on for weeks, so. . . how was your day?*

"Long," she attempted a small close-lipped smile. "And yours?"

"I can't complain. Where are the kids?"

"They're with Mum."

His brows pulled together momentarily as they reflexively did when he was trying to remember some plans he must have forgotten during his hectic day.

"Ah, alright."

Turning, he hung his coat on the rack and went to remove his work shoes near the door as he always did.

While he was distracted with undoing the laces, Perri took the opportunity. Knowing deep down that she could never initiate this conversation with him looking at her.

"I need to talk to you."

Lifting his head but remaining motionless otherwise, Ian attempted a smile but ultimately looked more nervous than anything.

"Should I sit down," he tried to joke, hoping that the gravity of her tone and statement was not as much as he now feared.

"Probably."

Came her single word reply, and it gave him little comfort.

Straightening, he made his way anxiously further into the house and sat down, "Are you alright?"

And of course, his first question, his first concern, it seemed, had to be of her. Even when she was about to be the one doing all the damage.

Not saying a word and unable to meet his gaze, Perri slid the papers across the table to him.

She left like a heartless coward. She was hurting him, and she couldn't even look him in the eye. He wasn't even going to understand why this was happening, and she couldn't even look at him.

Silence, like nothing that had ever been experienced between them before, reigned for several painful moments.

"Perri, I—," his voice wavered a little, "What is this?"

"You and I both know what it is."

Her tone came out much harsher than she intended, but she felt she had no right to cry, so a stiff upper lip it had to be.

He stared down at the papers, motionless, and Perri wished he would just say something. Be angry with her. Anything. Anything but silent and hurting.

"I—I don't understand."

He finally looked up at her, and she fought everything inside herself to keep from looking away.

"Are you really that unhappy?" The heartbreak in his eyes nearly killed her, "Just tell me what to do. Tell me, and I'll fix it. I'll do whatever, Perri, please."

She wanted to tell him. Wanted to tell him so badly, but she had passed up that chance long ago and made her decisions. Now she must move on with her choices.

"It's too late for that now."

* * * * * * * * * * * * *

Perri went to their room and pretended to sleep while waiting for Ian to come to bed. But he never came, and all of her pretending eventually sent her into a fitful doze. From which she woke very little, but when she did, she found herself reaching for someone who wasn't there. A moment or two would tick by, and she would remember. She had done this to herself, and this is what her new life looked like.

When the sun finally came through the curtains, Perri allowed herself to get up and go in search of her husband. She found every other room in the house to be empty, with the pillows and small blanket from the back of the couch put neatly in their places. Either he had left at some point in the night and not been there at all, or he hardly slept and left for work much earlier than necessary.

Either way, he was gone.

It wasn't until that evening, right before their children were to come home, that Perri and Ian encountered each other in the hall.

Perri placed her palm gently against his chest, stopping him as he tried to pass her by, "Ian."

His blue-eyed gaze remained focused on their feet and the old wood beneath. Perri, remembering that she most likely had no right to even touch him anymore, quickly retracted her hand as if she had been burned.

"Perri."

What was there to say? What is to be said after the night before and how she had left things.

"I don't want to fight you," Ian's voice was soft, "I'll give you whatever you want. I'm not ending it with fighting."

"I don't want to fight either," Perri almost reached out again to touch his arm, but she stopped herself and just continued to watch his face, "If we can just come to an agreement on things, I just want to. . . I want to be done with this as quickly as possible."

Ian tried not to wince at the last bit and lifted his chin to stare at one of the family photos hanging on the wall. One of the four of them from the last visit to Alaska, all of them bundled tight in ski wear and getting ready to take on the sloops together.

"I won't take both of the houses. I refuse. I'm not going to leave you without a home."

"Thank you," Perri murmured, feeling her heart break at his kindness and then shatter at the sight of tears sparkling in his eyes.

"Please," his voice broke, "*please*, don't take our kids from me. I can't lose all of you. I'd—I'd never make it."

"Ian," her voice was barely above a whisper and, even though she knew it wasn't right and probably wasn't fair, she reached up and cupped his cheek but didn't force him to look at her.

"I would *never* take them from you. I could never take your place in their lives. They need you as much as they need me, and I will not come between that. Just because we can't make it work doesn't mean their love for you doesn't matter anymore."

Ian nodded silently and swallowed once before asking softly,

"Do you love me anymore?"

Allowing her hand to drop, Perri looked away and sighed, "Ian."

"I take that as a no then?"

Before she had time to answer, the front door opened, and her mother looked inside.

"We're back, you two," she greeted, and Perri forced a bright smile.

"Hi, Mum!"

Ian had yet to move his gaze from where it had settled but called out a reply to her just the same, "Hey there, Mama L."

"The kids found the dogs first, so I imagine they're going to be a few minutes."

The couple shot her thin-lipped smiles and nodded. Understanding, Laurel went into the kitchen and set about opening the take-out she had brought.

After making sure the woman was out of earshot, Perri turned her attention back to Ian and continued softly, "Ian."

"Have what you want. I still want to be able to see the kids, and I just—I don't want to fight you."

With that, he turned and walked away into their room. That left Perri to stand alone in the hallway to try and blink back the tears stinging her eyes before joining her mother in the kitchen.

How am I going to tell her about this? What am I going to tell the kids?

* * * * * * * * * * * * * *

He had misplaced the papers twice.

"Misplaced."

But after the papers reappearing on his side of the dresser both times, Ian understood that there was nothing else to be done. He didn't want it to be over, hadn't even realized it was until he laid eyes on those dreaded forms for the first time. Hoping he could maybe salvage what was left of their marriage, he hid them until the third time they appeared, and he knew.

"I've, uh, I've signed them," he murmured one evening as they sat on opposite sides of the bed, backs toward each other. "What now?"

Yes, indeed, what now?

* * * * * * * * * * * * * *

In less than twenty-four hours, they would be leaving work to meet at the Register Office and put an end to their marriage in the same building where they started it.

Perri and Ian sat in bed, resting back against the headboard, both reading silently to themselves as they attempted to relax enough to try and get some sleep. But both of them, being alike in more ways than either of them realized, were not actually reading anything. They were simply skimming their eyes along the lines of words and would soon realize that they were merely seeing them and not retaining them.

Ian gave in first. Closing his book softly, he placed it down in the duffle bag in front of his nightstand. The bag that he would be zipping up the remainder of his things into the next morning and taking with him to what would now be his only home, back in Hoylake. It was the one of their two homes that was closest to his practice and their home in Liverpool was nearest Perri's architecture firm in Manchester. Both were within an hour drive of one another, so the children would never have to worry about one, or both, of their parents being there when they needed them. Life would continue on, just in a very different way than before.

Adjusting his pillows, Ian turned out his lamp and, leaning forward, planted a kiss on the back of Perri's hand that held her book. After the painfully familiar gesture, laced with the heaviness of finality, he laid down and turned away. Something which Perri was very grateful for because it meant that he wouldn't see the tear that escaped past her lashes to roll down her cheek.

Pure selfishness. She scolded herself. What right did she have to be crying? She had brought them here, to this point. Had she done it on a whim? Of course not. It was something she knew must be done, but that didn't make it any less painful when her chest felt as if it were being crushed at the thought of never waking up next to this man again. But it was for the best. She knew that. And so, she allowed herself a few tears at the loss she was about to suffer, even though she didn't regret her decision.

Perri waited until after she was certain she had given Ian enough time to fall asleep and then laid down herself. She felt the chill of the sheets, and part of her expected Ian to roll over and draw her close like he always did, even in his sleep. But no movement ever came, and with an unforgiving twist in her gut, Perri reached back to find the same cold space between them that had been there all evening. It was unfair of her to expect any different. After all, what had she done up to this point to be deserving of such treatment? That still didn't stop the ache in her chest and the stinging that it caused behind her eyes.

She sniffled quietly, not wanting to disturb what little sleep Ian may be able to get tonight. Because if she knew him, and she knew him very well, Perri knew he was not going to sleep well these next several hours. Or for a long while now perhaps.

After only a few minutes of lying in the darkness, Perri heard Ian take a deep breath, and she immediately quieted her quivering breaths and waited. Then there was the rustling of sheets and movement on the other side of the bed. An arm slipped around her waist, holding her gently but secure just like she had grown so accustomed to over the years, and pulled her flush against Ian's front.

She didn't deserve his kindness, but somehow, even after all this, he loved her enough to give it to her anyway. That knowledge alone was enough to make the damn break. Add being held so tenderly knowing the strength this man was capable of, and there was no way for Perri to hold back the gasping sob that escaped her. She laid her arm over his and laced their fingers together, feeling him rest his cheek against the side of her head.

"It's okay, Per," he whispered into the blonde hair now pillowing his jaw, "I've got you. You can cry. You're allowed to cry."

His words only made her cry even harder. He knew her so well, maybe better than she knew herself.

He was quiet again for a long time and simply allowed the darkness to hold them both as their thoughts were consumed with the same thing.

"It will be alright. Someday, love, it will be alright."

And for a moment, Perri wondered if it was too much to ask if, just for tonight, they could pretend that what Ian was saying could be true. Turning over, she wrapped her arms around his neck, pulling him in as close as she could. She allowed herself this one last time to hold him and be held and then no more. It wasn't fair.

All the while, Ian's pretty lies were whispered in her ear until sleep finally took her. She slept dreamlessly that night, not yet fully understanding how much her sleep would change once she was no longer sharing a bed with Ian. She had no idea how often her future self would end up reaching for her husband during the night, only to come up empty-handed as cold sheets met her touch. Or how she would have trouble falling asleep without Ian's arms looped around her and his presence behind her. How she would miss the comforting warmth of him underneath her and the soothing rise and fall of his chest that would lull her back to sleep no matter how much her mind was racing. Most surprising of all, she would long for the chance to wake up to the sunlight streaming through the sliver between the curtains and her arm draped over Ian's waist, her forehead pressed softly into the back of his neck. Long for the quiet moments following waking up, when she would lift her head just enough to rest her chin on his shoulder and fill her lungs with the peacefulness of their few shared minutes before their days began pulling them every which way.

Perri had no understanding of all the little things she had come to treasure so deeply and would find herself searching for long after Ian was gone.

* * * * * * * * * * * * *

Ian stood outside the Register's Building, waiting, hoping that maybe, just maybe, Perri had changed her mind and was on her way to tell him so. But he knew that to be wishful thinking, his wife was much too determined once she set her mind to something and there would be no changing her decision. Even if she had discovered every reason to decided differently, she wouldn't be able to shake the haunting of the first things that made a decision necessary at all.

He knew it was in vain, but he allowed himself the painful chance to hope anyway.

And there she was. Beautiful as the day he first saw her. No, that wasn't true. Somehow, even after all the years, Perri had just managed to become more beautiful in his eyes. Even more so than that first day when her dark eyes caught his gaze in the mirror of that crowded store. He knew it was because now he knew her. He had seen her heart and knew her mind in a way no one else ever had. He knew her love for their children, her work, and the strength of the love she had once carried for him. He knew her courage, her passion to create, and all the things that made Perri the woman she was. And she was breathtaking.

Her close-fitting outfit which he was well aware she saved for important meeting days, was not helping to tone down her beauty and save him just a little pain.

Looking up, Perri's eyes met his, and he attempted a smile in greeting but only got as far as a slight lift of the corner of his lips.

Once she finally came to a stop a few feet in front of him, Ian anxiously adjusted the collar of his shirt.

"H—how has your morning been?"

Perri was quiet for a long moment, a heaviness in her eyes, "Quick. It passed by. . . so quick."

Watching him fiddle with his collar, she took a step forward and reached out slowly, allowing Ian plenty of time to back away if he wanted. "Can I help?"

"Please," he replied, lifting his chin a fraction, "It's been a full day at the clinic already and I've been fighting with this shirt most of the morning because of it."

Reaching up, she folded it down properly and smoothed it out gently, her fingers lightly brushing the skin of his neck.

"There," she stated, moving back, "All better."

"Yes. . ." Ian looked down at her face, fighting the stinging behind his eyes, "All better."

People passing on the sidewalk not so far away watched as the couple stood in silence for a few minutes, unsure of how to proceed.

"I feel like I can ask just one thing of you before we go in."

Ian's voice was soft and broke Perri's heart.

"Of course."

"Can you. . . Can you just stand here with me for a few minutes more and just. . ." Laying his hands on her shoulders, Perri fought the urge to close her eyes and soak the feeling in. Instead, she quirked a brow and watched him smile, just a little and with a hint of sadness in his unusually dim eyes. Turning her slowly until her back was facing him, Perri almost whipped back around to question him on what he was doing.

"Ian, what—"

"Just trust me. Just for a minute more, if you can. Please."

His tender request was spoken in a voice barely above a whisper, choked with emotions he was trying to keep in check. His breath brushed against her ear, and Perri's eyes fluttered shut in response.

"Okay."

Then his hands were gone, and Perri wondered for a moment if he had left her standing there all alone. Just when she was certain that he was no longer there, she felt his back meet hers, and her heart plummeted to the tunnels hidden deep under the city.

They had stood in this same spot eighteen years before. Back to back, preparing to turn and see each other for the first time that day, mere minutes before they were to go inside and say their vows.

Tears stung her eyes and threatened to close her throat. Breathing deeply, Perri rested her head back against Ian's shoulder and closed her eyes. They had come full circle, just like Ian had promised they would, but definitely not in the way he had imagined. They had begun their married life here, and here was where it was coming to an end.

"It's not too late," he whispered, the breeze carrying the sound to her ear.

Squeezing her eyes closed just a little tighter, Perri clenched her teeth for a moment before answering softly, "It is. I—I wish it wasn't."

Feeling his shuddering breath against her back, Perri felt the tears escape past her lashes and quickly whipped them away.

"I'm so sorry, Ian."

"So am I," he replied, his voice low and tight.

Giving themselves just a few more moments, the couple eventually turned and headed toward the front doors. Both of them were trying so hard to think of anything but the day they had all but ran up the stairs with smiles so wide that their cheeks hurt later. Excitedly rushing into a side room to commit their entire lives to one another in front of their parents and friends.

Think of anything but that. Anything at all.

* * * * * * * * * * * * * *

It was over.

Their marriage was officially ended.

Perri descended the stairs with purpose, intent on continuing on with her day and the rest of her life. But how does one simply turn their back on something that has been so important for so long without wishing there was a way it could have been saved?

The tears flooding her vision were the original cause for Perri stopping. But it was the deep, twisting ache in her chest and the sudden heaviness of her feet were the reason she stayed. Slowly at first, unsure and knowing it would only make this all the more painful, she turned to watch Ian go. She had driven him away. After all, she should at least have to watch him leave.

But what she found was her husband—ex-husband—standing at the other end of the stairs, his bright eyes already watching her. As if being tugged by an invisible sting connected somehow to the rib protecting her heart, Perri took a small, uncertain step forward. Followed by another. Then, when she saw Ian doing the same—one unsure step after another—Perri sped up, closing the remained distance between them in mere moments.

Launching herself the final few steps, Perri collided with Ian and threw her arms around his neck. It wasn't graceful, or anything like the movies or even the books would have you believe. They crashed together, the air leaving their lungs and tears rolling from their eyes. Perri dug her fingers into the soft warmth of Ian's shirt, and his hand made its way up under her suit jacket to splay between her shoulder blades, holding her close.

"I told you not to turn around."

His voice shook softly as he turned his face to bury it in her hair.

Green apple. He wanted to remember that smell. Her shampoo and the soft sent of her strawberry soap that mixed so well with the smell that was naturally Perri.

I don't want to keep walking away from you. Perri thought as she shook her head gently. Clutching his shirt in one fist, she tunneled her fingers into the thick hair at the base of his skull and held him equally close. As close as humanly possible.

She couldn't remember when it was that they last held each other this way. She felt all the broken pieces mending and her heart shattering all at once. How could such a thing be possible? How could this moment be possible? Their younger selves would never have foreseen this happening to them one day.

Was it too late to change her mind?

Yes. She couldn't back out now. Her reasons were too strong. Besides, everything was signed and legal now, and setting fire to the Register Building just so that a small stack of papers would no longer exist was probably worthy of some time spent in The Big House.

"Perri, I don't understand," Ian whispered, his voice breaking.

"I'm so sorry."

She allowed a single sob to escape past her lips.

For the mixed messages. For hurting you. For not telling you the reason. I'm just so sorry.

Minutes passed in days, and yet somehow, it was over all too quickly.

Neither one was sure who began the parting, but they both slowly let go of the other. For a moment, they remained standing with mere inches separating them.

"Now," Ian spoke softly, and his eyes could not bring themselves to meet Perri's, "We go and we—we can't look back."

Perri nodded, her face crumpling for a moment before she forced herself to take a deep breath and straightening to her full, confident posture. Practiced as that posture may be.

"Good," she could almost hear the smile in Ian's voice, "Chin up, love."

Releasing the light hold he had on her elbows, Ian took a step back, and Perri was struck by the chill that hit her without having him so close. She gasped softly and lifted her eyes to meet his gaze for a fleeting moment before he nodded and gave her a sad, close-lipped smile.

That was the signal. It was done. Time to turn and not look back.

For both of their sakes.

So they did just that.

The couple turned their backs toward one another and set off in their separate ways to embark on separate lives.

But neither one would ever know that they had both cast one last look over their shoulders at the other, for just one last glance before they no longer saw the other's face every morning or fell asleep every night with the other being just a breath away.

Who's to say what would have happened had their gazes met in that final glance. Perhaps things would be different now, perhaps not. One can only wonder.

With the walls that separated them now, both the ones that made up their adjoined rooms and the invisible ones that existed between the two even in the closest of settings, Ian often found his thoughts wandering back. Favoring a certain night when the two of them were much younger, and he had finally acquired the spontaneous courage to ask a question that forever changed their lives. The one question that would make it where he never had to figure out how he would survive a day without Perri to face life with. Or at least that is what he had hoped for. But things do not always turn out the way we hope, something that Ian had been forced to learn in all areas of his life.

Getting ready to meet his family for their nighttime adventure, Ian knew it was more harmful than good, but he didn't stop himself from thinking back as he pulled on his snow gear. It seemed that being in such close proximity to Perri was awakening every memory that he had tried so hard to tuck away for the welfare of his own heart.

* * * * * * * * * * * * *

Sitting atop one of the surgery tables in a quieter part of the clinic, Perri worked on a condensed version of a sketch on a spare piece of paper she had found lying nearby. As long as she had this to keep her mind occupied, she was content waiting for Ian to get out of the emergency surgery that had interrupted their date.

During the time they had been seeing each other, more than one date had been not so gracefully interrupted by a call from the veterinarian that Ian was finishing his externship under. Tonight was certainly not the first time Perri had tagged along to wait for him either. Having only a silent and dark apartment to return to, she figured that waiting in an active clinic, with the occasional puppy to show some affection to, was a much better alternative. And knowing she would get to see Ian for at least a few more minutes afterward before going home made the waiting worth it.

So Perri sat in her usual spot and swung her feet gently back and forth as she thought about the details of her design. Hearing doors open and close in the distance, she looked up and was met with a familiar sound. The sound of Ian's footsteps coming down the hall made her chest warm, and a smile crept onto her face. Then there he was, rolling his tired shoulders and flexing his tense hands, always ready with a soft smile for Perri, whose impish grin he loved so much. Crossing the room, Ian slid his hands around her waist and pulled her forward, standing between her knees to have her as close as possible.

"Hi," he greeted, his voice a little gravely from lack of use but soothing as ever.

"Hello," Perri smiled, tipping her head back to look up at him fully and resting her forearms on his broad shoulders, "How did it go?"

Nodding slowly, Ian's eyes drifted downward in thought as Perri had noticed they always did.

"Good. The little guy should be fine by tomorrow."

"What happened to him?" she inquired, "Tell me how you fixed it."

She loved to hear Ian talk about his work and, more importantly, she liked him to know she cared and was curious about what his days consisted of. Ian always made her feel as if he valued her work just as much as she did, and sometimes he saw value in it that even she didn't. He was always so kind and attentive, and she loved to hear him talk so passionately about his work.

Shuffling his feet to be a little more widespread and easier on his body that had already been standing for hours, Ian began telling her about the dog that now lay recovering from surgery several rooms away.

"And then we closed him up, and hopefully when the little fighter wakes up, he'll be feeling better."

Perri smiled softly, her eyes shining with so much affection and admiration, and she pulled him into a warm embrace for a minute.

"You're amazing," she said, "You know that."

Ian chuckled, the sound rumbling in his chest, and his arms slid fully round her waist to squeeze her in return.

"Well, thank you, but I had plenty of help."

She hummed in response and planted a kiss on his temple before leaning back.

"Now, can I take you to dinner?" Perri smirked, "I'm hungry, and I can imagine you are too. There's not much left open, but I don't doubt our abilities to find food."

Ian smiled, and her chest warmed. The part of her that had been single for so long almost hated how much she loved his smile. *Almost.* In all reality, she was just happy to be near him, and when he smiled, it just made things even better.

"Can I ask you a massive favor?"

Taking his face in her hands and tunneling her fingers through his hair, Perri leaned down a fraction to be closer to him.

"Anything. Anything you want."

The fact that she felt safe offering someone anything they wanted from her, especially a man she had been seeing for what felt like a short time, was enough to almost shock her into hesitation. But somehow, it felt as if they had always known each other in a way, and offering him everything felt more than safe. Perri knew, without question, that Ian would never ask too much of her. No matter what he needed, he would never ask for more than she could easily do. In fact, up to this point, Ian had never asked her for anything. The things Perri had done for him were all because she had seen him needing help, even if it was just someone to sit back and hold him on the hard days.

"Will you marry me?"

His voice was soft and at the sound of his question, Perri's eyes stung and for a rare moment, she didn't know what to say. Ian noticed her eyes filling with tears and the panic settled on his face.

"I can't say that I'm sorry because I'm not," he began, his voice rushed as if trying to fix something he had broken, "But I can take it back. For now. I didn't mean to—well, I did, but—I didn't expect you to—"

146

"Don't you dare take it back," Perri cut in and pulled him in to crash their lips together.

The kiss wasn't fireworks exploding behind Perri's closed eyelids. It was soft tendrils of fire creeping up her body from the base of her spine. It was a breath pulled from the very back of her throat that she's been holding for hours, for months. It was Ian's hands rising to either side of her face, but not touching, not just yet. Just waiting. As though he didn't know where to touch first. Also, in disbelief that this moment was finally happening.

So began eighteen years of a shared home and a shared bed, with millions of moments and thousands of kisses that made them feel the exact same way as the first.

5

This is you, this is me, this is all we need
Is it true? My faith is shaken, but I still believe
This is you, this is me, this is all we need
So won't you stay a while?
And hold me while you wait
I wish that I was good enough.

— "Hold Me While You Wait"
by Lewis Capaldi

"Good morning, everyone!" Ian greeted, taking a seat in the only empty chair at their breakfast table. The only seat was beside Perri, as Aspen and Zayden made sure to claim their chairs before either of their parents arrived.

"You're late," Perri informed him, her gaze focused on the steaming mug in her hands.

Ian scoffed playfully, "Perri, it takes time to look like this"

Finally looking up, Perri chuckled but tried not to appear amused by his statement.

"Like *what?* You're wearing snow pants."

"Touché."

Aspen and Zayden immediately relaxed as their parents ended what could have been a disastrous interaction with smiles instead of one of them leaving the table with promises to meet up at the slopes later. She hated it because she didn't want to end up hurting herself even more, but Aspen couldn't help getting a little more hopeful as she watched them. Until it actually happened moments ago, she never would have imagined their parents walking out of *that* conversation being amused instead of fractious.

Aspen felt a tap against the side of her thigh, and, looking down, she found Zayden holding his phone just in her line of sight with a note typed out on the screen.

Who would have thought, yeah?

I just wish they wouldn't do that in front of us.

Lifting her eyes, Aspen's brows pulled together in question, and she shook her head just enough for him to understand her confusion. Taking his phone back, Zayden typed something else and passed it back into her view. Picking up her glass of orange juice, Aspen went to take a long sip, giving herself the opportunity to cut her eyes down and read what he had said.

Dad is looking at Mum like he could jump her right now and Mum is looking like she's sort of into it.

The sudden sound of Aspen choking on what was meant to be a peaceful morning beverage scared everyone at the table. With her eyes wide from both the shock of choking and her brother's observation, Aspen quickly covered her mouth, and Zayden set to hitting her a few times on the back.

"Baby, are you okay?!" Perri questioned, her eyes wide themselves from her own shock.

Both Perri and Ian appeared ready to leap out of their seats in a fraction of a second if they felt like they needed to. So Aspen quickly waved their concerns away with the hand that wasn't currently occupied.

"I'm fine," she managed between coughs.

The two settled back but remained alert as ever until Aspen's airway decided to quit being so angry with her.

"So sorry," she said, her voice strained a little, "I wasn't expecting all the pulp, and it surprised me is all."

"You're sure you're alright?" Ian asked.

"Positive," Aspen gave a decided nod.

Once their parents went back to looking at the menu, she cut her eyes over at her brother, who was fighting back a wicked smirk.

She would get him back for that later.

To fill the silence as they waited for their breakfast, they all started discussing which runs they would do that morning.

"Ooo, that's a difficult one," a mischievous smile grew across Ian's face, "You in?"

Aspen, as fearless as Ian and as impish as her mother, leaned in conspiratorially and replied, "I am so in."

Laughing, Ian reached over and tapped his finger against her nose, much like when she was small, and Aspen beamed.

"Mum, are you going to join us?" he asked his ex-wife, "I know you said you had had enough for a couple of days after last night's trip."

"I don't think I can keep up with you two," Perri shook her head.

Ian rested his arm on the back of her chair and leaned a little closer. "I don't know, Per. You used to keep me on my toes. Come on. Don't be chicken."

Perri raised a sharp eyebrow, "You can't bully me into skiing with you."

He smirked, "If you're scared, just say so, Per."

Perri's jaw dropped, but Ian could tell she was trying not to smile.

"Fine," she shrugged, "I was trying not to beat you in front of your children, but if you don't mind," Lifting her hands in surrender, "Then neither do I."

"Cocky," Ian commented softly, and his eyes dropped down, taking in Perri's frame before they shot back up to her eyes, "I like it."

Perri had learned over the years that no response at all always egged on Ian's not-so-subtle flirting, and she secretly enjoyed it. So she was grateful for the waiter's interruption. Once their orders were placed, they excitedly discussed the day ahead of them.

With breakfast finished, Ian headed out to the ski emporium to get their lift passes and rentals for the day. Heading up to their rooms, Perri, Aspen, and Zayden went to change into their own snow gear, much similar to Ian's.

Once they were all out in the snow together, Ian and Aspen had decided to snowboard instead, leaving Perri and Zayden to ski. The tram pulled into the station at the side of the hotel and took them halfway up the summit, where the lift would take them from there. Scooped up two at a time, they were all soon dropped at the top of the mountain.

"May the best skier win!" Ian shouted through his snow balaclava.

"Don't worry," Perri yelled back, "I plan to!"

With that, they took off down the hard-packed snow, their children just behind them. It was a complicated course that they had decided on, but Perri was determined to get through it faster than her equally competitive ex-husband. Bending her knees, she accelerated toward the mark on the path that was at least twenty-five meters away. In her peripherals, she could see Ian sailing smoothly across the snow, quickly closing in on her. Perri shot through the two poles that were the first gate just mere seconds before Ian. She took pleasure in the small victory but knew that Ian would not make it any easier for her now that she had bested him on the first turn.

The second and third turns were more in Ian's favor. He succeeded in passing through both gates just before Perri and was approaching the fourth when Perri flew past him in a cloud of snow that hissed loudly around her.

Zayden wasn't far behind, and together, the three of them raced toward the last gate on the trail. Perri had forgotten how exhilarating it was to rush so quickly down the side of a mountain with the freezing air whipping all around her.

Could it be? Was she actually having. . . fun? Part of her did wonder if maybe she had forgotten how. . . Just a bit.

Just as they got closer to the fifth gate and the final run-out, Perri saw it milliseconds before her skis touched it. She couldn't have avoided it if she tried, but she wished she had been able to dodge that death cookie somehow. Because she knew this fall was about to hurt like hell. Perri suddenly felt like she was skiing on marbles, and even as she tried to stop herself, she knew it was too late. Her skis slipped from underneath her, and she was forced to turn and just roll with the fall.

Ian, seeing her turn, tipped his board forward to pass the rolling blonde. She cut her off at the pass, effectively blocking Perri from tumbling down the remainder of the run. Unfortunately, Ian didn't have the chance to firmly mount his feet and gain his balance before Perri spiraled directly into his legs. The force caused him to fall forward on top of Perri, who lay motionless in the snow.

"Perri!"

Feeling the anxiety reach up and clamp down on his throat, Ian scrambled around to where he was face-to-face with Perri. Pushing her goggles and hat off, he watched as blonde waves unfurled against the pure white snow. Pulling off his own helmet and balaclava, his graying hair fell onto his forehead and curled in front of his panicked eyes. Removing his gloves, Ian's hands went to Perri's chin, moving her face from side to side, checking for any scrapes or cuts. Brushing the hair back from her face, his frantic eyes searching still.

"Per, are you hurt?"

"No," Perri replied, her dark eyes calming slowly, "No, I'm okay. . ."

She searched Ian's face, watching as his expression turned into something else altogether. A small smile lifted the corners of his lips, and Perri's heart fluttered in her chest, although she would never admit it. Ian watched in boyish delight as her gloved hands came up to rest on his in an attempt to keep him close.

"I'm fine. Really," she assured him again.

One uninterrupted moment later, Ian had tried to convey everything he was feeling in just one look. And Perri. . . well, Perri had, despite the skiing pole poking at her side, somehow managed to give Ian—.

"You're making kiss me eyes," he stated.

Immediately dropping her hands, Perri's brows pulled together, creating the adorable crease between them that Ian loved so much.

"No, I'm not!" she hissed.

Leaning just a fraction closer, Ian smiled, "I was married to you for eighteen years, I think I know a thing or two about that look."

Rolling her eyes, Perri pushed Ian off of her just in time for Aspen to come skidding to a stop not that far away from them.

"Mum!"

Feet still attached to her board, Aspen fell more than knelt beside her mother, eyes wide behind her snow goggles. Never in all the years, they had come here had she seen the woman have an accident this terrifying. She wasn't going to lie and act like it didn't shake her to watch, knowing the whole time that there was nothing she could do to stop it.

"Mum, what happened?!" Taking her mother's face in her hands, Aspen's eyes searched her face, and Perri couldn't help but think how much she resembled her father in that moment.

Reaching up, Perri gently wrapped her hands around Aspen's wrists and held her daughter's panicked gaze.

"Hey, hey. It's alright. I'm alright."

Sniffling back the panic and some tears, the girl took a deep breath.

"You hit hard, Mum."

Lifting her shoulder in a single shrug, Perri smirked a little, "That's what all the padding is for, love."

Shaking her head, Aspen did chuckle softly, "No, it's not."

From beside them, Ian laid a hand on his daughter's shoulder and shot her a quick reassuring smile. Looking back and forth between them for a moment, Aspen finally stood and, reaching out, helped them both to their feet.

"So what happened anyway?" she asked, "I was too far away to see."

"A Death Cookie almost wiped Mum out."

The moment Perri stood, she knew something was wrong, and with a gasp of pain, she quickly took all the weight off of her left foot.

Ian's hand was right there, balancing her and ready to take her full weight if needed. "What hurts?"

"Nothing," she insisted and attempted to put pressure on her foot again with the same results, "I'm fine." She winced and bared her teeth against the groan of pain that almost slipped past without her permission.

Ian wrapped his arm around her waist, "You're not fine. We have to get you off of the course."

Looking around, Aspen found a boulder not too far off the run, and together they waddled a protesting Perri over to sit.

155

"I'm going to run down to the emergency service tower so they can send an EMT." Ian began gathering his discarded gear and putting it back on.

"Looks like someone beat you to it," Perri replied, tilting her head in the direction of the bright red snowmobile that was racing the last stretch to reach them. On the back sat Zayden, his chest puffed out and a proud smirk on his face, like he was single-handedly rescuing a damsel in distress.

"I saw you go down. Figured someone had to get emergency services as soon as possible," he said, coming up to stand with his family, "You alright, Mum?"

"My hero," the woman smiled, "Yes, I'm fine, but your Father here is convinced I'm broken."

"I didn't say that," Ian protested.

Looking up at him, Perri countered, "You didn't have too."

Perri was placed on the back of the snowmobile and taken to the hotel's infirmary, where she was promptly diagnosed with a badly sprained ankle and wrist and possibly a small concussion. With ankle and wrist wrapped tightly, she was given some medication to relieve some of the pain and told to rest easy for the next few days at least.

Perri hobbled from the infirmary as soon as they would allow her to leave, followed dutifully by Ian and their children.

"I'm really alright," she smiled over her shoulder at them, "You don't need to worry."

"You really shouldn't be walking on it, Mum," Zayden said, watching how she favored her foot as subtly as possible.

Giving a tired chuckle, Perri shook her head, "I'm not an invalid, my love."

And with familiar bullheadedness, the woman turned toward the stairs and went to make her way up to them. Suddenly a strong arm was around her waist, and her feet were lifted off the ground just enough to stop her.

"Oh no, you don't."

"Ian Astankova, you put me down right now!"

"Agree to take the elevator, and I will."

Perri went still and seemed to be battling with herself on whether or not to give in.

Sighing, she caved, "Fine. Now let me down."

Turning her in the direction of the elevator, Ian lowered his ex-wife back to the floor, but he kept his hands lightly on her waist for a moment. She could feel the soft press of his grip through her snow gear, and Perri's heart stuttered in her chest.

Aspen looked over at her brother, smiling knowingly with a twinkle in her eyes that almost made Zayden laugh out loud.

Leaning down, he whispered, "You look so much like Mum when you do that."

Elbowing him playfully, she turned back to find their parents already heading to the elevator.

"You two coming?" Ian called over his shoulder.

Taking off, the two went to catch up as Ian held the elevator door, and their mother shook her head affectionately.

Helping Perri to her room had not been the easiest task, but they expected no less from a woman who didn't quite know how to accept help. Once they had her inside her hotel room, Perri plopped down on the sofa, still wearing her snow gear.

"You two go back and finish your morning on the slopes. I can assure you that I am fine. I'm all settled and can elevate and ice my ankle just fine without the three of you watching me."

Thinking about it for a moment, the two siblings shared a look. Then flying forward, they kissed her cheek, insisting that she did actually rest and assuring her they would be back to check in on her in a few hours.

"I'll be on my best behavior," Perri promised, and she watched as her children took off to return to the snow.

When they were finally alone, Ian and Perri shared the room in silence for a moment before he disappeared into the bathroom to draw a bath. He wasn't long, but he should have known Perri would start trying to do things on her own as soon as no one was around to make sure she behaved.

Bent down, she was struggling—at best—to remove her remaining snow boot with one hand. Her growing irritation was evident even though he couldn't see her face, and he did his best to stifle a small chuckle.

"Let me help," he said softly, crossing the room.

"I'm fine," Perri insisted, a little more harshly than she meant to, but the quiver in her voice was what Ian heard most.

Kneeling down, he caught her hand in both of his and held it for a moment before looking up to meet her eyes. "Let me help."

He waited for her permission, which came in a subtle nod, and then proceeded to finish unlacing her boot. Shoe placed aside to be returned to its mate later; he lifted his crystal eyes to her amber gaze once more.

"Pants next?"

She knew she would regret it later, but Perri nodded, unable to resist. It would be easier to accept help from the man she was still madly in love with than to tussle with the heavy snow pants all on her own once he was gone.

Offering a hand to steady her, Ian remained on the floor while Perri stood up. With all the hardheadedness she possessed, she stood on both feet and tried to hide the wince that crossed her face.

"Ah," he tutted gently and tapped the inside of her injured ankle with a feathery light touch, "Lift this one and use me for balance."

Rolling her eyes, Perri placed her hands on his shoulders and looked straight ahead as he helped her slide out of the thick material. As soon as the pants hit the floor with a weighty sound, Perri sat down, and Ian slowly got back to his feet.

"Can I help you with your coat?"

"No, I've got it," she replied, focusing her attention on the zipper.

She could already feel the heat crawling up her chest and turning her neck a soft shade of red.

"Please, Per, I feel terrible," Ian continued, "At least let me help you." Attempting a chuckle to try and lighten the mood, Perri tried to ignore the sadness behind his eyes as he continued, "I'd be willing to do your bidding for the next few days if you'd just let me."

The corners of her lips lifting a fraction, Perri's eyes danced, "It seems that you're willing to do my bidding any time. Especially if it puts us in a room alone together."

Shaking his head, Ian gave a small smile, "I'm being serious, Perri."

"As am I," she answered, looking up into his face with a reassuring look of her own, "I'm fine. And if it weren't for my horrible competitive nature, we wouldn't be here either."

Unzipping her coat, Perri tossed it across the back of the sofa. Ian sighed in knowing defeat and merely offered his hand to help his ex-wife to her feet as well.

"You could at least let me help you to your bath to assuage some of my guilt."

Sliding her arm around his shoulders, Perri reminded herself to breathe as his arm wound around her waist, "I will allow it, I suppose."

Making it to the bathroom without combusting at the nearness of Ian was an accomplishment, Perri felt, and one she deserved a medal for. Especially while only wearing her black Long Johns set and his hand sturdy and warm at her side.

Sitting down on the side of the tub, Perri smiled her thanks, and reaching over, she turned off the water before the bubbles began to overflow.

Ian placed a towel on the steps of the whirlpool tub, "Enjoy your bath. They didn't have strawberry scent, so I'm afraid vanilla will have to substitute. Don't get your wrap wet."

With a quiet click of the doorknob as he shut the door behind him, Ian left Perri alone in the bathroom. She looked at the vanilla-scented bath that could easily fit two and wondered if this was really what she wanted the rest of her life to be. Enormous baths always by herself. Constantly fighting the urge to just let her ex-husband see how badly she still wanted him. Hurting her own feelings and Ian's at the same time.

The vast loneliness of the warm bath sent her thoughts to old memories of the simplest things. Things she found that she missed more and more as time stretched on, and she was still alone.

* * * * * * * * * * * * *

Perri was always content to lay mostly atop her fiancé, be they on the couch or in the barn on fresh hay among the horses. It didn't really matter. If they were going to lay down, Perri was always going to end up on Ian's chest, somehow.

This moment found them on the couch, Perri's arms folded across his chest and her chin resting atop her arms to give her the best view of his face. Although she would never admit that was the reason for her specific position.

Ian smiled, running his fingers through her hair, and Perri gave a small smirk of her own in return.

"You know something, Perri?" Ian spoke softly, breaking the quiet around them, "You always try to hide that you like when I do this to your hair, but I can tell you enjoy it."

"Oh, yeah?" she commented, lifting a challenging brow, "How so?"

She could feel his laughter rumble in his chest, and Perri fought off the smile that threatened to brighten her quizzical expression.

"Because," he replied, "you're practically purring, idiot."

Drawing back a few inches in mock shock, Perri tried to appear offended.

"I do not purr!" she insisted, "And we both know I'm not the only wanker in this room."

His laughter drifting off, Ian's smile still threatened to outshine the sun, "Of course, darling."

Around lunchtime, Aspen reappeared in her mother's room and was happy to see the woman actually sitting with her ankle resting atop two throw pillows from the head of the bed.

"Did you get any rest, Mum?"

"Not really," Perri admitted, "My mind was far too full to fall asleep."

After being left with her memories and thoughts, Perri couldn't help but take a hard look at her life. What she had done, all the things she still wanted to do, and, more importantly, who she wanted to have with her.

Flopping down on the bed beside her mother, Aspen stretched out, "What have you been thinking about?"

Perri was quiet for a long moment, her gaze thoughtful as she watched the fire dance in the fireplace across from them.

"Time."

Aspen's brows drew together for a moment, trying to understand what her mother was attempting to say.

Turning her gaze to her daughter, Perri smiled a little sadly, "Just time."

"I don't know exactly what you mean by that," Aspen replied honestly, "But if it has anything to do with wondering about time for Zayden and I, you and Dad always make time for us. You were the perfect team. And look at us now, your both still making time for us. We're in the middle of freezing Alaska for two weeks, all of us, *together*. All because you two have always made it work for us."

* * * * * * * * * * * * * *

In the middle of Aspen's Secondary education, she found herself having her first set of boy troubles.

"He was a stupid one anyway," Ian made a face, "You're much too smart and far too pretty to cry over him."

He and Perri had crawled into Aspen's bed, laying on either side of her, despite the half-hearted protests of their emotional daughter.

"Also, he had stupid hair," Perri softly reminded the girl of her own words.

"Ooo, yes!" Ian agreed, eyes widening as he pointed at his wife in excitement, "Very stupid hair. He was going nowhere at all with that look."

"Not to mention that his parents are terrible!" Perri continued, "I mean, would you really want to marry a boy whose father is such a misogynist?"

Aspen considered her mother's words and then shook her head, rubbing the tears from her puffy eyes.

"No," came the murmured reply.

"Exactly," Ian's voice was softer now, "And why not?"

"Because women are the superior sex," Aspen stated through a sniffle. "Except for Zayden, he doesn't count. He's pretty okay."

"I mean, this girl," Perri looked across the bed at her husband, "She's a genius. We have literally taught her all she needs to know."

"I agree," he teased, propping himself up on his elbow, "She really does know her onions. Now all she needs is a job and her own apartment."

"Yeah. Get out of here so Dad and I can turn this room into a home office," Perri tugged lightly on a strand of Aspen's hair, making the girl giggle.

"Or something else."

Ian wiggled his eyebrows suggestively at Perri, who laughed.

"No! Eww! Get out!" the girl half-whined, half-laughed, using both her arms to push her parents toward the edges of her bed. When they didn't seem to budge, Aspen went to try and climb out of bed to get as far away from her parents as she could.

But Perri grabbed her by the back of her t-shirt and pulled her back down to lay between them.

"Ugh, Mum!"

"We love you, Penny girl," the woman said before she and Ian kissed Aspen's cheeks simultaneously.

"Yes," Ian then planted an extra kiss on his daughter's forehead, *"We love you so much."*

* * * * * * * * * * * * *

Perri smiled at the memory and the way Aspen told it.

"You know, we argued about an hour before that?"

"Really?" Aspen looked shocked. She had had no idea.

"Yeah, but for the life of me," Perri admitted, "I can't remember what it was about."

"Because it turns out that it wasn't important," Aspen shrugged, "I think that just goes to show that when you truly love someone, you can always come together for a common goal, even if you're mad at one another."

Perri looked at her daughter, soft awe in her eyes, as she reached out to stroke her hair before resting her palm against Aspen's cheek.

"You really are too smart for your own good."

The girl grinned, looking up innocently at her mother. "Thanks," she smirked, "I get it from my parents."

Perri sat quietly for a long moment. There was something she knew she needed to tell her children and now seemed to be the only quiet moment she may get to do so with Aspen. Taking a deep breath, her lips parted to finally confess what she had kept hidden for the last few months, and the door to her room opened.

"Wh—? How in bloody—How did you get a key to my room?" Perri questioned.

Her annoyingly handsome ex-husband dangled the key card from his fingers, then placed it in the pocket of his bomber jacket and patted it lovingly. "I told them I was checking on my near-crippled wife."

"Ex-wife."

Ian lifted his shoulder in a little shrug, dismissively. "Semantics."

Aspen bit the inside of her cheek to stop the laughter from escaping against her will.

"Ian," Perri said in warning.

"What?" the man asked, looking as innocent as possible as he crossed the room, "You could have fallen, and no one would have found your body for *days*, Per."

"Mm-hm." The woman quirked a brow, unamused by her ex-husband's antics.

"So, what were we talking about?" Ian inquired, taking a seat on the couch and settling in.

"I think Mum is having a midlife crisis."

"Aspen!" Perri scoffed. Though she had to admit, their daughter wasn't too far off; she was having a crisis of sorts. She was just trying to find the right time to tell her family about it. *Time.*

"Mum is not even middle-aged yet."

"Ian, please," Perri muttered.

"You know what your problem is, Per?"

"Oh, you mean, besides you?" she countered.

The door to her room opened yet again, and Perri could do nothing but throw her hands up in defeat. Her room would now be a high traffic area, and there was nothing she could do about it.

"So *this* is where the party is," Zayden greeted as he strutted into the room as if it were his own.

"How did *you* get a key to your Mum's room?" Ian asked.

The boy fell into the wing-backed chair beside the fireplace, slouching comfortably.

"Told them I was checking on my Mum with the gimpy leg."

"Hey!" Perri huffed. "I am not gimpy!"

The three turned to simply look at the woman whose ankle still remained a foot higher than the rest of her leg.

"Fine," she conceded after a long moment, "I'm a little gimpy. Please, continue on to something else."

"Catch me up," Zayden said, "What's the word?"

"Dad was about to tell Mum what her problem is," Aspen replied cheekily.

Zayden leaned forward in interest, his elbow on his knee, chin in his palm. "Oh, do tell."

Perri deadpanned, "Yes, we are all *breathless* to hear it."

"Your problem is that you need to just take a moment to remember that you have a beautiful family that loves you, a great job that you are excellent at, and not everything is always as hard as you like to think it is. So you need to just let loose and maybe be a little less hard on yourself."

Silence fell over the room.

The truth was: Ian wasn't wrong. He was only confirming everything that Perri had been thinking so deeply about a few hours before.

Perri shook her head and smiled softly, looking down at the quilt beneath her.

"The logical part of me tells me that you're right."

Ian froze for a moment, then scrambled to sit up.

"I'm sorry. Could you repeat that?" he teased, although part of him was serious, "I don't think I heard you correctly."

Perri's eyes reached the heavens she rolled them so hard.

"I am not repeating myself. Take what you can get."

And he would. For now. But Ian was suddenly suspicious. Something was off with Perri, and he decided that his new mission was to figure out exactly what was going on with his ex-wife. She had the habit of keeping things to herself, and, well, he had the habit of finding them out so he could help her. Whether she always wanted him to or not.

Perri could practically see the cogs working in Ian's head as he tried his hardest to gaze straight through her eyes and into her soul. And all of his suspicions were confirmed when Perri, who was never one to back down from a staring challenge, looked away.

Laughing softly, Perri had to break the awkwardness she was feeling. "Anyway, I'm sorry I ruined our trip with my ankle."

"It's not ruined, Mum," Zayden replied, getting up to grab the remote. "I say we order a ton of room service and watch horribly cheesy holiday movies for the rest of the day."

"If Mum doesn't mind." Ian reminded gently.

"I think it will be fun!" Aspen turned and gave her best puppy-eyed gaze to their mother, "If it's okay with you, Mummy?"

Perri nodded, "That sounds like fun to me."

The four of them spent the rest of the day in Perri's room, both siblings laying on the spacious bed with their mother and Ian stretched out on the couch.

But of course, that only lasted until lunch showed up when Perri was the first to invite Ian onto her bed so they could all sit together and eat. It was just like when they were all a little younger, only their children had grown some since then. Ian and Perri on either side, with Aspen and Zayden lying on their stomachs, heads at the foot of the bed and plates resting between their elbows. And, as it always had been, Ian's arm spread wide, resting against the wealth of pillows behind him and Perri.

They spent most of whatever cliché movie they were watching, cracking jokes or commenting, but with the ending fast approaching, everyone had gone quiet. Because whether any of them wanted to admit it or not, they did in a way care what happened.

When the snow began to fall and the girl got the guy, Ian absentmindedly twirled golden tendrils of Perri's hair around his finger. She looked over at him, at first to figure out what he thought he was doing, only to find that he was gazing directly at her. She lifted her brows in question, but Ian just kept staring. Blue eyes sparked a fire inside of Perri that began in her cheeks and worked its way through the rest of her body.

Uh oh.

Eventually, it was Zayden's stomach that growled first. He checked his watch and realized that it was already nearly half-past seven.

"I'm starving."

"Me too," Aspen agreed, turning her attention from the new film to her brother, "Dinner at Seven Glaciers?"

"Mum? Dad?" Zayden turned on his side and caught the tail end of Ian, pulling his arm back to his side of the bed.

"Yes?" The two answered in unison.

"Should we do dinner downstairs?"

"Ehm," Perri looked at Ian and shrugged. "You can, I don't think I'll—"

"I think we are going to stay here and finish the movie. It is just getting good; she's met the guy in the dorky sweater, and the love triangle has started even if she doesn't know it," Ian smiled, gesturing to the TV. "We will order something from room service again and let you guys know how this ends."

"Okay," Aspen smiled, probably a little more excited than she should have, "Come on, fetus, the first round is on you."

The door clicked shut behind them, their eyes met, and they walked a little faster to the stairs so they could talk without their parent's hearing.

Zayden was the first to speak, "Something is up with Mum and Dad."

"Oh yeah," Aspen agreed without hesitation, "They're definitely going to have sex."

"What?!" Her brother was not at all prepared for that, especially considering Aspen's reaction to his note just that morning, "No. Well, yeah probably, but that's not what I meant."

Aspen shot him a confused look as they started down the stairs.

"I mean, they're having their secret eye conversations."

"Like when we were kids? Those eyes conversations?"

"Yeah, but it's different," Zayden's brows drew together in an expression that was common among all four of them, "There's something happening that they're not telling us."

Aspen was quiet for a long moment as she thought about it. "Mum did seem like she was about to tell me something important before Dad came into the room."

"What do you think she was going to say?"

They finally made it to the floor and took a turn to enter the restaurant. She looked at her brother and shook her head, "I don't know, but I got the sense that it wasn't anything good."

Reaching out, Zayden looped an arm around her shoulders and pulled her close to his side for a moment. "Then we'll just have to figure it out and hope that it's not something that will hinder your plan of getting them back together."

6

I'll be waiting for you
Here inside my heart
I'm the one who wants to love you more
You will see I can give you
Everything you need
Let me be the one to love you more

— "To Love You More" by Celine Dion

Sitting in the quiet as the credits rolled past, Ian kept glancing over at his ex-wife. He would love to just ask her what was going on, even if she would just tell him what she was thinking about. It could be the weather outside, he didn't care, as long as she talked to him. But he knew the best way to get Perri to shut down was to ask her to talk, especially about things she was already keeping held so close, so secret. She reminded Ian of a child with their favorite stuffed animal squeezed tightly in their arms, and every time you asked them for it, they just hugged it tighter to their chest.

Yep, not going to ask.

His eyes drifted over to Perri once again, and this time she caught him.

"What?" she questioned, her tone cutting as always when she was feeling defensive.

Ian kept his tone soft, "Darling, you do know you're allowed to be in pain, right?"

Perri glared up at him but didn't respond.

Holding up placating hands, "I'm just saying that it's alright if you're hurting. I'm not assuming you *are*, I'm just saying."

Leaning back once again, Perri got comfortable and turned her attention back to the TV as the advertisement for the next movie came on.

"I'm fine."

"Alright," Ian gave a rueful look, "Do you want any pain meds, at least?"

"My ankle is fine. I don't need pain meds for that."

It was like pulling teeth with this woman. Ian fought the urge to roll his eyes at her stubbornness. "You see, you keep saying that your ankle is fine, but you forget you also have an injured wrist and a concussion. I know you don't *need* them. I asked if you *want* them."

Perri looked daggers at him for a second, nostrils flaring once, twice. Ian knew that face worked on most people, but he had learned how to wait Perri out. Raising an eyebrow, he did just that.

Perri maintained her glower for another few seconds before sighing.

"Yes, please."

"Okay," Ian slid off the bed and went over to the dresser where Zayden had put his mother's things. "How bad is it? One or two?"

"One. . . And a half?"

Ian chuckled quietly to himself, "Sure, Per."

Snapping one of the pills in half, he went to the small kitchen area and got a glass of water before returning to the bed.

"Sit up, please," he requested, and Perri cut her eyes up at him like a petulant child, "I won't have you choking on these. Especially not while I'm here. They will accuse me of doing it on purpose."

Pushing herself up, Perri sighed, "No one would ever think that. You're too good to kill me on purpose."

She had almost said, 'you love me too much,' but thought better of it. Neither of them needed a reminder of that. They both knew it was painfully true.

Looking over at the door that adjoined their rooms, Ian gestured to it with his thumb.

"So, is it okay if I go get into lounging attire so I can enjoy watching this new love triangle blossom in comfort?"

"I don't care." Perri's reply was simple, but inside she was just begging that it wasn't one of the shirts she loved him in.

Crossing the room, Ian waited for a moment on Perri's side of the door. "Can I. . . Can I leave this unlocked? Is that alright?"

Looking over, Perri met his gaze, an amused smirk hidden in her eyes. "If I said no, you would just use your card key to get back in the front, so I may as well save you some time and say yes."

Flashing a bright smile but quickly masking it with a very serious expression, Ian nodded once.

"Much appreciated. I'll be back soon."

Perri watched as the door shut behind her ex-husband and sat in silence for a minute.

"What are you doing, Perri?" she asked herself softly.

Sighing, she fell back against the pillows and stared at the ceiling for a long moment. The pain medication was kicking in, and it felt wonderful to not be feeling the burning aches in her bones and the throbbing in her head. Filling her lungs again, Perri felt herself relax fully into the bed.

The last thought she remembered was a simple one that didn't exactly have a place in her mind anymore, but it was always there just the same.

Ian will be back soon.

When you lay there and you're sleeping

Hear the patterns of your breathing

And I tell you things you've never heard before

Asking questions to the ceiling

Never knowing what you're thinking

I'm afraid that what we had is gone

Then I think of the start

And it echoes a spark

And I remember the magic electricity

Then I look in my heart

There's a light in the dark

Still a flicker of hope that you first gave to me
That I wanna keep

Please don't leave

— "Flicker" by Niall Horan

Letting himself back into Perri's room slowly, Ian slipped inside and looked over to find her lying down again. Crossing the room, he couldn't help but smile a little at the sight before him and the memories it brought back. Half covered by the blankets, Perri lay with her arm crooked, leaving her hand resting above her head and her injured wrist resting atop her stomach. He could tell by how still she kept her hand that it was still causing her some discomfort, but he was just glad she was finally sleeping.

Her golden locks splayed across the pillow like a hallow giving her an ethereal quality—a few rogue strands cascaded along her face, the curled tips setting on her shoulders. The smattering of freckles along her neck and shoulders, like constellations, mapped across sun-tanned skin, just beckoning to be traced by gentle kisses.

Subconsciously his hand moved up to rest along Perri's neck, his thumb resting on the base of her jaw. Ian allowed himself a few moments to brush his thumb tenderly over the soft skin just below her ear. It took all he had to not lean down and press a kiss to her hairline. But things weren't like that for them anymore.

He took a step back before his chest could explode with warmth and the longing to hold Perri close, hopping to soothe some of the discomfort somehow. But instead, he settled back in on the other side of the bed. Ian switched off the lamp and turned his attention to the film that was playing, content to just be near Perri for a while.

* * * * * * * * * * * * *

"I never noticed," Ian scrunched his brows together as he stared intently at Perri's nose and across her cheekbones. "You have some freckles right here." He reached out his little finger and followed the path across her cheeks. As his pinky slid over the bridge of her nose, it tickled and made her nose scrunch adorably.

"Guess you're learning a lot about me today," Perri replied, tapping Ian's nose in response, then letting her arm return to its position wrapped around his back.

But Perri had looked so startled and genuinely modest that Ian laughed. He studied her blushing her face, his eyes following the track of his finger, making note of the dappled pattern of freckles on Perri's skin. Entirely engrossed, Ian let his fingertips trace her cheekbones over again. "I love this."

Perri, soothed by his gentle ministrations, was disoriented for a moment before making the connection and grimacing. "Oh, my freckles, they're awful."

Sitting back a little straighter, Ian protested, "They're not awful. How can you even say the words 'freckles' and 'awful' in the same sentence? They're lovely. Like. . ." He thought about it for a moment, "Like stars on your skin. I know that sounds cliché, but it is what it is."

* * * * * * * * * * * * *

Ian had long since muted the TV just to sit and soak up the fact that he was once again sharing a bed with Perri. Even if it wasn't in the same way it had once been, they were still near each other, and he could listen to the peaceful patterns of her breathing.

"You want to know something?" He spoke softly, even though he knew that if he did speak at a normal volume, Perri wouldn't be waking up any time soon. "That day you left—the day we went our separate ways in front of the Register Office—I almost went after you. The only reason I didn't was because. . . well, you asked me not to. From the very beginning of that whole process, I knew I would have to face the moment where I couldn't run after you because you didn't want me to."

Ian sat with his own words for a moment before he continued. "So you coming back here—with me—and saying that you *want* to be here, you want to stay even though I'm here too. . . If this isn't a dream that I'm just going to wake up heartbroken from, I want that.

I want you to want to stay. I want you to want me to stay. Even if it's just like this, I want that more than anything."

There. He felt a little better having had the chance to say that out loud. If only she had been able to hear him, that would have made all the difference. But some things were just never meant to be.

Reaching out, Ian slid his palm beneath her fingertips and held just her fingers lightly in his hand for a moment.

Good. They're still warm. The wrap isn't too tight.

Or at least that's the reason he told himself that he had taken her hand.

Deep down, he knew the truth. Ian let go softly, and his head tipped back against the headboard, giving him a fantastic view of the same ceiling Perri had been gazing at as she fell asleep over an hour before.

He just wished he knew what was going on. What kind of secret had Perri hiding from him so hard?

"What is going on in that beautiful mind of yours?" His head lulled to the side. He couldn't tell anymore, and that knowledge created this cold, hollow feeling in his chest.

Then the chilling thought that what they had shared all those years ago, from the very beginning, was truly gone. Had their spark been snuffed out, and it truly had ended with the same quietness with which it had begun? Falling in love is very easy. But staying in love, well, that is something special. And he thought they had that. Could he have been wrong for all these years?

Looking back down at Perri, he felt his chest warm in that all too familiar way it did when she was nearby. His mind drifted back over their years together, and the echo of the everyday magic their love grew reassured him of one thing. Their story was far from over. Be it the story he longed for or not, it wasn't over.

I can feel you breathe

Hear your heartbeat

I love the sound, I'm hearing it loud

I don't wanna sleep

If I'm dreaming, I'll miss tonight

— "Everybody Knows" by Idina Menzel

Old habits die hard. It's an old saying, and Perri had heard it often, but she never realized how true it was until the next morning.

After just one night of sharing a bed with Ian again, even in her half-asleep state, she found herself falling into old habits.

Scooting close, she leaned up and planted a kiss on the side of his neck before laying back down. It was easy. A thoughtless thing.

She didn't even realize she was doing it when it happened. The curling toward Ian while she was in the sluggish moments of just barely awake and pressing the kiss to his neck. Then snuggling closer against his back, she rested her forehead between his shoulder blades, just out of old habit. In fact, she was so far from being fully conscious that it took her a few minutes before she realized she had done it at all.

But when her brain caught up with her actions, brown eyes snapped open, and she jerked away, putting space between them once more. Sensing her tension even in his sleep, Ian rolled onto his back and looped his arm around her shoulders to pull her close again. Although she knew she should, Perri didn't fight the motion and instead allowed herself a few selfish moments of taking the offered closeness. Laying her head on his chest, she inhaled slowly and closed her eyes. She was gently being lulled back to sleep by the rise and fall of Ian's chest and the soothing sound of his heartbeat.

You shouldn't be doing this. It's not fair to either one of you.

One part of her brain reprimanded with logic she knew to be true. But the other part fought back and with arguments just as compelling.

But it's been so long, and what harm can it do just for a few minutes. He's asleep, and you've missed this. Whether you're willing to admit it or not.

Perri had never really cared for physical affection before Ian. Whenever she had dated before, and any one of them had touched her, whether it was intimate or only a chaste hand on her back, she counted the seconds until they were no longer doing it. She was always much too uncomfortable, never able to relax into their touches.

For a while, she had thought that it was something wrong with her. As if she were the problem. Then Ian came along. With him, she swore she could have touched him forever and never wanted to let him go.

One of her favorite things about him—and there were a lot of them—had to be his hands. And not in the way people would immediately think if she mentioned it.

Ian was always gentle. That's what it was really. A hand on Perri's knee when they sat beside each other or rubbing small circles on her back when she was stressed.

Hands clutching Perri's arms when they kissed or cupping her cheek and tenderly running his thumb over her skin. Hands that ran down the bare skin of her back, which gave her chill every time, fingers that grazed her thigh ever so lightly and drove her mad. Her husband always held her like she was fragile. Not as if she would break easily if he didn't, he knew that was not the case, but as if she were something to be treasured, something priceless.

Ian was always soft until he wasn't. It always caught Perri by surprise when she remembered that the man she loved didn't treat anyone else with nearly as much care as he treated Perri. He was never cruel, and his kindness was always evident in how he spoke to others, especially those he loved. But there had been something different about how he was with Perri from the start. She was more precious to him than all the others and was treated as such.

Even after all this time and everything that had transpired, he still treated her the same way.

Perri quickly swallowed back the tears that threatened and quietly slid out of his embrace. Going to the bathroom, she hid herself in another warm bath and hoped Ian didn't hear her crying.

Once Perri left the safety of the bathroom, she found that Ian must have slipped back into his own room. She was relieved, all but for that stinging twinge of sadness she felt when she found herself alone again.

At least he didn't wait in hopes of something more than I could give him.

Perri settled onto the couch and swung her foot up onto the opposite arm, doing her best to get comfortable. Though she would deny it, she found herself listening to see if she could hear Ian moving around in his room. After several minutes, it was becoming hard to resist the temptation of simply hobbling over to the unlocked door and opening it just to see him for a few seconds more. Just as she was going to get up, she heard the soft beep that always followed someone running a keycard. She quickly settled back in so as not to look suspicious when one of her children invited themselves into her room.

It was Aspen who opened the door and looked around the quiet room in silence for a moment before turning to her mother.

"Don't tell me you killed Dad after we left, and that's why he's not here making sure you're staying off your ankle."

Perri scoffed a laugh at her smirking daughter, "I will have you know I was perfectly civil, and no one was hurt. . . too badly at least."

"Okay, Mum, whatever you say," Aspen's eyeroll mimicked her mother's almost identically, "But when the guests and staff start reporting a strange smell, don't come to me for help getting his body out of here."

"I'll remember that." Perri brought her leg down and patted the space next to her.

Crossing the room, Aspen made herself comfortable beside the woman. "So I think Zayden and I are going out to do some things this morning, but we'll be back soon. Oh! And tonight there is going to be a jazz band playing at Seven Glaciers that you would love. We heard them last night." Doing a little shimmy of excitement in her spot, Aspen eyed her mother hopefully, "Do you think you could make it down? Just for a few minutes?"

Looping an arm around her daughter's shoulders, Perri chuckled lightly, "You know what, I think I can manage to make it to the elevator and sit downstairs for a bit."

Giving her a quick but tight hug, Aspen then stood up and took off toward the door, "I'll make sure one of us comes up to see if you need anything later."

Before Perri could even reply, the door opened and closed behind her daughter, who was probably well on her way down the stairs. Shaking her head in amusement, the older woman stretched out across the sofa once again and opened up the book she was hoping would keep her entertained for a while.

The warm sun was beginning to settle into the frozen mountains in the distance when Ian slowly opened the adjoining door. Peeking inside, he made sure he wasn't going to disturb Perri getting some rest. Noticing his ex-wife out on the balcony instead, he entered the room quietly, admiring the way the orange rays of the dying sun outlined her form against the snowy background.

Coming up behind her, Ian leaned down and whispered softly against the chilled skin of her neck.

"Hello, Perri."

She could feel his breath brush the skin just below her ear. Perri's eyes fluttered shut, and all the air left her lungs in a soft sigh. At the feeling of his lips so close to her skin, her shoulder dropped, and her chin tilted up a fraction, allowing him room to move closer.

An offer Ian gladly would have taken had Perri not so quickly shaken herself and moved away, murmuring something about not liking him doing that. When the mortifying truth was, it drove her deliciously mad, and she loved it.

Clearing her throat softly, Perri glanced in her ex-husband's direction before looking back out at the scenery. "Am I to assume that our oldest sent you in here to help get me downstairs?"

Ian, who had taken a step back, rubbed the back of his neck, "Madame, I can neither confirm nor deny the circumstances that brought me to be here at this present moment."

"Of course you can't," Perri smiled, just a little, over her shoulder at him before turning to face him fully, her embarrassment fading. "Alright, I am going to need to change, so that means I need you to leave."

For a moment, Ian thought about making a remark about how she must be needing him to leave so that they would actually make it downstairs. But he decided that probably wasn't the best idea. With still trying to get her to tell him what she was hiding, a comment like that would only make her defensive. That was the exact opposite of what he wanted.

"As long as I am able to report back to my commanding officer that you are reporting for family time entertainment downstairs shortly, I will tear myself from your side."

Waving him away, Perri made her way to her closet, "Go report to the little hellions that I'll be down soon."

"With pleasure, m'lady."

Ian clicked the door shut behind him, and Perri began the process of shimmying out of her current lounge wear and into something that would actually be decent to wear down to a restaurant.

Mumbling curses and frustrations under her breath, Perri finally managed to get into some different pants and was pulling a soft turtleneck over her head when she heard the dividing door open.

"*Knocking*! Ian," she exclaimed in irritation and, though she would never admit it, slight embarrassment, she quickly jerked the shirt down to fully cover her body, "Would be great."

"I've seen much more than just your mid-riff before, Per," he observed casually, then paused for a long moment, "But if you want, I will knock from now on. I'm sorry."

Rubbing at her forehead in a way that was familiar to Ian, Perri sighed after a moment. Not looking up at him, she spoke, "No, I'm sorry. I didn't mean to be so snappy."

"Are you hurting?"

Could he not just be rude back sometimes? It would make things so much easier.

"I'm fine." Came the murmured response, as she turned her attention to adjusting her shirt before attempting to get to her feet.

Coming to stand beside the bed, Ian rested his fingertips on her upper arm, and Perri's attention immediately fell to his hand. The tension between them was electric. His gaze followed hers, and he could almost feel the heat rising on his neck.

"Do you need me to help you up?" he offered, his tone still soft and even.

Perri answered by way of standing, of course, but she promptly lurched forward into Ian, who gripped her hips. Fingers dipped under the hem of Perri's shirt, sending sparks through her veins as the pain in her ankle calmed.

"Just a head rush," she explained, her voice low and so very close.

"Mm-hm."

He didn't dare contest her statement, and he figured it would be more difficult to tease her right now anyway with how his thoughts were all chaotic, and his mouth was getting so dry. Perri was so warm and soft against his fingertips. It was something so little, but it was enough. Enough to satisfy his need to be near her and yet enough to drive him mad for more.

Holding on to his forearms, Perri took a step back and made sure she was steady on her feet before letting go.

"Are you okay?" Ian asked, leaning down a fraction to try and catch a glimpse of her face.

Raising her chin, Perri looked completely composed once again. "Yes, nothing to worry about."

"Alright then," he nodded once and turning, he offered his arm, "Let's get down there before our children come hunting us down."

Sliding her arm through his as if she had never stopped, Perri chuckled and agreed.

"Though I'm not sure how long I'll stay. You know I hate having to pass up the chance to dance to some good jazz."

Laying his hand over hers, Ian smirked down at his ex-wife, "I'm sure that even though you won't be able to dance, you can pull just fine tonight. What with these young waiters and all, you won't have any trouble finding someone to take you back up to your room."

In an attempt to not get jealous of this imaginary situation that he had just created with his own joke, Ian shot a wink her way. Perri laughed, much louder than she intended.

"I haven't even been kissed in the last six years, so I highly doubt I will be pulling anyone any time soon."

Just as he opened his mouth to begin asking questions, the elevator door opened, and Perri continued on as if she had said nothing of consequence. Falling back in step beside her, Ian stood in silence as they waited for the doors to open again.

Standing there, he caught the scent of a new perfume hanging on the air around them.

"Is that a new perfume?"

"Oh," Perri seemed surprised for a brief moment, "Yes, it's one my secretary has been wearing recently. It was different. I thought I would try it out. Get something a little more befitting to my age."

"You're not an old woman, Perri," Ian stated, taking note of the heavy floral scents that you would expect in the perfumes your grandmother would wear, "You don't need to smell like one. You should go back to the one you were wearing when we met."

Perri couldn't help but scoff softly, "I'm not exactly twenty anymore, Ian."

Once again, the opening of the elevator doors cut him off, and they were met with the sight of their children waiting nearby.

"We were about to come up and look for you," Zayden informed as the two siblings closed the distance between them.

Letting go of Ian's arm, Perri drew her children close and walked happily between them, "Well, we expected no less, so we beat you to it. Now, show me this band you've been going on about."

Perri grimaced and shifted in her seat for the fifth time in the last several minutes. She liked to fool herself into believing she was subtle, and maybe she was for people who didn't know her, but Ian noticed. He always noticed.

With a painful jolt of realization, Ian wondered; even though *he* knew that he noticed even the smallest things about Perri, did she know that he took time to see? He had felt as if it could go unsaid, but, like many things looking back, he questioned if that was something that should have been put to words.

Gazing across the table at his ex-wife, he longed to finally voice all the little things he still knew about her that he doubted she even realized he had taken notice of. But now was not the time, and with a heaviness in his chest, he knew that the time had passed him by.

So now, he did what he could.

Reaching slowly over, he laid his fingers against her arm and spoke her name softly into the space between them.

"Hmm?" Her warm chocolate eyes turned to meet his gaze.

"Are you ready to go back upstairs?"

Looking back at the performers and then toward their children, who were laughing at each other over at the bar, Perri nodded.

"Yeah, I think I need to head up," she admitted, "I'm getting sore."

Standing from his seat, Ian sent a quick text to their children, and the two of them waved when the siblings looked up from checking their phones.

"Shall we go?" Ian offered his arm once again, and Perri stood carefully.

They made their way to the elevator and waited as it came down from one of the top floors.

Feeling his phone vibrate, Ian pulled it from his pocket, thinking it was from Aspen and Zayden, but he was taken aback to notice it was neither of them. Instead, it was some news from his clinic back home. News that he wished he would have never gotten. Quickly sliding his phone back out of sight, he stared with determination at the still-closed doors of the elevator shaft.

Perri cut her eyes over at her ex-husband and watched him subtly for a long moment. She had felt the change in him almost immediately. But how do you say something like that after you were the one to leave a person seven years ago? Do you say that you still notice things like that, or would that be taboo?

Screw taboo.

Placing a hand on his chest, Perri caught his misty gaze with a concerned look of her own.

"Hey," she kept her voice soft, "Are you okay?"

His smile appeared too quickly and seemed too forced, "Yeah, fine. Why wouldn't I be?"

Her brows drew together momentarily as she studied his face, "It's just. . . For a minute there, you didn't look fine."

"I'm fine," he assured and walked them onto the elevator as it conveniently opened.

It was a peacefully quiet ride up. The two of them remained in their own thoughts even as they walked down the hall to their rooms.

Coming to a stop in front of Perri's door, they stood there a fraction longer than necessary. Finally, Perri moved to let herself in and only paused in the doorway when she heard Ian take a breath to speak.

"You were right," he said, and a look of confusion crossed her face. "About me not. . . being okay."

Leaning on the door, Perri's eyes softened, and she hummed in response. "Anything I can do?"

The corner of Ian's lips lifted slightly, and he shook his head, "Not this time."

His heart swelled with affection as he watched his ex-wife tilt her head much like a curious puppy. "Will you be alright?"

"Oh, yeah," he waved away her concern, "It was just a text from work—and I know we promised no work, but this—"

Reaching out, Perri rested her hand on his upper arm and gave a gentle squeeze.

"Ian, it's fine. Your work is different than my drawings."

Looking momentarily offended, Ian's brows pulled together. "That's not true. Your drawings are—"

Hovering her finger a breath away from his lips, Perri quieted him with a soft smile, "Ian, we can debate this later. What happened? If I can ask."

A deep sadness passed through Ian's eyes, and she fought the urge to hug him close until the sadness passed, but that was a right she had given up long ago.

"They were just letting me know that one of my long-term patients passed a little while ago."

She said his name so softly that he almost missed it, but he definitely felt the hand that slipped into his. Turning his attention to the floor for a long moment, Ian then cleared his throat and squeezed her hand before meeting her gaze once more. "Thank you, Per."

A single nod accompanied by a sad, close-lipped smile was the only reply she could manage, but it was enough.

"Sleep well. Come over if you need anything." And with that, he was turning to enter his room.

It had only been several minutes, but it still startled Ian when he heard Perri tap lightly on their adjoining door.

Crossing the room, he opened it and smiled down at her, "Miss me already?"

"I've missed you for a long time."

The words left her mouth without her permission, and she immediately regretted them. But there was no taking them back now. They had been released from deep in her subconscious to now exist in the air between them.

"M'sorry," she murmured, looking away and awkwardly tucking a loose lock of hair behind her ear. "I—I'm just. . . I'll just go—"

She gestured behind her, back into her room, and went to turn away without ever looking back up to meet Ian's gaze.

"Perri," Ian stopped her retreat, "It's alright. What did you need?"

Perri shuffled where she stood, wincing but hoping Ian didn't notice. "I, ehm, I can't get my ponytail out. . . It got all tangled somehow and. . . I . . . needed help. With having my hand wrapped the way it is and being. . ."

Perri could feel her face burn with embarrassment. She still found herself contemplating turning and locking the door behind her just so there would be a barrier between her and her ex-husband again.

Don't you think there have been barriers between the two of you long enough?

What a thought. Her brain really could betray her sometimes.

When she finally choked down her awkwardness, Perri looked up, expecting that charming smirk that always graced Ian's face when she got herself into these situations with him. But instead, she was met with a kind-eyed expression and a tender smile.

Slowly, Ian reached around to Perri's ponytail, and, in a moment of weakness, she rested her forehead against his shoulder. His fingers moved delicately, gently pulling at the elastic until it loosened from her curls and released a cascade of honey-gold hair around her shoulders.

"There," his voice was quiet so as not to break the peace of the moment, "All free."

Perri murmured a thank you and leaned away.

"I could, uh, I could help you with that."

She lifted her eyes to Ian's face in confusion, all thoughts of leaving his room escaping her mind.

Her eyes narrowed for a moment, "You already did, and I said thank you."

"No, I meant. . ." Ian paused, and this only proved to make Perri more curious and nervous, "You said earlier that you hadn't been kissed in six years. I could help you out with that. No one, especially not you, should go that long without a proper kiss."

Perri couldn't help how her eyes drifted down to his lips and held there for a moment. Then, in a voice barely above a whisper, "I don't think that's the best idea."

"Why not?" Ian couldn't help but smile just a little, "We both think about it all the time. What harm could it do."

Perri could feel the heat of excitement flushing her chest, "So much."

"But would you mind it so terribly?"

No, I wouldn't mind it at all, actually. So long as I got to kiss you again, it wouldn't matter how much it hurt me later.

"Perri?"

She shook herself from her thoughts and brought her eyes back up to meet Ian's, "Yes."

For a moment, Ian was convinced he had heard wrong.

"Yes?"

Perri nodded and repeated just a little louder, "Yes."

Her heart was pounding. She had been longing for this, but the logical part of her brain knew it would never happen, or at least that it should never. But at this point, she didn't care. She just wanted what was about to transpire between the two of them, and that was all that mattered.

Perri was worried that being too eager would make Ian back out and want to forget the whole thing. But his lips were within a whisper of touching hers now, and there was no hesitation in him yet. Something in her chest throbbed at the thought, and she aligned it to the fact that it had been *six years* since anyone had touched her this way. And the fact that the last person to do so *was* Ian probably didn't help.

They were smiling, of course, because they couldn't help themselves, even though they were standing in the middle of a slightly messy hotel suite. All because Perri was lonely, and Ian was kind. Or something like that.

So what if Perri was suddenly hyper sensitive to the feeling of Ian's arm wrapping tighter around her waist and pulling her flush against him? Or the feel of his palm tenderly cupping her jaw.

It would be a lie to say that warmth did not begin to slide down her spine. It raked down her ribs, and her eyes dropped to Ian's lips all over again, remembering all the kisses from the past that could still somehow leave her breathless. It shouldn't be this easy to want this. But it was so very easy.

Perri's lips parted, and with the same impatience that had followed her through most of her life, she closed the breath of space left between them.

The longing to have Ian close again was finally fulfilled. She could no longer tell where he began and where she ended. But feeling his lips moving against hers and the way he drew her in until he couldn't anymore just fanned the flames that still burned for him deep inside her chest.

Ian kissed messily without being sloppy, languid without ever being boring, insistent without being aggressive. Oh, she had missed this. The taste of their shared breath and the feeling of their combined heartbeats. Perri allowed her hand to slide under the collar of the robe Ian was wearing and press against the warm skin of his chest, and she sighed into the kiss. Ian's hand splayed out wide against her lower back, while the other moved to cradle the back of her neck, just desperate to keep her close.

Perri was unsure who moaned first, but one of them readily echoed the passionate sound and want poured through her body like molten lava. Before they could be drawn in deeper, she brought herself from the daze she had fallen into and suddenly knew they—or at least she—was in deep trouble.

Moving back slowly, she placed one last gentle kiss against his lips, ending the moment. Perri reached up to cup his jaw, and her thumb grazed his bottom lip as she tried to catch her breath.

"We should stop," she whispered slowly.

Ian's hand came to rest on her hip, flexing softly, and he left his hand behind her neck. Resting his forehead against Perri's, he nuzzled his nose tenderly against hers, "Okay. . . But if you change your mind. . ."

"I know where to find you."

Ian lay awake, gazing quietly at the door that blocked Perri from sight. His heart was still racing at the thought of what they had done. He could still feel the warmth of her palm against his skin and the feel of her under his hands. His mind swirled with emotions and thoughts as he listened to Perri move around softly in her room. He knew she would not be lying down any time soon. She was like a caged animal when she had a lot going on in her head.

She had always been a little feral to some degree. Ian couldn't help but smirk a bit, he loved the untamed energy that always seemed to hum just beneath the surface of her skin.

Ian knew from the beginning that that was one of the many things he would always love about Perri. When she had said she would marry him, Ian had felt a warmth like no other swell inside his chest. The moment that Perri, wild and free, had agreed to spend the rest of her life just letting Ian hold her close, his life was complete.

And then it ended, and suddenly he didn't know how to fix it this time.

What kind of man loses something he values so much?

But he couldn't think about it for too long. Instead, he rolled over and tried to sleep. He was here with her, and things were different between them in this place. Something about being here gave him a little hope. As false as it may turn out to be once they left here. Either way, he allowed himself the briefest indulgence to hope.

I'll come running when you call out my name
And it'll always be this way
I'll be there for you
No matter what you're going through
I'll be there with you
Anytime that you need me to
When there's no one else around
On your last breath, calling out
Trust me, my love won't let you down

— "My Love Won't Let You Down"
by Little Mix

Perri had eventually laid down after fighting the urge to just go back into her ex-husband's room and finish what they had started. When she woke with a smile lifting the corners of her lips, she was both surprised and concerned. She couldn't let anything start happening between them. It simply wasn't possible, no matter how much she wanted it to be. She had kept too much of a secret, and now it was back to haunt her steps even as she lay dreaming of a different future.

Caught up in her thoughts, Perri had missed the soft knock on the adjoining door and only opened her eyes once she felt a presence beside her.

"Per."

Emotions and feelings of so many kinds spread through her at the sound of his voice. She hated it, but only because she could do nothing with them.

It must have been something in her eyes that Ian could much too easily read. Kneeling on the bed beside her, Ian slowly laid down on top of her, holding himself up on his elbows so as not to have his full weight crushing her. Perri had allowed herself a few moments of vulnerability, but it was best to mask her expressive eyes before they got her in any more trouble. He smirked down at Perri's now pompous expression and slid his forearms up under her shoulders. Threading his fingers through her hair, Ian cradled the back of her head and looked deeply into her eyes.

"You're still so beautiful, you know that."

"Get off of me," she demanded, trying not to remember how much she missed being held like this.

* * * * * * * * * * * * *

Watching Ian come into the room Perri allowed a smile to creep onto her face as her eyes followed his movements. Looking up to find his wife awake and watching him, Ian smiled and crossed the room.

"What's this then," he greeted, "You're still up?"

"Mm-hm." Perri tilted her head back as Ian came to stand beside the bed, and he brushed back her hair gently. "Lay with me?"

Kneeling down, he took off his shoes and then laid carefully on top of her. Resting on his elbows, he hovered above her and cradled the back of her head in his hands. Leaning down to lay his forehead against hers, Ian couldn't help but smile at the wicked smirk growing across Perri's face. Her mischievous gaze brought him such peace after his long day. Taking a deep breath, Ian let it out slowly, and his eyes drifted shut.

"Hi."

"Hello," Perri whispered back. Reaching up, she tunneled her fingers into his hair, pulling him down a little closer, and tilted her chin up to brush her nose against the tip of his.

They were quiet for a moment until Perri's sharp eyes caught Ian's. "How tired are you?"

Ian chuckled low in his chest, "Not too much. How tired are you?"

"I'm not tired at all." Her hands slid up his arms and onto his broad shoulders, lacing together behind his neck. Lifting herself up off the bed, she pressed a softly passionate kiss to the corner of his lips. She couldn't stop the smile that grew across her face and wrapped her arms tighter around Ian's shoulders as he drew her close against his chest.

"Now, what have you started, Perri Vilein-Astankova," Ian purred in her ear.

She laughed and purred in return, "Nothing that I didn't intend to start."

* * * * * * * * * * * * *

Perri shook herself from her thoughts and focused on those same eyes from all those years ago, even if they appeared a little older these days.

"Ian."

"Alright, alright," he chuckled good-naturedly, obviously not too off-put by her demands for him to get up.

He offered Perri his hand to help her up, and in those few moments, she decided that she must get the upper hand once again.

Once she was steady on her feet, Perri lifted her gaze to Ian's and smirked. That same smirk that made Ian want to shuffle where he stood, but he merely lifted a brow in question instead. He didn't have to wait long for an answer.

Perri firmly grabbed two fistfuls of the cotton lapels on the robe he wore. She immediately felt a stab of disappointment that her thumbs did not brush warm, bare skin. But she quickly put that thought away. Leaning in by Ian's collar, she buried her nose in the fabric before taking a deep breath, inhaling the scent from deep within the fibers.

Ian instantly froze at his ex-wife's actions, taken aback at the boldness of her sudden closeness for some reason. His hands made their way to Perri's shoulders to give him some sense of control over the situation. Even though he knew he had such little control here. So, he relaxed into the touch, his chin slightly fell, briefly touching Perri's head.

Perri's eyes closed as she felt his chin graze the top of her head. She had to focus to continue to gain the reaction she wanted. Setting her mind to analyzing the scent emitting from the robe. The soothing aroma of his shower gel was most noticeable, but Ian's specific smell also filled her senses. Perri forced herself to push off of his chest after already taking more time than necessary.

"What. . .?" Ian looked down at her, utterly confused.

Perri smiled, "I was just seeing if you had borrowed my robe from in here because I couldn't find it last night."

Stepping back, she turned to pick up her phone as if nothing had happened.

"Oh. . ." Ian stood motionless in his spot, "Okay."

"Zayden texted," Perri said, looking down at her phone, "He said they are heading out to the slopes for a few hours and would be back for lunch if we wanted to order room service together."

Finally, taking a few steps away from the spot he had been planted to, Ian rubbed the back of his neck, "Yeah. Yeah, that sounds great if you're alright with it."

Perri sent a text and turned her attention back to Ian. She could just tell him that she wanted to be alone and rest her injuries more so she could get back up to the slopes with their children. But that invisible cord that seemed to tie them together at every turn tugged in her chest. Leaving Perri just longing to sit with the man who had once been the one her soul burned for. Still was, if she was honest. But she tried not to be when it came to this situation.

"Come sit with me on the balcony?" she offered, "It's a wonderful view."

Ian looked briefly surprised, his brows raising almost to his hair-line for a moment, and then followed her out.

Settling in, Perri leaned back in her seat and looked over to find Ian doing the same. She slowly turned her gaze to look out over the snow-covered mountains, and she wondered where their children might be. Ian followed her gaze, and the two sat in contented silence.

"You know," Perri's voice was quiet in thought and carried gently on the chilled breeze, "Aspen fell asleep on my bed with me the other night, and I was just thinking. . . I could never leave her—either of them—like my mother left me. I just love them so much. I could never leave them behind to wonder. . ."

Ian looked over at his ex-wife and entertained the image of Perri watching over their twenty-two-year-old daughter as she dozed off in bed beside her. His heart swelled at the thought but also ached at her words. That was something Perri had struggled with for so long, whether she talked about it or not, and Ian knew it was something that hurt her deeply.

"But as I have gotten older, I have come to believe that my mother did love me. I think she loved me with every piece of herself that she had left. But there just weren't enough pieces left to call her own. There were too many ghosts of things that I will. . . never even know about."

Her gaze never turned from the view sprawling out before them, and Ian's eyes studied her intently.

"Or at least that is what I tell myself these days."

He felt the deep urge to reach out and lay his hand on her arm, but he knew better of it.

"I'm so sorry," he spoke softly so as not to frighten Perri back into hiding.

She turned to meet Ian's eyes, "Why? You didn't do any of this."

Looking back out, Perri continued, "If anything, you helped me. Between you, Mum and Aliyah, I was broken, and I am healing. You have nothing to apologize for."

"I'm still sorry that you have had to carry this around all your life."

Shooting him a soft smile, Perri held his tender gaze and allowed a moment of genuine connection. "Thank you, but I don't regret it at all. If things had been different," she shrugged slightly, "I wouldn't be here. I wouldn't have our children, and I would have never discovered that I can be the woman I wish my mother could have been."

The contented silence settled between them once more, but one question kept eating away at Ian. One he knew was a danger to ask, but he had waited patiently for so many years, and he figured that this might be the only time relatively close enough to be "right."

"Perri, can I ask you something you might not like?"

The woman lulled her head to the side and looked at him with a surprisingly calm expression. It must have been the pain medication.

"Go ahead."

"So, hypothetically," he began, "If you still loved me. . . maybe we would have a chance? Hypothetically, of course."

"Of course," Perri repeated, holding his gaze as she thought about her answer, "If love was all there was to worry about. . . we wouldn't even be having to have this conversation right now. *Hypothetically*, if love were enough to keep two people together, we would have never been where we are now because nothing would have changed."

With a twisting ache in his chest, Ian knew love just wasn't enough for overcoming some things, and that was just the painful truth of life. Whether it was fair or not.

Ian nodded thoughtfully, the answer wasn't what he was expecting, and it was painful in its own way but bittersweet. If love was all that was required to make a life together, it would have been enough. Unfortunately, even for those who love as deeply as they did, there is still more to it than that.

"I'll just say one thing, and then we can drop it and act like the conversation never happened if you want."

Perri stayed quiet, giving him the go-ahead to say whatever he needed to say.

"I realized something as you walked away that day."

They both knew what day he was referring to. That day in front of the same building where they had once vowed to be together until they were separated by things beyond their control. The day they had signed the papers ending it all and turning to go their separate ways as best they knew how.

"What was that?" The question was so soft that Ian almost missed it.

"That. . . I would miss you forever."

Perri murmured his name and looked down at her wrist that was still in a brace.

"Please, I'm almost done, and we can not talk anymore. I just need you to know that I—I looked back that day. I looked back, and I knew that I would wait forever for you. I was willing to wait however long you needed me to. And, should you find that you have just enough love left for me that we could be friends, well, that would be enough for me, I suppose."

Quiet settled between them once more, and Perri fought the tears stinging her dark eyes.

"Just think on it, maybe?"

"Yeah," she nodded, still not looking up, "Sure."

Ian watched her for a moment, then spoke gently, "Do you want me to leave?"

To his surprise, Perri shook her head and looked back out over the mountains in silence.

7

'Cause I love you, more than you think I do
And I love you, now you don't want me to

— "I Love You" by Alex & Sierra

You are searching for something you are never going to find anywhere else.

Aliyah's words from a few years before echoed in Perri's head as she cut her gaze over at Ian. And she had found that her best friend had been right. When she had finally grown tired of being alone, she had begun searching for someone to remind her of Ian, even if she wouldn't admit it. Deep down, she knew that she was hoping she could find at least someone similar. Someone to bring her some sense of the happiness she had felt with her ex-husband.

Aliyah had been right, and Perri knew it even then, but she refused to act like she did. Instead, she tried to venture back out into the world and meet someone new.

* * * * * * * * * * * * *

Coming down the hall, Perri made the final adjustments to her hair as she rounded the corner.

"Where are you off to, chaton?" her mother asked from her place on the couch. The woman had been spending many of her nights at her daughter's house, especially when her grandchildren were off with friends. Perri hated being alone. Only a handful of people knew it, and she would never say that she did. But Laurel knew it would be over her dead body if she could be there for her daughter and chose not to be.

"I, ehm, I have a date," Perri smiled proudly, lifting her chin a fraction, but her mother noticed the nervous twitch of her fingers around her clutch purse.

Raising a brow and smirking in that wicked way Perri had mastered so well, Laurel eyed her daughter. "Oh really. With whom?"

Raising her own brows and smiling just a little, Perri replied, "Someone from work. That's all, Mum."

Lifting her hands in surrender, the woman looked away, "Fine, don't tell your mother."

Crossing the room, Perri chuckled and leaned down to kiss the woman's cheek, "You'll be alright. I'll tell you about it soon. Good night, Mum."

Rolling her eyes, the older woman tried not to smile, "Good night, my love. Have a good time, okay."

"Oh, I plan to try," Perri smiled, "Could you lock up when you leave? I don't know how late I'll be."

Sitting alone in the dark, Perri had turned on the tv for some soft background noise as she finished up the bottle of whatever kind of alcohol

she had grabbed from the cabinet. It wasn't late. In fact, it had only been dark out for almost an hour.

So it wasn't too much of a surprise when someone rang the doorbell. Assuming it was her mother, Perri pushed herself up from the couch and made her way to the door.

Opening it, she found her husband—ex-husband—huddled under the cover of the porch, trying to stay out of the onslaught of rain.

"Hi."

"Hey. . ." She began slowly. The word drug out a bit more than she intended, as she was trying to focus her blurred eyes and not sound too drunk. "The kids aren't here tonight."

"Oh, are they out tonight?"

"Yeah," Perri briefly scrunched the skin of her forehead between her thumb and fingers, "Friend's houses and sleepovers and such. Ya know, before leavin' for university and all."

Ian brows pulled together for a moment as he studied his ex-wife's tired face. Her accent usually wasn't so evident, but it was very heavy at the moment.

"Right, I had forgotten about that. Are you—are you alright, Perri?"

Leaning against the door, Perri sighed, "Honestly, I'm very sloshed at the moment."

"I can see that," he gave a small laugh, "Why? What happened?"

There was one thing he always admired about drunk Perri. She never minced words.

Straightening, she gave a sweeping gesture in his direction.

"You. You happened," she answered, "You made me love you."

Ian was beyond confused but didn't dare interrupt Perri once she was blustering.

"I went on a date tonight for the first time in <u>years</u>. I went out with this wonderful man who has been a good friend to me for a long while now and I should have had the best time. There was no reason why I shouldn't have. But the whole time I was there, the only person I wanted

was you. I wanted you across that table from, and I just couldn't get it out of my head."

Perri reached up and wiped at her misting eyes.

"He was early! He was <u>early</u>, Ian. Do you know how long it's been since a man has been early for a date with me?"

Pain came to rest on Ian's face. Not for himself, at least not entirely, but mostly for the woman standing in front of him. She had finally had someone pursuing her in a way she had felt like he had not in the last bit of their marriage, and now she couldn't even enjoy it because of him.

"I'm so sorry, Perri."

Perri just shook her head, "And now I'm going to have to tell this kind man that I can't see him anymore."

"You could though. Keep seeing him." He loathed even suggesting it, but if it made her happy, well, he would find a way to stomach it. He had done enough already to cause her hurt; the least he could do was let her find some happiness even if he couldn't.

"No!" Perri's irritation was visible for a moment and gone the next, "You don't understand. I can't see him anymore. Because I can't get sloshed every weekend when I'm with him just because I miss you."

The two stood in silence for a long moment until Perri pushed her thick curls back from her face.

"Look, I want to go upstairs for a lie down, but first, I really need to go to the loo."

Turning to walk away, she left the door open, and Ian stood awkwardly there for a moment until concern got the better of him. Following her inside, he shut the door and called after her.

"Go to the loo, how? Are you about to speak Welsh?"

"Of course not!" she called back, and he watched light flood the hallway from the bathroom, "What kind of airy-fairy do you think I am?"

"Okay, well, if you're sure you're alright," Ian stood just out of the line of sight in the hall, "I'm going to head home for the night. I was just popping in to say hello since I was in town still."

It was quiet for a long moment, and expecting that would be the only response, Ian went to retreat back to the front door.

"Could you—Could you wait a minute?" Perri's voice called hesitantly from the bathroom.

Ian paused, "What do you need?"

A moment later, there was the sound of a toilet flushing and a sink running, then Perri appeared in the hall once more.

"Could you, ehm. . ."

"Yeah?"

"Could you stay? For just a bit, not all night or anything!"

Ian shook his head slowly, "Perri, I don't think—"

"No funny business," Perri said, "Really. I just want to be held for a little while."

How could he refuse when everything he was wanting was being asked of him. And asked as if it would be an inconvenience in some way, despite the very real truth. He could never deny this woman anything, especially when she was looking at him with those soft, dark eyes.

After a few long moments, he conceded, "Just for a while because I still have to make the drive home."

Perri nodded a little more eagerly than she would like if she had been a fraction more sober. Then she took his hand to lead him to the bedroom they had once shared.

"I won't try anythin'," Perri reassured, as Ian cautiously climbed in next to her and pulled the covers over them both, "I promise. Just hold me for a little while, maybe until I fall asleep, and then you can leave, and we don't ever have to mention this again."

Rolling over to face the opposite direction, Perri relaxed into her pillows and nestled in contentedly. Breathing in a slow, deep breath and sighed happily as her eyes drifted shut.

Ian allowed himself to settle in close and, without thinking, he pressed a kiss to the back of her neck and breathed deeply the smell of her straw-

berry shampoo, mixing perfectly with the remnants of her perfume. The same as it was before. So little and yet so much had changed.

There were a few things that Ian loved about drunk Perri when he really thought about it. She didn't really change, she was still very Perri, but she cared less about what she was saying and just said whatever came to mind. She was also very snuggly and just wanted to be held. Sometimes, depending on what she had to drink, she was more flirty and handsy than normal. But above all, she was just super sleepy and could fall asleep in mere minutes if given the proper surroundings and a place she felt safe.

Much like now, for example. Pulling her back against his chest, Ian sighed and rested his chin on her shoulder, wishing she didn't have to be drunk to ask him to hold her again. But some things just could not be anymore, and as hard as that truth may be, there was nothing to be done to change it.

So instead of questioning it, Ian allowed himself this brief moment in time to enjoy what he had been offered. Little knowing that the "brief moment" would quickly turn into a whole night's worth of sleep.

Hours into a deep sleep, Perri turned over in Ian's arms so that she was facing him. She tucked her arms between their bodies and nestled as close as she could. She could feel Ian's arms tighten around her instinctively, and in her mostly asleep state, nothing seemed at all off about the situation. Her brain completely forgetting that she and her husband had been divorced for almost five years now, and he should not be in her bed, especially not holding her this close. But instead of any of this breaking through her blissful sleep, Perri settled back in. Softly she nudged his jaw with her nose, and even in sleep, Ian immediately lifted his head from memory, providing the room his ex-wife was silently requesting. She laid her head under his chin and breathed deeply, content to continue sleeping and, for mere hours, forgetting the truth of her reality.

The night sky was slowly drifting to life, the world outside turning a peaceful grey as the sun yawned just below the horizon. The once couple had eventually detangled from their position that had changed yet again over the course of the night.

From resting her forehead against Ian's chin and having her fingers tunneled into the thick hair at the base of his skull, Perri had rolled onto her back but still within arms reach. And laying there beside her, Ian laid his hand against her chest gently. His large hand covered most of the expanse just below her neck, and his fingertips rested on her collarbone, occasionally brushing along it soothingly. Feeling his presence even as she dreamed, Perri reached up to hold his wrist and keep his hand in place. Tranquility would be the best word to describe the sleeping pair.

Once the sun curled its rays of light through her curtains, creating a strip of warmth across her bed, Perri awoke to find that her limp hold on him had not made Ian stay. With a twist of pain deep in her chest, she knew it was best that he hadn't and was glad that he didn't. . . for the most part. And for a moment, she wondered if perhaps it had all been some sort of vivid dream brought on by the drinking.

Rolling onto her side, Perri found a glass of water sitting on her nightstand with a small bottle of pain relievers not far from it. With a sigh, she knew that Ian had most definitely been in her house last night and probably in her bed.

Sitting up, Perri took a sip of water and went to open the bottle so she could take something for the splitting headache she felt already coming on. The sound of her phone vibrating against her nightstand caused her to nearly choke and reaching recklessly to grab it, she instead knocked it onto the floor. Rolling her eyes at her own morning incompetence, Perri leaned down to snatch it off the floor before she missed whoever was calling.

"'Ello."

"Good, you're up."

The sound of Ian's voice shocked her almost as much as the loud ringing of her phone had moments before.

"I—I am, yeah."

"Did you find the—?"

"The things, yes," she smiled a little before quickly stopping herself, "Thank you."

"You're welcome."

A few moments of silence followed, and Perri rested her forehead in her free hand, elbow digging into her knee as she tried to decide if she should even ask about last night, considering she remembered so little of it.

"Nothing happened, Per," Ian said softly as if knowing what was eating away at her brain. "We behaved ourselves."

A wave of relief washed over her but was quickly followed by a wave of guilt.

"I'm so sorry, I—I thought it was a dream," Perri spoke softly, "I was terribly trolleyed. I really am sorry."

Ian remained quiet a moment longer, but she could hear the teasing smile in his voice when he finally did speak.

"So you dream about me, hm?"

Normally Perri's immediate response would have been to say no, and just no, but this was not a normal circumstance. Mainly because she was somehow still lacking the part of her brain that slowed down the words for processing before they came out of her mouth.

So instead,

"No. . . But I do think about you."

And suddenly, as soon as the words left her, that part of her brain caught up and her eyes snapped wide.

"Sorry! I'm sorry. I'm still very hungover and not quite myself yet."

"It's alright," Ian's voice was gentle as always, and Perri thought she heard a tinge of sadness in his voice, "I think about you too."

She had heard sadness, and she hated herself for it. Because she put it there.

Tears stung her eyes and blurred her vision before she quickly wiped them away. Then she saw her mother pull into the driveway and composed herself as best she could.

"I have to go," her voice was surprisingly stronger than she thought it would be, "Thank you again."

And she hung up.

Opening the door just as Laurel was about to knock, Perri practically threw herself into her mother's unexpecting arms.

"Perri, what's wrong?" Laurel questioned, both concerned and terribly confused, "What happened?"

Perri could only cry into the older woman's shoulder and simply move with her as Laurel maneuvered them into the house to shut the door.

"My love," the woman held her daughter tight and tried not to get overly fretted before knowing what had gone on, "Talk to me. Tell me what happened."

"I—I asked for this," Perri spoke between sobs, "In fact, I insisted on it because this is what I wanted. And—And now here I am. . . I'm miserable. I finally go on a date, and the only person I want is my husband. My husband who I left."

Laurel's chest felt a squeeze of pain for her daughter, her daughter, who had set out for what she thought needed to be done and broken her own heart in the process.

"Oh my darling," she held her tighter and cradled the back of her head, "I'm so sorry."

"Mum," Perri's voice and sniffles were muffled by the woman's soft coat, "What have I done?"

What have I done?

The question echoed in Perri's brain even all this time later. Even as she sat just a few feet away from her ex-husband, who had just told her that he could find a way to be content if she would simply be friends with him. But deep down, Perri knew she could never just be friends with this man. It simply wasn't something she would be capable of. And how could she possibly try while holding such a secret just out of his reach? That's not what friends do, and if she was even going to attempt to be his friend, she would not abide by being anything less than a good one. If she couldn't make it out of their marriage as a good wife, at least she could try and be a good friend to him now.

It was long past time for him to know the truth.

Looking over at the man she missed having so close every day, Perri took a deep breath. Now was the time.

"Ian. . ."

The cloud of her breath hung in the air for a long moment, and Ian turned his attention back to her.

"I, ehm, I want to—"

"Mum?" Aspen's voice called as she and Zayden entered their mother's room, cutting through her mother's serious tone.

Immediately distracted from all she was about to reveal, Perri looked over her shoulder, "Out here, babies."

The two crossed the room and came to stand dutifully beside their mother's chair.

"Hello, my loves," she smiled up at them, "What are you doing back so quick? We thought for sure you would be at least a couple more hours."

Zayden playfully elbowed Aspen and rolled his eyes, "Well, this one here decided she was too hungry and just *had* to come back."

"Yeah, and if we had stayed, your stomach growling would have brought the whole mountain down on top of us. So really, I was just saving everyone here. Honestly, fetus, these people are just trying to enjoy their vacations. Not die in a tragic accident because you won't admit that you're hungry."

Sometimes Aspen's quick wit was just too much for even her brother to keep up with, and he had been combating it for as long as he could remember.

Ian, who had finally recovered from the sudden interruption, chuckled, "So what you're telling us is you both came back only because you need to eat."

"Yeah, that's pretty much it," Zayden nodded until his sister reached over and backhanded him in the stomach. "We missed you, actually." He did his best to recover, hoping to avoid further abuse.

"And we wanted to see if you guys wanted to just order room service early?" Aspen asked hopefully.

"I think it sounds lovely," Perri agreed, looking around the two to see Ian nodding in agreement, "But first, let me change into some actual clothes, and then we can order something."

Getting to his feet, Ian looked down at his robe and smiled, "Yeah, I'll second that. Be back in a few."

Pausing momentarily, he let Perri enter the room in front of him and the two heading in opposite directions.

Minutes after, the normalcies of the interaction still had the siblings standing in the cold, a little confused and wondering what had happened before their arrival.

"Was Dad wearing his. . .?"

"Robe," Aspen cut in, "Yeah, yeah, he was."

"And were they both still in their pajamas?"

"Just sitting on the balcony of *Mum's* room. Again, yeah. Yeah, they were."

"Do you think they were. . .?" Zayden's words faded, and he looked down at his sister to waggle his eyebrows instead.

"Zayden, stop!" Aspen cringed, "I want them back together, but I can't handle the idea of them. . . being *together together*."

"You're right," he nodded decidedly, looking back toward the mountains they had just left, "Let's not think about that too hard. It kind of freaks me out. No matter how much we joke about it."

"What freaks you out?"

The sound of their father's voice startled them at first, and they quickly turned to face the room, feeling the warmth of it hit their faces.

"The people who come here and don't even think about skiing," Aspen quickly made up the response, and if Zayden had not been a part of their conversation seconds before, even he would have believed her, "It's half the fun, and they're skipping out. It's freaky."

Ian smiled at his children and looped his arms around their shoulders, "I knew we raised you kids right. That's definitely freaky."

Perri entered the room wearing a loose linen shirt tucked into a pair of faded jeans. She took a seat at the small desk in the corner and pulled the phone toward her.

"Alright, what does everyone want?" she asked as she started rolling up the sleeves of her black button-down past her elbows.

Gathering around the woman, everyone looked over the menu, and she placed the order before leaning back in that familiar content and confident air of hers to watch her family.

They did not have to wait long, and as soon as there was a knock on the door, Aspen and Zayden practically pounced. Ian passed the young man a tip and thanked him before closing the door. Perri snatched her hot chocolate from the midst of their children and retreated to the other side of the kitchen. Resting her hips back against the counter, she folded her arms across her chest and watched Ian interact with their children. Just so happy to be in the same room as these three and their wild antics.

Ian looked up from his finished plate and found Perri smiling softly at them, her eyes a little unfocused as her thoughts were far away. He missed those faraway expressions and the comforting presence of his wife—ex-wife—just sharing space with her family in her quiet way. And he knew he had told her earlier that he could be content with a friendship, but he also knew that would always only be just enough. He loved her too deeply for simple friendship to truly be enough. But if that was what she could give him, he would never say no. But he also wasn't going to deny how much he loved the game they had begun to play since their arrival here. The attraction between them was still electric and nearly impossible to overlook. So what would the harm be in continuing their little dance?

He didn't see any, and he knew that Perri would never object.

Crossing the kitchen to where his ex-wife stood, Ian moved swiftly into her space and looked down into Perri's face. He smirked as he watched her eyes snap open a fraction wider at his sudden closeness. If he had not been so close, he would have missed her soft gasp entirely. Placing a hand on her hip, Ian reached around her with his other arm, all the while leaving his gaze locked on hers.

"I just need a serviette," he remarked casually as if he didn't know exactly what he was doing.

Having had time to adjust to the unexpected action, Perri could never imagine allowing him to get away with it. With a wicked smirk, she lifted her chin and tilted her head just enough to give Ian access to her neck. Cutting her eyes up at him, she watched as he leaned down just close enough to inhale the scent of her perfume.

"Are you wearing it?" he smiled, and Perri shrugged before moving out of his reach. The interaction somehow went completely unnoticed by the siblings, who were playfully bickering just a few yards away.

It reminded Ian so much of when their flirtation first began and how incredibly unsure of himself he had been. Leaving him to only hope that Perri knew how desperately he wanted her despite his awkwardness.

* * * * * * * * * * * * * *

It was slowly getting dark outside, and the moon was shining brightly through the window across the room. Laurel had gone to bed a short time ago, and the two of them were seated across from each other with a chessboard between them, intense expressions on their faces. Laurel had 'gotten tired just watching them' and had left them mid-game and they were still determined to keep going.

After making a move, Perri got up to stir the fire as Ian stared at the board and she smiled to herself knowing she had trapped him. The logs hissed as they settled in the flames and sparkles flew up and out into the night sky, orange stars in a flight lasting only a moment. Perri turned back to face him, seeing he had yet to make a decision, and couldn't help take advantage of the opportunity she was being offered. Walking up behind Ian, she leaned down close, almost resting her chin on his shoulder.

"Your move," Perri whispered, her lips all but brushing the shell of his ear. She pulled away from him and returned to her seat, acting as if she hadn't a clue what she had just done. She tried to be as nonchalant as possible but touching Ian's skin, feeling how warm he was, breathing in the scent of his hair, made Perri a little dizzy.

Ian exhaled slowly; his eyes closed. After a moment, he looked up at Perri, cocking an eyebrow and sliding his queen over to capture an errant pawn. Raising her brows briefly in response, Perri turned her attention partially back to the board and thought about her next move. The game had begun.

* * * * * * * * * * * * *

So, of course, even now, once the game was started, neither of them could let it stop. Their competitive natures only made them want to continue out-maneuvering the other. And when Ian saw his chance, he took it, knowing exactly what would drive Perri mad in all the right ways.

Perri stood stirring her second hot chocolate, finally deciding that it was cool enough to drink, and Ian slid up close behind her. A mere breath away from touching her as he reached around to grab his own cup.

"Don't mind me. I just need this really quick."

His breath was warm on the shell of her ear, causing her eyes to flutter shut and her breath to catch in her chest. The nearness of him was almost too much for her to handle without reaction, especially for a second time.

Ian himself was struggling with not just wrapping his free arm around her waist and pulling her flush against him, just to revel in the sensation of holding her for a moment. But knowing the unspoken rules of their game, he instead took a step back and walked away without a word to rejoin their children.

Taking a deep breath, Perri braced her hands on the counter and pushed down the feelings that had boiled up inside her that were currently warming her chest and flushing her skin. The longing was the hardest part, but she knew the feeling well and knew that it would quiet from a scream to a whisper after a while. Turning to face the room, she caught Ian staring at her and held his gaze.

Both of them knew full well that they were playing in dangerous waters. But neither of them seemed to care.

It's a very surreal feeling, falling in love for the second time with someone you never fell out of love with in the first place.

There are many kinds of love, but, in the words of F. Scott Fitzgerald, "the same love never happens twice."

8

Hold me now
It's hard for me to say I'm sorry
I just want you to stay
After all that we've been through
I will make it up to you
I promise to
And after all that's been said and done
You're just a part of me I can't let go

— "Hard to Say I'm Sorry" by Chicago

"I have cancer."

Perri blurted the words before really thinking about it. All she knew was she couldn't hide it any longer. However, she had meant to approach the subject with a little more tact than she had just displayed.

The sky had darkened with the day having passed peacefully and contentedly. She and Ian were back on the balcony of Perri's suite, the glass fire pit burning between them to keep them warm. Perri sat in the lounge chair with the massive throw blanket that she had stolen from its place at the foot of her bed. While Ian stood at the railing wearing one of his shawl-collared Aran sweaters that she loved so much.

Perri noticed his grip on his mug had tightened at her words.

"Well, I think."

Eyes closed and lifting his face to the bitter night sky, Ian shook his head. "You *think*?"

"Well, they found another mass in my left breast. I had a biopsy done, and I'm just waiting on the results."

"How long?"

"How long what?" Perri answered his question with a question, something Ian typically found enduring, but not in this situation.

Ian turned to face her, crossing his strong arms over his chest. "How long have you known about the mass?"

He was angry. Perri hadn't really been prepared to deal with anger. She had so rarely seen him angry it just wasn't something she was expecting.

"Why are you mad?"

"How long have you known about the mass?" Ian repeated, annunciating each word slowly.

Perri almost wanted to ask *which one* but thought better of it and answered for the most recent.

"A few weeks now."

"A fe—." The exhale he blew out puffed his chill reddened cheeks and curled into the cold air in plumes. "When do you get the results?"

"They said anywhere between two or three days, but if the analysis was more complicated, it could take seven to ten," Perri replied, shuffling a bit in her seat.

"How long has it been?"

Perri looked into the mug that rested on her lap, watching the steam rise into the air above the warm liquid.

"Eight days."

Ian huffed a sigh, "Perri, why do you try to deal with everything by yourself?"

Her brows pulled together, "Ehm, because I have to!"

"No, you don't!" Ian almost shouted, "I am right here! I have always been right here, but you push me away just like you did when we were married!"

"I was trying to—I needed to know that you could step up when I needed you to."

"Step up? Perri, we were both there. We were a team."

"Yes, I know that!" Her voice was growing louder than she intended, "But what if I hadn't been able to be there? What then?"

"Why would you think you wouldn't be—?" The realization washed over Ian's face, and Perri watched as it began to process in his mind. Her chest ached, but she said nothing and simply waited. Ian took a deep breath, his eyes shut for a moment—then two—as he tried to compose himself. Finally, he opened them and still was no calmer than he had been. Now just with a shadow of something else behind his eyes as well.

"Tell me," he insisted quietly.

Perri was quiet for a long moment, none of this was going as she had hoped it would, and she suddenly wished for a rewind button so she could take it back and start over. And not just tonight, all of it.

"It happened before and—and I needed you to be the parent our kids would need if I was gone. I needed to. . . I needed you to be used to being the only one so that when you were, it wouldn't be such a massive adjustment."

Ian looked at Perri in disbelief. "What do you mean this happened before?"

He always just had to pay such close attention to what she said. It drove her nuts, in both good and bad ways.

Sighing, Perri explained, "There was another mass. Six months or less before we—before I—filed for divorce. I was scared, and I just—I needed to know that at least the kids would be fine if I was gone because you would already know how to care for them alone."

Ian shook his head, barely held back tears dancing dangerously close to falling off the edge.

"How could you. . . H—how could you ever think that I wouldn't be able to take care of our kids if something happened to you?"

"That's not what I—"

Ian held up his hand, "More importantly, how could you keep this *enormous* secret from me?"

Perri opened her mouth to reply, but the tightness in her chest had moved up to her throat, and the invisible hand was squeezing in a vice grip, making the words impossible to come out.

Ian was hurt. Truly, deeply hurt, and Perri would never be able to take that back. Not now, not ever.

"We were supposed to be teammates in everything," his voice was so soft, "We promised, Perri. When—When did you suddenly decide to become the captain?" Ian shook his head again and ran his fingers through his hair in that way that Perri knew all too well. He was trying to keep it all together long enough to leave.

"Ian—"

"I am tired," he stated, "I think I'll call it a night."

"Ian."

"Goodnight, Perri."

While her ankle was better, Perri was still slow to move when getting up. Which meant she had barely made it into the suite when she heard the heavy door adjoining their rooms click shut behind Ian, and then the lock fall into place.

That sound was probably what hurt the most. The lock was set, and this time it had been Ian to do it.

Perri stood silent in the center of the room, watching the door with misty vision, hoping that Ian would change his mind and come back. Even if it was just to be angry with her.

Had this all been her fault? Was the lack of communication all one-sided? Or were they both guilty in their own way? But she supposed it didn't matter now. They had both broken each other's hearts in ways no one else ever could. And how does someone begin to mend such breaks as that?

Perri was tired too. Exhausted, really. From constantly fighting a war with herself. From hiding for so so long. From maintaining the bloody façade. Honestly, she wasn't always sure who or what she was fighting anymore. She just always had to be fighting, and it was exhausting.

And if she really did have cancer this time, wouldn't it be better to have Ian as a teammate instead of an opponent? Or would he think that she was only using him as a crutch now? Only leaning on him because she was terrified.

The last time Perri had seen Ian so hurt was the night she had given him the divorce papers. She could barely stand under the knowledge that she had hurt him so irrevocably. Not once, but twice now.

Perri carefully turned and hobbled across her suite to shut the French doors that she had left open in her attempt to stop Ian's departure. Once they were secure, she made her way to her bedroom. She didn't even shed her clothes; she simply wrapped herself as tightly as possible in the throw blanket and laid down. It was a very poor substitute for Ian, and the memory of his arms wrapped securely around her the night before only served as torment now.

And Perri did something that she rarely did.

She cried.

She hadn't lied when she told him, not quite twenty-four hours before, that she had missed him for a long time. And now it was even worse.

I tell myself, tell myself, tell
myself, "Draw the line"

And I do, I do

But once in a while I trip up, and I cross the line

And I think of you. . .

Thought it was done, but I guess
it's never really over

Oh, we were such a mess, but wasn't it the best?

— "Never Really Over" by Katy Perry

The night rolled by in fitful minutes, passing as hours while Perri tried and failed to sleep.

She had figured out very quickly after the divorce that she had probably made a mistake, but now that the secret was out, the mistake was mocking her to her face. There were no longer any moments of doubt. She regretted what she had done. But, just as she had told herself after filing for divorce in the first place, it was too late now. She had to accept the life she had chosen for herself.

The sun stretched slowly over the horizon and taunted Perri with its existence. Today would be the first time she had to face the Ian who knew the truth. The Ian who would now look at her and only see a woman who had made decisions that greatly affected him without his knowledge and then ultimately ran away. Tears stung her eyes again, and she hated that the first thing she wanted was to wrap herself up in was Ian's old flannel.

But the sun continued to rise, shining its golden light in warm squares across the bed. For a moment, Perri was unrealistically jealous of and angry at the sun itself for having the audacity to not only shine so brightly on a day like today but to also be warm and seemingly content. She knew it was foolish, but she was angry just the same.

Having promised their children she would be at breakfast, Perri got up, and, after making herself presentable, she made her way downstairs. As she walked to the elevator, she tried to smother the hope that Ian would come out of his room at the sound of her movement and ride down with her. At the same time, she dreaded the idea of seeing him after the revolution he had endured the night before. To be locked inside an elevator with him now would be both heaven and hell. But the opportunity for either passed her by as Perri boarded the elevator alone.

Nervously rubbing the sleeve of her sweater between her thumb and fingers, Perri waited for the doors to open. But the moment the elevator stopped, her mask fell masterfully in place. The façade must continue. She couldn't lead him on, especially now. And she couldn't take him back, not with the threat of cancer looming over her again. She wouldn't put him through that. And now, she doubted he would even take her back. Even if part of her still wanted to hope.

So I'll remain within your reign
Until my thoughts can travel somewhere new
My mind is blind to everything but you
And I wonder if you wonder about me too

— "Wonder" by Lauren Aquilina

Coming up the front steps of Aliyah's house, Perri smiled a little, already hearing the commotion of voices inside. Opening the door almost hesitantly, she peeked her head inside and immediately saw one of the hosts.

"Hey, Ali."

Turning at the sound of her best friend's voice, the woman's face broke out in a bright smile.

"Perri! Come in, come in!"

Fully opening the door, Perri was wrapped up in a tight embrace before she could even get inside.

"Ya know you can jus' let yaself in, wha' were ya doin' lurkin'."

"I know," Perri answered, "I just figured I'd be a little more formal since this is a party and all."

"You and I 'ave never been formal," Aliyah held her at arms length, "Ya came into my 'ouse at midnight without so much as a ring to warn

227

me and wearin' pajamas to boot. Ya can most cer'ainly jus' let yaself in my home always, no ma'er wha's goin' on inside."

Laughing, the two looped their arms together and integrated into the festivities taking place a room away.

Perri's sharp eyes scanned the room of familiar and unfamiliar faces, searching for one person.

"He's 'ere," Aliyah's voice broke her focus.

"Hmm?" Perri turned her head partially toward her friend but kept her eyes moving along the path she had started. "Who?"

The other woman stopped their movements and, with that, received Perri's full attention.

"We both know who you're lookin' for," she answered, squeezing Perri's arm gently. "He is 'ere."

Perri nodded, turning her eyes back to the room, "Okay."

It was a while before she spotted him, but once she did, Perri struggled with remaining where she was and not running to him just so she could share the same air as him.

When she had accepted the invitation to the New Year's party, she suspected that Ian would be present, considering they had both formed friendships with Aliyah and her husband. But this being the first time she would see him outside of things involving their children, Perri hadn't quite known what to expect. Despite it all, she had convinced herself that she would be fine, and now that the moment had finally arrived, it almost proved to be too much. Especially when their eyes would meet, even from across a crowded room. Then they would hold in the way they always had when they went out together before. . . well, before she had ended it all. But lingering gazes and soft smiles would have to be enough. It was almost too much.

The gravitational pull the two seemed to have for one another kept them in close range of each other constantly, like a perfectly choreographed dance. It wasn't until an hour or so into the gathering that they truly encountered one another.

Perri turned from the champagne table when she felt a tap on her shoulder and smiled.

"Winston!" she greeted and gave the man a quick hug, "How are you? When did you come back home?"

"Oh, I've been back in ol' Blighty for a few months now," the mustached man replied, "Having the whole pond between me and my home turned out to be too much for this old git."

"Well, it's good to have you back," Perri looked around, "Have you seen Ali yet? She's really grown up since our Primary days." She winked and chuckled because they could both see how the years had definitely changed them.

"I hunted her down first thing," Winston answered and stroked his mustache, "Had to show her that it turns out I can grow facial hair after all."

Sharing a laugh for a moment, the man continued.

"Look, Blondie,"

The use of her Primary school nickname made Perri shake her head but smile just the same. Winston looked over his shoulder and waved someone over. Now Winston was not a small man, he was tall and round and impossible for Perri to see around to identify whose attention he was trying to attract.

"I've been watching you two look at each other all night long, and I thought I'd do you both a favor and introduce you."

Brows pulling together briefly in confusion, but also a touch of intrigue, Perri waited as Winston took a step aside to reveal who he was referring to. Just breaking through the crowd to come toward them was none other than Ian looking as handsome as the day Perri first saw him so uncertain and uncomfortable in the middle of a clothing store. She couldn't help the close-lipped smile that lifted the corner of her lips, and she knew her eyes had taken on that familiar softness that she should be trying to hide. But she just didn't have the want to, especially when

Ian smiled that schoolboy smile that somehow still remained just a little lopsided.

"Ian, chap, now <u>this</u> is a woman for you," Winston said, "She'd cause you trouble, but she'd be worth it to you."

"I have no doubt that she would be." Ian's voice was warm and smooth and made Perri's chest clench.

"And Perri, this ol' boy is as good as they come, I assure you. He and I were good friends during the first years of Veterinary school before I had to transfer."

Perri's dark eyes held Ian's gaze, "I'm sure he is."

Winston smiled brightly, obviously pleased with himself, "There, now that you two know each other, you can stop just glancing in each other's direction."

"Well, thank you for the introduction, but. . ." Ian couldn't help but smirk, "We've already met."

"Oh?" Bushy brows drew together.

"You see," Perri continued, "We were married."

"For eighteen years, in fact," Ian finished.

Winston's face dropped, and a mortified expression crossed it instead.

"I—I don't even know how to—What I mean to say is—I had no idea, I've been away much too long, I—I'm so sorry."

Perri laid a hand on his shoulder and smiled reassuringly, "It's alright, Winnie, really."

"You've helped us honestly," Ian agreed, "We hadn't quite figured out how to approach each other at a gathering like this yet, and you just bridged the gap. Thanks, chap."

"I still hate that I didn't know," he said, running a hand over his mustache, "I—I wish I had so I wouldn't have. . . I'm really sorry it didn't work out."

Perri and Ian nodded once in agreement, smiling sadly.

Gesturing at the table where he had found Perri, Winston began to walk away, "I—I think I'm going to get a drink now."

The two watched their old friend go, chuckling a little at the whole situation.

Perri finally turned her eyes up to Ian, "I had no idea you knew Winston."

"We were dormmates at university," he replied, "I missed him when he left. It was shortly before I met you, in fact."

"The world really is a small place after all, I suppose."

The pair stood quietly for a long moment, simply remaining in each other's presence for as long as they could. But time was quickly running out for them to just stay standing in the same spot saying and doing nothing, but they couldn't bring themselves to part just yet.

"Can I get you a drink?"

Perri smiled up at him, "I doubt I need much more, but yes, that would be nice."

Filling two flutes and plucking them from the table, Ian turned and offered one to his ex-wife. "One more for us both. We'll bring in the New Year and then go home like two sensible people."

Clicking the rim of their glasses together, Perri smiled, "Sounds brilliant. Cheers."

From somewhere in the middle of everything, Aliyah's voice could be heard shouting above the rest.

"It's almost time, everyone!"

Liam was spotted making his way through the crowd to reach his wife in time for the count down, and Aliyah readily drew him close.

"Here we go! Five!"

The room was filled with the sound of voices mingling together in a chorus as the New Year rapidly approached.

"One!"

All around them, couples were embracing and welcoming in the new year in the arms of their lover. Perri looked up at Ian, and her heart ached that she had given up the right to kiss him right now like she so desperately longed to.

Instead. . .

"Happy New Year," she said softly, and then his piercing eyes were on her.

"Happy New Year."

Perri watched in shock as Ian began to lean down, and her skin hummed in excitement when he placed a hand lightly on her waist. Without thinking, she lifted her chin a fraction and waited for their lips to meet. But the moment never came. Instead, Ian placed a lingering kiss on her cheek. The air around them alone was enough for anyone to sense how badly the two of them wanted to take the whole interaction to the next level. It was nearly driving Perri mad, and she couldn't help but touch him, sliding her hand under the lapel of his dinner jacket to rest against his chest.

"Can I take you home?" Ian whispered against her skin.

Her eyes fluttered shut once more at the thought, and it took everything she had not to say yes and drag him from the house. One deep breath and Perri turned so that she felt her nose brush his cheek.

"No, I don't think so. . ." she replied so only he could hear, "You would hate me in the morning."

"No, I swear I wouldn't," Ian promised, his voice earnest as he leaned back to cradle her face in his hand, "I could never hate you."

Flashing that close-lipped smile once more and allowing the flash of sadness to pass through her eyes, Perri shook her head and gently moved his hand, "I won't chance it. Not when we've just made it to being able to look at each other again. I won't do that to us."

"Perri—"

"Not tonight, Ian. Maybe one day, but not today."

Hanging his head, Ian leaned slightly into the brush of Perri's fingers along his jaw.

"I am sorry, Ian."

"Me too," His voice gravelly with emotion.

"Ian," Perri said his name with such gentle purpose that he looked up and met her gaze, "Thank you."

He nodded and delayed only for a moment longer. Both of them knew what had to happen next. They turned and walked away from each other, just as they always did now since that day months before in front of the registers office.

As she passed through the hall looking for her best friend, quickly flicking a tear off her cheek, Perri felt someone snatch her arm and pull her into a secluded room.

Whipping around to see how had grabbed her, she was met with the exact woman she had been searching for.

"Bloody hell, Ali, I nearly throttled you."

"I think I could take ya. For a bit a' least," Aliyah smiled.

"Probably," Perri replied, her tone sharp and quick, "Now, what did you need so urgently that you pulled me in here like this?"

Crossing her arms, Aliyah's playful air changed a bit, "Don' get shirty with me now, princess."

"I'm knackered, a'ight."

"Are ya? Or are ya upset from spendin time with Ian? I saw you two in the back of the room tonight."

"We weren't snogging, for bloody sake," Perri huffed like a teenager caught on the pull with her boyfriend.

"Ya didn' have to be, love," Aliyah replied gently, and reaching out, she gave Perri's upper arm a squeeze, "Babe, ya cannot expect 'im to sit around and pine after ya for the rest of 'is life. It's not fair."

"I'm not!" Perri angrily stepped out of her friend's reach, "<u>I</u> divorced <u>him</u>, remember."

Sighing, Aliyah nodded, "I do and I think that's the stupidest thing you've ever done. And I 'ate to say this; but yes, ya do. And if ya don't want 'im, if ya won't take 'im back, it's time ya let go and allowed 'im the chance to move on to someone who does."

Crossing her arms defensively, Perri quirked a brow, "Oh, you mean someone like you." Her dark eyes flashed with accusation.

"Now <u>you</u> remember somethin', I am still happily married to my husband," Aliyah's voice was calm and level.

"I'm sure you two can find a way to make it work."

Taking a step forward, Aliyah tried not to snap, "Now you're jus' bein' childish and cruel. So, I am goin' to stop talkin' before I say somethin' I'll regret later. I'm goin' to leave and you can brood all you wan' and jus' think about wha' I've said. Because you and I both know that I'm right."

Sweeping past the blonde, Aliyah left Perri standing dumbfounded in the room alone. Of course, she knew Aliyah was right, would she admit it to anyone—including herself—most definitely not. At least not right anyway. She was much too stubborn, but she was also willing to admit when she was wrong. Once she had time to get over the fact that she was.

Perri wasn't sure how long she had spent in the darkness of the secluded room, but she knew it had been some time because the sounds of people had slowly diminished. Feeling a little ashamed of her behavior earlier, she was cautious about leaving the safety of the room. But she would have to one day and she may as well get it over with.

With a huff much heavier than necessary, Perri went out to find Aliyah and apologized for accusing her best friend of wanting to sneak around with her husband—ex-husband. She grimaced when she thought about how she had let her emotions carry her away and had opened her mouth without thinking. Walking the house like it was her own, when Perri entered the foyer she heard familiar footsteps. But they were not the footfalls she was hoping for.

"Perri," Ian's eyes immediately brightened, "I didn't know you were still here. Did you go fall asleep in Ali's room again."

His teasing wink made Perri smile brighter than she intended and then Aliyah's words echoed in her mind.

Don't drag him along. It's not fair.

"No," she stated, her expression falling blank, "Where is Ali? I need to talk to her before I go."

Confused by the sudden change in Perri's behavior, Ian blinked twice before pointing back over his shoulder into the other room. Nodding her thanks, Perri brushed past him only to feel his hand gently grip her upper arm.

"Good night, Ian," she said, barely turning her head to cut her eyes down at his hand.

Ian withdrew his hand, all the while staring at his ex-wife's stoic profile, not understanding what had happened since their last interaction. "Per, did I—"

"Good night."

Sighing, Ian felt the now all-too-familiar stab of pain twist between his ribs.

"Good night, Perri."

And he watched as she hesitated only momentarily before continuing down the hall.

As soon as she entered the other room,

"I swear on my mother's grave, if I am grabbed one more time tonight," Perri threatened when she felt Aliyah grip her arm.

"You have to stop," Aliyah insisted, letting go once she had her friend's attention.

"What?!"

"You were being an arsehole," she answered through clenched teeth.

Throwing her hands up and letting them fall back to her sides, Perri's mouth dropped open. "You told me not to be so nice!"

"I told you not to drag him on! There's a difference."

The ticking of the clock on the wall was the only sound as the two locked stares. It was Perri whose gaze flitted away first, but only for a moment.

"It's either be an arsehole or show that I'm still madly in love with him. There is no in-between right now," lifting her chin, Perri took a

deep breath to collect herself and attempted to prevent her tears from making an appearance. "Anyway, I came to apologize for what I said earlier and to tell you I have taken to heart what you said. As you can see, I'm not dragging him on anymore. So. . ."

Looking at her friend for a long moment, Aliyah knew she would never be allowed to look her directly in the face when she was emotional like this. Her eyes softened, and she stepped forward to pull Perri into a tight embrace which her friend surprisingly relaxed into. Planting a kiss on the side of her head, Aliyah rubbed her back soothingly.

"I'm sorry, chick," she said quietly, "I can't imagine how hard it must be. . ."

"Ali, sweetheart—" Liam cut himself short at the sight that greeted him.

Looking over Perri's head at her wide-eyed husband, Aliyah subtly waved him away and almost chuckled at how he awkwardly backed his way out of the room once more.

Things had changed since then. Well, some things. She was still fighting not to drag him on and trying to give him the chance to carry on with someone new. Even though she knew she would hate the very day he did. Most times these days, she wasn't as heartless in her ways toward her ex-husband, but bridging the gap between ruthlessness and strictly friendship was much harder when you happened to be in love with the person.

Finally spotting her children, Perri waved and crossed the room to the table where they sat. Her eyes immediately fell on the empty seat where Ian would normally be, and she wondered if she would be the reason he stayed away this morning.

Because you've been an arse. . . As usual.

"Look at you, Mum," Zayden beamed up at the woman as she pulled out a chair across from him, "Hobbling much faster these days."

Aspen slapped his arm, but couldn't keep herself from smiling, so she hid behind her glass of orange juice.

"Very funny, you two," Perri cut her eyes up at her children as she looked over the menu to pick something different for breakfast this time. If she had chocolate chip pancakes once more, she feared she would be sick. "You'll regret teasing your mother once I'm back out on the slopes with you."

"Where's Dad?" she inquired after a time, trying to seem casual in her questioning.

Aspen shrugged her shoulders, "He said he wasn't hungry and that we should go ahead and eat without him."

Looking over at his sister in confusion, Zayden dropped his menu, "Dad is always hungry."

"Maybe he's coming down with something," Aspen suggested, "He didn't look his best. We should probably go check on him after breakfast."

"We have a spa appointment, Penny," Zayden rolled his eyes, "And you were the one who *insisted* I go with you. We are not skipping out on it now. I want it over with. Mum can make sure he's okay."

"It won't take five minutes, fetus, let's just—" Aspen's words faded as she noticed her brother's raised brows and his slight head tilt in their mother's direction.

Catching on slowly, her eyes brightened, and an impish smile grew across her face, "Yeah. Yeah, you're right. I completely forgot about that. What do you think, Mum?"

The woman lifted her head and looked back and forth between her children. Having been so suddenly drawn from her thoughts she realized she was painfully behind on the conversation. "Hmm?"

"Could you go check in on Dad, just really quick after breakfast?"

Sure, if he even wants to see my face. Perri thought. But instead, she just smiled softly.

"Sure. I'll go check on him. You two go to your, ehm. . ."

"Spa appointment," Zayden filled in dryly as he lifted his glass to his lips.

Chuckling a little, Perri smiled teasingly in her son's direction, "Yes, your spa appointment."

"Don't make fun, Mum!" he looked up at her with pleading eyes.

Holding up her hands and shaking her head, Perri did her best to hold back her laughter. "I'm not, my love, I'm not! I don't see anything wrong with it. You just—you just seem *so pleased* about it I couldn't help myself."

When their breakfast arrived, Perri took a few bites and then just ended up pushing the remainder of her meal around the plate. It just wasn't going to do. Perri had to fix this. . . If she could.

She wasn't an idiot. Perri knew how she felt for Ian. It was the same way she had *always* felt for him. There was just so much that they needed to communicate with one another. As openly and honestly as possible for a change. The only question that remained; would Ian be open to it after everything that had happened between them?

9

Come my love our world's would part
The gods will guide us across the dark
Come with me and be mine my love
Stay and break my heart

— "Tir Na Nog" by Celtic Woman

Knocking on Ian's door, Perri could feel her insides doing flips and yet somehow clenching themselves into tight knots. It was ridiculous, really. Ian was her ex-husband. They had seen each other at their best and their worst, worst predominating on occasion. But still, they loved each other so much that they had gotten married and made a family Perri could never even imagine living without. They had laughed and argued and always managed to come to some sort of middle ground. That is until Perri was too focused on doing what she thought was the only right thing and took matters into her own hands instead of just letting Ian be there like he always wanted to. In the end, all it got Perri was. . . well, divorced. Not to mention it made her incredibly lonely. And unhappy some of the time.

And for bloody sake why isn't Ian answering his door? Get it together, Perri.

Doing her best from falling down her rabbit hole of regrets, Perri knocked again.

Still no answer.

It was a good thing that she had stopped by the front desk on her way up to ask the concierge for Ian's room key. Utterly pleased with herself, the corner of Perri's lips lifted just a bit as she let herself in to find Ian buried under the heavy duvet.

"Ian?" she called softly, trying not to startle him.

Nothing.

"Ian," taking on a sing-song tone Perri sat on the bed and poked at the lump hidden beneath the blankets, "I'm not leaving until you talk to me."

Silence.

Fine, Perri didn't mind too much, considering she knew exactly how to get her ex-husband's attention: The Mum Voice. That always whipped everyone into shape.

"Ian Vilein-Astankova, you come out from those covers right now!" Flipping the comforter back, she was greeted by feet where a head should have been. Jerking back in shock, Perri blinked a few times, unsure of what to do next. Movement at the end of the bed drew her attention, and she watched as Ian struggled to push the blankets off.

Finally, his head popped out, silky dark hair tousled from sleep. He turned to face his ex-wife, a hilariously thunderstruck look on his face.

"How did you get in here?"

Perri held up the room key and grinned wickedly, "You're not the only one who can play the concerned spouse card, you know."

"Ex-spouse," Ian mocked, only half teasing.

To which Perri grinned even more and waved his words away, "Semantics." She enjoyed throwing Ian's words back at him, almost as much as Ian did with her.

"What do you want?" he questioned, still not recovered from last night. If he would ever be.

"To talk." Came the simple statement.

"*Now* she wants to talk," Ian said to the air around him, "The woman divorces me first, and *now* she wants to ta—."

"I'm sorry."

Ian shifted in the bed, gathering himself and sat up, pushing the blankets away as he went. He said nothing but stared so intently at Perri's face she knew he must be thinking he was hearing things.

"I am sorry," she repeated.

Ian crossed his arms and eyed her suspiciously, "For what?"

"For talking *at* you instead of *with* you before I made decisions that hurt us both."

"And?"

"And for making myself the captain instead of just staying your teammate like we promised."

"*And?*" Ian urged, cocking a brow expectantly, causing Perri to wonder what more she could apologize for.

Then it hit her.

"And for not telling you about. . . about my health scare."

Satisfied for now, it seemed, Ian crawled up the bed and sat next to Perri against the pillows. "Can I ask you something?"

Perri nodded.

"Why?"

Squinting her eyes a bit, Perri shook her head in lack of understanding, "Why what?"

"Why did you keep it from me?"

Perri looked down at her hands and was quiet for a long time, but Ian was a patient man, as he had proven time and again over the years.

"I think. . . I think I just didn't want you to see me like that."

"Like what?"

"Sick."

"Why not?" Ian couldn't understand, "We vowed that we would care for each other 'in sickness and in health,' Per. Did you not think I could handle it? I could have helped you."

"No, no, that's not it. I—," Perri sighed, "I didn't want you to have to handle it or just be forced to help me die."

And she meant it.

If Perri was being truly honest with herself, she would admit that if she *had* been diagnosed with cancer all those years ago, she never would have wanted Ian to watch her die. It simply wasn't fair to him. He was in a struggle against death every day at work, granted it was with people's pets, but she couldn't bear the thought of him coming home and doing the same thing in the place where he was supposed to be able to rest. Ian was still young and had his entire life ahead of him. He could remarry, and their children would still have had a family, regardless if she was gone or not. That was simply how she had seen it.

And she told Ian that. All of it.

When she had finished, Ian merely stared at her in wide-eyed disbelief.

"Are you insane?"

"Ian—"

"No, I am serious," he knelt on the bed, turning his body to face Perri. "Do you need to get your head examined next?"

"It's just how I felt. . . well, how I *feel*."

"You still feel this way?" Ian's voice was so soft she would have missed it had he not been so close. "Do you *actually* believe that if you died, I would be able to move on? Find someone new? Even now, with how you've treated me all this time, I haven't been able to even stomach the thought of ever trying to find someone new. How is that supposed to get any easier if you died?! How does that help?"

Perri shrugged, "I—I would want you to."

"I don't care!" Ian exclaimed, "Besides, we both know that's not true. You're skin just crawls at the idea of me being with someone else. Don't make me bring up that time you came to the clinic and met that client of mine and lost your shite on me after."

Perri's eyes dropped, and she tried to chuckle, but it came out as more of a swift release of the air from her nose that she had held in her lungs for too long.

Ian, in all of his gentleness, brushed his knuckles tenderly down her jaw until his index finger came to rest under her chin.

"What, in all of our years together, would make you think I would be able to ever stop loving you?"

Perri was unsure if the question was rhetorical, but she didn't have to wait long to find out that it wasn't. Which was good, because if he had stayed quiet waiting for her to answer too long, she would have completely lost her train of thought in the feeling of his skin against hers, little as it was.

"I need an answer, Perri," Ian remained close, leaving his index finger beneath her chin so she couldn't look away.

Giving a half-hearted teasing smile, Perri attempted a chuckle, "Why? So you don't do the same thing with the next woman?"

"Stop," his tone was assertive but tender, "Diverting."

Lowering her gaze to stare at the familiar scar on the inside of his wrist, that being the only way she did not have to hold Ian's intense gaze, Perri shook her head, "I know. I'm sorry."

"Don't apologize. You didn't do anything wrong. I just need you to answer the question," Lifting her chin just a bit to regain eye contact, Ian smirked a bit and tossed her a wink, "And seriously, for that new girlfriend I have lined up."

Searching her face, Ian wanted nothing more than to hold her close and wipe away the tears that had welled up in her dark eyes, but he didn't want to cross any lines and make Perri retreat back into herself. Reaching up, Perri wrapped her hand around his wrist to keep him from pulling away.

"I—I don't—"

"Is it because you stopped loving *me*?" A tear escaped past Ian and made its watery trek down his cheek. Perri thought she was hurting before, but now she could almost hear her own heart breaking. Immediately, she took his face in her hands and brushed the warm liquid from his face.

"No. No," she assured him, "I never stopped loving you. Not for a moment. You have to know that."

And as if the mountain itself had fallen to rest solely on Perri's chest, she realized. The fact of the matter was Ian didn't know that because she had never really told him. She had never expressed to Ian that their falling part was not really his fault at all. She had made decisions that forever altered their lives and had hidden so much under the disguise of "protecting" Ian. She had done so many things that made the harmonious life they had created together so much harder to maintain until it could no longer be what it had once been. Even though all of it was overshadowed by the fact that she would always be so desperately in love with Ian, he never knew that.

"Then why did you leave me? I know I am not perfect, but if you were sick, I—I would have loved you through it all."

Voice cracking and throat painfully tight, Perri managed, "I just couldn't put you through it. I am so sorry."

Without another thought, Ian gathered Perri close and wrapped his arms tightly around her, tucking his face in the curve of her neck.

Perri, who couldn't help the half-laugh, half-sob that escaped her lips, held Ian equally as tight.

"I am sorry too," his voice was muffled by her sweater.

"For what?" Perri genuinely had no idea why Ian would feel the need to apologize, especially after all she had revealed to him over the last twelve hours.

"For not seeing what was right in front of me," he answered, "For not picking up on your subtle hints of what was happening and what you needed from me."

Perri leaned back enough to shake her head, "No, I shouldn't have expected you to read my mind."

"I *am* good at *many* things, Perri," Ian teased, "But I am unfortunately not clairvoyant."

This was far from the happy ending one would expect from a moment like this. There was still so much to talk about. Still so many years of hurt and misunderstanding to work through to do what they could to make things right. Still even more to figure out. But this, this is what one could call a good beginning. And for the moment, this was enough.

Simply studying his ex-wife's face for a moment, Ian felt a small smile lift the corners of his lips, "Do you want to watch a movie with me?"

Chuckling at the simplicity of the question, Perri nodded, "Yes, I'd love that."

Adjusting the blankets around them, Ian placed a pillow near the foot of the bed and gestured for Perri to bring her feet down.

"Move the pillow," she said, not wanting to just throw her feet on it.

"No, you have to elevate your ankle."

Perri's heart squeezed in her chest, and she smiled at the sweet gesture. This man was beyond good.

Once they were both settled in, Ian clicked on the TV. Searching through the channels and debating about what to watch proved to be yet another rhythm they fell back into so easily they didn't even notice. Finally agreeing on another cringy Christmas film, they prepared to spend the next hour and a half making each other laugh with added commentary.

It was about halfway through, after coming down from a fit of laughter, Ian's hand landed on the bed between them, exceptionally close to Perri's. Subconsciously, he linked his pinkie with hers, and Perri couldn't help the soft smile that grew across her face as she curled her own finger around his in return.

10

So lay here with me
Let down your guard
Let's take off our clothes
And quit making it so hard
'Cause you don't wanna go
And I don't want you to leave
So why don't you stay, please
Lay here with me

— "Lay Here With Me" by Maddie & Tae

Perri awoke with a start, a sharp pain shooting through her ankle and a deep ache in her wrist. She and Ian had dozed off at some point and had turned to face one another even in sleep. With one arm pillowed under his head and the other draped over Perri's waist, Ian was the picture of tranquility. And Perri couldn't deny that she felt she had gotten more rest in the last couple of hours than she had in the last seven years. At last, there was peace. No secrets, no facades, just Ian and rest.

Looking down after several long seconds of her gaze being locked on Ian, Perri searched for the source of the pain. She found her legs entangled with her ex-husband's and her wrist trapped beneath her own body as she had attempted to roll closer to Ian. Her healing injuries would continue to complain until she moved them, so she took care not to disrupt Ian as she rearranged herself. It was only a coincidence that she ended up lying closer to her ex-husband in the process.

Looking back at Ian's sleeping face, Perri noticed the change in his once peaceful expression. His brows were pulled together briefly, his expression still remaining more of a grimace once his brows relaxed. Then his brows knit together again, and he hummed softly in distress. He was dreaming, and obviously, it was nothing good.

Reaching up, Perri pressed the pad of her thumb gently to the center of Ian's forehead and rubbed softly until his face relaxed. Perri smiled. It always worked. The corners of Ian's lips twitched upward, and for a moment, Perri forgot the dull ache of her ankle and wrist.

Ian had always had that effect on her. Even the smallest smile from the man and everything in Perri's world was right again.

"Perri," Ian muttered.

Her smile grew wider, and she ran her fingers down the soft expanse of Ian's face. An action that earned her a soft moan and Ian's head tilting into the touch. Because even in his sleep, Ian longed to be close to Perri.

"Are you awake?" Perri whispered after a moment.

"Mm. No." Ian wrapped his arm tighter around his ex-wife and threw his leg haphazardly over hers to affectively trap her in place.

With a purring little laugh in the back of her throat, Perri quirked a brow. "Very believable."

"I am a very good actor, Perri. You know this."

Blue eyes opened slowly and almost immediately found Perri's. Ian slid his fingers gently around the delicate hand on his face and squeezed.

"Perri," Ian murmured, "When I said, 'in sickness and in health, until death do us part', I meant it. I still do. You know I would go to hell and back for you."

It was much too soon for tears to be stinging her eyes again, but here they were. "I know." Her voice trembled.

Ian turned his head against her hand and planted a kiss in the center of her palm. Followed by each of her fingertips. Her wrist. Her cheek. That spot on her neck that drove her wild.

"Ian," Perri whispered.

He kissed up her neck to her ear and then her cheek once more. He felt Perri's fingers ball into a fist, tugging at the material of his shirt. Neither of them knew when it happened, but the energy in the air suddenly shifted. Their hearts started to race. Breath mingled between them, their lips all but colliding.

Perri's head tilted upward a fraction of an inch. She wanted this. She wanted Ian to kiss her. Because, for her, a single kiss from Ian Astankova could cure anything.

But then what about the ailment her body was most likely facing? Could she really put Ian through the pain of watching her die? The thought wouldn't leave her. Then Perri had started to understand that the question was not whether or not *Ian* was strong enough to handle it. . . The true question was, could Perri.

"It isn't wrong to have what you want, Per. The world will not end because you kiss me," Ian spoke softly, and it sounded almost like a promise. "You *know* we are right for—"

Ian's words were cut off when Perri shot forward, pressing their lips together in a searing kiss.

Ian moaned into the kiss, and when Perri's tongue made its way into his mouth, he could have died a happy man. She deepened the kiss, pulling Ian even closer somehow, and Ian's hand tangled itself into Perri's hair. Perri echoed his moan when Ian pulled away from her mouth and focused his energy on her neck. She readily tilted her head to the side, giving him more room. He sucked at her pulse point and then took the soft skin between his teeth before pulling slowly away, just the way Perri liked. Her hips bucked once—twice—as the moment only got more and more heated.

"We—we should stop," Ian managed to choke out, despite how much he was enjoying touching his ex-wife this way again.

Perri hummed her disapproval and lifted her chin, tilting her head wordlessly, begging for Ian to continue his glorious caresses on her neck. And damn his lack of willpower because Ian would never deny Perri whatever she wanted.

Time. Horses. The moon. The stars. The whole galaxy if she wanted.

Divorce.

Whatever Perri wanted, Ian gave it to her, so willingly. Even if it meant Ian hurt for it. If Perri was happy, Ian could breathe. The problem was now, it seemed like Ian finally realized that he hadn't been breathing properly for so long. And now, here in Perri's arms, Ian felt his lungs had been given new life all over again. Perri was here, willingly, and she was happy. Finally, Perri wanted him again, just him.

No sooner had Ian's hand slipped under Perri's shirt and splayed wide against the warmth of her back, a knock ripped through the otherwise quiet of the room. A call of housekeeping followed, and waited for entry to be granted.

Perri chased after his lips when Ian pulled away. Both of them quickly—or at least as quickly as they could—shook themselves back to reality.

"Go away!" Ian yelled, "I'm naked!"

He looked at Perri as soon as the words left his mouth, eyes wide and shocked at his choice of action to send the intruder away. It was Perri's who cracked a smile first, and the two fell into a fit of laughter. Her cackling laughter that he had missed so much made Ian almost double over in mirth.

When they had gathered themselves, Ian cradled Perri's face in his hand and brushed his thumb tenderly against her cheek. His expression was gentle and serious as he gazed into Perri's chocolate eyes.

"We really should stop."

A flash of sadness passed through Perri's eyes, and Ian hated himself for being the reason it was there. But she nodded in agreement, an understanding but regretful smile barely lifting the corner of her lips. Her hand trailed down Ian's arm, and she followed its path, finding herself unable to look into his eyes. Taking a deep breath, Perri rested her forehead against his collarbone. Just for a moment, she told herself. Just so she could revel in the closeness a bit longer.

Then swinging her leg back over, Perri removed herself from where she had straddled Ian's lap and settled in beside him instead.

The moment was over.

Stupid housekeeping. Perri huffed to herself.

They sat beside each other for several minutes, content with the quiet between them, until Ian looked over at her.

"Do the kids know?"

"No, of course not," she answered, "If I had told them, they would have needed someone and would have gone to you. Exactly as they should have."

"Or Ali."

"Or Ali, who *definitely* would have told you. Either way, you would have known before *I* could even break the news to you if I had told the kids."

"Did you. . . Did you tell anyone?" Ian asked, worry shadowing his eyes when Perri hesitated, "I know you, Perri, how did you manage without someone to—"

"Talk me down?" Perri's expression flickered with tired amusement, "Honestly, it did drive me a little bit mental sometimes. But I was alright. I'm alright. I never got fully lost in the plot," Perri nodded slowly, thoughtfully, turning her eyes forward again to study the wall across the room.

"When things would get hard, and I would get scared or overwhelmed with all the waiting and not knowing, I would. . ." she paused, and before Ian knew what he was doing, his hand had reached out to cover hers that lay on the bed between them. Perri did her best to give him a small smile, and the quick release of air from her nose, Ian assumed was an attempt at a chuckle. But it gave her the ability to go on,

"I would think about you. What you would say or do, and I would be able to make it. You asked me, shortly after the divorce, if you ever crossed my mind."

Perri paused to take a deep breath, and her eyes drifted shut momentarily, "You don't cross my mind, Ian. You live in it. Especially during those times. I needed someone, and you were it, but I didn't have you so. . ."

"Perri, you could have had me," Ian turned his body to face her.

Hanging her head, Perri lifted her injured hand to cover her misting eyes, "I know, Ian, I know."

"Even after everything," he said softly, wanting her to know he wasn't being condescending about her leaving him, "You could have had me whenever you wanted me. All you had to do was ask. Even today, with all these years between us, you can still have me. . . If you want."

"Don't believe for one moment that I didn't think about it. I wanted you *so* badly most days. But it would have been selfish of me, and I had already been selfish enough. I wasn't going to do that to you."

Perri drew a shuddering breath and refused to lift her head, brushing his hand away when Ian tried to uncover her face. She hated this. But she couldn't help it.

He was her safe place, and somehow it was still that way even after all this time apart.

Perri whimpered softly and did her best to continue avoiding Ian's gaze, making sure her tearing eyes remained covered. It was all too much for her to handle. She had only felt this much on a handful of other occasions. And she couldn't handle being dissected under Ian's piercing eyes. Eyes that made her feel like he could see all of her, her vulnerabilities, her flaws, her fears. She most definitely couldn't handle feeling all those things and still seeing in his eyes how much he loved her and, even after everything, only saw perfection. If she looked at him now, she would never be able to get herself back together.

But ever persistent, Ian gently took her hand away from her eyes and pressed a lingering kiss to her palm before carefully threading their fingers together.

"You don't have to hide from me, you know."

It took every ounce of willpower she had not to ask Ian to hold her.

Just hold me. I'm lonely and so afraid, more than I will ever admit.

As if hearing her thoughts, Ian arranged himself differently beside her, and for a moment Perri panicked and thought he was leaving. But instead, she felt as Ian slid an arm behind her shoulders and the other behind her knees, scooping her into his arms and placing her in his lap. Cradling the back of her head in his hand, he drew her close and rested his chin on top of her head. Perri gasped against his collarbone, simultaneously shocked by the gesture and yet feeling the wave of relief and gratitude crash over her. She would never recover from this man; it simply wasn't possible. She could never deserve him either, but she would never stop trying. Even if she had given him up years ago.

"Do you think we should try marriage counseling?" Ian asked.

The two of them were still sitting in the same position. Perri nestled close, never wanting to move, and Ian was content to hold her for as long as she would let him. Her tears had dried, Ian's too, and they had simply remained sitting there for a long while.

Perri chuckled a bit, "Well, maybe not, considering we're not married."

Tightening his arms around her just enough for her to notice, Ian's voice took on a different tone, sad in a way and even more serious.

"We'll always be married, Per. You know it, and I know it. Even if you married someone else, I would always be in your head. Just like you would always be in mine."

"I don't think I could ever meet anyone else," her words were quiet and thoughtful as she drew random patterns on Ian's chest with her fingertips. "Let alone marry them."

Perri could feel Ian trying not to be too delighted about her statement, and the right side of her face curled upward in a devilish smirk.

"I don't think you would let me."

Momentarily surprised, Ian quickly recovered and laughed, "You're right. I would definitely object at the wedding."

"If you didn't scare him off before we even made it to a wedding."

Well, she wasn't wrong, and Ian couldn't fight it. He liked to think he could let Perri move on so long as she was happy, but he knew deep down that he would cause more mischief than anything to see if the man was even worthy of being near his ex-wife.

Shrugging in acceptance, they left the conversation behind in favor of comfortable silence.

"You know. . ." Perri's voice was soft against Ian's chest, "All of our problems always seemed so small whenever we were here."

"Maybe it's the mountains," Ian suggested, "And the feeling of being so far away from reality."

"Bloody Hotel Alyeska," Perri said with a small smile and a shake of her head.

She felt her ex-husband nod in agreement, "Bloody Hotel Alyeska."

How many nights does it take to count the stars?

That's the time it would take to fix my heart

Oh, baby, I was there for you

All I ever wanted was the truth, yeah, yeah

How many nights have you wished
someone would stay?

Lie awake only hopin' they're okay

I never counted all of mine

If I tried, I know it would feel like infinity

— "Infinity" by One Direction

Perri had discovered her new favorite place, and for a while after the realization, she uncomfortable with it. But as time went on, well, she just decided she might as well embrace it.

Taking advantage of the moment—like she did as often as she could with the reality of both of them returning to university looming in the very near future—Perri made herself comfortable laying on Ian. Her chin resting atop her arms that were folded across his chest. She could feel the soft rumble of his voice against her arms, and she loved it.

Ian looked up into her dark eyes, and Perri smirked a little, confidently holding the eye contact he just initiated.

"Perri?"

She hummed in response and repositioned her head to lean a little closer to him.

Resting his hand lightly on the dip of her back, Perri nearly purred in pleasure at the feeling.

Pushing herself up off of his chest, Perri moved up and hovered over him on her elbows. Chocolate eyes met blue for a long moment before her eyes glided slowly down to gaze at his lips.

Perri leaned closer to him until they shared the same air. His eyes drifted shut and her whisper of his name was the only thing that caused them to open, slight as it may be. Her lips all but brushed his when she spoke.

"Tell me to stop, Ian," she whispered, dragging her eyes away from his lips to hold his gaze once more and wait for his protest.

An impish smirk of his own grew across Ian's face and he shook his head, "No."

A purring chuckle came from the back of Perri's throat, and she smiled. Painfully slow, she closed the remaining distance between their lips and finally got to kiss the man she had been falling for over the last months. She gave a blissful hum as Ian's fingers tunneled into her hair to draw her closer.

Months later, the semester in full swing, both Ian and Perri found a weekend to get away and go home for a couple of days.

Ian glanced at the clock ticking on the wall across the room.

Midnight. *He thought.* Finally.

Looking down at the blonde head pillowed on his chest, Ian's lips lifted in a smile. She was sleeping so well, and she had been through such a long day, he hated to wake her. But wake her he must.

"Hey," he spoke softly, so not to scare her but rouse her gently, "Perri."

Perri felt more than heard his voice as it vibrated in his chest against her ear, and she hummed, taking in a deep breath as she woke. And, oh his cologne. It filled her senses and caused her to sigh in pure content.

"What time is it?" she inquired, still laying in his arms and in no rush to move. Honestly, wishing there was a way to sink a little closer and go back to that wonderful sleep she was just catching up on.

Ian reached up to smooth her hair back away from her face, "A little passed midnight."

"Oh!" Perri was suddenly a little more awake than before. She hadn't realized how late it had gotten. "I'm sorry. Give me five minutes to wake up, and I'll make tracks." She pushed herself up, yawning as she went.

Ian chuckled softly, sitting up with her so he could pull her close again. "Hang on. Come here," he gathered her back into his arms, "You can stay, that's not why I woke you up."

With a hint of that wicked smile that first got his attention, Perri's eyes met his for the first time since she had woken up.

"Not that I'm opposed to the idea at all, but I'm not staying the night with you. Your mother likes me, and I intend to keep it that way. And me staying over will not be helpful to that goal."

"That's not what I meant," Ian smiled, shaking his head and that tantalizing curl of his fell onto his forehead. "Though I am not opposed to the idea either. Just not tonight. I don't think we're there yet."

Now, don't misunderstand. He thought about Perri staying the night, both in innocent and not so innocent ways, often. But he had yet to even tell her that he had fallen in love with her and anything more than what they had now seemed unfair to allow to take place. Especially if Perri didn't even know how deeply she was loved.

He was about to make sure she knew, though.

"I was actually wanting to tell you something and, as long as it's alright with you, I would like to hold you while I say it."

That familiar anxiety leaped to life in her chest, and Perri tried not to let the fear shine in her eyes.

This may be the beginning of the end and she wasn't sure how she would handle it if it was.

So, she nestled close and allowed herself to be held. Taking a deep breath, she tried to soak it all up, hoping to give herself enough to live off of long after Ian was gone. Just in case this was the last time she was held this way by this man who had come to occupy her cautious heart, she wanted to savor it.

"Remember when you asked me to be <u>very</u> certain that I meant it before I told you that I loved you?"

Perri nodded, curling her fingers a little tighter into the softness of his sweater. Memories of their conversation flooding back. Her own voice echoing back in her head, "My own mother told me she loved me and not thirty minutes later threw herself in front of a train!" *Perri's eyes twisted shut at the words. But she was quickly drawn from out of her own thoughts by the sound of Ian's voices once more. Yet another thing she had come to love about him. His ability to draw her out of her own head with just the sound of his voice.*

"Well, I'm glad you did," he said, "But now we have a problem."

Perri felt the tears stinging the back of her eyes and a close-lipped smile spread slightly across her face to match the sadness in her dark eyes, "Oh no."

"You see, the problem is. . . It's been ten months and twenty-three days since you asked that of me, and I've discovered that. . ."

Perri closed her eyes and held her breath, she wasn't ready for this. She had told herself and told herself not to get attached because things hardly ever last. But here she was, and she suddenly realized that she had gotten very attached to this quiet veterinarian without her own consent.

"I never even needed that long to know that I was in love with you. But it gave me time to find even more reasons that I do love you. I held off out of respect of your request and understanding that it mattered to you to know that I truly meant my words. And now I can assure you, Perri Vilein, that I am not going anywhere if I can help it or unless you tell me to go."

He kissed her. He kissed her because he had nothing left to say. He kissed her like he had never kissed any woman before. With such tender promise. His hand cradling her chin. And it wasn't like any fantasy he had ever played out about this moment. It was so much better, because it was real.

Ian slowly leaned away, separating their lips but still close enough to where he could feel Perri's breath.

"I've loved you for so long," she whispered, her eyes welling with unshed tears.

Perri nuzzled her nose against Ian's and leaned in so their lips could collide. It was delicate, almost, but passionate in a way that made Ian's whole body tingle. Perri proceeded to lay back on the couch, keeping their lips locked, and her fingers tunneled deep into his hair, drawing him down to rest on top of her that made him erupt in an all-encompassing heat.

It was the barely-there hint of salt that drew Ian's attention away from the fire coursing through his veins and pulling back he found the source of the taste. Taking Perri's face in his hands, he wiped away the tear trails on her cheeks and laid his forehead against hers.

"You okay?" he asked, his voice barely above a whisper.

Perri nodded reassuringly, though her eyes remained closed, and her fingers curled into his shirt. It was an unconscious thing that she even dared do, but it felt possessive enough that he was charmed by it.

"For a minute there, I wondered if I should have held your hands so you didn't hit me, in case it was too soon and all."

"I love you," Perri said through her laughter and then stopped short. She had not said that phrase exactly yet and now, outside of the moment, well, let's say it made her a little anxious.

Ian felt her tense, and he pushed himself up a little straighter to stare down at her, knowing for certain now after hearing it a second time that he had not imagined it.

"You mean that?"

Ian leaned back down a fraction to hover over Perri as she tugged a bit at his sweater. Holding his hand against her cheek, he smiled the widest, brightest smile he had ever smiled in his whole life it felt like.

Locking eyes with him, so he understood the depth with which she said these next words, "I've never meant anything more."

Sighing in relief, Ian chuckled in an almost giddy state, resting his forehead against her shoulder for a moment as she wrapped her arms around his broad shoulders.

Breathing in the scent of her perfume, Ian couldn't help but smile until his cheeks hurt. Raising himself back up, Ian found Perri's expression to be one of perfect content, and the warmth that spread through his bones was a feeling that he knew only Perri's happiness could give him.

"I love you too, Perri Vilein."

Perri lifted her head and slipped her hands back into Ian's hair. Allowing her eyes to drift shut, she kissed him slowly and purposefully for a long time. When they finally separated to catch their breath, she grinned sheepishly, and a small giggle escaped her lips.

"Say it again," she whispered.

"Per," Ian's voice was close and warmed Perri in a way she had not been warm in years. Sliding her hand up from his chest to rest on his shoulder, she hummed in response. She had so deeply missed just being held by him that she dared not speak too loudly, in case it was all a dream.

"You need to tell them."

His words were heavy, and Perri's eyes twisted shut, her brows knitting together as she dreaded the thought of telling her children her secret.

"I—I know," she murmured.

"Soon."

Perri dropped her forehead to Ian's chin with a grunt. They stayed there for a few minutes, Ian's arms still wrapped around her, holding her, and Perri's palm resting softly on his shoulders. It was nice. Calm. Content.

"They'll be up here soon," she remarked, glancing over at the clock on the nightstand. "I don't know if I'm ready for this."

"You are," Ian assured, "They'll be alright. They have us. And you'll do fine. Maybe just. . . break it to them a little easier than you did me, yeah?" He tossed her a teasing wink.

Chuckling nervously, Perri rubbed at the scar through her eyebrows, "Yeah, that didn't go exactly how I planned. Like, at all."

"Well, I'm glad to know you didn't intentionally set out to kick me in the chest with bluntness."

"Of course not," she replied, returning the wink, "It was only meant to be a small shove."

Feeling content in a way she hadn't in such a long time, Perri couldn't help the smile that broke out across her face. As for Ian, well, he suddenly felt as if he was breathing fresh air once again and not the stale air he had been holding locked up in his lungs since the day Perri left him.

Sitting up, knowing they were quickly running out of time, Perri pulled him closer so that their foreheads were touching, and their noses brushed for a smoldering moment. Somehow that said it all, and Ian let out a shaky breath. His shoulder finally relaxed, and with the last bit of breath leaving his lungs, he laughed softly.

"You know, you're going to give a man a heart attack if you keep up this shite."

Leaning away, moving to slide off his lap and then the bed, Perri looked over her shoulder at him, and her eyes danced mischievously.

"Oh, Ian darling, I know exactly what I'm doing. Always have."

Perri had not been back in her room long when she heard the approach of their children, and her stomach dropped like a ball of lead through the floors beneath her. With timing as perfect as ever, Ian knocked on the adjoining door and waited a few moments before peeking inside.

Perri sat, a little less graceful than usual, down in one of the chairs across from the sofa. As the door opened, she quickly masked the dread that had worked its way into her features.

"Hello, babies," she greeted.

Aspen and Zayden smiled brightly, hugging their father as they crossed the room to embrace their mother.

"You're both freezing," Ian remarked.

"Don't tell me you've been out in this without jackets of some kind, at least."

"We were wearing our thick sweaters, Mum," Zayden replied, "We weren't planning on being out that long, but Penny here thought it would be a good idea to start a snowball fight with me and, well, we got a little carried away."

"Sure, blame it all on me, fetus," Aspen rolled her eyes good-naturedly, for the most part, "It's not like I'm the one who couldn't accept defeat and just let us go inside."

Shaking her head in amusement, Perri tried to ignore the nauseating twist in her stomach. Sensing her anxiety, Ian came to stand behind her chair, resting his hands on the back, not quite touching her but letting her know that he was right there.

Leaning forward in her seat, Perri rested her forearms on her thighs and held out her hands for her children. They each took one of her hands in theirs, and she immediately began rubbing her thumbs back and forth across their knuckles.

Taking a deep breath and lifting her head from staring at their joined hands, Perri began.

"I have something I need to tell you both, but there is no reason to worry, okay." Her voice was steadier than she thought it would be, and it carried that calming tone that she always used when talking about serious things with their children.

Aspen tilted her head a fraction, her brows drawn tight together as if trying to read her mother's thoughts before she voiced them. "Mum?"

"A while ago, I had a suspicious mass appear. It turned out to be nothin', but the doctor told me I should be cautious from then on, just in case," A small slip of the tongue and her accent appeared, tipping everyone off that she was much more nervous than she would lead them to believe, "so I was careful and watched and recently another little mass showed up. . . It's, ehm, it's not lookin' good this time. I don't have any results yet, but I wanted you both to know in case somethin' did happen to come back this time."

She made sure to make eye contact with both of them as she spoke, and now that she was done, Perri waited for one of them to say something. Anything.

"So. . . you have cancer?" Zayden stated more than asked as if trying to comprehend.

"It's possible, darling," she nodded, squeezing his hand.

"When will the results be in?" Aspen asked, her face serious.

Perri gave her daughter's hand a squeeze as well and held her intense stare, "I could have some answers before we leave here, but it's looking like it will be once we return home."

The silence that hung in the air was almost suffocating, but Perri knew that they needed time to process what she had just told them.

"I will let you know as soon as I have some answers, okay," she promised.

The siblings nodded, a couple of tears escaping their eyes without permission. Perri reached up and brushed them tenderly away, utterly gutted by their lost expressions.

"Hey, now," she scolded playfully, "I don't have any results yet, so technically, I'm not even sick until they tell me I am. So, we have nothing to worry about right now, a'righ'."

The two of them nodded once again, neither of them trusting their voices at the moment.

"We are going to be just fine," Perri assured them, and standing up, she gently tugged them to follow suit so she could wrap her arms around their shoulders and hug them close. The three of them stood, latched on to each other for a long time until finally, the siblings took a step back.

"On a better note," Perri informed cheerily to try and bring up the mood, "My ankle is feeling much better, and my wrist feels practically normal again, which means I can go back to gallivanting around with you for the last little bit. But for now, I'm hungry, and

I'm sure you're both starving after raising hell with each other. Ian, fancy a cuppa, at least?"

"I do, actually," he replied, straightening from where he had leaned forward on the back of the chair. "But what I really fancy is getting to beat you racing down those slopes again."

Perri waved away his words as she crossed the room to call in room service, "Unlikely, but you are entitled to your dreams."

11

You're in my arms
And all the world is calm
The music playing on for only two
So close together
And when I'm with you
So close to feeling alive. . .
So close was waiting
Waiting, her with you
And now, forever, I know
All that I wanted
To hold you so close

— "So Close" by Jon McLaughin

The remaining days of their getaway passed much like the first once Perri had an easier time leaving the confines of her room. But now, the days were both familiar and yet entirely different. The shadow of the unknown always loomed in the corners of every activity and made its ominous presence known in the quiet moments. The shift between Perri and Ian was noticeable and something that never failed to thrill their children, who watched delightedly from the sidelines. Aspen was practically floating at the idea that her scheming just may pay off by the end of their vacation. There was much that needed healing and mending between the couple, but finally, having the truth between them instead of secrets was a step.

Some nights found Aspen and Zayden sleeping in their mother's room. Not remotely ashamed to admit that it wasn't at all by accident. One sharing the bed with her, and the other sprawled haphazardly across the sofa. On those nights, Ian couldn't help but peek into the room to take in the peaceful sight of his family. In the peaceful quiet, his chest would swell with unimaginable love for the three of them.

This morning though, found Perri alone in her bed and simply enjoying lying under her thick blankets past seven a.m. But she couldn't seem to keep herself from hoping that a certain someone would make his way into her room. Perri laid there as time ticked by and tried not to think too hard about how much she missed Ian's morning greetings.

* * * * * * * * * * * * * *

"Good morning," Ian whispered, sneaking up behind Perri and pulling her back against him.

"Morning," she tried not to smile too wide, "I missed having you do that."

She shivered when she felt Ian's lips against the soft skin of her neck.

"You're telling me," Ian squeezed her tight for a moment, "A conference that lasts a fortnight is much too long."

Planting a kiss in the slope of her shoulder, Ian buried his nose there for a moment, and Perri couldn't help but sigh contentedly.

Finally realizing what his wife was doing, Ian perked up immediately, "Can I help you make the French Toast?"

* * * * * * * * * * * * * *

Sighing as the memory faded, Perri rolled onto her stomach and persuaded herself to get a little bit more sleep before they started their last day at Hotel Alyeska.

Ian knocked on the adjoining door and waited a moment. When there was no protest or invitation inside, he slowly opened the door to find his ex-wife still asleep. Entering the room softly, he crossed the room and did his best not to wake her too abruptly. As he rounded the edge of the bed, he noticed that her arms were resting above her head, and her fingers were clenched lightly into the pillowcase. It stirred old memories of how she used to hold on to his t-shirt the same way when she slept on his chest. There had been little else in the world that he loved more than that feeling.

Kneeling down to wake her, something familiar caught Ian's eye. A flannel folded neatly on the nightstand, with a sticky note from the hotel's stationery attached to it and his name scrawled across it in Perri's handwriting. Waking his ex-wife momentarily forgotten, Ian turned and took the shirt in his hands. The soft material was vagally recognizable, and the pattern was similar to a flannel he had not seen for lord knows how many years. In fact. . . he had not had this flannel in his closet since the night he had helped Laurel and Perri deliver the colt before they were even officially dating.

Ian's head snapped up, and he turned to look at Perri, who was still snoring softly. Could this really be that same shirt? Had she actually kept it all this time? After everything? A small smile crept onto his face, and his chest warmed at the thought. But with the note accompanying the shirt, he assumed that Perri was going to try and sneak it into his room before they left tomorrow. That was something he couldn't allow her to do. So, he gently removed the note, sliding it into his pocket and looking around, he stashed the flannel deep inside one of her already mostly packed suitcases. He would not be taking that with him today.

The sound of an alarm going off nearly made Ian jump out of his skin. With adrenaline now pumping through him, he made a mad rush back to his room like a child caught with his hand in the cookie jar just before dinner.

Ian walked pointlessly around his room for a few minutes, not wanting to appear creepy as if he had just been in Perri's room to wake her up right before her alarm went off. Which is exactly what he had been doing, but he didn't want to make Perri uneasy like that. So, he waited. Much like he always was, just waiting.

Then he heard the sound of her door opening and closing, followed by the muffled sounds of voices. Moving closer to the door, Ian went to knock but paused when he heard Aspen's voice talking to her mother.

"It's our last night here, Mum, you and Dad should come down to dinner with Zayden and I. And you and Dad should definitely dance one more time before we leave."

Ian smirked a little and shook his head.

"Penny."

He could see Perri shaking her head and trying to fight off the amused look on her face.

"You're flirting with him, Mum. You might as well dance."

"I am not."

Her tone was very insistent, and Ian chuckled quietly.

"That's bullocks. But whatever you say, Mum."

Gathering himself so that they wouldn't know he had heard their conversation, Ian waited a moment then knocked.

"Is that Dad?" He could hear her excitement and knew the impish gleam in her eyes must be looking exactly like her mother's.

"Well, my love, I'm not really sure who else it would be." The statement was followed by a small laugh before she called, *"It's open. Come on in."*

"Good morning, ladies," Ian greeted, "Lovely day to be on the slopes."

Smoothing out the soft wrinkles in her dress, Perri turned and analyzed her appearance in the full-length mirror. Turning this way and that to see all angels. She smiled a fraction, having not expected it to look this good on her. But even she had to admit, this was a great dress, and it fit her perfectly. It hugged her form in all the right places, and Perri could feel her younger self's slightly cocky nature coming up for air.

About that time, Perri caught sight of movement in the doorway and met Ian's gaze in the mirror just over her shoulder.

She knew that look.

She loved it.

So Perri turned to face him and smirked, her brow quirking slightly as she watched her husband's face with sharp eyes.

"What do you think?"

"Um, I . . ." Ian fumbled for words as his eyes slowly raked down and back up her frame a time or two. "I really love it. A lot."

Perri hummed her approval and closed the distance between them. Reaching out, she rested her forearms atop his broad shoulders and tunneled her fingers into Ian's hair. Leaning in close, she lifted her eyes to meet his gaze and whispered, "How much?"

Ian's arms wrapped around her middle, and he captured her lips in a deep, searing kiss. A kiss that he didn't allow to last too long, but that definitely promised more.

"You know, when you say things like that we never get anywhere on time."

Chuckling softly, more like a purr, Perri's head tilted forward, and her forehead met his shoulder.

"I know."

* * * * * * * * * * * * * *

Perri stood studying her reflection in the mirror. Her daughter had been very persuasive this morning and convinced everyone that their last night should be spent in the restaurant downstairs, enjoying the atmosphere for a while longer. At Aspen's request, they were all dressing up a bit for the occasion and, if Perri was being honest, she was quite relishing it.

Deciding that she was finally pleased with how she looked, Perri grabbed her room key and went out into the hall. She tried not to seem too happy when Ian exited his room at the same time, dressed in her favorite suit of his.

"Hello," she greeted, and Ian's eyes snapped up from adjusting his jacket.

His arms dropped to his sides as he took her in, and Perri couldn't help the way her chest swelled just a bit at his attentions.

Ian cleared his throat, "Um, hello."

Shooting him a charming smile, Perri gently bumped the back of her hand against his and tilted her head in the direction of the stairs. As if nothing had changed, Ian followed willingly.

As they crossed the restaurant to their table, per usual, they saw their children were already seated and waiting a little impatiently to order. The siblings watched as Ian said something that made Perri laugh and reaching out, she brushed her hand down his arm. To which Zayden elbowed his sister in the side and she looked over at him with excitement dancing in her eyes.

Greetings mingled as Perri and Ian sat down, and Aspen seized her opportunity.

"Mum, you are a shameless flirt."

Looking at her daughter with a wide-eyed expression, both shocked but knowing exactly what she was talking about, Perri gave an awkward laugh.

"What?"

"But only with Dad, which I find very interesting," Aspen continued and then brought her attention to their father. "Don't look so smug, Dad. You're as bad as she is."

Perri turned, and that wicked smirk which first got his attention spread across her face. Her dark eyes squinted, just a fraction, with pleasure that it was obvious he was just as bad. Her single dimple appearing in her right cheek as she smirked.

By the grace of God, their waiter appeared, and their conniving children were distracted by the prospect of food.

Dinner carried on with conversation about the day, their favorite parts of the vacation, and what was coming up when they got back home. Everyone avoided bringing up what was next for Perri, besides her catching up on designs for some grand hotel in Dover. As the evening went on, they moved over to the bar side of the restaurant and settled in to listen to the music.

While their children were up at the bar to order more drinks, Perri slid out of her seat and came to stand behind Ian. Resting her hands on his shoulders in a feather-light touch, she leaned down to where her lips were all up brushing his ear.

"Dance with me? It's our last chance."

The sound of a piano intro started, and Ian stood, offering Perri his hand as they walked out onto the dance floor. Then the soulful voice of Gwen McCrae came over the speakers, and Perri's heart clenched tight in her chest. Maybe she should have waited to see what song was going to play next before she got so eager to be in Ian's arms.

Maybe I didn't treat you
Quite as good as I should have
And maybe I didn't love you
Quite as often as I could have
Little things I should have said and done
I just never took the time
You were always on my mind, yeah
You were always on my mind

Perri wrapped her arm around his shoulders and held herself close so he wouldn't see the mist in her eyes. It still thrilled her how Ian was just the right height for her to rest her nose atop his shoulder and breath in the smell of his cologne. His scent was what she chose to focus on as she tried not to think too much on the words of the song they were now dancing to.

Maybe I didn't hold you
All those lonely, lonely times
And I guess I never told you
I'm so happy that you're mine
If I made you feel second best
I'm so sorry, I was blind
You were always on my mind, yeah

You were always on my mind

Ian was idly running his fingers up and down the expanse of Perri's lower back, and he could feel the warmth of her skin radiating soothingly through the material of her dress. Without thought, he mimicked an old habit of his from years gone by. Ian leaned in and softly nudged just underneath Perri's ear, inhaling her perfume. He knew he had to savor this moment for as long as he could because God only knew when he would have this chance again. If ever.

Tell me
Tell me that your sweet love hasn't died
Give me
Give me one more chance to keep you satisfied

Perri drew their interlocked hands in close and held the back of his hand against her chest. The song was quickly coming to a close, and all she could think about was how tomorrow they would be returning to reality.

Little things I should have said and done
I just never took the time
You were always on my mind, yeah
You were always on my mind

"You were always on my mind," Ian's voice was gravelly in her ear as he spoke the last line of the song.

Reaching up, Perri cradled the back of his head in her hand, just to keep him close a moment longer.

"Me too," she whispered, her voice trembling a bit more than she would have liked.

Not wanting to make a scene, Perri ripped herself away from Ian and somehow felt her heartbreaking all over again. Still holding onto his hand, she gathered herself and walked them back to their table in the corner where their children sat waiting.

"Who's dancing with me next?" she smiled, and both of them shot up at the same time. Laughing, Perri gestured for them to sit back down. "No more slow songs, though. I want to bust a move or two before we leave here."

A handful of songs played until finally a good beat started, and the three of them were headed for the dance floor with what some may deem "too much" enthusiasm. Ian turned in his chair, smiling as he watched his greatest loves dance together like there was no one else in the room. Memories of him coming home to dance parties in their living room and, as their kids got older, "dancing it out" sessions in the kitchen. Perri knew the power of dancing, and she made sure to pass it on to their children.

Ian recalled driving home with Zayden for the first time. The two-year-old was sleeping soundly in the backseat, and one of the first things Perri said was how they would have to start teaching him how to dance. Ian smiled at the memory of her reason why they had to, because "I love Drake and Shonda, but I know neither one of them could dance, so they definitely couldn't teach him". At the time, that was the best way they knew how to cope with their friends shocking death, remember the funny things and raise their orphaned son as their own.

Someone coming to stand beside his chair interrupted Ian's thoughts, startling him a bit.

"Can I join you?" the woman asked.

"Actually, the table is full," he replied politely, trying not to be rude, "They're just out dancing." Shooting a quick, almost panicked look into the crowd, he hoped one of the three saw it.

"Well, I doubt they'll mind if I keep their spot warm while you wait."

Taking a chair, she moved it a few inches closer to Ian's and sat down. "So, how long are you staying?"

Just as Ian opened his mouth to excuse himself, he felt a familiar hand come to rest on his upper arm.

"He's here with someone else," Perri informed, her brow raised as she subtly staked her claim, and Ian quickly stood. Sliding her hand up to his shoulder, she lifted her eyes to meet Ian's grateful expression. "Take me upstairs?"

"Of course," Ian offered her his arm, "Excuse us."

Perri shot the woman a very quick, very small smile before they turned to walk out of the bar.

Ian came to a stop just outside the doorway, and Perri looked up at him in confusion. Immediately reading his sudden halt as displeasure with being pulled away, she was a little surprised.

"I'm sorry, the kids and I saw your face, and I just thought that—"

Ian leaned down and brushed his lips against Perri's. It was featherlight and over before she could even react, but that didn't stop her heart from racing in her chest.

"Thank you," he said, and Perri could feel his breath brush over her lips.

The only response Perri could muster was a soft, "Mm-hm."

The sound of someone clearing their throat behind them made the pair jump apart. Their attentions ripped away from one another immediately.

"So sorry to interrupt," Aspen smirked wickedly.

Ian closed the gap between them and hugged their children, "No, I'm sorry for interrupting your dance, but I cannot tell you how grateful I am that I was rescued."

"The song was almost over anyway," Zayden laughed, "And you looked pretty panicked, Dad. We couldn't exactly just leave you there."

"It just wouldn't have been fair," Perri agreed, "As much as I was amused by watching your squirm."

That was very much a lie. As soon as she noticed the woman talking with her ex-husband, Perri was immediately burning with that same possessiveness she could never seem to get under control, especially when they had been together. And as soon as they had seen Ian's silent cry for help, the three of them had sprung into action, and Perri was more than happy to interrupt whatever that woman thought she was doing. It was currently taking every bit of willpower Perri had not to still be holding on to Ian in some way, but she had to remind herself that she didn't have that right anymore. As much as she may want it, she had given it up.

They all began making their way upstairs slowly, talking and making plans for tomorrow morning. Then went their separate ways with mingled good nights and sleep wells filling the stairway.

"You nearly killed me the way you got me away from her," Ian remarked as they went down the hall toward their rooms.

"What do you mean?" Perri asked, then thinking about it for a moment, her face flushed just a bit. "Oh. . . That."

"Yes," Ian chuckled, "*That*. You can't look at me that way and then tell me to take you upstairs."

Shooting him an apologetic face, "Sorry. I didn't think that one through. But I got you away at least."

Ian nodded in agreement, "That you did."

Perri unlocked the door to her room and took a fraction of a step inside. "Do you want to maybe. . . come in for a minute? She cut our night much shorter than I thought it would be."

"If you would like I'll come in for a bit." How could he refuse?

Smiling brightly, Perri opened the door fully, and they walked inside. "I'm going to change. I'll be right back."

The bathroom door clicked shut, and Ian took off his jacket and shoes, getting comfortable himself before settling in on the sofa. He didn't have to wait long and Perri exited the bathroom in her blue pajama set he had bought for her shortly before they separated. But Ian didn't notice that, he was much too taken with the woman wearing the clothes. This was the Perri that so few people saw, soft and content to be quiet. The Perri who wanted to be held and leave the control of the room to someone else for a change.

Don't misunderstand. Ian first fell smitten with the confident and almost cocky Perri. But when he finally got to meet soft Perri, well, he knew he was done for then. This woman had bewitched him, and he absolutely loved it. There was no side of Perri he did not adore, it simply wasn't possible for him.

"Ian?"

Snapping to reality, he met Perri's amused gaze, "Hmm?"

"I said do you want to go change while I put on a movie or something?"

"Oh, yeah," Ian got up and grabbed his jacket, "Yeah, I'll be right back."

He so badly wanted to add, "please don't change your mind," but one look at Perri's face, and he knew she was as desperate to spend their remaining time together as he was.

"He's still watching," Perri said, and Ian went to look over his shoulder, "Don't look! Don't look!" She chuckled a bit, "He'll leave eventually."

Hearing that quiet laugh and seeing the way her eyes danced in amusement, it brought back that burning in his chest, and he just stared in awe.

"Do I—Do I have your permission to make him jealous?" Ian asked softly in her ear, and it was a question that had Perri jumping back just a few inches to look into his face. Mischievousness and badgering were two of her favorite things after all and who was she to pass up such an opportunity.

"Yes," her response was instantaneous, and Ian felt a smile tugging at the corner of his lips.

Even though they were seated, Ian was towering over Perri in the most attractive way. His eyes were gleaming with mischief as he moved his knees between Perri's.

Ian slid his knuckles along her jaw, so light it almost tickled. His fingers caressed down her neck, his eyes focusing on the freckle just to the left of her throat. His hand around the base of Perri's throat, it was gentle but possessive and totally inappropriate for public viewing. But her ex was watching, and Ian was prepared to give him a show.

Perri's body ignited, and she shivered as she waited for Ian to close the distance between them. She noted the soft smirk on his lips as she listened to his breathing intensify. She was almost certain Ian could feel her heart beating through her dress. It was not on account of Luka watching their every move, either. It was her body's instinctive reaction to just being close to Ian.

"You look so lovely in this dress," Ian murmured against her lips, his free hand idly sliding around Perri's waist. This man's accent was lethal, cutting through Perri like a knife through soft butter.

Would Perri even be herself if she did not take initiative and try to gain the upper hand in whatever game they were playing? Of course not.

She wrapped her hand around the back of Ian's neck and crashed their lips together with a loud, satisfied sigh. She had not kissed him since that night a few weeks ago when they had been lying on the couch. Ever since she had been starving to feel his lips against her own again since the moment, they had draw back for air.

Ian was momentarily shocked, though he wasn't sure why. He should definitely be used to Perri's assertiveness by now, but then again, he wondered if he would ever not be surprised by her.

Their lips moved in chaotic harmony. The slow tenderness of their first kiss was long forgotten. This kiss lacked restraint and modesty, and Perri found that she couldn't resist the urge to draw Ian as close as possi-

ble by wrapping her arms around his shoulders. The kiss tasted like new beginnings, and she could not wait.

Ian pulled away first, and he stared at Perri for a long time. They shared the same shallow breaths as they made up for lost oxygen. Ian's pulse was drumming in his ears as he tried to reorient himself. The air between them was thick and hot and made of pure electricity.

"Is he still watching?" Ian inquired after a time, still trying to will his pulse back to its normal rhythm.

"Who?" Perri replied, dazed.

* * * * * * * * * * * * * * *

Perri smiled to herself at the memory. That was the first time they had helped each other when they were receiving unwanted attention. And something in Perri knew that tonight's intervention still would not be their last.

The adjoining door opened and in came Ian, looking comfortable and just as appealing as ever.

"There you are," Perri greeted, "I was beginning to think you had bailed on me and decided not to come back."

"Not a chance," Ian replied, crossing the room to sit back down on the sofa. "What are we watching?"

Coming to stand beside him, Perri laid a hand on Ian's shoulder and directed him to rest his back against the arm of the couch. Not yet fully understanding, he swung a leg up to stretch out across the cushions. Nodding once in approval, Perri rounded the sofa and sat down between Ian's legs, laying back against his chest.

Ian merely sat there for a moment, surprised and a little unsure of what was happening maybe, but definitely not complaining.

Once she was comfortable, Perri sighed and answered his previous question, "I don't know yet. I hadn't seen anything that caught my interest."

Finally deciding on National Lampoon's European Vacation, Perri couldn't hold back one last sigh at the feeling of Ian stroking her arm absentmindedly. His fingertips grazed up the front of her arm from her wrist to her elbow, and then he would run the back of his fingers down her arm. Again and again. A peaceful pattern that made Perri want to melt and sink further back against him.

They eventually migrated to the bed and had a different movie playing in the background as they simply sat together, alone with their own thoughts.

"We've raised some pretty smashing kids, Per."

Ian's voice broke the silence, and Perri hummed in reply.

"Yeah, we really have. They're probably too smart for their own good, though."

Ian's soft laughter reverberated through his chest, and Perri tried to memorize the feeling of it.

"You're probably right," he agreed, "You know, I had a thought the other day that maybe they planned for this to happen all along."

"What?"

"*This*. Us. Again."

Perri's insides went cold, and her stomach dropped. If anyone knew their children, it was her and Ian. He thought that a few days before, and Perri had become a little suspicious of it herself with Aspen's bold commentary about her flirtatiousness with her ex-husband.

Oh no. This can't be happening. I didn't bring them here to disappoint them.

Perri hummed again in response, her mind running a thousand miles a second, though she did well hiding it.

* * * * * * * * * * * * *

Ian pressed a kiss subtly to her hair, the woman now resting gently against his shoulder pressed her nose into his neck, humming softly.

"If someone cut me into pieces," Perri began, rolling a lock of thick hair at the base of his neck between her fingers, "And all that was left of me was my hands, would you know that they were mine?"

"Yes," Ian replied without hesitation, his eyes closed contentedly as she snuggled against him. "Why'd you ask?"

Perri shrugged, "I watched a Dateline London episode."

"Ah," Ian nodded in understanding, holding her against his chest a little tighter.

"How would you know?"

Ian opened his eyes then, "Well, I'd start by looking for the smudges of ink and lead all over the skin." He teased, taking Perri's hand in his own and playing with her sketch blackened fingers tenderly. "There is also a small scar on your right index finger. Just across your knuckle. And you have a small birthmark almost shaped like a flame on the pad of your left pinky."

Perri glanced at her hands, and her brows pulled together as she wondered how they were her hands and yet these were things she had forgotten.

"And if those were impossible to see, I would look for a torn thumbnail on our right hand," Ian continued, "Because you chew at it when you're agitated—"

"I do not," Perri insisted.

"Yes," he laughed, "You do."

Perri said nothing as Ian wrapped his hand around her wrist. Their eyes met as he brought her hand to his lips and placed a lingering kiss in her palm, before lacing their fingers together.

"Or perhaps I'd use muscle memory," he stated, giving her hand a gentle squeeze.

"You would hold my cold, dead hand, would you?"

"If that's what it took to find you."

She seemed pleased with that, and Perri moved to kiss him. One hand sliding into his hair while she shifted them a little on the couch beneath them. After a few minutes of languid kisses, Perri laid her head back against Ian's chest as their fingers danced together.

Her wedding ringing catching the light, Ian smiled softly, and he twisted it on her finger. "Or I could look for this, I suppose."

"One would presume that anyone who dismembered me would strip me of my jewelry first," Perri remarked.

"I'd look for the tan line then," he shrugged, "Given how you refuse to take it off, it would be there."

Pushing herself up off of his chest just enough, Perri looked down at him.

"Are you complaining that I never remove the wedding ring you gave me?"

"Complaining? Definitely not," Ian answered. "I'd prefer that you never removed it ever."

"That's what I thought," she smiled a little smug.

* * * * * * * * * * * * *

She stayed lying on Ian's chest for a while longer, her mind slowly quieting but never stopping. Perri was content in her ex-husband's embrace, and she wanted to enjoy it for as long as she could, so she tried not to let her thoughts get the better of her and ruin what little time they had left away from reality. But, as it had always been, Perri's mind was too loud and her heart too afraid of being broken beyond repair.

"Ian," her voice held a note of hesitancy.

He hummed, a habit he had picked up from Perri many years before, and she could feel it against her cheek. His arms tightened just a fraction, and she fought the urge to just nestle closer and forget everything she was about to say.

After a few long moments, Ian's eyes opened, and he tilted his head to look down into her face.

"Per. . . What are you thinking?"

She could see the anxiousness in his eyes and she hated herself all over again.

Why did I do this to us.

Her fingers curled into the soft fabric of his shirt, and her eyes darted away from his to instead focus on the rise and fall of his chest.

"We've rekindled something that cannot survive outside of this place."

"Perri, I—I don't understand, I thought—" Ian began.

"And I wish you had been right." Perri forced herself to sit up and look away.

"Perri, if this about—"

She did not let him finish, "It's not. You know the truth now, but that doesn't make it any less difficult for—" she gestured in the air between them, "*this* to work in the real world."

"But, Perri, we did it before," Ian said, smiling hopefully, "We can do it again."

"I don't think I—" Perri's voice broke, and she found she didn't have the words. At least not the words she could say out loud.

I just can't let you watch me die.

Silence reigned for only a moment, but it was a suffocating moment. Ian broke through it with the heavy sigh of a man who had seen his future, had it within reach and lost it all over again. Hanging his head, Ian ran his fingers through his hair in that familiar way that made Perri then want to reach out and fix what he had tousled.

And with words that would haunt Perri much longer than she would have liked, Ian looked up at her.

"I understand."

Oh, how she wished he would be angry or yell. *How could she do this to them?! What was wrong with her?!* Anything but this sad acceptance of the fact that she was so afraid of breaking them both that she couldn't even allow them their second chance at happiness.

"Good night, Perri," Ian leaned forward, placing a small kiss against her temple, and he walked out.

The door clicked shut delicately behind him, and the dam broke. Baring her teeth and twisting her eyes shut in an attempt to stifle her sobs, Perri clamped a hand over her mouth as the tears fell at their own will.

She had done exactly what she had promised herself she wouldn't, she had dared to allow herself to hope for more. Blinded by the glittering snow and peaceful air of the one place they had always come to escape life.

She had done this to them and despite her hopes of leaving here having mended some of the damage she had caused, somehow she had made more.

But it didn't matter. Very soon, they would be returning to ordinary life, and things would repair themselves in time.

Or at least that was what she had to tell herself.

12

Someday I might find myself
looking in your eyes
But for now, we'll go on living separate lives
Yes for now, we'll go on living separate lives
Separate lives

— "Separate Lives" by Phil Collins

The plane ride was quiet, and not much was said between any of them. A sadness hung in the air as they all began trying to readjust to the coming life outside of Hotel Alyeska. Perri and Ian would once again be separated by both space and relationship. Aspen and Zayden would be heading back to their universities to pursue their careers. The happy family that existed while in Alaska seemed to only be able to exist while frozen in the midst of the snow-covered mountains.

Luggage wheels rolling across pavement was the only sound among them as they made their way to their train platforms. Perri and Ian were seeing their children off to Manchester, where Aspen would spend the remainder of her vacation terrorizing her little brother.

The train whistle blew loudly, and hearts sank like stones to a river bottom.

"This is it then," Aspen turned teary eyes to her parents and hugged them both. Locking her arms around her mother, she whispered, "Thank you for agreeing to this."

"My darling, I had the best time," Perri assured, "Thank *you*."

Taking a step back, Aspen hugged their father and tried not to think too much about how her plan had failed. Their parents were not back together and now seemed as if they were hardly speaking all over again. Her lungs constricted in her chest, and she sniffled softly before letting go and allowing Zayden to take her place.

Perri reached out and took her hand, drawing her close.

"Baby, come here." The woman held her tight, and Aspen cried quietly into her mother's shoulder. Zayden came to stand beside them, to which Perri opened one of her arms and pulled him in as well. "My little darlings, you have no idea how much I'm going to miss being with you all every day. We'll do this again, yeah? Next year, huh. If you two aren't off taking the world by storm, of course."

Both of them leaned back to meet their mother's own tearful expression. Cradling their faces in her hands, Perri smiled reassuringly and planted a kiss on each of their foreheads. "We good?"

They nodded.

"Good. Alright, babies, I will see you in a few weeks when I come up to see that you're getting settled for classes."

Ian approached and laid a hand on Perri's shoulder, to which she tried not to react.

"And I'll be popping in shorty. As soon as I make sure that no one has burned down my clinic while I was away."

"Let us know when you make it home, okay." Perri adjusted her son's jacket, pulling it close around him to protect him from the misting air of London. "Try not to cause too much trouble. Both of you."

"Don't worry, Mum," Zayden teased, "We will leave Manchester in one piece. For now, at least."

Rolling her eyes, Perri sighed good-naturedly, "Oh wonderful. I'm so relieved."

The last call whistle blew, and Perri ushered them forward, "Now, on with you both and we'll talk to you soon. I love you."

The siblings jumped up onto the entrance car just as the train began to slowly pull away. Farewells and I love you's mingled as Perri and Ian waved, watching their children until they could see them no more. The two of them already feeling lost in a way without their children nearby.

They remained silent but lingered, not really wanting to say goodbye.

The unexpected ringing of Perri's phone ripped them away from their thoughts and frightened her into action.

Quickly pulling it from her pocket, Perri stared at the screen in silence.

"Let me guess, they left something with you, didn't they," Ian chuckled, expecting it to be their children.

"No," she answered slowly, her eyes never leaving the screen, "No, not the children."

"Perri?" he asked, his suspicions making him anxious, "Who is it?"

"It's, ehm, it's my doctor."

"Perri, answer it!" Ian insisted, and she turned to him with a panicked expression, "I'll stay right here until you're done."

Nodding mutely, Perri answered the call on its last ring.

"Hello. . . Yes, this is she. . . Yes, I'm so sorry, I only just got back into the country. . . Okay." A long silence followed as Perri listened to what the person on the other line was saying. She nodded slowly, thoughtfully, as tears formed in her eyes. "Yes, yes, ehm, thank you. I will—I will be in touch as soon as I get home."

Hanging up, Perri's hand fell to her side as she stared down the tracks.

"Per?" Ian felt his stomach knotting and the knowledge of what she was about to tell him, freezing the blood in his veins. "What did they say?"

"I—I have cancer."

The world came crashing down around them, and yet somehow both of them could not find the ability to cry.

"It's, ehm, it's small so. . . Hopefully with surgery to remove the mass and it being in early stages and all, a few rounds of medication should do the trick. But I have to make an appointment to discuss things more fully with her soon."

There was nothing to say. The moment had come, and there was nothing to be done.

"Can I. . ." Ian hesitated to ask, "Can I hold you for a minute?"

Perri nodded and turned to face him finally, allowing herself to be gathered close and held tightly for a time as everything sank in.

She felt as if she were reacting all wrong to the news. She felt numb and yet so afraid, all in the same terrible moment. She had known this was the most likely result, but that one small corner of her mind had dared hope that she was wrong. It's that one small corner of hope that is always so so dangerous. But how else would we survive this troubled world without it.

"Do you have a train to catch?" Perri asked as she moved out of his arms, wishing somehow that Ian's answer would be no.

"I do," he answered, his eyes studying her profile, "What about you?"

"Mm-hm," she nodded slowly, looking back at the train tracks briefly.

"Will you be alright?" Perri could sense the concern in his question and met his gaze.

"Yeah," she smiled fondly, but the touch of sadness in her eyes dimmed her usual glow, "Yeah, I will be."

Neither one made any attempt at moving away from each other, if anything, they somehow drifted closer. Their hearts were so deeply and irrevocably intertwined that they couldn't help themselves.

"Thank you."

The corners of Perri's lips lifted slightly, and her brows pulled together in a confused expression. Tilting her head a bit, Ian's heart all but ruptured in his chest.

"For these last two weeks," Ian continued, "And for. . . For telling me. I wish it hadn't happened to us, but now at least I understand. So. . . thank you."

Tears filled Perri's eyes, and she nodded, "Yeah. I'm—I'm so sorry about. . . You deserved to know much sooner."

"Well thank you for telling me now," Ian gave a small smile.

As he turned to walk away, Perri felt for sure that she would never breathe again if she had to watch him leave at this moment.

"I—" she hesitated. Did she dare voice what she was feeling? Would he understand what she meant? She was willing to chance it and hope he knew what she really wanted to say. "I wish we had had more time."

Seeing his eyes soften and watching as he closed the distance between them once more, Perri knew he understood. Just as he always did.

Leaning down, he cradled her face in his hand and placed a lingering kiss on her cheek. Perri fought the urge to lean into him, but she couldn't stop the sigh that left her lips as her eyes twisted shut. If only they had just had more time.

It took everything she had not to fall to pieces, and it didn't help that the London sky had decided to start watering the earth with its own tears.

"Do you want my brolly?" Ian offered, taking a step away, and Perri liked to imagine his heart was breaking as badly as her own. As awful as that was.

"No," she shook her head and wiped her eyes, "Thank you, but you have more of a walk than I do."

Nodding once, Ian gave her one last smile, "See you around, Per."

"Bye," she gave a small wave and watched Ian turn and leave.

Th rain was now pouring in sheets, cold and cutting as most London rains were. Stinging the skin of the people caught in its onslaught, whether they were wearing coats or not.

And Perri stood there.

She hated herself for it, but she couldn't bring her feet to move from the spot where they had said goodbye.

Am I willing to let him walk away all over again?

She missed Alaska so much. The place where things were so simple and the real world seemed further away than it did standing here in the chilled rain.

Well? Are you going after him or not?

Was she willing to swallow some pride and go find him before he boarded his train?

Do you think love could be enough again for us one day?

His voice echoed in her head as she remembered their conversation while lounging in her room alone. She could almost feel the warmth of his hand against her cheek.

"Bloody splendid," she huffed. Her mind was made up.

The thing about you,
Got me believing
That all my leavin'
Was much too soon
And the thing about you,
I can't deny it
And I can't hide it
That's why I'm coming home
The thing about you

— "The Thing About You" by Chloe Agnew

Ian drew his coat tighter around him as he made his way through the crowd. His shoulders felt heavier than before, carrying the weight of losing Perri a second time. But at the same time, they were lighter at the knowledge that it wasn't because their love had died. It was still there. He knew it was alive and well deep beneath the surface of many things. Just not strong enough to keep them together in the end. Life and its struggles were too much and too terrifying.

He hated it.

But there was little he could do. Perri had made her decision and once she did that, there was no changing her mind. Now at least with the truth out, they could form some sort of bond. Little as it may be it would have to be enough.

Enough could get him through.

Couldn't it?

Taking off, Perri ran through the rain. Splashing through puddles that had grown in minutes, she paid no mind to the way the water was soaking the edges of her jeans.

She knew Ian's platform well and the fastest way to get to it, even though a sea of people. Coming up on it, Perri searched the crowd of hunched figures and hidden faces. She knew Ian had to be here somewhere waiting.

"Did you change your mind about the umbrella?" Ian's voice came from close behind her, and Perri whipped around.

"I don't want your bloody umbrella, barmy," she stated, "I want you."

A confused look crossed Ian's face, and Perri did her best not to get irritated. But here she was, running through the rain like some lovesick idiot from those dramatic movies that she hated. Then to really finish it off, she was about to have to bear her feelings in the middle of a crowded train station. And here he was, looking confused.

"I never wanted to be this way," she said, her voice stern as she tried to figure out how to put into words what she wanted to say, "I *never* wanted it. But here I am because I can't—I'm not sayin' let's get married. I'm sayin' that. . ." Lifting her eyes, she met Ian's gaze as the realization was just beginning to brighten his features. Perri couldn't help but smile just a bit, and her tone took on a softer edge, "I can live without you. I just really don't want to anymore. So please, when we walk away from here, I don't want this to be the last I see of you for the next six months. I—I miss you, and I want to. . . I want to try."

Without a word, Ian took a half a step closer, leaving little space between them. Perri's breath hitched in her throat at the feeling of his finger sliding under her chin, tilting her head up just a fraction. Leaning in ever so slowly, Ian gave her time to turn and run away if she wanted to. But she didn't move. She didn't dare. She wanted this too much. Perri's eyes drifted shut, and she waited for the feeling of Ian's lips moving against her own.

Lips met and warmth coursed through their veins, the rain chilled world fading away around them. Ian's hands came to splay wide against Perri's back, pulling her in as close as possible. Perri responded in kind, gripping the lapels of his coat to keep him as near as she could. Time went by like the dripping of thick molasses from a spoon, but it was never enough.

Finally breaking apart for air, Ian's hands slid over the slope of Perri's back to skitter up and cup the jut of her elbows. Giving her the knowledge that she was free to go if she wanted, but he didn't want to release her entirely just yet.

"Are you sure?" he asked.

Perri answered his question with her own, "Have I ever ran after something I wasn't entirely sure about?"

Laughing, Ian shook his head, "No, no I don't think you have."

Perri had the brightest smile. You wouldn't always know it, especially recently, but Ian felt as if he could combust when her face broke out in the widest smile he had seen in many years.

Smiling his own megawatt grin, Ian brushed Perri's wet locks from her face, "Well, I suppose they were successful after all. Even though they will never admit, that was their goal with this trip."

Perri laughed, "Oh no, they'll never own up to that. But I can guarantee they will be ecstatic when we show up together at their dorms in a few weeks."

"Already making plans, are we?" Ian waggled his eyebrows teasingly, and Perri purred a chuckle, smoothing out his lapels as she leaned in close.

"Oh, I have many plans, darling." She let the air between the crackle with attraction for a long moment before swiftly moving away, "But for now, I have a train to catch."

Blinking a few times, Ian shook his head to clear his thoughts as Perri turned to leave.

"I'll see you around, love," she smirked.

"Cheeky!" Ian called over the crowd and the train whistling loud.

Tossing a wink over her shoulder, Ian watched Perri and her devilish smirk walk away into the hoard of raincoats and umbrellas.

For the first time in seven years, one of them walking away did not cause their chests to ache with that hollow emptiness they had become so painfully familiar with. For the first time, this parting of ways held promise for more.

Maybe it's time that we
Gave it another chance
Look at how far we've come
Don't say that we can't
And ev'ry time I take a breath
It's you... It's you

— "The Thing About You"

The weeks had passed, plans were made regarding Perri's condition, and a surgery date was set. Designs for the hotel were sketched, and Ian's clinic had survived his absence. All the while, the two of them remained in contact throughout their days.

Finally, the day arrived, and the two of them met at one of their favorite restaurants just outside of Liverpool. Both hoping that they could eat in peace without being recognized by too many and being peppered with questions.

Perri sat at a booth toward the back, waiting for Ian to arrive. Not even having to look up from her menu, she slid her feet out of the booth across from her, opening up the seat for her husband as he rapidly approached.

"So sorry, I tried to make it on time."

Lowering the menu, she gazed at him with her intense dark eyes for a long moment before smiling, "Don't worry, you're not late. I was just able to get out of work a little earlier than I originally planned."

Ian released a sigh of relief and reached across to hold her hand, "How are you feeling?"

"Better now that we have an actual plan and things in motion. The kids are feeling a little bit better too, I think."

Bringing her hand to his lips, Ian pressed a kiss to the back of her fingers, "Do you. . . Do you want me there? You know, on the day of everything."

Her eyes softened, and Perri nodded, "I really do. As long as it's not too much trouble."

"You are never trouble, Perri Vilein," Ian assured, kissing her fingers once more, "Well, except for that one time—"

Perri cut him short with a quick slap across the arm, and he laughed, holding up his free hand in a placating manner.

"Alright, alright, you win. You've never been any trouble in your life."

"That's right," Perri replied, looking superior for a moment before her façade cracked with her own laughter.

The sound of the little bell on the door ringing as someone entered drew Perri's attention over Ian's shoulder. Immediately her eyes widened a fraction as she recognized the gaggle of old ladies walking.

"Perri, what—?"

"Don't! Turn around," she instructed softly, "We will never have any peace while we try to eat if you do."

"What are you talking about?" Ian questioned.

"Mrs. Owens and her friends just came in."

Picking up a menu, Ian held it up to appear like he was looking at it while really he was just hiding Perri's face.

"Can you still see them?" he asked quietly.

"Yes."

"Where are they?"

There was a pause.

"Per?"

Lowering the menu just in time to catch his ex-wife-turned-girl-friend sliding out of her booth.

"What are you doing?" he hissed urgently, visibly resisting the impulse to grab her wrist and pull her back down.

"I am going to hang myself in the bathroom," she answered, turning tail and not making any attempt to soften the reverberating clack of the heels of her boots as she practically ran out of sight.

Not a minute passed;

"Ian Astankova, is that you?" Mrs. Owens crooned, coming to stand beside Ian.

Sometime later, having gone miraculously undiscovered by Mrs. Owens, the couple stood from finishing their lunch.

"I'll get lunch, considering I sacrificed you to the vultures earlier," Perri made an apologetic face.

Ian's hand slid across the small of her back as he walked behind her, a kiss landing on her shoulder as he fell in stride beside her.

"It's alright," he replied, "I would take on more than a few pesky old women for you."

"My hero," Perri chuckled, linking her arm with his.

Opening his wallet at the register, a familiar image caught Perri's eye, and she couldn't help but take a closer look. Tucked in the heart of his wallet was not only a picture of Aspen and Zayden on their first days at university but one of her as well.

It wasn't a posed picture at all. Instead, it was one snapped at random while Perri was laughing at something Ian had done. Her blonde hair was tied back in a ponytail, but the wild curls were still everywhere. Her dark eyes were dancing with amusement, and her smile was beaming.

Quickly looking away, when Ian went to close the wallet, Perri acted as if she hadn't seen a thing. Although she couldn't deny the rush of warmth it sent through her knowing that Ian had probably never once removed that picture from his wallet. This whole time, all these years later, after all the years of coldness and secrets, Ian had kept that picture. Not only had he kept it, he had it with him every day.

Maybe I've broken your
Heart once too many times
Maybe you've moved on
Or maybe you'll still be mine
And ev'ry time I take a breath
It's you... It's you

— "The Thing About You"

The madness that followed their arrival at their children's dorms was ecstatic beyond words. To say that Aspen did not cry would also be a lie. But some moments in time are just too personal and priceless to share with the rest of the world. That being said, we will turn our heads and give the family their privacy as we skip ahead to that same night.

Having decided it was much too late to make the trek back to their homes, with the last train having left hours before, Perri and Ian had put themselves up in a hotel. When the woman at the front desk assumed they wanted a room together, well, they did not correct her. Once they had a room, the couple went to a nearby store to buy some things to sleep in and the other necessities they would need. With plans to go directly back to their room interrupted by the smell of a hole-in-the-wall restaurant, Perri and Ian found themselves waiting for their dinner.

Turning from the old jukebox near their table where she had been choosing some familiar songs, Perri nearly collided with a man standing in her path.

"Blimey!" she exclaimed and took a deep breath.

The man gave a charming smile that, without question, would have worked had Perri not been more charmed by the man just a handful of steps away.

"I couldn't help but notice you over here picking music, and I wondered if you would care for a dance."

"No," Perri answered, still trying to recover, "Ehm, thank you, but no."

"Well, I'm right over there," he gestured with his thumb, "if you change your mind."

Perri nodded once and gave a polite smile before closing the remaining distance between herself and where Ian sat at their table.

"You could have said yes, Per," Ian chuckled a little, knowing how much she loved to dance but also finding it amusing how much the man had managed to surprise her.

Settling back in her chair, Perri shot him a smile with a contented look in her dark eyes, "I came here with you."

Ian didn't quite know how to voice what he wanted to ask, and so he let the moment pass into silence.

It wasn't long, though and Perri turned her eyes back to Ian. "I would really love to dance, though."

And an echo from the past brought a smile to her face.

"I could never deny you anything, Perri Velien."

As they entered their hotel room, they divided up their things they had bought, and Perri took the bathroom to change. Once they were both in something more comfortable, their eyes locked from across the room and the air between them became charged with that familiar, undeniable attraction.

"I—I kept telling myself that it wasn't a date," Ian finally said.

Perri purred a chuckle, "Oh, it most definitely was a date."

Crossing the room with purpose, Ian came to a stop mere inches from Perri.

"I just really want to kiss you right now if you'll let me."

Perri's gaze darkened as she laid her hand against his chest and brought her body almost flush against his, "I certainly won't object."

Crashing together, the couple was immediately locked in a passionate kiss, complete with wondering hands and soft sounds of encouragement. Hands slipping under shirts just to feel the other's skin warm against their palms. Open mouthed kisses traveled to jaws and necks, finding all the familiar sensitive places that made the other gasp and moan with want.

Their feet began moving of their own accord in the direction of the bed. Occasionally stumbling here and there in the unfamiliar room, eventually Perri's knees hit the edge of the mattress, and she readily sat down, pulling Ian down with her, not wanting to waste a single second not kissing him. Shimmying her way up the bed, until her back met the headboard, Ian crawled up with her, continuing his desired attentions to her neck.

You know the hinge during passionate interactions. That second where a decision is made either to continue or to stop. The time for decision-making had arrived, and Perri had no intention of putting a stop to anything. Ian, on the other hand, slowly broke himself away to catch his breath, resting his forehead against Perri's.

"I—I don't want our first time back together to be in some random hotel we didn't even make plans to stay at."

Sighing, Perri tried not to show her disappointment. She also couldn't help but feel a soft warmth spread through her that contrasted the burning flames that had been coursing through her seconds before. This man was too much. Her eyes misted over at the feeling of being so valued and Ian wanting their time together to be special. Even after the countless times, they had had one another and the way they still had the other's bodies memorized, he still wanted this moment to be something to remember.

"Okay," Perri whispered and, opening her eyes, met his gaze. "I suppose I can wait."

Leaning down, Ian kissed the dip between her collarbones as they both waited for their hearts to slow back to their normal pace.

Moving from on top of Perri, Ian sat down beside her and angled his body toward her, stretching his arm out across the low sitting headboard.

Not hesitating a moment, Perri slid closer so that she was nestled comfortably into Ian's side. She felt his nose in her hair and Ian's hand coming to rest on her shoulder, fingers drawing small circles on his bare skin.

"You know," Ian's voice was muffled by her thick hair, "I may have seemed calm, but I saw red when that man asked you to dance. And then he kept staring at you the whole time we were there. Perri, I don't enjoy fighting, but I could have killed someone."

Shaking her head and rolling her eyes, Perri straightened somewhat, although she didn't break the contact between their bodies for an instant. "Shut up," she chuckled, "You're not going to murder someone just because they are a leering pig."

Ian was the one to break their connection, leaning down to place a soft kiss on Perri's cheek, then her brow. "Oh, you don't know, Perri, I would for you."

You always find the exit sign in a crowded room
Everybody wants their shot,
but you're bulletproof
Don't like the feeling when your arms unfold
A fire's burning, but your cave has gone cold
And you know you can't stay here forever

So you're scared, you don't think you're ready yet
We'll take it slow, I'll walk with you on the edge
Paint the colors on top of the sunset
I can do this all for you

— "Avalanche" by Fletcher

The next few months were harder ones. With surgeries and recoveries, medication, and a lot of time spent resting, Perri would have gone mad had it not been for her family making sure she stayed sane. Despite how much she hated them watching her struggle, Perri was grateful for their nearness. She tried not to think too hard about all the pain she had put everyone through. All of it because the thought of Ian watching her waste away was something she couldn't bear. Now here she was, having faced what she thought was coming years before and coming out the other side alive and on the road too well. She was more ashamed and remorseful than she would let on, but time would help heal those wounds, and Ian, always kind and gentle never once mentioned it. He was just glad to be allowed to walk with her when she needed someone.

As celebration of her full recovery from the last surgery she would hopefully have to have, Ian drove into to Liverpool and took Perri back to his place in Hoylake for the weekend.

Ian couldn't help but be relieved when Perri had asked to go see what pets he had at the clinic. And Perri, knowing he needed to go check on the sick animals, had not minded letting it be believed that she just wanted to pet some dogs. When really, she just hadn't wanted Ian feeling guilty that he had to go to work for a bit.

Their time at the clinic was short, and they were soon enjoying the gentle roll of the Irish Sea while their old dogs lay sunbathing on the back porch of Ian's home not that from the water. Being out on their old sailboat was almost as peaceful as being back in Alaska. The two of them worked like one mind inhabiting two bodies. And there was nothing quite like sailing with your soulmate.

They spent hours roaming the waters. Perri stealing Ian's "Sailing Hat" right away and only threatening to throw him overboard twice. It was times like these that Ian felt like as long as he was with Perri, he would be young for the rest of his life. Even with grey hairs slowly making themselves known on both of their heads, Ian couldn't bring himself to really care. When he was with Perri, he didn't feel any older than the day he first met her. He didn't know if she even realized she had that effect on him, but something in Ian knew that Perri felt the same.

The soft rumble of thunder in the distance brought Perri out of her sleep, and she listened to the rain pounding against the roof. Humming softly, Perri nestled a little deeper into her pillow.

"Ian," she murmured, waiting for his arm to wrap around her waist and draw her close. He had always held her during storms. It wasn't that she hated them; she actually enjoyed them. It had all started when they were only dating, and she had gotten a little chilled during an unusually vicious storm one night. Ever since, even though both of them knew the truth, Perri allowed Ian to believe she always got a little cold and needed to be held during a storm. When, in all honesty, she just liked the excuse to be close to him and all wrapped up in his arms without having to ask.

When Ian's arm didn't wrap around her, Perri rolled over to drape her arm over him instead. But her hand met cooling sheets instead of Ian's warm chest. Eyes opening, Perri sat up and looked around.

"Ian?"

At the sound of her voice, their age greyed Anatolian Shepherd came into the room as fast as her arthritic legs would carry her once strong frame. Licking her hand, Darci went back toward the door and looked over her shoulder at Perri.

"A'ight, let's go then," Perri encouraged.

And with that, Darci lead Perri out into the pouring rain. Holding a hand above her eyes, she strained to see through the blinding downpour. Finally, lightning ripped through the black sky and lit up the night. It was then that she caught sight of a shadow shaped like Ian running through the rain carrying something to the water's edge and running back to the small shed not too far from the porch.

Immediately Perri realized what he was doing and ushered Darci back inside where it was safe. She ran out into the rain, getting soaked as soon as she left the shelter of the house. Finally making it to the shed where Ian kept the sandbags for flood season, Perri pushed her hair back from where it clung to her face, and she waited for Ian to come back from the shoreline.

"Perri," Ian stopped short, surprised by her sudden appearance.

"When did it get this bad?!" she asked over the deafening sound of the rain hitting the metal roof above.

"I woke up to it barely starting, and then it was like the bottom just fell out of the sky," Ian answered, as stunned as she was, "This wasn't supposed to hit until next week."

He pushed the hair back from his eyes, "You don't have to help with this. Go back inside, and I'll be in later." Ian wrapped his fists around another sandbag.

Bending down, Perri laid her hands over his and wrapped her fingers around his wrists to stop him.

"Ian," she said softly, gaining his attention, "Let me help."

Wanting to make her go back inside, Ian paused for several seconds.

"You don't have much choice, darling," Perri smirked. The rain that had caught in her eyelashes fell to roll down her cheeks like the drops that fell from the tip of her nose, "I'm helping you whether you want me to or not."

Shaking his head but smiling all the same, Ian lifted his hands and let a triumphant-looking Perri take hold of the sandbag.

"Where have we started the line?"

"Just down to the shoreline and to the left, after that the ground gets higher," Ian gestured.

Without hesitation, the two of them went out into the storm and secured the wall around their home.

It was the early hours of the morning before the wall was complete, and the storm was still raging, the waters lapping at the edges of the bags they had placed.

Looping his arm around Perri's shoulders, Ian tucked her into his side and did his best to shield her some from the unforgiving rain, even though she was already soaked through. Racing to the house, they were greeted by two sleepy-eyed dogs, and finally looking at each other in the light of the warm house, they couldn't help but laugh. Doing their best not to leave a trail, the couple raced to the bedroom to get some dry clothes, laughing the whole time and leaving muddy footprints in their wake.

Dry and slowly thawing, the two collapsed in bed after opening the curtains of the window that faced the sea. Laying on Ian's chest, Perri sighed and reveled in the feeling of his arms wrapping around her like she had wanted hours before.

"Comfortable?" Ian asked.

"Very," Perri replied just as her eyes were drifting shut and sleep overtook her.

The heat of sunlight coming through a window was what finally woke them, much to their displeasure. But waking up next to each other seemed to make it a little less irritating.

Smiling softly down at her, Ian rested his hand on Perri's cheek before brushing his fingers over the soft skin there.

"We really should have closed that window," he whispered, his eyes dancing over Perri's face.

"Mmm-hmm," she hummed, her eyes shut as she enjoyed the tenderness of Ian's touch on her face.

"You're staring," Perri spoke after a few moments of silence.

"I'm admiring," Ian corrected, his smile brightening as he delighted in Perri's hearty laugh.

"Wow. That was smooth and probably one of the most romantic things you have said to me in a bit," Perri told him, her eyes opening to meet his gaze.

"Oh, you know me," Ian chuckled, "Just trying to up my game so our kids will quit making fun of me."

"That will never happen," Perri remarked, smiling in amusement as she sat up to get out of bed.

"Where are you going?" Ian asked, following suit even as his tired body protested.

"I mostly want to lay here all day, but my body is demanding food, and I must answer."

Perri stood to walk over to her suitcase and rummage through it, while Ian decided he may as well get up too since his reason for staying in bed had gotten up and left.

Coming out of the bathroom a few minutes later, Ian found that Perri was already gone and making noise in the kitchen. Shaking his head, Ian got dressed and made his way down the hall to see if he could help. Rounding the corner, he watched as Perri flopped the sleeve of the flannel she was wearing down over her hand and used it as a makeshift potholder to lift the shrieking tea kettle from the stovetop.

"Isn't that my flannel?" Ian inquired, squinting his eyes and acting like he was unsure, even though he knew exactly which flannel it was.

"No, of course not," Perri replied, simply, "It's mine."

Looking over her shoulder a moment later, she flashed him a smile, "After all, someone put it back in my suitcase on our last day in Alaska. Kind of seems like someone wanted me to keep it, don't you think?"

Shaking his head, Ian crossed the room and planted a kiss on the cheek that was offered up to him, "It certainly seems that way, doesn't it. Now, how can I help?"

Staring at the waves, but you
don't wanna drown again

Wish that you could feel the
water come pouring in

The blood is rushing, but you're paralyzed

Defenseless, but you feel so alive

I think that you can love me forever

We can let our hearts run free

Baby, you can have a life with me

— "Avalanche"

The months passed, and life continued on as it was, all except for Perri's growing longing to be with Ian. But she decided that she couldn't be the first to make a move toward making their relationship something more. That would need to be something that came from Ian. So, she waited, and time seemed to drag on as she hoped for the day he would make a move.

Perri had begun to fear that he would never want them to be any more than they were now. The thought made her heart twist, but she could endure it so long as he never left. Then just as she had resigned herself to it, the moment happened.

Ian came to stand beside Perri as she was filling the dog's bowls for dinner, and he watched her for a long, quiet moment.

"Ian, if you're that hungry, all you have to do is ask, and we can fix that," Perri teased, thinking that he was staring so intently at the kibble she was pouring out.

"I think. . ." Ian looked away hesitantly, and Perri suddenly realized that he was much more serious than she thought. Putting the dog's bowls aside, she gave Ian her full attention.

"I think I'm falling in love with you, Perri."

"Good," she said right away, not giving him another minute to doubt himself or be nervous or any other emotion that would scare him off. "Because I've already fallen in love with you."

Blue eyes snapped back up to meet brown, and Perri's gaze didn't waver. She knew that Ian wouldn't find anything other than the truth in her eyes, and the truth was what Ian deserved, always. She always did her best to learn from her past, and that meant no more secrets from this man. So when it came to displaying true feelings, she let her eyes speak for her as she was not always good with words in moments like this. And this time, the truth was simple, she loved him. Madly, deeply, truly loved this man standing before her. It was the most peaceful she had felt in ages.

Instead of responding, Ian moved forward and pulled Perri into a kiss. Perri knew she had been in love with Ian again for months now, but she hadn't wanted to say anything before he was ready for fear of scaring him away. Now that he had said it, though, Perri felt as is she were floating through clouds, and she couldn't help but smile into the kiss. At first, Ian kissed her in a soft, barely-there kind of way. Tentative and cautious. He pulled back a moment later, nervousness fluttering in his chest, reasons that really made no sense, but he could not control.

Then he heard Perri's breath, a shaky exhale escaping from her lips, and he knew there was no reason for him to be nervous at all. Ian kissed her again.

They kissed like two lovers reunited after a long time apart, whose bodies fell into old rhythms with practiced ease. Just like every other time before, it came naturally to them. Ian's desire to trace his fingers along Perri's jaw, to press soft kisses on the corners of her mouth when they drew back to catch their breath, was fanned into a flame all over again. Their familiar, passionate dance that only they knew.

He grazed Perri's cheekbones with his lips, trailing feather-light kisses up to her ear, sending shivers down Perri's spine as he whispered her name like a mantra.

After a time, Ian went to draw back and end the moment, but Perri took a fistful of his shirt in hand and pulled him close again.

"Do you really think I'm going to just let you go after that?" she purred in his ear. Feeling Ian's hands come up to tangle in her hair, Perri sighed and locked her arms tighter around him to keep him close. Their lips collided, and the rest of the day was forgotten as they made their way to the bedroom they had once shared years before.

And for the first time in a very long while, everything seemed right with the world from the safety of their tangled bed sheets.

So give me one night, one minute

And I'll watch you fall like an avalanche

Let your walls down, I swear you won't regret it

Hold on tight, baby, if you can

We'll be rolling fast, and crashing hard

Hear the mountains roar to the beat of our hearts

And we'll be falling like an avalanche

— "Avalanche"

The one-year anniversary of their vacation to Hotel Alyeska was rapidly approaching, and the kids were already abuzz with plans for this year. Both of them making sure to be free for at least a week.

So much had changed in these last three hundred and twenty-two days. Perri had faced her greatest fear and come out the other side. Ian had not only learned what had torn him and his ex-wife apart years before but had been able to heal what was broken. Now he had fallen madly in love with the woman Perri had become over those seven years they were apart. She was somehow entirely different and yet entirely the same, and he was awed by her as always. Aspen had gained honors in her classes and was scheduled to graduate with a degree in Journalism next semester. Zayden was moving remarkably quickly through his Peace and Conflict studies and had somehow found the time to have a steady relationship with a girl he met at university. Dani was her name, and his family was certain that she was the one. Now, how quickly they would marry was something no one could guess, but they knew somewhere in the future, these two would end up together for life.

But that was all in the future. For now, the family had been celebrating Guy Fawkes Day with bonfires at dusk to usher in the night of fireworks.

As the dark was settling its cool blanket over the sun, the siblings went off to watch fireworks with friends, leaving their parents on their own for the night. Shouting their good nights and 'don't wait up's, their children disappeared into the dusk, leaving Perri and Ian to relax back in their chairs for a while and listen to the sounds of the night.

Looking at his watch, Ian stood from his chair and offered his hand to Perri, who looked up at him, confused.

"What?"

"I have a date planned for us tonight if you would be so kind as to come with me, m'lady."

The corner of her lips lifting in a surprised expression, she tried to read his expression. But without hesitation, Perri took his hand and got up, "Ooooh, I'm intrigued. Where are you taking me?"

"It's no fair to ask questions, woman," he laughed, "Just know that you're going to love it."

Driving to a pier popular for yachts, Ian pulled them to a stop and smiled over at Perri.

"Are you ready?" he asked, and she shook her head, smiling brightly.

"I have no idea."

Exiting the car, he went around to open her door, offering Perri his arm. Leading the way to a yacht with Edison lights weaving their way around the railing, Ian tried not to seem overly excited about the whole thing. But no one would have blamed him if they knew how much time and effort he had put into preparing for this night.

"Ian?" Perri smiled up at him while still keeping an eye on the yacht they were approaching, "What are you planning?"

"I was thinking you and I could go out on a yacht for a change, instead of a small sailboat, and—oh what a coincidence, it's Night of Fireworks—" Ian shrugged, trying to play off like it was all an accident, "Well, I guess we'll just have to watch the fireworks from the water."

With a childlike squeal, Perri bounced on the balls of her feet a few times before launching herself into Ian, throwing her arms around his neck.

"You do understand that I will be spoiled worthless one day, right," she said, her voice muffled by his neck where she had tucked her face.

Wrapping his arms around her back, Ian laughed, "Worthless? Never. But should that ever be the case, I suppose I'll just have to have a talk with whoever is causing me such trouble."

Ian could feel Perri's laughter against his own chest, and bending down, he scooped her up into his arms bridal style, carrying her the rest of the way to the yacht.

Perri ran excitedly around the deck of the yacht as Ian tapped the window twice to let the driver know they were ready to go. Coming to stand beside her, leaning forward on the railing, Ian felt his chest swell with affection for this woman who still got so excited over fireworks.

"We have a while yet until the actual show starts," he informed, "But there will be plenty of civilian fireworks to see."

Perri scanned the shores and looked for the dark, ghostly outlines of other boats, waiting for the distinct *pop* of fireworks blasting into the sky.

Her excitement slowly became less elated and turned to more of a pleasing hum under her skin as she anticipated the magic. As she and Ian stood so close together, leaning on the rails of the pristine yacht, Perri's thoughts turned to the man who had planned this. By far one of her favorite people and beyond thoughtful, even remembering how much she adored fireworks. His kindness never seemed to run out, even when it should, and he never once made Perri question whether or not he loved her. Despite all the trouble they had getting here again.

Turning her attention to Ian, Perri found herself unable to think about ever going back to daily life without this man in it.

"I keep trying to imagine the future," Perri began softly so as not to disrupt the peacefulness around them.

The thoughts were too much to unravel in her brain, too many things she wanted to say and understand better herself, so she had to think out loud. "I ask myself, what I will do when our children leave to different parts of the globe to pursue their careers, where is my career going, what does my future hold? But any time I try to answer those questions, all I see is you next to me."

The more she spoke, the faster her words came. "I was stupid before, and I regret everything I did to us, but somehow I think it has just made us better suited to one another. There is no other option for me. There is only one thing I am sure of right now, and it is that I need you in my life for more than just a couple of days a week. I want your every day, selfish as it may sound. Ian Astankova, I don't want to possess you," Perri echoed Ian's words from many years before when they had been so young and knew nothing of what all they would face, "I want to love you and be able to call you mine again."

Hands trembling, Perri pulled a ring Ian had bought long ago off of her thumb and held it out. He looked down at it, confused almost.

To Perri's own surprise, her voice came out steady and strong as she said, "Let's get married."

"You just had to, didn't you," Ian sighed, "You just had to ruin it."

Her brows knitting together, Perri jerked back, offended at his response. "Bloody hell, you could have just said no."

"Do you even realize how you've ruined everything?"

"Ruined?!" Perri shrieked, "I'm trying to save it! I *thought* we were two people in love who wanted to get married someday, and I couldn't imagine going through life much longer not sharing it with you like we used to. You wouldn't be so offended if you thought it through!"

Ian laughed, "She thinks I haven't thought it through."

He stalked over to the cabin and shouted below deck, "You might as well come out now. It's all spoiled."

Perri's bewilderment only grew as Aliyah and Liam emerged from the cabin, both of them wearing captain's hats and grinning like children. "Did it happen?! How the hell did I miss it?!"

"No," Ian snapped and pushed his hair back from his forehead, "Perri got ahead of me, and I couldn't catch up in time to salvage it."

"Wait a minute! What is going on?" Perri demanded, "Liam, Ali? Since when did you start sailing yachts?"

"We moonlight," Aliyah smiled with a shrug.

"Penny! Zayden!" Ian yelled through the cabin door.

A few moments later, a sound like elephants stampeding through a very small space met their ears, and their children came up from below.

"Congratulations!" Aspen exclaimed, but Zayden clutched her arm, putting a finger to his lips.

"What's happening? Why are you all here?" Perri asked, still trying to make sense of what was going on. She must be dreaming. She had fallen asleep beside the bonfire, and her subconscious was drawing a scenario that she could only wish would happen. She idly began pinching her arm, but she did not wake. Suddenly feeling self-conscious, Perri tucked her ring away into her palm.

"This is how much I have *thought it through*, Perri," Ian said, a little defeated as he gestured at the crowd of people around them, "Everything was going to be perfect, but you had to go and get too excited."

"I don't. . ." Perri couldn't even come up with a question to ask anymore.

Ian pulled something small from his pocket and offered it to Perri. "I'm sure you understand what this is now. Just take it."

"Blimey," Perri exclaimed quietly as she took the box, but she couldn't bring herself to open it. Not that she needed to open it anymore to guess what was inside.

The hinged box was about three inches, square, and covered in the softest blue velvet.

The surprise date. The yacht. Their family all hidden away close by. It was all coming together and suddenly making perfect sense.

"Open it," Ian prompted.

"No."

"You can't say no, not after already proposing to me before I even had the chance. Open it."

"No, no, I want to," Perri explained, "Shite. I'm sorry. Can we rewind? You take the box, I'm gonin' to put this back on. . ." She slipped her own ring back on her right hand. "And everyone else will go hide because I'm assuming they weren't supposed to be here for this part."

Nodding dutifully, Aspen ushered her brother, along with their Aunt and Uncle, back below deck, flashing a beaming smile and a thumbs-up as she went.

"There," Perri said, turning her full attention to Ian, "Now, we can pick up where we left off. Take two." She took a step back over to the railing, just as she was before, "Come on."

Ian followed slowly, rubbing the back of his neck awkwardly, "It's not the same. It all sounds stupid now."

"I know it isn't," her voice soft and apologetic, "But none of it is stupid."

Ian sighed and leaned on the railing once again, staring out at the sea. "I knew from the first moment I saw you walking across the airport that we would end up here someday."

"Shut up," Perri interrupted, "No, you didn't."

Ian shot her an are-you-serious look, "Perri."

"Sorry," she said, "It's just, I remember that day, and I was windswept, and I looked a mess. I get being romantic, but there was really no way you could have known then that we would end up here and you would—"

"Are you trying to ruin this a second time?" Ian questioned, chuckling a bit.

"Sorry." Perri closed her mouth and gestured for his to continue.

"I knew from that moment that I was going to do everything in my power to convince you that we were made to be together," Ian continued, "But you didn't need my convincing, and we both know it wouldn't have mattered anyway. You had to make up your mind. I just needed you to know that this—us—was different from anything I had ever had before. And even after being separated for so long, I couldn't bear the thought of letting it go. Of letting you go again. Plus, I was really hoping for a day when I wouldn't have to have so much self-control with you."

Looking down at her with his piercing blue eyes, Ian took her hand, "I love you." Reaching into his pocket with his free hand, Ian pulled out the ring.

Although Perri knew what was happening, she couldn't stop her face from breaking into a smile as Ian got down on one knee on the wooden deck.

Ian opened the ring box and took Perri's breath away for the second time. There was a white-gold ring etched with mountains that looked awfully familiar. As she plucked it from the cushion and looked closely, she confirmed—it was a horizon view of Mount Alyeska. In the center of the mountain range, as if setting on the tallest peak, was a brilliant, round diamond. Small but bright.

"Perri," Ian said softly, all the string lights reflecting in his eyes like stars, "Will you marry me?"

It was the easiest question Perri ever had to answer. For the second time in her life.

"Yes."

Beaming, Ian took Perri's left hand and slid the ring into place. It fit perfectly, to which Perri was not surprised. Just another detail that Ian had thought of ahead of time.

Leaning down, Perri took Ian's face in her hands and kissed him, their lips fitting together perfectly, just as it was meant to be.

Calling everyone back up, Ian held Perri close, resting his cheek against the top of her head.

"Did it work the second time?" Liam asked, peering around the corner cautiously. "Can we celebrate now?"

Holding up her hand that now glinted with the ring, Perri smiled until her cheeks ached. Then all four of them rushed out. Their children shrieked with pure joy and danced around the deck. Their friends exchanging congratulatory hugs.

Aliyah threw her arms around Perri and hugged her tight.

"I can't believe this is happening," Perri said, muffled by her friend's shoulder.

"Oh darlin' I knew ya would end up together in the end, whether ya ever realized it or not," Aliyah laughed and held her friend at arm's length, "I just hope I ge' to be a bridesmaid for this weddin' and ya don' just run off to the registers office."

Meanwhile, Ian had pulled out his phone and was exchanging a very businesslike command.

"Operation Foxtrot is a go. I repeat we are a go. Execute."

Hanging up, he grinned at Perri's curious look, clearly enjoying himself. He slipped his hand around her to rest on the small of her back. Guiding her over to the side of the boat, he pointed at the shore.

"Watch."

The sound of fireworks whizzing through the sky and then exploding with that thrilling *pop* made Perri's heart beat a little faster all over again.

"Wave hello," Ian said, waving his arm high in the air.

Perri squinted and could just barely make out three figures on the shadowy shore, waving just as excitedly.

"Who?"

"This is the one part your Mum desperately wanted to help with," Ian shook his head, "I tried and tried to get her on the boat with us so she could be here, but she just loves to set off fireworks for her girl. And we all know that Gemma and Lena love exploding things and getting to play with fire."

Turning to face Ian, Perri studied his face as the ever-changing colors of the fireworks lit up his features.

"When did you. . .? How?"

Ian smirked, "Well, what did you think I was doing all those days I couldn't be with you?"

Perri slapped his arm playfully, "All those times when you weren't working, you could have been with me."

"I had to plan!" Ian replied, "I didn't like being away from you either, but to trade some lonely nights planning, for forever," he shrugged, "It wasn't so bad."

"Forever."

The words felt so big and yet so perfect.

Perri stretched her fingers out in front of her, turning the ring so the diamond caught the moonlight and the sparkle of the fireworks.

"I hope it isn't too much," Ian said softly, "I thought you wouldn't want anything too big, but I had to go a little expensive. Forgive me for splurging on the quality."

"You're forgiven," Perri shot him a smile. "It's gorgeous."

Leaning in close, Ian whispered, "You should read the engraving on the inside."

Curious as always, Perri slid the ring off her finger and tilted it so she could read the inscription.

Bloody Hotel Alyeska

Throwing her head back, Perri laughed until her sides hurt.

Finally calming enough to speak, Perri placed the ring back on her finger, "Ian, *this* is perfect. Thank you."

Then she remembered, and taking her own ring back off her finger, she held it up to the light. Positively dull with age and obviously a size or two too large for even her thumb, Perri removed the ring spacer.

"This, ehm, was actually yours," she explained, "I found it in the back of a drawer after we had separated, and I always seemed to forget to get it to you, so I ended up wearing it instead thinking that would help me remember. Obviously, after a while I just ended up keeping it for myself. I think I want to give it back to you now."

"Give it here," Ian said, holding out his left hand.

Sliding it onto his finger, Perri sighed happily.

This was really happening.

Liam ducked back into the cabin and steered the boat in a lazy arc to pass closer by the shore where Laurel and the girls were still launching fireworks. Aspen and Zayden came running up, looping their arms around their parents and hugging everyone close.

Perri leaned into Ian as they stared up at the night sky with their children nestled close. Light blossomed over the dark sea, leaving sparkling trails of all colors in their wake.

It was extravagant and nothing she ever expected. But it was so Ian with the perfect touch of everything she loved most.

The fireworks whistled through the air and exploded, one after another. *Whoosh! Bang! Crackle!*

And Perri realized she had not felt so at peace in a long time.

For the first time in years, they had time. As much time as they needed. Time to fall deeper in love. Time to be a family again.

Finally.

Alternate Ending

Time, sometimes the time just slips away

And you're left with yesterday, left with the memories

I, I'll always think of you and smile

And be happy for the time I had you with me

Though we go our separate ways, I won't forget

So don't forget the memories we've made

-"Please Remember" by Leann Rimes

Placing the stack of pages on the table between them, the publisher smiled.

"Well, Aspen, I don't even know what to say."

"I hope that's a good thing," the woman laughed, trying not to appear anxious even as she reached up to rub her eyebrow. A habit that she had picked up from her mother, despite not having a scar of her own.

"That is probably the best compliment I could give you," Jamie answered, "You started out with something great, but you've grown it into something even *I* never imagined it could become. It's not often a piece leaves me without any commentary at all, but *this* is something special. Some real ace work."

Aspen's cheekbones darkened a fraction, and she gave a shy smile, looking down at the stack of pages she had put her blood, sweat, and tears into.

"Blimey," tucking her hair behind her ear, she sat there for a long moment, "Well, thank you. Now *I* don't know what to say, and being my mother's daughter, that's unusual for me."

Relaxing back in her seat, Jamie smiled in wonderment, "So how do your parents feel about you putting their whole love story in print for the world to read?"

"They don't mind so much," Aspen shrugged, "They're actually just excited that I'm finally doing something with all of it."

"I just can't believe you managed to get your parents back together in basically two weeks, after years of them being separated."

Aspen gave a bark of a laugh, "I can't either."

"Astounding," Jamie shook her head, "Can you imagine how many children are out there who would love to be able to pull that off? How many who wish they could have done it themselves?"

Aspen nodded thoughtfully, "I know how they feel."

"Well, of course! With how long it took you to actually be able to make it work out, I bet you thought it was never going to happen at all."

Now it was Aspen's turn to rest back into her seat and smile. But her smile held a hint of something else, an accepted sadness.

"Author's secret?" she offered.

Instantly intrigued, Jamie leaned forward once more and rested her forearms on her thighs, "Sure. Of course. I keep them all the time."

Picking up her glass from the side table, Aspen took a sip and tried to rein in her emotions. She hated talking about this. In fact, she rarely ever did.

"We never made it to Hotel Alyeska. Not all of us anyway."

Jamie's face fell as the words settled in.

"My brother and I went, of course. And even now, we go with my family and his fiancé. . . But Mum and Dad, they. . . They both had good reasons why. Even though now I. . . I can't even remember what they were." Her brows pulled together briefly in thought, trying so hard to remember what had kept them away, "But they never got back together. It was all imagination and Chinese whispers."

Silence reigned for a long time between them. Aspen gazed at her book of lies that had somehow helped her cope with the fact that she could never get her parents to reunite, and now it was just too late. While Jamie stared in almost open-mouthed shock at the woman sitting across from her.

"So, you're telling me that. . . it never happened?"

"Exactly," Aspen replied, her dark eyes coming back up to meet Jamie's, "It was all dreamings from the mind of the little girl locked up inside me who only ever wanted her family together and never got her wish in the end."

"I—I don't know what to say. . ."

"Twice in one day," she smirked, much like her mother, "I must be real special."

A few moments passed quietly, and Aspen glanced at her watch before beginning to gather her things.

"We can talk about details sometime next week, for now, I have a wedding I have to get to, and I cannot be late," Looking up, Aspen shot her that charming smile, "Thanks so much for all your help and remember, that's our little secret."

"Yes, yes," Jamie replied, standing to walk her out, "I'll see you next week. The secret is safe, I swear."

Turning to shake her publisher's hand, Aspen took a moment and held the woman's gaze, "Thank you."

Jamie now knew one of Aspen's best-kept secrets; the fact that she struggled so deeply even after all this time, with her parent's separation and the knowledge that she was never able to help them mend it.

But, she supposed, there was only so much one desperate young woman could do, and she had tried everything. Or at least that is what she told herself.

Goodbye, there's just no sadder word to say

And it's sad to walk away with just the memories

Who's to know what might have been?

We'll leave behind a life and time
we'll never know again

-"Please Remember"

Standing at the front of the church waiting, Aspen smiled when her brother appeared.

"What do you think, little brother?" she asked, holding out her arms to show off her freshly tailored suit. "Am I Best Woman material?"

"Oh, Penny," Zayden approached her in awe, holding out his hands, and she squeezed them in her grasp, "You look amazing!"

Lifting his arm, he gestured for her to do a turn.

When Zayden had asked Aspen to be his "best man" and she told him she was going to wear a vibrant red women's tuxedo, he had thought she was mostly joshing with him. But obviously, that had not been the case. If he were being honest with himself, he wasn't sure why he ever expected less.

"Thank you," she shot him a winning smile, "I thought Mum would approve."

Zayden laughed, "She would. She always said that there was nothing like a fine red suit."

Aspen's smile softened, and she held her little brother's gaze, "She would love this. All of it."

Zayden looped his arms around Aspen's shoulders and pulled her into a lose but comforting embrace. Looking around, he could feel his chest swelling with so many emotions.

"You think so?"

Giving his waist a tight squeeze, Aspen nodded, "Oh, I know so. Mum loved you too much and adored Dani so much there is no way she would be disappointed about any of this finally happening."

Standing in front of a mirror, Aspen adjusted her jacket and gave herself one last look over before going to make sure her children were ready and not causing trouble instead. But she knew in all reality, they were probably half-dressed and running around, causing chaos. They were her children after all, and their father had no desire to tame the wildness they had obtained from her, he liked it too much.

Turning to walk out, Aspen's face broke out into a smile at the sight of her father rounding the corner. Ian stopped abruptly and took in his daughter.

"I, ehm, I had it designed after Mum's," she explained, looking down at the suit she wore, "I thought it might be appropriate. Bad idea?"

Ian quickly closed the distance between them and hugged her, "No, no! I think it was a wonderful idea. You look so much like her it just shook me for a moment."

Taking a step back, Aspen reached out and began untying her father's tie, "How's Zayden doing?"

Ian lifted his chin and chuckled, "Well, I just left from helping him fix his tie, so you may want to check my work there in a bit. But otherwise, he's just excited. So, I thought I'd come to see how my girl was doing."

"Ya know, I'm ready to have a sister. That also means half the work for me, because now fetus will have someone else watching him too to make sure he doesn't get into too much trouble," she replied, smoothing out the wrinkles she had created, "And it's not every day I get to dress up this nice and dance at a party."

* * * * * * * * * * * * * *

Ian stepped out of his car and waved at Perri, who was working in her sketchbook, soaking up the evening sun from the patio.

"I came to get my suit approved," he said in greeting.

Perri chuckled, "Well, you may have to wait a bit for the approval. Our little perfectionist is out with her brother, and who knows where they ended up."

"Is it alright if I wait here?"

Perri quirked a brow and then tilted her head in the direction of the chair opposite, "You may as well come up and sit down."

"Thanks," Ian sat down and leaned back. He missed evenings like this. "What are you working on?"

"I'm trying to become inspired by these ideas this man gave me for this ridiculous building he wants, but honestly. . . I've got nothin'."

Ian made a face, "Sorry, love."

Perri head snapped up, and she met Ian's wide-eyed gaze. Neither of them had expected the use of the old pet name.

Somehow it was Perri who recovered first, and she shrugged, "It's alright. I just hope I never work with him again. He lacks. . . creativity."

Turning her attention back to the sketch in her lap, she continued, "Tell me something about your work. How's the clinic?"

"Surprisingly busy for this time of year," Ian replied, "But nothing too out of the ordinary."

Lifting her eyes briefly, Perri took in his expression to decide if he was trying to spare her sad details and could tell in that half a second he wasn't.

"Your hair is getting long," she remarked.

Reaching up, Ian pushed it back from his forehead, "Yeah, things have been so hectic lately I haven't had the chance to go to the barber."

Sitting in silence for a moment, the two listened to the sound of the night creatures slowly making their evening appearances.

"You want me to cut it for you?" Perri finally asked, "Won't take a minute, and I'm sure the kids will still be a while."

"Um, sure," Ian replied, a little surprised by the offer, "Yeah, that would be great actually. Thank you."

* * * * * * * * * * * * *

A few days later, freshly trimmed hair combed back and wearing his approved suit, Ian walked up the front steps with flowers in hand. Ringing the doorbell, he waited a moment until Zayden opened it.

"Hey, Dad!" the boy greeted and hugged him quickly, "Mum and Penny are upstairs finishing up. They should be down in a minute." Turning, he called up to them, "Dad's here!"

"So mate, you and Mum doing anything special tonight?"

"Yeah, I think we're going to ride horses for a while and then probably to dinner."

High fiving his son, Ian interlocked their fingers and smiled proudly at Zayden, "That's my boy."

The sound of someone coming down the stairs caught their attention, and they turned to see Perri taking the last few steps.

"Ian," she greeted, and he smiled at her.

Looking him up and down, Perri had forgotten to disguise that she found him incredibly attractive in this new suit.

"Honey, come here," she closed the gap between them and began adjusting his tie without thinking.

Ian stood utterly motionless and looked down at the focused expression his ex-wife was wearing. Finishing up, Perri tenderly patted the center of his chest where the tie now lay smooth and lifted her gaze. As soon as she did, the realization hit her and her eyes lost their softness, becoming guarded as before.

Quickly looking away, Perri turned to face the stairs.

"You're taking our daughter out. I can't have you looking like you can't do your own tie," she remarked.

And with perfect timing, Aspen appeared at the top of the stairs.

"I don't know how well I'll be able to dance in this dress, but I am so excited!"

* * * * * * * * * * * * *

In a room not too far from Aspen and Ian, Zayden was sitting down with a letter their father had left for him to read.

I was once told by my grandfather that the thing that ultimately ended his and my grandmother's marriage was that he stopped noticing her. He got to know her as the woman she was when they first met, and after that, he just thought he knew her. He didn't take into account that people change all the time. He stopped noticing her, and then one day she was gone. And when he was forced to open his eyes and really look at her, he no longer recognized her.

I didn't want that. I never wanted to have to look at my grandchildren and tell them the reason I lost their grandmother was because I didn't take the time to know her after I married her.

So now I pass on an addition to my grandfather's advice and ask you not to do what I did.

I noticed your mother. I made sure I knew her as a woman, as her own person, even after we married. But everyone has their times when they forget to do important things, and I failed to notice when things began to fall apart for your mother. And because I failed to notice, she made decisions without me that I cannot truly hold against her, but that hurt me—hurt us—just the same.

Looking back, though, I think things would have been much different if I had told your mother that I still noticed her. So that is my addition. Don't just notice Dani. Tell her that you notice her.

Because even today, I can tell you things I noticed about your mother that she never knew I had taken time to see.

She loved to stand in the rain. That's right, just standing there. I asked her once if she ever felt like one of those shite movies for TV characters that dramatically ran out in the rain to chase after someone before they boarded a train to leave forever. She looked me dead in the eyes and said she 'would bloody die before she ever did anything like that'. And if she did, well, I won't write exactly what she said, but I knew that I would never have that woman chasing me down in the rain. Unless it was for a damn good reason. Like helping her catch a stray dog all quick like before I left.

She played pretend better than most kids do. Her creativity was mind-blowing. You could almost watch the thoughts forming and the millions of ideas working themselves out inside her head. It's amazing. She loved playing pretend with you kids. Sometimes I think she just used it as an excuse to embrace her inner child without other people asking her what made her go daft.

No matter the situation, she could make you feel comfortable. She listened carefully to everything, especially when she cared about the person talking.

She knew when to push and when to let something rest.

She was always brewing a cup of tea and ultimately leaving cups to get cold in random places. Often left beside an abandoned pencil or resting atop a serviette with a small sketch in the corner.

She was there. Present. All the time. She never said it was too much, even though sometimes it must have been.

She was such a great dancer. Definitely made me wish I could dance better. But she taught you kids at least. I could not be rescued from my mediocre station, but she danced with me anyway.

She took all of our moods in stride. She didn't give in, but she also didn't make anyone feel bad about what they were feeling.

She preferred to wash the dishes in the dark. Either you kids were in bed or heading that way. When I say dark, I mean that it was dark outside, and the only light in the kitchen was the small light above the oven that was across the room.

Zayden looked up from the letter and wiped the tears from his cheeks, taking a deep breath.

He recalled something his mother told him once, and it caused a twisting ache in his chest.

"I fell in love with your father, so so quickly it rocked my world. And I'll never stop loving him. . . even though that doesn't make sense anymore."

Sighing, Zayden stood up and went to stand in the hallway outside of Dani's room so he could talk to her for a few minutes before the wedding. Someone might kill him if he saw her before the wedding, but he also knew she would never turn him away.

"Dani, you still in there?" he asked softly.

"Zayden?" she called, surprised he got past her bridesmaids, "Give me a second."

Chuckling, he leaned back against the wall and smiled. This chaotic woman was about to be his wife, and he couldn't be more thrilled. Part of him still couldn't believe that she had said yes.

She rounded the corner, and Zayden's hand immediately flew to his eyes.

"Dani! You know we can't see each other before the wedding. I just wanted to hold your hand and talk to you for a minute."

"Well, it's too late now," she smiled, "Come on, that's an outdated tradition that was brought about by brides who were traded by their fathers for goats or something."

Zayden's face brightened a bit with a small smile, and Dani took in the half of his face that she could see with adoration.

"There it is," she remarked, "My favorite smile."

"Really, Dan," Zayden insisted, "I want to be surprised. Can you put something over the dress for me?"

Rolling her eyes playfully and making sure it could be heard in her voice, Dani gave an exaggerated sigh, "Fine. I'll be back."

Finally lowering his hand from his eyes, Zayden waited and listened to Dani rummaging through the small room.

Coming back into view, Dani was now wearing the tan trench coat Zayden had let her barrow on one of their first dates. She had never returned it, and here she was wearing it over her dress so he couldn't see.

Looking up at him, she smiled softly and adjusted his lapels. "Uh oh," her voice barely above a whisper, "You saw me. Looks like a thousand years of bad luck for us."

Looping his arms loosely around her waist, Zayden attempted to return the smirk, but there was a cloud behind his eyes that his smile couldn't quite make it past.

"Hey," she spoke gently, concern evident in her eyes, "Are you okay?"

"Yeah," he assured, "I just wanted to talk to you for a minute."

"So you said," she took in his expression thoughtfully for a long moment.

Nodding in understanding, Dani took a step forward and wrapped her arms around her soon-to-be husband. She was so small compared to him, but she knew just how to wrap him tight and make him feel seen. Immediately Zayden curled around her, and she tenderly rubbed his back, holding him close. Today was harder for him than it should be, and she knew there was nothing she could do but be here for him while he faced it.

Please remember, please remember
I was there for you and you were there for me
And remember, please remember me
Please remember, please remember
I was there for you and you were there for me

Please remember, our time together
The time was yours and mine
and we were wild and free
Then remember, please remember me

-"Please Remember"

Vows taken and promises made, memories and emotions dancing in the form of teary eyes for everyone present. The room was filled with family and friends who had waited for this day. But as Zayden and his new wife looked out at the cheering witnesses, what stood out to them was the few seats remaining empty for those who could not make it to this moment.

"All good?" Dani asked gently, squeezing Zayden's hand.

Her husband smiled down at her, "Wonderful."

Looping her arm in his, the couple excitedly took off back up the aisle to get ready for the reception.

After mingling with guests and sharing lingering glances from across the room, the newlyweds finally sat down together and immediately fell into easy conversation.

Soft music began to play, and the projector brightened the suddenly dimly lit room with the words "Mother-Son Dance" written in Perri's handwriting, which caused Zayden to halt mid-sentence.

"Uh, Dani. . . What. . ."

His wife turned to meet his curious gaze, and she shrugged, attempting to look innocent but not really succeeding.

Then Aspen appeared on his other side, her hand resting on the back of his chair in a comfortingly familiar way.

Turning to look up at his sister, Zayden gestured around her to the screen, "Hey, Penny, do you know what's going on here?"

"Actually, I do." she replied, coming around to face him fully.

"I just thought we took this out because. . ."

"Look, I know I'm not Mum," Aspen shifted a little on her feet, "But I am a mum to three amazing children, who were just in your wedding, I might add. And while I know there is not a single person out there who can try and stand in our Mum's place. . . I would love to give you this moment on your wedding day. I may not be as great a dancer as Mum, but I can still 'bust a move,' as she would say."

Aspen met her brother's gaze, "So, what do you say, fetus? Will ya dance with me?"

Zayden looked down at his sister's hand that was being offered to him and his eyes glossed over with tears.

"Penny, I don't know what to say, you. . ."

"It seems I'm having that effect on people today," Aspen smirked and waited patiently for her brother.

"Just go dance with your sister, Zay," his wife's voice came softly from behind him as she squeezed his shoulders, encouraging him on.

Taking her hand, Zayden got up, and the siblings walked out onto the dance floor. Aspen shot him a reassuring smile as they fell into step with the music.

Looking up at Zayden, she tilted her head toward the head of the dance floor, "Hey, watch the screen. I made you something that you may want to hit me for."

"Wonderful," Zayden laughed and wrapped her up in a tight hug for a moment while still keeping them swaying to the music.

"Please don't be mad at me, mate," Aspen's voice was muffled by his shoulder, "You could kill me right now if you squeezed any tighter."

"Sorry, Penny," he released his sister, and they fell in step with the music just like their mother taught them.

Watching the pictures of their life with their mother float by, the two teared up and held onto each other's hand a little tighter.

"I miss Mum," Zayden finally said softly.

"Me too," Aspen replied, sniffling quietly, "Especially on days like this."

As they watched the pictures come and go across the screen, they commented quietly between themselves. When pictures came up of them dancing with their mother, the siblings couldn't help but laugh and say how lucky it was that their mother taught them otherwise, they'd look real barmy right about now in front of all these people.

"Yeah, dead from the neck up, for sure," Aspen laughed, allowing the moment to pass as the pictures changed.

"Now tell me something," Zayden smirked knowingly and jerked his head in the direction of the table where he had left his now-wife sitting with their father, "Was she in on this too?"

"Oh yes," Aspen nodded without hesitation, "I could say it was more her idea than mine, but that wouldn't be *entirely* true. She's a real ace, that one, and she came up with the whole video idea to begin with."

Zayden let out a booming laugh, "Ahh, I'm going to have my hands full for the rest of my life, aren't I?"

"Especially with both of us around," she confirmed, looking mischievous as ever. "You put a ring on a wild thing, fetus. You better hold on tight."

They watched a few more pictures go by and listened to the crowd behind them make soft sounds or murmured comments with each new image.

"Which reminds me. . . I, erm, I did a thing today."

Looking down at her with an impish twinkle in his eyes, Zayden smirked, "Yeah? What did you do this time?"

"I went and spoke to my publisher," she looked a little self-conscious, "We are getting together next week to talk details."

"Penny!" Zayden stopped mid-dance, "Oh, Penny, that's—You finally did it!"

"Keep dancing, you fool!" Aspen slapped his arm, "And quiet down! I don't want everyone knowing!"

"Why not?! This is amazing!" He fell back into step and shook his head in awe, "Penny, you really did it."

"Yeah, looks like it's finally happening." A little uncertainty flashed in her dark eyes.

"What's the face? You should be proud!"

A little sadness swirled with the doubt in those eyes so similar to their mother's, "Do you think. . ."

"Ah, Aspen," Zayden hugged his sister close, "Mum would be so proud."

Returning his embrace, Aspen rested her chin on his shoulder, "Are you sure? I mean, I spend years at university for journalism, and I end up writing a fictional novel about our parents getting back together."

"I have no doubts, Penny girl," he gave her a good strong squeeze, "I think we've done our parents pretty proud, ya know. . . Even if things didn't turn out the way we always hoped they would, you have made something beautiful out of it anyway. And *that* is definitely something Mum would be proud of. And besides, where would the world be without a little fiction."

"Thank you," Aspen whispered, tightening her hold before taking a step back.

As the song changed, the siblings watched their father stand from his chair and offer his hand to the bride. Ian escorted her onto the dance floor with as much charm and poise as they had not seen him put to use in a couple of decades, and their hearts warmed.

"Well, looks like you're stuck with me for another go-round, fetus. What do you say?"

"My pleasure," he answered, "I am dancing with a soon-to-be world-famous author, so why would I say no?"

Rolling her eyes, Aspen laughed, "You don't know that yet. Besides, you better watch out. Dad may steal your bride yet with those moves."

"Hey! He had his chance to object," Zayden replied, looking over his shoulder at the two, "She's my girl now until one of us kicks the bucket."

"Which may be sooner than we all think if you try any more of those daft tricks skiing this year."

"Ah, Hotel Alyeska," Zayden chuckled, "There's no place quite like it."

Aspen hummed softly in reply, "Ya know, I think you're right."

And how we laughed and how we smiled
And how this world was yours and mine
And how no dream was out of reach
I stood by you, you stood by me

We took each day and made it shine
We wrote our names across the sky
We ran so fast, we ran so free
I had you and you had me

Please remember, please remember

Glossary

The Nick — Can refer to prison.

Shirty — Someone short-tempered or irritated.

On the Pull — Someone that's "on the pull" has gone on a night out with the intention of attracting a sexual partner.

Mad as a bag of ferrets — Crazy

Wanker — Idiot

Sloshed — Drunk

Tosser — Supreme Asshole or jerk.

Shove off — Go away.

Chav — White trash or low class.

Slag — Whore of the worst kind.

Fit — Used to describe someone physically attractive, usually referring to their physique.

Faffing — To "faff" is to waste time doing very little.

See a man about a dog — Attend a secret deal or meeting or to go to the toilet.

Fais de beaux reves — Sweet dreams in French

Down below with the brown bread — Down with the dead. "Brown Bread" is Cockney for dead.

Pea-souper — A thick fog, often with a yellow or black tinge.

A dog's dinner — is a mess or fiasco - sometimes also referred to as a "dog's breakfast."

Whinging — To "whinge" means to moan, groan, and complain in an irritating or whiney fashion.

Bagsy — Calling "bagsy" is the equivalent of calling "shotgun" or "dibs" when something is offered up to a group.

Blimey — To express surprise, excitement, or alarm.

Manky — Disgusting

Poppins — Perfect

Moxie — Force of character, determination, or nerve.

Bollocks — Often meaning "nonsense".

Snogging — Making out

Chunder — To vomit

Know your onions — To be very knowledgeable.

Chaton — Kitten in French

The loo — Bathroom

Speak Welsh — Vomiting

Airy-fairy — Not strong, weak.

Trolleyed — Drunk

Serviette — Table napkin

Ol' Blighty — An informal and typically affectionate term for Britain or England.

Git — A stupid or worthless person.

Brilliant — Something amazing or awesome.

Shite — The best way to say "shit" without getting told off. You can simply say you were trying out being Irish for the day.

Lost the plot — Gone crazy, stupid, or mad.

Fancy a cuppa — "Would you like a cup of tea?"

Brolly — Umbrella

Barmy — Stupid or crazy

Cheeky — An act that could be deemed as impolite or shameless but for some reason comes across as funny or endearing to others.

Ace — Excellent or wonderful.

Chinese Whispers — watered-down stories until they only vaguely resemble the truth.

Dead from the neck up — Stupid

Daft — Crazy

About the Author

Ashlynn lives in her hometown with her sister and their many pets. She's a proud Shih Tzu Mum, who works as a veterinary technician and moonlights as an author. In her spare time, she enjoys building projects of all kinds and hours spent working in her garage.

CPSIA information can be obtained
at www.ICGtesting.com
Printed in the USA
BVHW081212260422
635364BV00001B/73